THE
FIRST CENTURY
CHRISTIAN
SAGA

BOOK TWO

BISHOP OF THE NILE

BISHOP OF THE NILE

A Catholic Christian Novel by
JOSEPH L. CAVILLA

With the exception of historical events and personages, all the characters and events in this book are fictitious, and any resemblance they might have to actual persons, living or dead, is purely coincidental.

September 2016

"For the Greater Glory of God."

ACKNOWLEDGEMENTS

Once again, thanks to my son Paul, for his encouragement, and his dedication in formatting, and publishing of this book. Thanks also to my brother Charles for his enthusiasm and the proof-reading of the book.

FOREWORD

This book, is meant as a sequel to Simon of Cyrene, and expounds on the life of Simon's younger son Rufus, with whom my esteemed reader, is well acquainted.

The expansion of the church in Egypt is the main theme of the story, in which Rufus features prominently under the direction of John Mark, (later St. Mark the Evangelist) who was the first to take the teachings of Christ to Egypt.

Since the apostles, constantly dedicated themselves to spreading the Word of God and converting people to Christianity, they did not have the time to build 'stone and mortar' churches, and to set out a Liturgical procedure for the performance of the services particularly the 'Breaking of the Bread' service, which would be the Eucharistic service of today's Liturgy.

The setting up of those services, and the furthering of religious instruction was left to the bishops, which the apostles consecrated during their travels, and who had been carefully chosen and taught by them as they stopped at the various places during their missions.

The church in Rome which had grown in the midst of much antagonism and constant persecution, was unable to provide permanent places of celebration for their services, which were held where convenient and safe at the particular time.

The Roman church was truly a church militant during the first century, thus allowing Cyrene, Egypt, and other more peaceful places within the Roman Empire to propound their faith and establish 'stone and mortar' churches for their services, with continuous growth and stability in their parishes.

The provision of an orthodox Liturgy was of paramount importance, and Rufus, under the direction and encouragement of John Mark embraced that as his goal, as he strove in his missionary work up the the river Nile, and throughout his life wherever he went. His pioneering efforts to establish and run churches in the upper Nile, in the face of many difficulties and how he achieved it, is the backbone of this story. It presents many exciting and romantic situations, whilst once again opening for you my dear reader, a window, into the day to day life in that first century of ardent, vibrant, joyful, Christianity with all its hardships and perils.

CAST OF CHARACTERS

The main characters such as Rufus, were all introduced to the reader, in the book "Simon of Cyrene" of which this is a sequel.

Senh's — Antiquarian and Rufus' assistant.
Annianus —Assistant to John Mark.
Miriam —Rufus' second wife.
Aunt Miriam —Miriam's aunt.
Ita —Aunt Miriam's maid.
Manetho —Landlord in Akhetaton
Phile —Manetho's wife
Pah —Manetho's adopted son.
Demetrios, Sosigenes, and Sophia —Parishioners and Greek friends of Rufus.
Melech, Esther, and Jeth.....Parishioners and Judean friends of Rufus.
Tertius —Rufus' partner in Rome.
Octavius —Priest and leather carver in Rome.
Linus, Cletus and Clement — Roman bishops.
Athena —Christian maiden in Rome.
Aemilius—Legate. Friend of Senator Linus.
Publius —Island Chief and Bishop of Malta.
Drusa —Publius' wife.
Vibiana —Publius' daughter.
Cato —Village chief fisherman.
Crispinus —Villager fisherman.
Hemon—Senh's father.
Laret —Senh's mother.
Naporaye —Senh' sister.
Merenre —Senh's brother.
Nebitia —Merenre's girl friend.
Anen —-Archaeologist and Senh's friend.
Ensaf—Crooked business man.

Priests
Bek —Missionary.
Alceres —Missionary.

Iteti ——Missionary.
Addaya —ex.Isis priest.
Ahmes —ex.Isis priest.
Djidi — ex.Isis priest.

BIBLICAL CHARACTERS

Joseph of Arimathea — Councillor in Sanhedrin
Nicodemus — Councillor in Sanhedrin
Gamaliel — Councillor in Sanhedrin
Peter — Apostle
James — Apostle
John Mark — Evangelist
Mary — Mother of Yeshua
Mary — Magdalene
John — Apostle
James — John's brother (apostle)
Judas Barsabas — Disciple (minister)
Rhode — Door-keeper
Cornelius — Centurion in Caesarea
Paul — Paul of Tarsus (Evangelist)

DAYS OF THE JUDEAN WEEK

Dies Solis — Sunday
Dies Lunae — Monday
Dies Martis — Tuesday
Dies Mercuri — Wednesday
Dies Joves — Thursday
Dies Veneris — Friday
Dies Saturni — Saturday (Sabbath)

ROMAN TERMS

Palla — Shawl
Stolla — Outer garment
Cena — Supper
Peristyle - An open colonnaded courtyard decorated with plants and flowers, and covered by a surrounding inward sloping roof all around. A pool which was actually a cistern, called an 'impluvium' for storing rainwater was normally located at its centre. It was the preferred living space of the house, all bedrooms and kitchen opened into it, and it was located at the rear end of the house.

Atrium - A courtyard similar to the peristyle, situated near the entrance to the house and decorated more formally.
Visitors and business personnel were received and entertained there. It had a small opening in the ceiling, a sloping roof all around, and an impluvium much smaller in size than that in the peristyle.

MAP GLOSSARY

Genua — Genoa
Nicea — Nice
Arelate — Arles
Narbo — Narbonne
Tarraco — Tarragona
Sagantum — Sagunto
Carthago Nova — Cartagena
Pillars of Hercules — Calpe — Gibraltar
Tingis — Tangiers

BISHOP OF THE NILE

CHAPTER ONE

SAD RETURN

Letitia stood at the window looking out on the garden where her two daughters were happily playing under the watchful eye of Zaphira. A great longing to see her parents and spend time with them once again, had taken root in her following the death of her mother-in-law Ruth, which had devastated her beloved husband Rufus. He was still struggling to accept his loss and get over the feeling of guilt in not having visited his mother sooner, giving her an opportunity to enjoy little Letitia, her new five year old grand-daughter.

It was now over ten years since their having moved to Rome, and she had only been back once. Her mother Julia had however been over to see her once also, when her eldest daughter Marcia was born. It was now coming on to six years since she had been back to Cyrene, and she was most anxious to visit again.

'I could be faced with the same tragedy as Rufus any time, since my parents are also getting older,' she said to herself.

"Zaphira! please bring the girls in now. Lunch must be almost ready for them."

Rufus sat at his desk in his office, twiddling his stylus around and staring into space; his thoughts flying off to Cyrene and his mother's dying face.

'Why is it her dying face that keeps haunting me? Why can I not see her as she always was; full of life, a loving smile constantly on her beautiful face, fussing around us all with that love and enthusiasm she always felt for her family.'

Lately he was having much trouble concentrating on his work, which was strikingly apparent to his partner Tertius, who approaching him, put his arm around him and said:

"You have come back to work too soon. You have not recovered from your great loss. Why don't you stay home and amuse yourself with your children for a few more days? All is well here, there is nothing urgent, and one of us suffices to handle things."

Rufus agreed with his partner; Vibia's new husband of only two years.

He was a quiet and considerate person and the two partners got on very well together. They were almost the same age and understood each other very well. He was tall, though not as tall as his father-in-law had been, and was rather thin and slight of build, with pleasant features and a good sense of humour.

"I shall take a walk and perhaps it will pull me out of my lethargical state of mind," he said as he got up, walked out the door, and went off to visit Drucila. He had not seen her for quite some time even though she was just down the road from his office. She might be able to console him, he thought, as she used to in his younger days.

He knocked at the door and waited. Well remembered footsteps were heard descending the stairs, and a few moments later Drucila appeared at the door.

"My goodness! Rufus, is it really you? Where have you been? I have so often thought of you. But you have been too busy and forgotten your friend Drucila."

"No, I have not, I have thought of you often, but with one thing and another, I have neglected you. I hope you will forgive me."

" Come in, sit down," said an older looking woman than Rufus remembered. " I hope you are happy and enjoying your married life."

"Thank God, yes, but I have recently lost my dear mother, and I am very saddened as a result. I do not seem to be able to concentrate on my work. I find it so disturbing."

"I am sorry to hear that my dear young friend. I sympathise with you. It will take some time for the immediate shock to pass, but I assure you it will.

You remember how much I used to miss my son. He was always away, and I was lucky if I saw him once a year."

"Yes," answered Rufus.

"Well, he was killed last year in some sort of brawl in Crete."

"Oh my," said Rufus with true feeling, and going over he hugged his old friend.

"I, like you, was totally devastated by the news," she said with tears in her eyes.

"I had always prayed to the goddess Diana to keep him safe, but it was not to be. It has taken me the whole year to get used to the idea that I shall never see him again; but now I am resigned to it. That's life."

"It is so horribly sad though, losing someone you love," asserted Rufus.

"You must stay and have lunch with me, and bring me up to date with your adventures."

"My days of adventure are over. I am a settled and contented family man now.

You must come and visit us. Next week, on *Dies Saturni*, I shall call on you and take you to meet my family. Would you like that?"

"It will give me great pleasure my good young friend, and now that you are here, let me thank you on Erasmus' behalf, for the way you have looked after his family since he died. As you know he was a dear friend of mine from our youth. He courted me for a while and then circumstances worked against us. But again, that is life."

When Rufus left Drucila's house he felt more comforted, knowing that she too had experienced the sadness that he now had. He made his way home instead of returning to the office. He felt the need to be near his beloved Letitia, and his two lovely little girls whom he adored.

Rufus, arriving at his house, rang the bell that hung outside the wall. Festus the gate keeper and gardener, opened the gate for him. The master nodded, as he walked past still lost in his thoughts. Two little girls, fresh from their lunch, one blonde, and one brunette, ran over to him and warmly embraced him. He, embracing them with a smile on his face, swung them round and round much to their delight.

"We are so glad that you came home early today Daddy. Come and see the present that auntie Lavinia has brought us," announced the elder one, parting her long, wavy brown hair. So saying, they took him by his hands and led him to their favourite little arbour hideout, where a tiny white puppy was tied to the leg of the iron bench.

"If we let him loose, he runs into the flower beds and we have trouble getting him out again without killing the flowers," said ten year old Marcia with a responsible look on her pretty face, as little Letitia was busy untying the string that restrained the pup; her large blue eyes full of mischief.

Rufus sat on the bench. He played with the dog and the girls for a little while, and then leaving them with Zaphira, made his way to the house where he found Letitia and Lavinia having an animated chat in the peristyle.

"This is a nice surprise," said his wife as he walked in.

"To what do we owe this honour?" asked Lavinia jokingly.

"I could not concentrate on my work, and Tertius suggested I come home and spend the day with you all."

"Linus is planning to go down to the circus and watch the horses race later this afternoon. Why don't you go with him? It will cheer you up a bit," suggested Lavinia, with a look of sympathy in her attractive eyes.

"That's a good suggestion," agreed Letitia, getting up and giving her husband a kiss and a hug. "In the meantime," she continued, "let us go out into the garden with the children, and enjoy the lovely afternoon."

They all went into the garden conversing frivolously; trying to cheer up the master of the house as best they could.

Rufus and Letitia's house, was comparable to that of her father's in Cyrene. It fulfilled an old promise that a younger Rufus had made to himself. It was much the same in size and design, including a Venus pool which brought back dear memories to them. The gate was an exact copy of the one in Marcus' house as their romantic natures delighted in reminiscing about the hours that they had spent at that gate; some happy and some sad. They enjoyed entertaining friends, and had as a result become fairly well known in the neighbourhood. Their friend Cassius had visited them on two occasions, and they had enjoyed his company immensely. He was still supplying them with silver, which was stored as always in Erasmus' house.

It took the best part of a month, before Rufus accepted his loss and embraced life once again; even if without much enthusiasm.

At work, he and his partner were concerned that a couple of shipments of grain from Alexandria were substandard in quality. A voyage would have to be taken by one or the other in the future, to find a more reliable source. Vibia was expecting her first child, and Rufus felt that Tertius should stay in Rome to look after her needs. However, that was still a little ways off as they still had some grain in storage.

Now that Vibia was married, her friendship with Rufus had rekindled in a sisterly way as the latter had always hoped. She owed much to him for the way that he had looked after her mother Gaia and herself after her father's death, and prior to her getting married. However, her jealousy for Letitia had never totally disappeared.

Rufus had taken the larger share of the business, as he had had to manage it and take the responsibility for its continuing success. But had been more than fair in the portion he had allotted them. He felt he owed it to Erasmus, who had been so good to him and whom he had grown to love.

Rufus' life slowly returned to normal as the year ran its course. The new business year promised to be even more successful than the old one. Their imported goods were in high demand. Tertius was a good manager, and with the two very competent clerks they employed, made for a strong team and gave the firm great stability.

Letitia continued to nurse her desire for a trip to Cyrene. She knew that Rufus had now accepted the loss of his mother with resignation, and she finally decided to propose her much anticipated trip to her husband who rarely denied her anything. She opened the subject at the cena one evening as spring arrived.

"Rufus, I would love to visit my parents and take the girls to see them again."

"I have no objections to that. I just wish my mother was still alive to enjoy the visit too," said her husband with sadness in his eyes.

"We shall have to send word to your father and get him to send a cargo of barley over here with Marius, so that he can take you with him on his return, along with a cargo of roof tiles which I shall send him."

"That will be wonderful. Thank you my love," she said; her beautiful blue eyes bubbling with enthusiasm. The girls will have such a great time with their cousins, that they will want to stay there, and you, will have to go over yourself to coax them back."

All was made ready for Letitia's departure. Zaphira was saddened by their going, and suggested to her mistress that she would be quite content to stay out on the ship's deck if allowed to go.

"I need you to stay and look after the master whilst I am gone," pointed out Letitia, with a benevolent smile which made the servant (for she was no longer a slave) realise her role of responsibility in the household. "If I need you, I shall send for you, but you will serve us best by staying."

Six weeks later, in answer to his request, Rufus received a message from Marcus informing him that the *Stella Maris* was undergoing extensive refurbishing and repairs in Carthage. It would be out of commission for another two weeks at least, after which, it would be four or five weeks before it could get to Rome.

"I shall have to send you off with Silas who is due into port at Ostia within a week or so," said Rufus as he gave Letitia the news.

"Marius will take too long to get here and it is already past the middle of spring."

"Oh. I was banking on Marius coming for us. What a pity," she pouted.

"You will like Silas too. He has such a pleasant and jovial nature, that I am sure the girls will take to him easily. He is a good captain, highly experienced, and a good friend of mine. The children will enjoy his stories of the sea, and he will treat you all like family."

The *Pretoria,* now berthed at Ostia, awaited the arrival of the family to set sail. Rufus dropped into Neta's, where Letitia and the girls were introduced to the dear and congenial landlady. All, including Silas, had a very enjoyable luncheon before they finally boarded ship.

Neta and her daughter Lydia, who were very taken by their favourite lodger's family, accompanied them to the wharf, where Rufus bade a loving fare-well to his wife and daughters.

The ship pulled away gracefully on a calm blue sea and lightly clouded sky. Letitia and the girls waved back until they were out sight. Rufus, offered a prayer to Yeshua for his family's safety, bid goodbye to Neta and Lydia, and jumped onto the cart he had hired; the driver hurrying the horses so as to get back to Rome before nightfall.

A week passed since his family's departure. A lonely Rufus paced up and down the garden thinking of them, and at a loss as to what to do with his leisure time. Zaphira had outdone herself, fussing over every little item which would give him pleasure, and the cook had also excelled in the preparation of his meals.

'I miss them more than I thought,' he mused to himself, as he walked around the garden that Letitia had created with the help of Festus, and which reflected the happiness which comprised her life.

The pool of Venus with its life size statue, was the centre and heart of the garden, but was shaped rather differently from that of her parents' house in Cyrene. Following her request, her brother-in-law Alexander had sent her a design that was quite unique and beautiful. He had also sent a plan suggesting the way the various pathways, shrubs, trees and flower beds, could be organized; along with statuary, benches, and even arbours. The colour and choice of plants and flowers, he had left up to her, as he knew that she had excellent taste in that regard, and they should be to her liking in any case.

These things held Rufus' attention as he walked around, and from a myriad of thoughts and considerations, came the decision to finally travel to Alexandria, now that his leisure hours were dragging. That nagging bit of business regarding the substandard grain had to be dealt with once and for all.

The following morning he made known his intentions to his partner and after some discussion, it was agreed that this would be the best time to tackle the problem.

A corbita, fitted with a passenger cabin was said to be lying at anchor in Ostia, and Rufus was resolved to take passage on it if it was bound for Alexandria. As it happened the vessel was on route to Caesarea, but would touch at Alexandria. That route required it to stop at a number of ports: Rhegium in southern Italy, Phoenix in Crete, across to Alexandria, and finally following the coast of Egypt, to Caesarea. On the whole, a long journey on mostly open sea.

If all went well, he could be in Alexandria in thirty days at most. Hopefully less. His route would be almost the same as that which Silas had taken, as Phoenix would also have been the last port he touched at before crossing to Cyrene.

As provisions would be replenished at each of these ports, Rufus took only enough food for the first leg of the journey, with sufficient to last three days more than required, in case the winds should prove unfavourable.

He would enquire at the registry office in each port with regard to the *Pretoria's* progress, it being a week ahead of his ship which bore the name of *Nimbus.*

As Rufus boarded the ship, at Ostia, he looked at the passenger cabin, which he was to occupy, and said to himself in disgust:

'There is a good chance that this cabin, which I am about to inhabit for the duration of the trip, has been built by my thieving partner here in Ostia.'

The ship wormed its way out of the crowded harbour, bound for Rhegium, further down the coast. Its first port of call.

Being late spring, the weather was fine. They duly left Rhegium behind, having replenished food and drink, and made for the island of Crete.

The Rhegium Registry office had confirmed the arrival and departure of the *Pretoria,* and Rufus' mind was quite at ease that all was going well for Letitia and the girls. He hoped that the little ones would not be sea-sick.

The journey along the coast of Italy had been very pleasant. The passengers had been entertained by the view of forests, mountains and villages, as the ship kept close to, but at a safe distance from shore. Now they were out in open sea. The movement of the ship increased somewhat as might be expected, but by the same token, their speed also increased thanks to the stronger wind.

Finally the island of Crete crept into sight on the distant horizon, and the passengers eagerly awaited the opportunity to stretch their legs on dry land once again if only for a few hours. The *Nimbus* pulled into port at midday and allowed the passengers to disembark. They spent the next three hours procuring their victuals for the next phase of the journey, admiring the scenery, and stretching their legs.

Rufus made for the Registry office once again, where they confirmed the arrival and subsequent departure of the *Pretoria.* He then took a walk around the ancient town, ate, and bought food and wine for the final leg of his journey.

Phoenix proved to be a large city, offering every type of commodity to the traveller. The streets were packed with people. The well stocked and interesting shops and bazaars carried on a brisk trade. Its strategic location in the Mediterranean made it the hub of commerce, and very cosmopolitan. Many languages could be heard as traders bought and sold products from all over the world.

By the ninth hour the passengers of the *Nimbus* were all back on board, the captain and crew making ready to sail once again. Slowly the ship made its way out of the harbour, gliding past the many vessels at anchor, and out into the open sea.

Our galant Cyrenean stood at port-side, admiring the cliffs, beaches, and mountain ranges beyond; their soft purples broken up occasionally by masses of dark green forest and cultivated land that completed the background, framing in sharp relief, the houses that animated the landscape with their diversity of colours.

Soon the island faded into the afternoon horizon behind them and all became water once again, as the ship continued on its course to Alexandria.

The third day out the weather changed. The Sirocco wind increased and the sea became choppy. There was no rain, but the warm humid wind that accosted the ship caused it to roll around quite noticeably as it continually tacked, causing some passengers to become seasick. This condition lasted for two days and slowed down the ships progress considerably. At last the wind changed and the ship picked up speed again much to everyone's relief.

Alexandria finally loomed into view after thirty three days at sea, with food supplies having been exhausted three days earlier for a good many of the sixteen passengers. Fortunately the water supply had held. It was a hungry Rufus, who on disembarking, quickly made his way to the nearest food shop and appeased the uncomfortable feeling in his starving stomach.

There was to be no trip to the Registry office this time, as the *Pretoria* would now have been in Cyrene for over ten days or so. There was no way of verifying it for the time being. It could very well take a couple of weeks for news to arrive.

Rufus found a good inn and proceeded to make himself comfortable.

The following morning being the first day of the week, or 'Dies Solis,' Rufus went in search of a Christian place of worship as was his custom in Rome. There, they met every week at some predetermined, secret spot; usually in the garden of some large house or in some rented building. There were as yet no organised churches in Rome, such as his father and brother had built in Cyrene, and he wondered whether there were any in Alexandria.

He walked around the very impressive city all morning, gingerly asking someone every now and then, if they knew of a Christian Church. But to no avail. He then decided to try the Synagogues where he suspected that some Christian might be preaching outside the building, as his father had done in Cyrene before old Rabbi Elias had died.

There were many Judeans in that large and cosmopolitan city, and it did not take him long to find a Synagogue. However there was no preaching being done outside the first or even second that he encountered. After a quick stop for lunch, he continued his search. He was on the point of calling it a day, when he came across a crowd of people assembled outside of one to which he had been directed by a local.

As he drew closer, he saw a man standing on the steps, enthusiastically addressing an attentive crowd. The man was speaking in Greek, and as Rufus listened, he knew that at last he had found fellow Christians.

The preacher having finished the Baptisms that normally followed the preaching was walking away. The young merchant approached him.

"I am a Cyrenean and I have just arrived from Rome," he said in Greek.

"I have been wandering around looking for a Christian church, seeing that today is our Sabbath day."

The man looked at Rufus with a quizzical look and asked:

"What name do you go by?"

"My name is Rufus! I am the younger son of Simon of Cyrene. And who do I have the honour of addressing?"

"I am, Annianus! answered the tall, slim, preacher with a welcoming smile.

"An assistant to John Mark who is our bishop here. If you care to accompany me, I shall take you to him, since he has on many occasions mentioned your father and brother, praising them both for their excellent work in Cyrene. I am indeed very pleased to meet you."

He gave the newcomer an animated embrace.

The pair walked off together to where John Mark had set up his church.

It was an old, plain looking building of fair size, with a row of high windows and a large arched entrance with a great wooden door. On the door, the name of the church was inscribed in gold letters. 'Christian Church of the Redeemer,' appeared in Latin, Egyptian, and Greek. This massive door contained another smaller door through which they entered.

Rufus found himself in a very large well lit room. The high windows allowed the sunlight to light up the long wall opposite, which was decorated with colourful murals. These depicted many episodes in the life of Yeshua, and greatly resembled those that Alexander had painted in their church back home. There was also an altar at the far end of the room with a tabernacle on it. From the ceiling hung a number of oil lamps running down the centre of the room. They were suspended by ropes tied to hooks positioned along the window wall, allowing them to be raised or lowered as required. The wall behind the altar was also colourfully decorated. It depicted the figure of Yeshua with welcoming outstretched hands. A number of benches had been placed in front of the altar, presumably for the comfort of the older members of the congregation. Altogether a very beautiful interior he thought.

The pair walked down the entire length of the room, and Annianus entered a narrow door by the side of the altar, followed by his newly found friend. There, sitting at a desk and writing diligently was John Mark.

The bishop got up and saluted Annianus, who putting a hand on Rufus' shoulder and with a broad smile on his thin friendly face said:

"You will never guess who this is?"

"I am John Mark! who have I the pleasure of addressing?" Asked the bishop with a smile, as he awaited the visitor's mysterious introduction.

"I am Rufus! younger son of Simon of Cyrene. My father has often spoken of you and I am sure he wishes me to convey to you his love, along with my own respects, since we are meeting quite by chance, or perhaps providentially."

The bishop was stunned by the presence of the unexpected visitor and embraced our hero with great affection.

"The Lord be praised, what a wonderful surprise!" cried the bishop, clapping his hands, and turning to his assistant.

" Annianus! have I not talked to you often of this excellent family, and the wonders that Simon and Alexander have performed in my country?"

"Yes indeed bishop, and we have adopted many of the designs and formats that his family formulated with regard to the liturgy," replied Annianus, stroking his dark bushy eyebrow and smiling at his new friend.

"Quite so," confirmed John Mark with enthusiasm."You have no doubt noticed a large similarity between you father's church and ours as you walked through it?"

"The interior is indeed beautiful, and greatly resembles ours. How my brother in particular would enjoy seeing it," assured Rufus with sincerity.

"And how is your lovely family?" continued the bishop.

"Alas, I have sad news," announced the visitor with a lowered gaze and hastening to explain.

John Mark's face sobered to display utter sadness, at hearing of Ruth's painful death, and embracing our hero, said:

"I am so very sorry to hear that. She was a wonderful soul, and perhaps the most beautiful woman I have ever encountered."

He hugged his young friend again.

"She will be in our prayers always," he continued, "though we know that she is now in the arms of Yeshua, where we all hope to be in time, when it be his divine will to have us."

John Mark invited Rufus to dine with him and Annianus, who was close to the visitor in age. The evening proved very entertaining, as Rufus recounted many of his adventures, his reason for visiting Alexandria, and the fact that he was waiting for news of his family's arrival in Cyrene. In return, the friendly bishop recounted his own experiences whilst spreading the good news in Alexandria, and expressed surprise as Rufus informed him of the lack of churches and liturgical services in Rome.

"Paul, Peter, and indeed all the apostles," continued the Bishop, "have been very busy establishing the various communities, and have not had the time to settle down and build actual brick and mortar churches as we have done. However as they ordain bishops to look after the converted flock they leave behind, those good and holy men themselves will be setting up the churches. I have already talked to a couple of the apostles about this, but they are all too busy with their mission of 'fishing for men,' which keeps them constantly on the move. I have also talked to a few bishops, including our countryman Lucius of Cyrene, who is the Bishop of Antioch, and given them details of the liturgy as your father, brother and I are doing. It must in the end be an orthodox liturgy, where we are all doing the same thing so as to be faithful to our divine Lord's teaching, with the 'Breaking of the Bread,' and reading of the gospels. These, I am at present writing through the guidance of the Holy Spirit. Indeed a few others are writing them also, following the teaching of the apostles, and by inspiration from the same divine source whose presence we can palpably feel. When the apostles are all gone to their reward, the words of Yeshua must be, as 'set in stone', never to be tampered with throughout the generations to come, for in those words and by the grace of God, lies our salvation."

Rufus visited with John Mark and Annianus almost every day, as he went around Alexandria sourcing new grain suppliers. He had quickly dispensed with the people he had been dealing with. These, he soon learnt, were not considered reputable in the trade. Actually the suppliers he settled with for future consignments to Rome, happened to do business with his good friend Cassius, from Hispania. This gave the Cyrenean merchant much confidence, and set his mind at ease.

His business deals finalised, he spent a little more time with John Mark. The bishop was hopeful that he might convince the young merchant to train for the priesthood, and have him and his young family come to Alexandria, to help him Evangelise further into the country.

Rufus politely refused the offer. He had a strong business in Rome, for which he had worked very hard, and a very satisfying family life. He would not change careers, or move from the Imperial City.

Rufus had now been in Alexandria for fourteen days, and as yet had no news of the Pretoria. It being the Christian Sabbath, he attended the service. He passed up Annianus' invitation to lunch, and made his way once again to the Harbour Registry office to obtain confirmation of his family's arrival in Cyrene.

The clerk on duty, recognising him from his earlier visits, pulled out a scroll, and with a sad expression on his face, handed it to him to read. Gingerly, Rufus unrolled the parchment and read.

'The *Pretoria* sank after a collision with a larger vessel at night, as it approached Apollonia in Cyrene. Several lives were lost. Underwriters have placed the blame on the other vessel the ....' Rufus was overcome with grief. He read it again, and again. He could not believe it.

The blood drained away from his face giving him a deathly look. The clerk quickly pulled out a wine skin from under his desk, and gave the stunned visitor a drink. Rufus, in his dazed condition, lent heavily on the counter to keep himself from falling. The kind man found him a stool, and sat had him down.

"Take it easy please. You obviously had a loved one on board," stated the clerk with great sympathy. "But you despair too soon, not all lives were lost, surely you have hope?"

Those words of the clerk plus the swig of wine that he had taken, brought the blood back into Rufus' face, as he realised that all might not be lost. At last he felt able to speak, and with a broken voice, he asked the clerk for further and more detailed information. The clerk shook his head, but promised to question each captain as they arrived.

Rufus asked him when the next ship that would be bound for, or touch at Cyrene was due. The man checked his records, and replied that a ship would be sailing within the next day or so, and gave him its name.

Our distraught hero gave the good man five denarii for his kindness and took his leave. He sadly made his way to his inn, where falling on his bed he burst into tears, and lay there for the rest of the afternoon, praying that his beloved family might have survived.

Later that evening, he found the ship which was to sail the following day and bought a passage on deck, as it had no passenger cabin to offer him. It was bound for Carthage, with a brief stop-over in Cyrene.

He spent the last few hours with John Mark and Annianus. Both men tried their best to give him hope, but it proved to be a very sad evening indeed.

Next day, his two cleric friends saw him off at the wharf in Alexandria, promising him continued prayers, and asking him to send them further word as soon as possible.

CHAPTER TWO

FAREWELL ROME

Rufus, baggage on shoulder hastily approached the gate of Marcus' house.

His ship had just berthed on the wharf in Apollonia Harbour and it would surprise no one that he had been the first person to disembark.

As usual, the gate was closed and not a soul in sight. He rang the bell and waited impatiently for Tecuno to come and open it for him. Moments later, the servant appeared, displaying a fallen countenance, trying his best to smile, his eyes wide with surprise, his mouth blurting out his normal greeting.

"Welcome young master," as he opened the gate, his head down, to avoid looking him in the eye as he took the baggage.

"Daddy!Daddy! Daddy!" came the high pitched excited voice of little Letitia, who appeared from nowhere it seemed, and ran into her father's arms.

Rufus' face lit up with joy as he embraced the lively little form which he found in his arms. He kissed her over and over again, tears of relief streaming down his face, as he walked up the path to the house with her in his arms. Tecuno, leaving the gate ajar, ran on ahead to alert the family of the young master's arrival.

"Where is Mummy and Marcia?" asked the jubilant father.

"They are with Yeshua, and I miss them so very much," replied the innocent little voice with a pout on her lovely mouth and tears brimming in her large blue eyes.

Rufus froze. He let the child slide down slowly to the ground, his eyes transfixed on the roof of the building, as Julia and Marcus appeared at the front door.

He turned of a sudden, and ran to the gate.

"Rufus! Rufus! wait. Please wait," shouted Julia and Marcus simultaneously as the latter ran after his son-in-law, who speeding through the gate, disappeared round the corner to the sound of, "Daddy! Daddy!"

"Let him go," said Julia catching up with her husband, and taking the little one by the hand. "He will be back when he gets over the shock."

Turning to her grand-daughter, Julia asked:

"Darling, did you tell daddy where mummy was?"

The girl, with tears falling down her beautiful little face answered:

"Yes, Gramma."

Tecuno picked up Rufus' bag with one hand and little Letitia with the other, and feigning a big toothy smile, his eyes dimmed with tears, said that her daddy would be back soon; he needed time, he told her, to think about mummy and her big sister. They all went back into the house, praying that God would give Rufus the strength and consolation that he needed, to come to grips with the tragedy.

At his masters request, Tecuno took a horse out of the stables, saddled him, and took it to the front of the house, where Marcus quickly mounted it and galloped off to Simon's house.

Rachel opened the door in answer to Marcus' knock.

"How lovely to see you Marcus," she greeted as she embraced him. "What brings you here?"

"Your brother Rufus has just arrived. He heard of the tragedy from little Letitia, who was the first to see him at the gate. He put her down, as he had been hugging her, and ran back out the gate. We don't know where he has gone. I did not pass him as I came up the hill."

Rachel who had been praying constantly for her brother, burst into tears and called out in an agitated voice for the rest of the family to come, as she showed the visitor into the house.

"Rufus is back," she cried, as Simon, Lucila and David entered the room, followed by their daughter, little Ruthie.

When the shockwave had passed, they all sat down to plan what they would do.

First, he had to be found, and that would not be easy. Our hero's present state of mind was unpredictable. It was decided that they would all disperse in different directions, and start an immediate search for him before he got too far.

Simon got Pepper out of the stable, saddled him, and made ready to go. David took his horse and trotted off to his parents' house as his first stop, to see, though unlikely, if perhaps he had gone there. Marcus went back down the hill to Apollonia to search around the harbour area and the beach, whilst Simon opted to ride up to Cyrene and elicit Alexander's help in the search.

It was late in the afternoon when the party met at Marcus' house after a futile search.

"Soon it will be dark and then we will have to wait until morning," pointed out Simon showing signs of fatigue. "God alone knows where he will be then."

They all knelt in Marcus' atrium and prayed to Yeshua for help. Midway through the prayers, Alexander got up and made for the door.

"I think I know where he might be," he shouted back and disappeared.

He rode up the hill until he was about half way to Simon's house, and dismounting, he led his horse into a neighbour's field from where he could see the sea. He approached the boulder that he and his brother had sat on a few years back, contemplating the sea. On that memorable evening, Rufus had been distraught because of Letitia's impending banishment to Rome by her mother. There was no one sitting on the boulder, but as he approached, he could hear someone crying. He looked over the large fieldstone and there on the ground, lay his brother shaking and weeping in great anguish, his heart breaking. Alexander dropped down beside him, a great lump in his throat as he fought back tears of sympathy, and picking him up, held him as the pitiful crying continued.

The brothers sat there for a long while. Rufus, slowly and with great difficulty, recovered his composure.

"She was everything to me," he wailed.... "Everything! How could Yeshua do this to me? How could he allow this to happen when we believe in him and he is supposed to love us? Is God getting back at me for all the Sabbaths I broke?

You are a priest. Tell me. Is that why?...And my little one too. What could she have been guilty of? She was only eleven years old. As if having taken our mother was not enough grief for me."

The questions kept coming. Alexander did not try to answer any of them. He simply continued to hold his brother, letting him feel his love.

It was late that night, when Alexander arrived at Marcus' house with a mentally exhausted Rufus in tow. Little Letitia had been put to bed, and Julia had already prepared a room in anticipation of his eventual arrival. All in the house dispersed so as not to intrude on his private grief until the following morning, when hopefully, he would have recovered somewhat from the terrible shock.

Alexander decided to stay the night with his brother at Marcus' house. He sent word to Hannah with his father, who rode up to Cyrene on Pepper.

Julia and Marcus had great difficulty in keeping little Letitia away from her father's room next morning. Alexander who had not slept all night, appeared at breakfast time in the atrium. He informed the family that his brother had finally fallen asleep just a couple of hours earlier, and should be left unmolested until he awoke on his own. He badly needed his rest.

It was a bitterly sad day that followed Rufus' appearance at noon. As you, my sympathetic reader can well suppose, an indescribable scenario unfolded in that beautiful little dining room that had been Letitia's favourite, and which brought back so many memories. Little Letitia would not leave her father's side and insisted in holding his hand all the time.

Eventually the sadness in the room subsided enough that Rufus was brought up to date with the particulars of the collision. It had become evident from witnesses on board the larger ship that their helmsman had been drunk, and it being a dark night, he had not seen the *Pretoria* in time to alter course. The latter ship, had been struck at midships toppling her over and damaging the hull very badly. All the passengers on board had been hurled into the sea and more than half of them had drowned.

Silas desperately trying to find Letitia and the children who he knew were asleep in the cabin, managed to pull out little Letitia through the window as the ship rolled over, taking her mother and sister with it. Silas had been ill for days after, and had stayed in bed at Marcus' house until the ship's owner had taken him away to attend the enquiry up in Cyrene. The bodies had been recovered later, and both mother and daughter had been interred in the garden that Letitia had loved so much. Tecuno placed fresh flowers over her grave every day. He and Silia mourned the loss of their beloved mistress, to whom they had been so devoted. Alexander was carving a small monument to put over the grave.

Little by little, Rufus recovered in the bosom of his family, and began to accept his misfortune. Simon and Alexander ministered to him with great patience and love, making him realise that God had a plan for him now that his life had changed. Just as his father's had changed when his mother died.

'Yeshua certainly has a plan for him and all will be very clear in time....God's time,' thought Simon to himself from the depth of his sorrow and hope in his big heart.

Over the next month, Rufus made some progress with his recovery. He visited Silas up in Cyrene, and found a very different man than he had hitherto known. The distraught captain kept blaming himself for not having been able to save Letitia and Marcia. Rufus had to put his grief aside for the moment in an effort to console his sick friend.

Two weeks later, the *Stella Maris* pulled into port, and a very sad Marius paid his respects to his adopted family. The captain accompanied Rufus on his visits to Silas, greatly consoling the ailing mariner, and starting him on the road to recovery.

Shortly after, Marius sailed for Rome with a cargo of barley and our recent widower on board; the latter intending to dismantle the remnants of his life in that city, and return to Cyrene for good.

"Are you really going to sell your business as well as your house?" enquired the captain asserting what Rufus had just told him, as they stood on deck, awaiting the berthing of the *Stella* by the longshore men, who were pulling her onto the quay at Ostia.

" Zaphira will most likely go back with you," said Rufus, "I am sure she will want to look after little Letitia and tutor her as she did her mother."

He put a hand on the Captain's shoulder.

"Please send word to my office when you load up with the tiles," he continued.

"I can get her here within five hours or so."

Rufus took leave of Marius, and walked off to Neta's house to inform her of his great loss.

Our hero spent the night at Neta's, sharing his sadness with his friend who was greatly shocked by the tragedy that had befallen him.

Back in Rome, Drucila was similarly shocked and distressed at hearing the sad news. She invited Rufus to stay for supper with her, and did her best to cheer him up.

Finally, late in the evening, he arrived at his house. Festus opened the gate for him and expressed his sincere condolences as Rufus greeted him. Entering the house, he called for Zaphira, who came running and threw her arms around his neck weeping bitterly. He, with tears in his eyes, returned her embrace.

"What are you going to do now young master?" she asked, withdrawing from his embrace.

"I am selling everything; business and house. What do *you* want to do? Do you want to stay here, or do you want to come back to Cyrene?"

"I want to go back to look after my little Letitia, of course, and take care of you. My dear lady would have wished that."

She broke into tears again.

"What is there to keep me here?" she wailed.

Rufus nodded solemnly.

"Captain Marius is in Ostia and will take you back in perhaps five days. I was pretty sure you would want to come back. I am very pleased that you agree. You are family, and we all want you with us."

"Who is going to look after you when I am gone?" she asked. A concerned look in her dark eyes. "It will take a while for you to arrange all the things you are planning."

"I shall stay with my old friend Drucila," answered Rufus, "my old room there will be comfortable enough. I do not need much of anything any more.... Though Lavinia and Linus might insist I stay with them. That will be more painful for me. They, being family, will remind me of many things which if I do not put aside for the moment, will drive me mad."

It took Rufus the best part of a month to settle all his affairs. He sold his share of the business to Vibia and Tertius, agreeing to let them buy him out over a period of three years as they did not have the money to buy it outright. They too, were very saddened not only by his tragedy, but in losing him as a beloved friend and partner.

The toughest farewell was with Lavinia and family, who had grown to love our hero, as well as being devastated by their great loss. Despite his reticence, he had found himself obliged to stay with them. Linus, had been instrumental in the sale of his house to a friend.

A month from the date of his arrival, Rufus was bidding sad farewell to Bashir and Aula on their barge in Rome, assuring them that business would continue as hitherto with both Erasmus' firm and that of Marcus' also.

As always, his last stop before embarking on the *Felicia,* which was now captained by a much recovered Silas, was at Neta's place. He went a day ahead of his departure time so as to have a final cena with her, her daughter, and Silas. The latter, was now a welcome visitor to that house, and would be the means of her keeping in touch with Rufus. Silas had Caesarea as his destination, but would make a stop at Cyrene to allow Rufus to disembark, and have David build a passenger cabin on his new ship.

The trip went well as far as the weather was concerned. However, the trail of sadness followed, as the two protagonists of the tragedy at sea, mulled over and over, the circumstances that had devastated their lives.

In Rufus' case, a total change was about to occur, though during that dismal voyage his mind had lost all desire, and he simply existed. He spent his hours sitting behind the captain's cabin by the 'Swan's Head,' staring into the depth of that cruel blue sea passing under him, without generating a single thought for the future; his precious memories crowding his mind, to the exclusion of everything else.

Silas fared somewhat better. The necessary routine on board ship diverted his attention from his haunting thoughts. The vessel had as yet no passenger cabin, but now, he had the owner's permission to have one built, and that kept his mind occupied.

"Perhaps you can help David build the new cabin for me," volunteered the captain.

No amusing smile cheered his face now. Since the tragedy, he had developed a nervous tick, which made his nose twitch at intervals, interfering with his speech. He spread his arm over his friend's shoulder as he spoke, and hoped that his suggestion if accepted, would go far in diverting the latter's depression by his being gainfully employed.

"The sea mesmerizes me," remarked Rufus, continuing to stare down into the wake of the ship and ignoring his friends suggestion. "It seems to promise eternal tranquility after just two breaths of torment to those it claims. Like a powerful wild animal whose beauty and graceful movements inspire admiration, and when it kills, it does so in one quick lethal moment, causing his prey a minimum of anguish and pain."

"Your two loved ones did not suffer much. As you infer, they died quickly."

"For that at least, I have to be thankful to God," was the reply; with a tone of protestation and a faltering voice.

Silas left him to himself. But going over to his helmsman, he quietly briefed him to keep a vigilant eye on his disturbed friend.

Day after day, the troubled Rufus continued to spend his hours by the 'swan's head,' looking down as if mesmerised by the water; head bowed, and without eating. Sometimes, he would stand up, and lean dangerously over the side; alarming the helmsman on duty, and putting him at the ready.

The *Felicia* finally pulled into Apollonia harbour, and tied up to the wharf, much to the relief of the crew. There it would remain for at least a week.

The returning father quickly disembarked, and made his way to Marcus' house to be with his little girl. She ran into his arms the moment he entered the gate. Once again shouting,"Daddy! Daddy!"

He picked her up and carried her into the house. Julia came across the atrium and embraced him with tearful eyes, and a loving smile on her handsome face.

"Oh, Rufus my boy, what a difficult time you must have had in Rome. Did you manage to sell the house as well?"

"Yes, Lionel found me a buyer among his friends. The business, I sold back to Erasmus' daughter Vibia and her husband. He is an excellent manager and a fine fellow. They will be paying me over the next three years, as they had not the funds yet. I got a good lump sum from them though, for the time being."

"That's great. I am relieved to know that at least, you will not have any monetary problems."

"I shall arrange everything with Marcus, so that little Letitia will have her own money when she grows up."

"But you will be around, and all that we have will be hers too," she affirmed; stroking his cheek and giving him a kiss.

At this point, Marcus entered the atrium and approached his son-in-law.

"Rufus my son, you are home again....How wonderful!" he said, tightly embracing him. Then, bending down, gave his little grand-daughter a hug as well. She, taking her father's hand, pulled him away to her room to show him something that her uncle Alexander had given her.

Little by little, our hero began to adapt to his new life. His father, the bishop, seeing how pointless his son's life had become, got him involved in church affairs, in which he seemed to show some interest. Alexander and Hannah had him help them duplicate the gospels that they knew of; he being such a gifted scribe. He lived in Marcus' house near little Letitia, but would ride to either his father's house or up the long hill to Cyrene to work with his brother and Hannah. He often passed Simon the tanner, as the latter rode downhill on his way to his tannery in Apollonia.

One day, Simon invited Rufus to accompany him on a mission to a remote village up in the mountains beyond Cyrene. It was not often visited by the bishop, but his young assistant Saul would go there once a month, and perform the 'Breaking of the Bread' service for some of the villagers. The service was performed in a large house which was always at the priest's disposal.

The first night of their journey they spent out in the open. They reached their destination around noon the following day.

Father and son were heartily welcomed by the little congregation who rejoiced at seeing their beloved bishop. They quickly made their way to the house where they normally assembled.

Three of the villagers took charge of the preparations, and that same evening, the Christian service was held. The liturgy, with which Rufus was now acquainted was performed. Simon officiated, with his son attending to his needs.

The Blood of Christ had just been distributed. Rufus was holding the metal container, in which the cloths that dried the little silver cups were to be burned. He was about to go outside, when all of a sudden, a commotion was heard.

A woman was carried into the house on a stretcher, interrupting the final stages of the service, as she was placed in front of the makeshift altar.

Simon stepped around and looked at the sick young woman, who could not have been more than twenty. Her brown eyes which appeared very large in comparison with her thin pale face, were encircled with purple rings, and her lips were colourless. Her body shook as if from the cold. He was about to address the little congregation and ask them to join him in prayer for her, when he was overcome by the calm feeling that occasionally gripped him. He found himself saying.

"In the name of Yeshua, and by the power of the Holy Spirit, be cured."

The gathering held their breath, as the young woman's face took on a healthy rosy colour. Straightening her clothes, she arose with a look of surprise and elation. Only to fall again at Simon's feet weeping thankfully.

The good bishop picked her up, and in his customary manner, informed her that it was not he, but Yeshua, who had cured her. The assembly broke into a hymn of joyful thanksgiving for the miracle.

Rufus was stunned beyond words, and going over embraced his father with great reverence, realising how Yeshua had worked through him.

This was to be the turning point in our young hero's life. From that day on, his enthusiasm for the faith became his prime preoccupation. For the next two years, he learnt all that he could about Yeshua's life, and the interpreting of the gospel messages as taught him by his father and brother.

As the winter of the second year ended, Rufus was keen to have his father the bishop ordain him with the 'Laying of Hands.' Alexander felt very strongly that his brother was now ready for the priesthood, and urged Simon to perform the ordination.

The bishop consented to his sons' request, and a date was set to coincide with Marius' arrival, as was their custom when any important event was to be celebrated by the family.

The *Stella Maris* berthed in Apollonia three weeks later. The 'Dies Solis' following the captain's arrival, was the day set for the ordination.

The 'Christian Church of Yeshua of Nazareth' in lower Cyrene, filled to overflowing for the celebration of that sacramental service.

Little Letitia now eight years old, was thrilled to see her daddy made a priest like her uncle, and grandfather. Now she could boast to her cousin Simon, who was five years older, that her daddy was the same as his.

After the beautiful and moving service, the family celebrated the bittersweet event in Marcus' house, where Ruth, Letitia, and Marcia were often mentioned, and lovingly remembered by all those present. They would now continue their lives without them, in the service of God.

Hannah, Rachel and Lucila sang a special hymn that Hannah had composed to celebrate the occasion, accompanied by all the children: Simon, Bart, Judy, Ruthie, and Letitia. Simon, listened with moist eyes as the young voices sang. He remembered his beautiful Ruth, when she sang with her girls at

John Mark's farewell supper on his memorable visit to Cyrene. The evening reached its climax, when Marius requested Baptism much to the joy of every one. He was immediately baptised there on the spot, by his beloved and overjoyed friend, the bishop.

It was not until a couple of days later; two days before the *Stella Maris* was due to sail, that Rufus announced to the family his intended departure for Alexandria to work with John Mark as he had been invited to do.

Everyone, with the exception of Simon, was taken by surprise. The bishop knew instinctively that this was the Lord's doing, and thanked Yeshua for strengthening his son's faith and making him also 'a fisher of men.'

Little Letitia was heart-broken when she heard of her daddy's pending departure, and insisted he take her with him. It took a lot of convincing and a promise to return soon, before Rufus managed to appease her. Zaphira promised to continue instructing her as she had done for her mother. The new priest with the love and affection of his wonderful, dedicated, Christian family, sailed away with his friend Marius, to face whatever God had destined for him as he ventured to spread the good news to the Egyptians.

CHAPTER THREE

MISSION

The redoubtable *Stella Maris,* plied its way across the Mediterranean Sea once more on its way to Alexandria with two of our heroes on board. One of the two, feeling at home with his surroundings which engendered a certain permanency to the course of his life, found contentment, which at his age was perfectly desirable. The other, welcoming a new and unpredictable life, braced himself for a challenge of a most important nature. Such as would reshape his entire life, by its profound spiritual demands on his youthful abilities and commitments.

Marius, now a baptised Christian, which gave further stability to his contented existence, was most anxious to learn more about the faith that God had finally given him the grace to accept. Doubtlessly, the prayers of Simon over the years had had much to do with his conversion.

The parables of Yeshua in the gospels were to intrigue and excite him, as Rufus made a great start to his priestly career, with the instructing of this excellent human being. In the course of the voyage, the priest taught him as much as he could; which was considerable. Simon and Alexander had worked hard to educate him in matters of the faith.

"Tonight," began Rufus one afternoon as they both sat in his cabin.

"I am going to perform the 'Breaking of the Bread,' the origin and importance of which I shall now explain to you."

The eager captain listened attentively. He remembered all the times when Simon had had to refuse him with great regret the participation in that Sacrament, as he had not been a Christian at the time.

"Yes," said Marius, "you need to explain to me what sins there are that I may have committed. As you say, I have to be absolved of those before I can receive the 'Body and Blood' of Christ in that hidden form."

It took the rest of the afternoon, for Rufus to explain to his hitherto pagan friend, the origin of sin; the Ten Commandments; and Yeshua's condemnation of sin; particularly against one's brother, which poised the most common challenge to human weakness.

"There are many sins which we commit every day that are not really serious, and those are forgiven you without being confessed to a priest. They are forgiven directly by Yeshua; provided that you pray to him; feel repentant for having hurt him who loves us so much; and resolve to try to correct your behaviour in the future; asking for his grace to accomplish it. Remember that without His grace, we can do nothing that is meritorious.

"I was not aware that so many things were sinful. What you call serious sins, such as can lose one's soul, I mean. I have not committed any of those, except for the worshipping of a false god. Though not having been a religious person, I really did not worship any god in particular until now that I believe so strongly in Yeshua.

Yes. I have fought other people," he continued. "I have spoken ill of them if I felt that they were behaving badly. I have been with a good number of women. But most of the time I keep to myself, and mind my own business. I do not cheat anyone, and I do not lie. Except in commercial matters, when it would be foolish to be too truthful."

So ended Marius' confession. His good friend the priest, soon realised that new converts coming from a pagan background and not having ever heard of the ten Commandments, or anything that was morally restrictive in their lives, were perhaps blameless. They were following their inclinations without any rule whatsoever, and therefore to a large degree, ignorant of their wrongdoing.

"So then," added Rufus. "you have not committed any of the big sins that I have mentioned to you?"

"Coming to think if it,...I guess I have sometimes envied other people for having beautiful wives, and things which I do not have. It is hard being a bachelor you know. But I have never attempted to rob a man of anything, far less his wife."

"You then repent of all those sins?"

"Yes, of course. As you say. Our souls must be pure before receiving the Body and Blood of Yeshua."

"I absolve you of your sins; in the name of the Father, the Son and the Holy Spirit," said Rufus making the Sign of the Cross.

As promised, the 'Breaking of the Bread' took place that evening. It was the first time that Marius had participated, and it made them both very happy.

Seven days later, the pair embraced, as they bid each other farewell at the Harbour in Alexandria. The captain, having instructed Rufus to leave messages for him at the Registry Office as usual, wished him God's blessings in his endeavours.

John Mark was very surprised at Rufus' reappearance. Once again he was busy with the writing of the scriptures in his little room behind the altar when the latter arrived.

"Welcome! Welcome! my dear friend," greeted the bishop as he quickly got up from his desk and embraced Rufus.

"What brings you here again?" asked the surprised bishop.

"I was quite devastated at the news you sent me, telling me of the death of your wife and child. I hope the Lord has calmed your tormented mind and given you peace in your acceptance of that terrible tragedy. We have been praying that Yeshua might give you the strength to bear it, and also that they may both be enjoying His company as also your mother's."

"Thank you. I am most grateful," replied Rufus. "I came to assist you as you once proposed to me. I was too absorbed in my worldly occupations to consider it at the time. God drives a hard bargain though, and so here I am, an ordained priest, entirely at his disposal and yours."

John Mark looked at his prospective assistant with a knowing look.

"As your father has probably told you, Yeshua has a plan for your life which in the end will be a saving one as far your soul is concerned. Just as he had planned for your sister Rachel, your father, and your brother. The future of the Church, depends on all of us pulling together on his behalf, and he will give us all the help we need to keep it on a straight course with the assistance of the Holy Spirit, who will be our constant inspiration and guide."

"Eventually," said John Mark, as he conversed with Rufus one evening. "I would like you to start a mission in Memphis if you are up to it."

"That would suit me very well," replied our hero, with enthusiasm.

"Very well then," said the bishop with a smile. "Once you are acquainted with the ways of this country and have a passable command of the language, I shall send you off to Memphis where you can make a start."

Rufus and Annianus became very close friends, seeing as they shared the same room at the back of the church next to the bishop's room. Rufus gave John Mark most of the money he had with him, but asked that he be reimbursed with some of it whenever he needed to visit his daughter, or to buy tools which would enable him to find employment as a carpenter in Memphis when the time came. The carpentry would provide him with a means of livelihood until his ministry flourished, as had occurred with his father.

For the next two years, the Cyrenean priest served faithfully under the Cyrenean bishop. Annianus who was gifted with a good sense of humour, would jokingly refer to the two as the ' Cyrenean conspiracy,' when things did not go his way.

However they got on very well, as they all kept in mind their mission.

John Mark, had ample time to assess his countryman. His suspicions were now confirmed in that the latter had been endowed with a very practical, outgoing personality, and gifted with many talents. He decided that it was time to probe further into Egypt's interior by using Rufus to launch the evangelical mission, he the bishop, had come to that country to accomplish. The endeavour, being plagued with many problems and dangers, he was reticent to send Annianus, who was more reserved and introspective, though equally as devout and dedicated as his Cyrenean colleague.

During those two years of service to the bishop, Rufus had been learning the Egyptian language from a native member of the congregation. As a result he had a fair command of it though he was by no means fluent as yet. He preferred to preach in Latin if it was understood, or Greek if he had to. As was the case in the majority of instances, the people of the Mediterranean were able to converse but not necessarily write, in a number of languages beside their own, especially the Greek and Latin. Egypt had a Greek heritage from the time of Alexander, and was presently a Roman Province.

One Sabbath day, after a solemn service for the success of his mission, and dedicated to the Holy Spirit, the young Cyrenean priest set out across the Nile delta on foot to begin his work in the Memphis area, about one hundred miles inland from Alexandria.

He was conversant with Egyptian history, customs, and ancient religious beliefs, and was well prepared for the battle ahead with a people who worshipped many gods, and held a strong conviction with regard to the Afterlife. He was also aware that Gnosticism had made some inroads there, and if encountered, he would also have to deal with that.

There was much tension in that country between the Greeks and Judeans especially in Alexandria, and Rufus had to be careful not to get entangled in that squabble. He carried some money; enough so as not to have to depend on people's charity, and to buy tools with. He plodded on in the heat of the day through the fertile fields of the delta, stopping at night in villages where he would eat frugally and find humble lodgings. As he travelled along that beautiful Nile Delta, rich in produce, he purchased freshly baked bread, delicious goat cheese, and dried fish and meats, in the villages that he passed. Fruit such as dates and figs, were usually given him by farmers along the road with whom he occasionally stopped to talk.

Rufus chose to follow one of the seven tributaries of that famous river; its banks profusely covered with papyrus plants. Children swam near the shore and played in the morning sun. Women washed their clothes in the river, whilst chanting their high pitched trembly melodies. Riverboats floated noiselessly on their way to Alexandria, loaded with the grain that would eventually reach Rome, making Ostia the bedlam of activity that it was. Wheat fields abounded; their golden hue colouring the landscape, livening all the other colours around them. Fig trees were everywhere, and the majestic date palms punctured the serenity of the golden horizon, their fanning branches swaying interminably in the gentle, warm breeze. Water, for which he carried a metal cup, was never refused him as he passed the many wells along the way. In this manner, he reached Memphis in four days and nights.

The splendid, ornate dagger that his friend Cassius had given him in those adventurous days of his youth, he still carried with him; no longer for protection but mostly as a means of cutting his food. It was the envy of all who saw it. The dagger was one of the things that Rufus cherished; not so much for its beauty and usefulness, as for the memories it recalled.

Though he had been briefed to the contrary, his trip had been a safe one. It was with relief, and thanking God, that he finally entered the ancient city of Memphis; now merely a shadow of its former glorious days, when it had enjoyed for a period, the status of capital of Egypt. The villages on his route, though small in size had been located close together. Thus, cutting down considerably, the length of desolate, unguarded roads, as had been the case in Gaul and Hispania. Doubtlessly, the good Lord had kept him safe in answer to the prayers promised him by John Mark and Annianus.

The evening of his arrival, sitting under an unusually large fig tree in the backgarden of his lodgings, Rufus contemplated the next step of his mission.

His train of thought was interrupted by the approach of a well dressed man in his mid thirties, of average height and medium build. He had a long face, dark in complexion, with refined features, and he wore a short pointed beard. His eyes like his plentiful tightly curled hair, were very black and had an intelligent, enquiring look about them.

"May I keep you company for a while, or is my intrusion into your deliberations unwelcome?" asked the man with a smile, exposing a fine set of very white teeth which lit up his whole face.

"You are most welcome," replied the priest returning the smile with his own habitually charming one.

"I go by the name of Senh, and I come from Karnak in the Upper Nile," announced the newcomer, and stretching out his hand, met with Rufus' who introduced himself as he pressed it.

"My name is Rufus. I come from Cyrene by way of Alexandria."

The newcomer, sweeping away some leaves that had fallen from the tree, sat on another bench opposite our hero's.

"I am a merchant of sorts," volunteered the man. "I deal in antiquities.... This city has much to offer in that regard."

"That sounds like a most interesting line of work," commented the priest. "Those commodities offer much variation, and are quite lucrative I have no doubt, since the buyers are wealthy and generally enthusiastic."

"Indeed you are right. However, much depends on the trader's expertise, as there are many worthless pieces around which have been made to look like originals. Some expert craftsmen employ their talents to trick people out of their money. It takes the likes of me to ensure their authenticity," explained Senh with a touch of pride.

"I have been a merchant too," remarked Rufus, "though a carpenter by trade. I owned a business in Rome importing grain, wine, olive oil, silver, and other goods that were needed there."

"Are you here to buy grain then?"

"No, I am now on a mission to preach Christianity in Egypt."

A look of surprise covered the Egyptian's face and shifting slightly on his bench said.

"I have heard something of your faith, and it has certain similarities to the faith of the Jew has it not? Though they vehemently deny it."

"You are correct," agreed the priest. "In essence, Christianity is a continuation of their faith, since Yeshua the Christ was a Jew himself. He claimed, and we believe him to be the Jewish Messiah and the Son of their God, and this they could not accept. Alas! They crucified him."

"As you probably know, our Egyptian faith is based on the belief in an Afterlife, as I think yours, and the Jewish faith also are."

"That is so," continued Rufus, leaning forward hands joined. "However, it seems that to attain that happy Afterlife to which your faith aspires, one is required to be properly and ceremoniously embalmed."

"Yes, true. It is absolutely necessary," conceded Senh with a nod of the head.

"Have you nonetheless stopped to consider the plight of most of your population who would not be eligible to enter into that happy Afterlife, as they could never afford the high cost of embalming?"

The Egyptian looked at Rufus with a surprised look on his handsome dark face but kept silent.

"I hope I have not offended you my friend," said the priest as he in turn had kept silent awaiting the other's reply.

"By Horus!" exclaimed the antiquarian of a sudden after a very long pause.

"We are so comfortable in our own precious lives, that we do not often stop to consider others who are not so fortunate. No! I must be humble and agree with you. But what would your religion do to remedy that tragedy for poor souls, who are certainly worthy of consideration?"

Rufus got up, sat beside Senh, and looking at him with a faint smile said,

"For me it is quite a simple matter. Christ came to save every single person from his sins, regardless of his status, so as to allow him or her to enter the Afterlife. There, He, his Father, and the Holy Spirit reign in a perfect, loving, and just world where happiness is forever guaranteed."

"How do you know this is so?" asked the Egyptian, after some consideration.

Rufus remembered his father recounting to him his talk with Ahmed on the road to Joppa, and he gave the same answer,...saying.

"Because, Yeshua the Christ rose from the dead after having said that he would.

His apostles were witnesses to his resurrection. He visited them many times, and he even ate in front of them on one occasion after his death, to show them that he was no spirit, but flesh and blood. His tomb had been found empty three days after his death even though the Jewish authorities had sealed it after his burial, and placed guards around it. Forty days later, he had his disciples accompany him outside the city to watch him ascending to his father in heaven, and disappearing from their sight with a promise of returning."

The antiquarian stared at the priest for a few moments. Suddenly, he got up, and walked away without a word. He almost bumped into the landlord who was standing there and had surely been listening to their conversation.

Rufus remained sitting, somewhat confused by the abrupt departure of his new acquaintance.

Next morning, Rufus was awakened by a gentle knock on his door. He got out of bed, put his tunic on, and opened. There stood the Egyptian with a tired look on his face.

"My apologies for disturbing you," he said, as the priest motioned him in.

"I have not slept a wink last night after what you told me."

"Oh dear, I did not mean to upset you," said Rufus throwing a friendly arm over his new friend's shoulder.

"What you told me last night is a powerful thing, and I am still trying to adjust my thoughts," said the antiquarian with a perplexed look, and crossing the room, sat on the bed.

"The great difference in our faiths," began Rufus, "lies in the fact that yours is based on a hierarchical structure, much as all societies in this world are based. The poor man is totally overlooked. Yet, he is the doer in everything, whilst the others command. Anything that is accomplished, is by his labour, which translates into sweat and blood. However, their merits are ignored and taken for granted. Yeshua came with a different message. He came to help the poor particularly, so that they would have the same right in the heavenly kingdom as his masters here on earth. His precepts are based on love. '*Love your neighbour as yourself.*' He said. And things like; '*no greater love does a man have than he lay down his life for his friend.*'"

"You must tell me much more about Yeshua," begged Senh, rising and placing a friendly hand on Rufus' shoulder.

"I certainly will," assured Rufus. "But now I have to get out of here and see how I am going to earn my bread whilst I preach Yeshua to the people of Memphis.

"You are going to make many enemies as well as friends," warned Senh. "I shall help you as much as I can. I am coming to believe in your loving God. It makes much sense to me, especially as he said he had come to save everyone."

The man left. Rufus performed his ablutions, and after breakfasting at his landlord's table, went in search of a carpenter who might employ him.

After two days of searching Rufus found an employer who was impressed with his experience, and willing to take him on. This saved him from having to buy tools and paying for a workplace of his own. The preaching, he would have to do in the evenings after his day's work.

'But then, that is how my father did it,' mused the priest, 'and there is always the Sabbath when I can dedicate all day to it.'

For the next week, Rufus worked with the carpenter who had hired him. At night he would be found preaching atop a little mound that was part of a garden near his lodgings. Because people promenaded there, it was lit by a number of torches courtesy of the city for the benefit of the general public.

Rufus had as yet not baptised anyone. But he noticed as days went by, that many of the people came every single evening to hear him. By their questions and general demeanour he was very optimistic with regard to their impending conversion.

The landlord of the lodgings where the priest was staying was a Jew. Though he had treated his lodger with apparent kindness he was resentful of his faith, and even more of his intentions of spreading it. He had overheard the conversation between him and the Egyptian under the fig tree in the garden, and witnessed his preaching from a hidden vantage point after having followed him secretly in the evenings

Senh who was a prime candidate for baptism, had left left for one of the archeological digs, the day following their first meeting, and had not yet returned. In the meantime some of those who had been attending the Cyrenean's sermons were asking to be baptised, which gave the priest a problem as to where to perform the sacrament.

He was walking home alone one night buried in his thoughts regarding the expected converts, when he felt a sharp pain in the head.

Rufus awoke to find himself in the dark. Not a sound could be heard. His head ached badly, and he hastened to examine the location of the pain. His fingers felt a massive bump which hurt sharply to the touch. The area was dry showing no signs of bleeding. He got up and started to probe his way around. He could not make up his mind whether he was in a cave or a room. Eventually he found a door. There was no handle on his side of it and he could feel where the nails that had held it had been pulled out. After further probing, he discovered what could be described as an opening; most likely a window, rather high off the sandy floor on which he stood. The opening, large enough to crawl through, he supposed, since there was no light from the moon that night, was obstructed by two iron bars. These proved to be well embedded. Having allowed him to raise himself up by hanging on to them.

After he had inspected every surface of his cell, Rufus sat down, and began to think who could have wanted him out of the way. He checked to see if his money had been taken. It was still there. Then a panicky thought crossed his mind and he quickly searched for his precious dagger. It was there too.

'Thank God!' whoever has kidnapped me was not interested in robbing me. They just wanted me out of the way. Do they mean to leave me here to starve to death? Someone in the park must have taken offence at my preaching and planned to get me out of the way before I spread my message. It could be anyone really,...Jew, Egyptian, or Gnostic.'

Seeing there was nothing he could do for the rest of the night, he prayed to Yeshua for help. A little later, in an effort to relieve his headache he allowed himself to fall asleep.

The morning light streaming in through the window woke Rufus up, and he once again surveyed his surroundings. He needed to find out even if vaguely, where he was. One jump got him a good grip on thc window bars and he pulled himself up. His head which had now recovered except for the large swelling, pressed painfully against the bars as he took stock of the exterior. He could see a number of ruins and some desert beyond. Nothing else caught his eye. Down he flopped again as he realised that he was in a truly isolated spot, and had no idea whether his captors would return or not.

Jumping back onto the window, he yelled a number of times for help in all the languages he knew. No answer came back. He let himself down again, and continued praying. Whilst he prayed, Rufus began to examine the door with great care. It opened to the inside, the hinges being on his side. His precious little dagger would be no match for those iron hinges nailed in with hefty nails and he did not want to damage it. He then knelt down on the floor to take a better look at the lower one. As he did so, his foot sank inordinately into the sand and made him wonder as to its solidity.

The bright Cyrenean, began to clear sand away with the help of the dagger, his hands following the contour of what seemed to be a rock. Before long he discovered that the floor below the sand was made up of stones which must have been placed there many years ago. They had been laid down to form a makeshift floor, without any mortar to join them. They were it seemed, of a size that he could move if not actually lift, and they did not fit tightly with one another.

Working diligently for the next hour, he managed to pull out three of the stones located in close proximity to the door. He then began to remove one of the two that straddled the bottom of the door. Because half of the stone was on the outside of the cell, he had to work lying on his stomach, reaching as far as possible. By digging further on his side and creating a slope, he was eventually able to make the stone respond to his pull; sliding it under the door and into the cell. There was now a large gap under the door and by persevering in his digging, Rufus made it possible to slide back the final stone, clearing his intended exit.

Finally after two hours of work, our diligent hero was ready to escape. Lying on his back, he managed to squeeze himself out head first under the door and up some steps to freedom. The room must have been used as a storeroom for the workmen who had at one time been digging in the ruins.

Shovels, levering bars and other iron tools were all piled up outside.

Rufus looked around the area. There was not a soul in sight. He had no idea where he was. He climbed up a high mound of rubble behind the ruins, and to his relief, saw the city.

As he found his way to his lodgings, he mulled over the possible identity of his captors. Suddenly he stopped. It dawned on him that his landlord being a Jew might have a hatred for him though he had not shown it, and could have set up the kidnapping.

He approached his lodgings stealthily, and with apprehension. Hearing voices coming through one of the windows, he drew closer to listen.

"No. From what he told me, he was going to look for work as a carpenter."

"No. No. As I told you, he left in a big hurry," the landlord was saying. "He would not even tell me where he was going."

"That is very odd," said the other, who Rufus recognized as Senh. " I am very surprised. I think he would have told me. He seemed like a very sincere man."

In a flash, Rufus jumped in through the window, and quickly took hold of the landlord, overpowering him. He held the man down, and explained to the antiquarian, the kidnapping that the guilty rascal had masterminded. They bound him with his own belt, and laid him on the floor on his stomach. The irate priest sat on him until the Roman soldiers whom Senh went to fetch, arrived and arrested the man.

The place of Rufus' detention was visited by the Roman authorities that same day, accompanied by both Rufus and Senh. It bore out the story given them by the former. The trial was set for two weeks, during which time the identity of the other two culprits who had actually done the kidnapping became known and were both apprehended. All three were eventually sentenced to fifteen years hard labour under Roman Law.

Both Rufus and Senh found a new home with an Egyptian family. Thus they continued to share common lodgings, allowing them to further their friendship; the antiquarian becoming a Christian soon after.

The preaching on the mound in the little public garden continued. The Cyrenean priest made many converts. He went to preach armed with a water jug, and towel, which became his hallmark, and were transported on a donkey that he had bought. His friend Senh would tease him about riding around on a donkey. But he would answer, that if it was good enough for Yeshua, it was good enough for him.

A few months went by, and Rufus had won many souls for Yeshua, including his new landlord and family who had grown quite fond of him.

CHAPTER FOUR

THE CHURCH

John Mark was beginning to be a little concerned about our hero, as he had not heard from him for over two months.

"I wonder if Rufus is alright?" he said to Annianus. "We do not know whether he is still in Memphis, or has moved on beyond."

Coincidently, at the same time as John Mark was becoming concerned about Rufus, the latter was saying to himself.

'I am no longer my own boss. I should send word to John Mark giving him news of what I have been doing here. It is my duty.'

That same evening, he got down to writing out a message to his superior, and sent it off five days later with a pedlar who also acted as a courier, and carried messages to Alexandria once or twice every month.

"Aha!" exclaimed John Mark. His assistant stood beside him waiting expectantly, as he read the parchment from Rufus.

"He has been having trouble over there," said the bishop, with a serious look on his face, and stroking his short trimmed beard.

"They actually kidnapped him, but he escaped. Yeshua be praised. He has won a good number of people for the Lord already, and he is now trying to buy or rent some place that he can convert into a church so that he can celebrate the 'Breaking of the Bread.'"

Annianus was shocked at the news of his friend's kidnapping incident, but knowing Rufus' history he was not really surprised. It seemed that the man was prone to unusual events. John Mark agreed with his assistant, and nodded his head in agreement.

" He will need some money. Perhaps, Annianus, you can go visit him soon and take him some of his own which I have saved for him. I knew that sooner or later, he would be in need of it."

Annianus was delighted at the idea of visiting his friend, but it would be a few more weeks before he could be spared by the bishop to embark on his trip.

Finally, permission was given him, and he was able to journey to Memphis. Since he was carrying a good sum of money, he took the precaution of travelling with a guarded caravan, though it would take him longer to get there.

* * * * *

Rufus was overjoyed to see Annianus. He introduced him to his landlord's family, and with particular pleasure to Senh, who had become a close friend.

The two priests were soon absorbed in their planning of the new church's activities. All that remained, was to find an appropriate location for the church, as near to Rufus' lodgings as possible. The new converts were all from that part of town, which Rufus knew well, and had got quite used to.

The constant hatred of the Jewish community for the Christians in other parts of the Empire, including his beloved Cyrene, made Rufus very aware of the perils of maintaining an active church. However, not withstanding these fears, the determined duo embarked on their hopeful search. If the building could hold three hundred people, that would do for a start they reasoned. The new disciples to date numbered a mere thirty or so, but with hope, prayer, and dedication, plus the ever present assistance of the Holy Spirit, they believed all would be accomplished.

As they walked around the area they favoured, they became aware of being followed. They ignored the matter not letting it interfere with their quest.

Encountering a large building on their way, they stopped to examine it. A row of high windows ran along its entire length, much like John Mark's church in Alexandria. The door was not large, and had no embellishments whatsoever. The deserted appearance of the place made them suspect that it was for sale or rent, but the owner would have to be found. They knocked loudly on the door in the hope that someone would be there, and could inform them further.

They continued to knock at intervals. Receiving no answer, they were on the point of leaving, when the door opened. A very old man leaning heavily on a staff, asked what they wanted.

"Is this building for sale?" asked Annianus in his fluent Egyptian.

"You will have to speak up," said the man. " I am deaf."

The priests were aware that whoever was following would now be listening, so they asked the man if he would permit them to enter.

"First you must tell me what you want," said the old man stubbornly.

Seeing that they had no option, Annianus repeated his question.

"What is that about the building?" asked the old man loudly.

"Is it for sale?" shouted the exasperated priest with concern on his face. His partner, whose sense of humour was ever part of his amiable personality, turned away as he giggled, inadvertently spotting the man who had been following them.

The old man bade them go in. The spy disappeared from view, lamenting the fact that he had been seen.

"You can go ahead and look around," said the old man. "The owner is not here. His name is Menes and if you are interested in buying or renting the place, come back tomorrow at this same time. I shall see that he's here."

The two men, took a good look at the interior. There was a similarity between this building and the one in Alexandria, except that this one was much smaller.

Unexpectedly, at the rear of the church proper, there were five rooms, an enclosed garden with a well, and a colonnaded porch which provided shade during the day. One of the rooms was next to where the altar would be located which was a good feature. It would serve as an office and daily storage for items connected with the services, and would also give Rufus a place to receive people. The other rooms would be used as living room, kitchen and bed rooms.

All things considered it would make for a good church if the price was right.

Some renovations would have to be made however and that would strain their budget further, but the priest could live there and save the rent from his lodgings.

They agreed to come the next afternoon, but an hour later. Rufus who had got away an hour earlier with his employer's permission, could not expect to repeat it.

The following day, late in the afternoon, the pair left their lodgings immediately on Rufus' arrival after work. Shortly after leaving their house, they had the feeling of being followed once again.The two clerics, put their heads together and came up with a little plan to lose or trap the spy. They split up, each taking a different route. Soon it became apparent to Rufus, that the spy was following him.

From his many meanderings around the area Rufus had become very conversant with its streets and houses. There happened to be a house on his daily route to the carpentry shop, whose owners he knew, and who allowed him to cut through his property occasionally when he was late for work. He would otherwise have had to go right around that street.

He had been cautioned by the man of the house, who happened to be a stone mason, that on crossing his backyard where he had made a very narrow stone pathway cutting through the pig sty, he should take care to avoid stepping on a treacherously loose stone. It was the only black one there; it wobbled badly and needed stabilizing.

" I never seem to get around to fixing it, despite my wife's constant nagging," the mason had told him.

That day as Rufus sought to shake off his pursuer, he realised with mischievous intent, that perhaps with a little ingenuity, he could shake the man's resolve in following them.

He made for the back of the house ensuring that the spy had seen him. He reached the backyard, and stepped his way through the sty with confidence; skipping as usual over the loose black stone, and making his way towards the next street.

The spy who had seen him vanish behind the house, came running and did likewise. At this point the wily Cyrenean allowed the man to get a glimpse of him as he turned into the street. There, he hid, and waited.

He held his breath for a few moments,...and then...."Ah! Ah! Ah!" came the expected and very audible confirmation, as the hapless spy found himself examining in the closest possible manner, the repulsive, foul smelling, sloppy ground, whilst being cordially,..if a little roughly greeted, by the sociable inhabitants of the sty.

It took Rufus enormous willpower to restrain himself from looking back to enjoy the amusing sight. He proceeded with the broadest of smiles on his handsome face, along his now unencumbered route to Annianus and the prospective building.

The visiting priest, walking around the building with the owner discussing its condition, wondered why Rufus was taking so long.

"Here I am," came the jubilant voice as the latecomer appeared in the doorway with a satisfied look on his face.

"You look like the cat that swallowed the canary," commented his brother priest.

"I've had a very amusing experience," said our hero. "I shall tell you more anon."

Annianus introduced Rufus to the owner of the building, and all three began their negotiations in earnest. It took all the bargaining skills that the two clerics possessed to cut down the price of the property from two thousand denarii which was the asking price, to one thousand seven hundred; an amount closer to what they had offered.

The priestly pair walked away satisfied with the transaction which was to be completed within two days as per their agreement.

"I wonder," began Rufus as they sat outside in the back porch of the their lodgings, "if perhaps I should try and get John Mark to give me permission to visit my little daughter in Cyrene, before I get to building this church, which will keep me here for the Lord knows how long?"

"That is a difficult question to answer," replied Annianus, smoothening his eyebrow, "especially as we now have the chance to get this building at a good price."

"Oh no! We would still buy the building, but I would not start the renovations until I got back," pointed out the Cyrenean.

"Mmmmm....well, I shall ask him when I get back, and we shall send news back by the courier."

The pedlar courier previously mentioned, was the only reliable way to get messages from Memphis to Alexandria and vice versa, even if only once every three weeks or so. Rufus used the trustworthy man to take news, and occasionally scrolls for his family, to the bishop. John Mark, would then pass them on to Marius when the latter visited him on his infrequent stops at Alexandria. This way, Rufus had kept in touch with home and little Letitia, who was for ever enquiring when daddy would be coming home.

Memories of his beloved Letitia, occupied his mind every vacant moment. He still missed her and the children terribly, and now, little Letitia being the only living member of his beloved threesome, he was guilt ridden at neglecting her. Any other occupation would not have warranted his having abandoned her. But the service of God, he felt, was of paramount importance, and other considerations of this life would have to be subservient to such a vocation.

'After all,' he said to himself, 'my little one is surrounded by love and affection; is receiving a good education, and has every advantage that anyone can desire. I must take solace in that. Please the Lord I shall be able to visit her when he sees fit'.

With these thoughts he consoled and justified himself, and decided to stay and build the church.

The two days of grace came due. Rufus completed the transaction, and now he owned the building.

"No.... I shall be going back to Alexandria," said Annianus, in answer to his brother priest, who had just asked him to stay a little longer.

"The bishop expects me back. After all, I only came to see you, and to bring you your money," concluded Annianus, his fingers smoothening his eyebrow.

Though he was telling the truth, he could have stayed a little longer. However, Annianus had recently met a woman whom he had fallen in love with, and he had as yet not had a chance of telling her. He suspected that she favoured him, but since there was nothing certain in their relationship, he did not mention it to either the bishop or Rufus. That, was really the reason for his hurried departure back to Alexandria.

Senh, volunteered to help with the renovations to the building.

Rufus' friend, the stone mason, would be hired to repair all damage to walls and stone floors. All the carpentry was to be done by the priest himself, as often as he could, without cutting down too much on the hours of his preaching in the park. His new disciples in Christ also volunteered their help. Since some of them owned donkeys and carts, the transportation of materials back and forth from the construction site would present no problem.

No sooner had the Jewish community heard that the building was to be a Christian church by the name of 'The Holy

Trinity,' than they started throwing stones through the windows, injuring two of the workers. Rufus, remembering how close his father's church had come to being burned, appealed to the Roman authorities for help. A soldier was temporarily assigned to guard the church and arrest anyone attempting to vandalise it.

It took two full months before the building was made habitable, but there was still much to do in the way of carpentry. Rufus who was then working part time for his carpenter employer, could only devote two afternoons a week to his carpentry. The remainder of the time, he was obliged to work at night by the light of oil lamps, following his preaching in the park which took precedence over everything else.

The altar, built on a three step high platform, had a tabernacle secured to it following the same design that Alexander had devised for the altar in Cyrene. Some temporary benches were made for those older members of the little congregation who would find it tiring to stand for the duration of the service.

Two of the back rooms were cleaned, the existing walls and ceilings repaired, whitewashed, and each fitted with a bed, bedside table, chest for clothes and ablution stands. A workable kitchen was built. A cook was hired and paid for by Rufus and Senh.

The antiquarian, being a bachelor, had left his lodgings and moved in with his friend to keep him company, and help with the expenses. Rufus had allowed himself enough money to last them three months if they lived frugally. A bonus feature of the building was a well in the gated backyard which provided the two occupants with good fresh water. A small stable to accommodate the donkey was built there. All things considered, the carpenter priest was well pleased with his purchase.

The second Christian Sabbath day of the fourth month of construction, which happened to be the feast of the

Resurrection, (in future times it would be known as Easter Sunday,) saw the church opening, with a total membership of forty seven baptised souls all eager to receive the 'Body and Blood' of Yeshua.

Rufus, with Senh assisting him, performed the service. It was a very joyful congregation, who joined in on the final hymn to the music of a harp and lute, provided by two young women who led the singing, much as the priest's sisters did in his father's church.

This was a far cry from their previous meetings in an old warehouse that a member of the little congregation had kindly permitted them to use over the past few months.

* * * * *

Six months passed, the congregation grew a little larger. All the carpentry work had been completed, but no decorations had yet been carried out on the walls of the actual church, which had simply been white-washed. It looked stark, as opposed to those of Alexandria and Cyrene. Rufus, was not too concerned about that however. It would come in time as the congregation grew, and perhaps, the Lord would provide a good artist. Maybe even from the congregation itself, as it was growing so steadily.

'If only Alexander were here,' was often on the priest's mind in that regard.

One night, Rufus woke up as a result of a dream he had been having, and thought he could smell burning. He sleepily made his way to the church. To his horror, it was full of smoke. The benches, and a whole stack of wood debris from the construction which was sitting there waiting to be carted away, were on fire, with the flames threatening the altar.

He quickly ran to the well, and taking the bucket that hung there, he shouted for Senh to wake up.

"Fire! Fire! shouted Rufus. There's another bucket in the kitchen!"

Pandemonium took over for the next half hour, as the friends ran back and forward filling their buckets at the well and and throwing water on the fire.

Fortunately the shutters of the window closest to the altar had been closed, and this prevented the torches that had been thrown through the other windows from setting the altar and tabernacle on fire.

The fire was beginning to travel along the floor towards the altar platform. The desperate pair soon realised that oil had also been thrown in to help spread the fire. The water was not halting the advance of the flames. Senh ran back to the garden, found a spade, and quickly began to dig up earth with which he filled the buckets. Simultaneously, Rufus ran back and forth dumping the contents on, and ahead of the flames.

At last after almost an hour of battling with the flames, the fire was extinguished. The exhausted duo sat down in the back porch inhaling the fresh air their lungs were craving for.

"The Jews are back to their dirty tricks," said Senh scratching his beard; a look of disgust on his face.

"I forgot to close the shutters," sighed the priest with much regret.

"It was a good thing that the one by the altar was closed, or they would have burnt the tabernacle and the consecrated bread and wine," said the Egyptian with concern in his eyes.

"Yes," agreed Rufus, "I shall have to be more careful with those shutters in the future."

After a long wait the smoke cleared completely. The whitewashed walls and ceiling, were a sorry site all stained by the smoke. They would have to be painted again. The shutters were then closed using a long pole with a hook at the end, that stood by the back wall solely for that purpose. Having done that, the two men went to the kitchen to relax with a glass of juice and some fruit.

"There is no one to accuse this time. We saw and heard nothing," pointed out Rufus, taking a mouthful of the juice.

"Even though we know who they were," commented Senh sarcastically.

Suddenly there was a loud knocking at the door, and both friends got up and rushed to the church door.

"Who is it?" enquired Senh .

"Open up, it's us," chorused voices which belonged to two members of the congregation, one by name of Melech, and the other Jeth; both Judeans.

The door was opened and the two men entered. They brought the news that a bunch of Jews laughing and bragging about having set the Christian church on fire, had woken Melech up as they passed by his house in a drunken state.

"We had suspected as much," said Rufus, "but we have no proof, as we didn't catch them in the act."

They talked for a while, surveying the sorry condition of the church with its sand covered, soaked, stone floor. The two men then departed, promising to return the following day to help with the clean up. The exhausted priest and antiquarian were left to their much needed rest.

The following morning, it was rumoured throughout the city, that the Greeks had attempted to burn a Christian church. No one knew who had started the rumour, but the Jews were suspect. It did not take long for a bunch of Greeks to attack a group of Jews and soon, city wide street battles erupted. The Roman peace-keeping force moved in, a number of people were arrested, many were injured, and two lost their lives.

Rufus was extremely unhappy on learning of the loss of life and injuries, as it was all because of his church burning that the rioting had occurred. He went to the Roman authorities accompanied by Senh, and explained the whole situation; including Melech's evidence, with regard to having heard the Jews bragging. The authorities who did not want another riot on their hands, informed the priest, that since they had no names or adequate descriptions, they could do nothing, and to consider the matter closed.

Shortly after the riot had been put down, Rufus received a message from John Mark, requesting him to visit Alexandria.

The bishop had just received a scroll from Lucius of Cyrene, Bishop of Antioch, containing some proposed changes to the existing liturgy, and wanted to consult with his Memphis pastor, prior to giving his approval.

Annianus, who was about to marry, invited Rufus to the wedding which had been arranged to coincide with his visit.

Rufus entrusted the church to Senh, and two parishioners; Demetrios and Sosigenes, and left for Alexandria. This time by riverboat, which was somewhat slower but safer than travelling by land. He had had to terminate his employment with the carpenter, which he regretted. On his return, he would buy some tools, and start on his own, since he had two spare rooms in the church where he could work, and the use of the backyard as well. The donkey's stable would be enlarged, and the wood required for his projects, would be stored there. A cart would be the only other thing needed.

* * * * *

As our hero, embarked on the riverboat, to Alexandria. I invite you, my esteemed reader to visit with me a secret underground Egyptian temple beneath the ruins of an ancient temple of Amon in the desert just outside of Memphis. The worshipers in that temple, were a sect who called themselves ' Amonites'. Not because they worshipped the god Amon (which meant 'hidden,') exclusively, but because they considered themselves, 'The hidden ones.' Their traditional god was Ptah, but as in many other cases, a number of gods were worshipped in unison and Isis, was their preferred goddess.

The solemn service having just ended, three priests, their heads and eyebrows, shaved, and clad in their leopard skin ceremonial tunics, walked off to their room behind the large statue of Isis to change. Bare-breasted women, eyes heavily outlined in black, their jet black hair falling limply over their shoulders and all in immaculate white robes with elaborate necklaces, fussed around the statue of their goddess Isis. They were busily putting away ceremonial vessels, tidying up, and extinguishing lamps, and torches.

Two bronze cauldrons that stood on each side of the statue burning herbs, were being covered and their fire extinguished by bare headed male assistants also clad in white linen robes. Their eyes smarted from the smoke which ascended up the stoney vortex overhead, sucking it to the exterior where it merged inconspicuously with the night air. Other assistants were busy extinguishing the many oil lamps that had illuminated the temple during the service, leaving only a few to light the priests' exit and to burn themselves out overnight.

The faithful began to leave. They slowly trudged their way up the winding ramp that would lead them to the secret entrance, well hidden among the ruins of the ancient temple. They dispersed in small groups so as not to attract attention.

"Before we break up for the night, let us discuss this business of the new Christian temple," began a man called Addaya, the eldest of the priests, removing his leopard skin robe, and looking at his two colleagues.

"Something has to be done," commented the youngest of the three, scratching his shaved head."But we have to plan it very carefully. The last thing we need are the Romans interfering, and finding their way back to us here."

"I think we would be wise to watch and study their comings and goings for a while, until we are thoroughly acquainted with their daily habits," suggested the other, who went by the name of Ahmes. There was malice in his eyes, as he struggled to remove his robe.

"Then," he continued, "we can strike with certainty and kill as many as we can".

"If we can eliminate the priest who is causing all the trouble, I think that, will put an end to them for the moment," pointed out Djidi, the youngest one.

"We are not looking for a temporary solution," pointed out the older priest, with a look of exasperation in his wrinkled face. "There is no point in getting rid of their present priest if they are simply going to continue sending other priests."

"We shall not know, until we have tested their metal," asserted the younger one. It seems that they were unshaken by the Jews when they tried to burn them out."

"Buildings can be replaced, but devoted men are much more difficult to replace," stated Addaya, lifting an index finger in a gesture of admonition."

"Regrettably, these Christians are not like the Jews, whom we can afford to ignore. They keep to themselves, and do not attempt to convert any one."

Ahmes, finally free of his leopard skin robe, which had got entangled with his sandle straps, solemnly declared with hatred in his dark eyes:

"The Christians are a real menace both to the Jews and us. They are constantly trying to convert everyone to their ridiculous faith. We have lost at least eight of our people to them already."

"Allocate someone to keep a constant watch on the building," said the elder, addressing Ahmes the middle aged priest. "Have him report back to you on a daily basis."

With these words, they all prepared to leave their subterranean temple.

* * * * *

Rufus' arrival in Alexandria, was celebrated with love and great enthusiasm by both Annianus, and John Mark. That evening, after a good supper, the three clerics, sat until well into the night, exchanging views regarding the proposed new changes to the liturgy, and listening to all of Rufus' difficulties in the building and maintaining of his church.

"I shall have to send a scroll immediately to your father and brother regarding the changes to the liturgy. As you can see, they are very minor. Mostly a matter of sequence, and a slight change to the closing prayers. Otherwise all remains the same," explained John Mark with a smile, looking at Rufus, who nodded his head in concurrence.

"They will both be very happy to learn that the Bishop of Antioch is also a Cyrenean," remarked the pastor with a touch of national pride.

"The Jews attack us at every opportunity," lamented the bishop, remembering Rufus' recent experience. "We are a constant thorn in their side, and the more of their people that we convert, the greater their hatred of us becomes. There is no reasoning with them, they are so set in their ways."

"Still," pointed out the Memphis priest, "we continue to attract many of them; by the grace of God."

"We too have had many problems here, caused by them and the Greeks," said Annianus, smoothening his eyebrow with a look of concern. "They are forever at each other's throats regardless of the cause. My future wife is Greek, and I am worried about her family's safety."

"Have you heard from Captain Marius lately?" Asked Rufus hopefully, at the mention of family.

"He is due in within the next two weeks or so I think," replied Annianus.

"We can visit the Harbour Registry office tomorrow and find out."

The following morning the two priests made their way to the Registry office, chatting enthusiastically about the impending wedding which was to take place three days from hence.

"The *Stella Maris* is expected in port five days from now if all goes well for it, reported the clerk with a smile on his face, as he recognised Rufus and remembered the generous tip that he had once received from him.

The priestly pair thanked the man, and at Annianus' suggestion, they went in the direction of his betrothed's house which was located at a fair distance from the church.

The future husband knocked confidently at the door and both waited impatiently for someone to open. A rather unremarkable but pleasant looking girl of about fourteen, opened the door, and seeing Annianus, produced a big smile and called for Euthalia to come to the door.

"Annianus is here!" added the young Helene as she showed them in.

Rufus was introduced to Euthalia and her family, and both were cordially entertained. A nice lunch was given them, as they became acquainted with our hero.

The bride-to-be, was pretty and petite. Her future husband towered over her as they stood beside each other. Her hair was dark brown, as were her large eyes, which looked at Annianus with admiration, as he talked about Rufus' church in Memphis, and the difficulties that he had had to overcome in setting it up, and keeping it going.

Both the sisters accompanied the two men part of the way on their walk back to the church. Euthalia was twenty two years old and very talented. She could read and sang beautifully. So, she was described for Rufus' edification, by her doting espoused who happened to be seven years her senior.

Two days later, the happy couple were married, and a great feast was given them following a beautiful church service. The congenial bishop had officiated with Rufus' assistance, and a good portion of the congregation was there to enjoy the ensuing celebration.

The newly weds left for Gizeh by river boat, to see the pyramids and the sphinx, which Euthalia had always yearned to see. They would then go on to Sakkarah and lastly to Memphis. There, they would stay at the church as Senh's guests for a few days, enabling them to visit the sites in that city before returning to Alexandria.

Once the couple had left, Rufus got down to the business of letter writing to little Letitia and his father Simon; sending him the changes to the liturgy. Marius would take the scrolls back to Cyrene with him.

The good bishop John Mark, was overjoyed to have Rufus with him, and he talked about the Simon family with regret at not being able to visit them; his work being so very demanding and restricting. He reluctantly admitted that in his weaker moments, he envied Marius the freedom he enjoyed in his career as the captain of a ship. Travelling however was now a risky business for any bishop, not only because of the usual perils that it posed, but because of their responsibility to their congregations and the supervision of their churches. There was always the fear that in their absence, their enemies who would stop at nothing, could destroy all that they had worked for on Yeshua's behalf.

'The Evangelist,' as John Mark was later to be known, had written many stories and parables of Yeshua's life, which were being known as Gospels, and he read quite a few of them to Rufus. They enjoyed discussing their message and how best to present it to their respective congregations. It was critical that they be interpreted in an orthodox way; all priests being of one mind. Not a single word would be changed once it was written down. After all, it was the written word of God, and the Holy Spirit was its inspiration and guiding light; all of which was readily apparent in the evangelist's enlightened eyes. Rufus was transfixed as he listened to the saintly bishop expound on the texts as he read them. He knew that like his dear father, John Mark had been singled out and privileged by God to carry out the mandate of His divine Son in a very special way, and had given them special powers even to heal people as Yeshua himself had done.

A day later, Rufus was embracing Marius on board the *Stella Maris,* and trying to catch up on all the news from home that he thirsted for. The ship remained in the harbour for five days. The two friends enjoyed much time together, as the kindly bishop allowed Rufus every possible free moment.

Not too much had changed back home, Marius had told him. With one joyful exception. The birth of a son to Lucila and David. They had named him Rufus, which produced a lump in the priest's throat, as he remembered his mother, and how she would have enjoyed seeing her latest grandchild.

His father was well; just getting older as was Marius himself. The latter happily informed him that he had lately married Sarah in Joppa, and would be taking her to live in Cyrene. There, he would rent a little house near Hannah and Alexander. The captain was contemplating selling his beloved *Stella* soon, and retiring in Cyrene.

Little Letitia was growing up very quickly as Rufus could see from a small portrait that Alexander had painted of her. She looked more like her mother every day, and the proud father treasured having it. With eyes threatening tears, he asked Marius to thank his brother for his thoughtfulness, and Lucila and David for the honour of naming their son after him. He sent much love and blessings to all the family, whom he greatly missed and continually prayed for.

Marius, and the *Stella Maris,* sailed from Alexandria with scrolls, best wishes and prayers from Rufus, who resigned himself to the will of God, and made ready to return to Memphis as soon as Annianus arrived back in Alexandria.

CHAPTER FIVE

THE FUGITIVE

There were many people milling around the riverboat that Rufus was intending to board, as he left Alexandria by himself. Both Annianus and John Mark, who had bidden him farewell at the church, were busy helping some members of their congregation who had got into trouble with the local authorities.

The travellers who intended to board, were impatiently waiting for those disembarking to clear the way. There were still a few animals on the boat, and some of their owners were having difficulties getting them onto the jetty. They all had to be lifted over the boat's railings and restrained.

A gentle tap on his elbow distracted Rufus for a moment, and turning, he encountered a young woman of considerable beauty. She quickly explained that she was escaping from her pursuers, and would he kindly accompany her on board; as she would be too conspicuous by herself.

"Here is some money for my fare to Heliopolis," she said, as she attempted to give him the money.

He, whose mind was still trying to adjust to the situation, was anticipated by his natural chivalrous nature.

"No, no, keep your money for now, we can talk later."

The woman who was in her early twenties could not keep her feet from fidgeting with fear and impatience, as they both waited to board. She kept looking back over her shoulder as if expecting her pursuers to appear at any moment.

"I am being pursued," she said, with fear, looking into Rufus' eyes. "Please act a as my husband. I shall explain later."

Rufus smiled, and nodded in the affirmative.

After some further waiting, their turn arrived, and they were motioned on board by the captain who took our hero's money as they boarded.

The boat was about to pull out of the stone jetty, when of a sudden, a man jumped into the boat. Another man who had arrived with him, remained on the the jetty and took hold of the vessel's cable which was being untied by one of the crew.

"What is this?" asked the irate captain. "We are not taking any more passengers. We are full and in the act of sailing."

The man put some money into the captain's hand and asked him to wait for a few moments. He was searching for a woman he said, who was absconding with his money.

There must have been at least sixty people on board and a number of small animals, goats, dogs, sheep and so on. It was difficult for any one to move around.

Rufus could feel the young woman shaking with fear. She took his waiting hand and they squirmed their way to the starboard side of the boat, which fortunately was only a few paces away. They both pretended to look out across the river, staying very close to one another. She kept her face averted, but he turned every now and then and could see that both the man on the boat and the one on the jetty were scrutinising all unaccompanied women.

Moments later, the pursuer got quite close to them. Rufus decided to confront him, as the man was actually pressing up against him.

"Watch it friend," he said, "my wife is not well, and she needs a little room." He gently but firmly held the man at elbows length. The man probably in his mid- forties and of a slender build, looked at the pretending husband, and attempted to look at her. She put her head on Rufus' shoulder hiding her face from the man, who was left with no option but to move away.

"Please leave my ship now!" shouted the captain. "I must sail."

Reluctantly, the intruder pushed his way slowly back to the jetty side and climbed out of the boat. He and his partner, continued to examine the passengers as the boat floated away. Frustration registered strongly on their faces.

The riverboat serenely glided along; Alexandria now half an hour behind. The woman, having regained her composure, introduced herself to her rescuer whose gaze showed admiration and kindness.

"My name is Miriam, and I am a Jewess, though I was born in Alexandria," she said, accompanied by a beautiful smile which displayed her excellent teeth.

"My name is Rufus, and I come from Cyrene. I was also a Jew," he said smiling at her.

"I have not given you the money," she said with a concerned and lovely pout on her beautiful mouth, which brought his beloved Letitia to mind. He involuntarily winced at the thought.

She, thinking that he was annoyed at her forgetfulness, quickly apologised.

"No, no," he replied, "I shall not take your money, it is my pleasure to treat you. I have not been in the company of a woman for some time now, and I am enjoying yours."

"You looked rather sad a moment ago, and I thought it was because I had not reimbursed you for my fare."

He looked at her for a moment and with a tender smile, he said.

"The beautiful look on your face as you spoke, reminded me of my lovely wife, whom I lost in a ship wreck at sea close to four years ago."

Miriam was taken aback by this piece of news from the handsome stranger, and was eager to find out more about his life. The next few hours went very quickly for the pair, as they talked, and came to know more about each other.

Since we are well acquainted with our hero Rufus and his very active life, let us now dear reader learn something of Miriam; the daughter of Samuel the tailor of Alexandria, and who we now welcome into our story.

She had had a happy childhood. Her father, a well known tailor in the city, was a reasonably wealthy man with a good and loving wife. They had two children, a boy and a girl. The boy was eight years older than the girl who had come late in the marriage. She was named after a maternal aunt who had married, and moved to a town named Hermopolis in the Upper Nile, when the girl, whom she dearly loved was but eleven years of age.

A few years after her aunt's departure, Miriam's mother died. The girl was then fourteen. Her father, much saddened by his wife's demise, lost his enthusiasm for his work and left much of the responsibilities of the business to his son; who was twenty one at the time, and like his father, an accomplished tailor.

Miriam now ran the household and devoted herself to her father, who relied on her more and more as each day passed. He became a difficult man to live with after his wife's death; given to long periods of depression that killed his desire to work. As a result, she spent most of her life at home. She had been well educated; had learnt to read and write, and like many well to do young women, she was proficient in the arts. She played the lyre, which wiled away many unhappy hours, and she was particularly good at sketching and painting.

Her life changed once again, when three years later, her father died. He had been drinking more and more in an effort to fight his boredom and depression. One day, he unwittingly walked in front of a four-horse chariot travelling at high speed. His badly broken body was buried beside his wife. His two children were left to battle life as best they could.

Miriam's brother ran the business. He gave his young sister only enough money to look after their basic needs, leaving her very little for herself. Eventually, he married, and his wife moved into their house. Miriam then became a virtual maid to the married couple. The new woman of the house was envious of her sister-in-law's good looks and talents, and made life unpleasant for her.

Pestered constantly by his nagging wife's groundless complaints regarding his sister, the young man, who's name was Jacob, tried whenever the occasion presented itself to bring home some friend whom he could get interested in her; with the hope of marrying her off.

Miriam proved very difficult to please in the eyes of her brother and wife.As a result, she had to put up with some very harsh and uncharitable treatment. The straw that broke the camel's back for the twenty two year old, was, that without her knowledge or consent, her brother had promised her to a friend; who as his familiarity increased became very belligerent in his dealings with her. This led to her decision to run away and secretly find her aunt in Hermopolis. She had learnt recently from an old friend of her mother's, that her aunt still lived, and she knew her brother would never suspect her going there. The escapade was financed with money her father had given her, and savings she had cleverly accumulated over the years from her household money.

Rufus listened to her story with great sympathy, and promised to help her in her quest for her aunt.

Many of the passengers being on shorter runs, had disembarked and gone their different ways taking their animals with them. As night fell, only a few 'long distance' passengers remained. A stop was made at one of the villages, to allow passengers to disembark, stretch their legs, see to their necessities, buy food, and return to the boat.

As the passengers left the boat, the members of the crew busied themselves in their absence. They swept and scrubbed down the deck which having served as a temporary stable for the animals that day, was quite filthy. There was enough room on the newly cleaned deck, to allow the passengers on their return, to sit on cushions provided gratis by the captain.

Three days went by in similar fashion. Crowds and animals were the order of the day, and more roomy and comfortable accommodations in the evenings. At that later and more tranquil time, the serenity and mystical beauty of the Nile under a deep blue star studded Egyptian night, would work its magical enchantment on any soul appreciative of God's creation.

Rufus and Miriam immersed in quiet mature conversation, discussed the many difficulties they might encounter on their quest for her aunt. Rufus also wondered if any problems had arisen in the church in his absence, and grew impatient to arrive.

He talked to her of Yeshua, and explained many things that she wanted to know. Miriam listened in awe, as he preached in a quiet loving way the things he believed so strongly, and were so close to his heart. As the voyage neared its end, she expressed great interest in the new faith that he expounded to her. She felt admiration, perhaps even love, for the handsome man by her side, who had been through so much and yet, was still so full of life and capable of so much love.

It was almost noon when Rufus and Miriam arrived at the church. As the priest had no idea if anyone was there, they went around to the back of the building, and looked through the garden gate to see if Senh was in any of the back rooms. He called out, but got no answer. He did not have the key to the church door, which made for a problem. They returned to the front of the building, and knocked loudly on the door. There was no response. At a loss for what to do, he decided to make his way to Demetrios' house. The man would not be there as it was only the middle of the day, but with a little luck his wife Sophia would be at home.

Stopping at a food shop near the park where he preached, and which was on their way, he bought lunch, and they ate sitting on a nearby bench.

"They may let you stay with them whilst you are in Memphis," said Rufus, referring to Demitrios and Sophia. Both friends, and parishioners. "They have no little ones as yet, having been married only a year or so, and I know they have a spare room."

"I also have an extra bedroom in the church house, but I don't think you would be at ease with two men and no other woman in the house."

"I have come to trust you in every way, and if the other man is as noble as you, I would not hesitate to stay there."

"There is a woman also, who comes and cooks for us. She might talk to her friends about you, and I do not want you to acquire a bad reputation."

"I shall not be staying long enough to enjoy the bad reputation," laughed Miriam looking at Rufus' concerned face. "The important thing is that we trust each other to behave honourably. For the thoughts of others I care but little."

As expected, Demetrios was at work, but Sophia had just got home from the market. She welcomed them both with joy, casting a look of admiration and perhaps jealousy at Miriam's beautiful face.

"Welcome my good friend," she greeted as she embraced Rufus and smiled at Miriam.

"I want you to meet Miriam!" said a smiling Rufus. "I had the good fortune of meeting her on the riverboat coming home."

"You are very welcome also," said Sophia as she stepped forward and embraced the newcomer.

"Come, sit down, and let us have some refreshments, it's a hot day out."

The visitors settled down on cushions which were strewn around the floor. Sophia made haste to put together some delicacies and juices, and placing them on a low table, sat down with the pair. They chatted amicably for a while. Then Rufus asked.

"Do you know where Senh is?"

"He had to go up to Akhetaton to inspect something or other in an old temple."

"Oh dear," sighed the priest, "that complicates things."

"How so?" asked the hostess

"What do I do with Miriam for accommodation?"

"Ha! Ha! Ha!" laughed Sophia," you men are so naive. What if he were in town, what difference would that make? A woman in a house with two men, that is even more scandalous than being with just one."

Miriam joined in the laughter, but when it had died down, she looked blandly at her hostess as if asking, ' what do I do now?' Which did not escape the intelligent Sophia.

"You will have to stay here with me," she stated emphatically, with a smile.

"It is simply Christian charity. Is it not Rufus?"

Demetrios arrived at his usual time from work, and gave Rufus the key to the church. He explained Senh's trip to Akhetaton and his expected return some time later that week.

Rufus took his leave for the moment, inviting Miriam to accompany him to the church, which he wanted her to see whilst Sophia prepared supper for all.

As he opened the church door, Rufus, turning to talk to Miriam, caught a glimpse of someone ducking behind a wall on the other side of the road. Asking her to stay where she was, he ran across the street and peered over the wall.

He saw a man running away. Realising that he had been spied on, he returned to Miriam and both went into the church locking the door behind them.

"Why did you run across the street?' she asked somewhat alarmed.

"Someone was spying on me and ran off."

"Why would anyone be spying on you?"

"We have enemies who resent us Christians because I am converting some of their people to Yeshua's teachings. Some of the Jews tried to burn my church down just after I bought it. They are not the only ones. I heard just before I left for Alexandria, that an obscure Egyptian sect, some of whose members I have converted, was keeping an eye on my progress and might make trouble for me in the future."

"That sounds quite frightening," said Miriam with a concerned look.

"As the size of my congregation grows, things should get better. We shall be stronger, and have more people to keep watch."

Miriam was reasonably impressed with the church, the house and backyard, though she remained somewhat shaken by the spying incident.

They visited the stable to check the donkey. It was asleep. Demetrios who kept an eye on him, had left the animal clean water and some oats. On the way out, she asked what the box on the altar contained. He told her that at the moment it was empty. Then, taking her over to one of the benches and sitting down together, told her the story of the last supper: Yeshua's ensuing Passion, and finally his Resurrection. All in more detail than he had already explained to her on the riverboat. He also quoted to her from the prophets as he knew she would understand. It was dusk, before they left the church to go for their 'cena' at Demetrios' house.

Rufus returned to the church after supper, leaving Miriam in the good hands of Sophia who had taken a liking for her. He was resolved to leave for Hermopolis with the endearing fugitive as soon as Senh returned. The sooner he got her to her aunt, the sooner he could return to his preaching, which had now been neglected for a number of weeks.

'It's too late to go to the park tonight, but I shall start again tomorrow Lord,' he prayed, as he knelt down in front of the tabernacle as was his habit.

As Rufus prayed, an impromptu meeting was taking place in a large affluent house at the other end of town, precipitated by the arrival of the man who had been watching the church. He had come to notify his employers that the Christian priest was back and in the church.

"I wonder where he went?" asked Djidi, the youngest of the three men whom the spy had come to see.

"I don't know that, but he had a woman with him," reported the informer.

"Perhaps that is his wife, and he went somewhere to fetch her back," commented Ahmes, the middle aged member of the trio; another of the party who had consorted together after the solemn service to Isis in that underground temple.

"We shall find out more in time. For now, continue to keep us informed of his every move. We shall have ample opportunity to strike when the right moment presents itself," assured the old priest Addaya, with confidence in his voice.

"I shall need assistance if we are to watch him day and night," said the spy, as he prepared to depart.

"Choose whom you will, and we will cover the cost," directed the old one again as the visitor walked away.

* * * * *

Senh, finally arrived, and Rufus began to prepare for his departure. The antiquarian had just finished an important piece of work for a client. He had been well remunerated, and consequently was in very high spirits as they all met at Demetrios' house.

Miriam was introduced to him, and he was stunned by her beauty as the others had been. He looked at his friend Rufus with a quizzical eye as he listened to his intentions of accompanying her upriver to her aunt's.

"You are needed here my friend," pointed out Sehn without malice, and stroking his short black beard. "I shall be more than happy to accompany this lovely lady on her journey. I know Hermopolis well, and I shall assist and protect her just as ably as you," assured the antiquarian.

"I heartily thank you, but Rufus promised to take me to my aunt himself, and I would prefer that he be the one to accompany me," cut in Miriam with a sweet smile; a touch of nervousness in her voice.

"As you wish," replied Senh returning the smile with a slight bow of the head.

He, and Rufus, left for the church a little later leaving Miriam in the good hands of Sophia and Demetrios. Rufus would come for her, the next morning, and go directly to the riverboat from there. The journey to Hermopolis would take two days and nights. The priest expected to be back within six days at the most.

The next morning found Rufus and Miriam embarked on the riverboat; travelling more relaxed than on their previous trip. They had left from Demetrios' house, and the priest was confident that the spy would be busy watching the church and would not know that they had gone. He was not taking any chances though, and kept a vigilant eye for anyone on the boat who might be behaving suspiciously around them.

The last evening of the journey, they were both quietly absorbed by the beauty of the Nile at night. They passed many little villages. Their quaint little houses, illuminated by the full moon, took on a silvery aspect. The golden light from their oil lamps warmly defined their window openings, engendering in the two weary travellers, a feeling of homeliness and security. The silhouettes of the tall ever present date palms, swaying in their mysterious and ghostly dance, fanned by the gentle night breeze, lulled their senses into peaceful meditation, as they glided by. The silence of the night broken only by the mild splashing of the oars.

"No doubt, you are thinking about your beautiful wife and child. Or perhaps your little Letitia," remarked Miriam.

"I think of them a lot. But no,... this time I was thinking of you," he said with a warm smile as their eyes met. "After tonight, God knows when I shall see your lovely face again."

"I had the same thought about you, and it greatly saddens my heart. I have never met a man like you, and I am going to miss you terribly," she said laying her hand on his arm.

Rufus did not say anything further other than place his hand on hers, but when their eyes met again, they both knew that a bond had been established between them which would give both their lives new meaning. In her case, she knew she had fallen in love with him. In his, a terrible feeling of betrayal. The memory and love for Letitia, still loomed big in his heart. Miriam's feminine intuition told her not to press him further at that time. The future lay ahead of them, and hopefully in time he would make room for her in his life....'Yes! she would wait.'

Finding Miriam's aunt was not easy. Hermopolis was a fair size town, and they feared it could be days before they would find her.

The hopeful niece had been so absorbed in Rufus and his teachings, that she had not given much thought to the actual whereabouts of her aunt. The one important clue that had stuck in her mind since childhood, was that her husband was, or had been, a government official; a Jew, by the name of Aaron.

Eventually, after much searching, and patiently following the frustrating labyrinth which is the time honoured route for governmental enquiries, they were given particulars regarding Miriam's uncle. He had, until two years past, held a high post in the Ministry of Agriculture. A sickness of the liver from which he had suffered for some time had finally claimed his life.

It was a tired pair of travellers who knocked on the widow's door late that afternoon, with very hungry stomachs, having had very little time to eat.

A middle aged matronly woman with lingering good looks and a very friendly smile, attended to them as the burly maid who had let them in, disappeared into the house.

"How may I help you?" she asked, searching the two handsome faces before her.

"Aunt Miriam, it's me. Miriam!" answered her niece with much emotion in her voice, her lovely eyes brimming with tears.

"Oh! my darling niece," cried the aunt as she stepped forward and embraced her, a flood of happy tears running down her plumpish cheeks.

"You are so beautiful, my darling. I have thought of you often; as I have no children of my own, and I lost my poor Aaron two years ago. I live a very lonely existence. Come, let me look at you," she said holding her niece at arms length admiring her exceptional face.

"You have grown into a very beautiful woman my dear," she exclaimed.

Miriam smiled and said.

"It will be better for you now Auntie. I would like to stay here with you if you will have me."

"Oh, you are most welcome. You are a God send." They embraced again.

"And who is this handsome man?" asked the aunt casting a look of admiration at Rufus.

"This is Rufus!...my hero. He has been helping me since I escaped from my brother's house in Alexandria. Jacob, and his nasty friend whom he wanted me to marry, pursued me until we baffled them posing as husband and wife on the riverboat for Memphis."

The happy aunt embraced Rufus, and thanked him for bringing her beloved niece safely to her. An excellent supper was served them, as they both relaxed in that lovely house after their gruelling day.

Miriam, whose happiness matched that of her long lost aunt, soon brought her up to date with the main occurrences of all the years that she had missed in Alexandria. Her aunt in turn, reciprocated with her own history, narrated between smiles and tears. Soon, it would be apparent to no one that they had been separated for so many years.

Rufus, sitting on a very comfortable cushion, sipping a very good wine, had been very quiet and attentive during the disclosure of the family history. His congenial hostess, on finishing her story, asked him to tell her about his life.

They entertained each other all evening, and late into the night, when Rufus with the help of the maid, carried a bed into the aunts room which the two Miriam's would share. He was given the guest room. It was arranged very comfortably with many soft, plump, floor cushions. Rufus fell asleep as soon as he lay down.

Shortly before mid-day the following day, our hero was awakened by the sound of music coming from the opposite side of the house, across from a little central garden.

Though the rooms were spacious enough, the house was not large. It had been cleverly planned to follow a 'U' design, with rooms along three of its sides. All had high exterior windows fitted with ornamental ironwork for security. Interior windows, and doors opened on to the garden. The entrance to the house, which comprised a slightly elevated hallway, was located at the centre of the lower portion of the 'U' shape with the kitchen and bedrooms on the right, and the living area and maid's room on the left. In the middle and stretching back to a high rear wall which joined the two legs of the U, was the garden; a tall date palm tree at its centre.

Forming part of the rear wall and integral with it, stood a rectangular well, decorated with coloured glazed tiles following a very beautiful design. That delightful design was mimicked on the portion of wall which constituted the back wall of the well and was enclosed by a rectangular arch in semi relief. The entire configuration was reflected to great effect in the small pool immediately in front of it, and surrounded by potted flowers. There was a particularly comfortable and shaded nook in the garden between the living area and the maid's room. In it were two stone benches facing each other and separated by a stone table; all under a tiled roof and surrounded by blood-red bougainvillea that boldly climbed the wall creating the effect of a scented arbour.

A well rested Rufus, crossed this enchanting and colourful garden, in the direction of the music with enthusiastic anticipation.

To his surprise, it was Miriam's aunt who was playing the harp. The niece sat there enthralled and happy. The music stopped abruptly as he entered the room; both women rising to greet him with radiant smiles. Young Miriam approached and hugged him warmly, her aunt following her example.

"My apologies for sleeping in so late," he said with a smile. "I must blame those most comfortable cushions, and your soothing music for my tardiness."

'We were just whiling away the time until you appeared. Now, we shall have a nice lunch, since you have missed your breakfast," said his hostess, taking off to the kitchen as the two sat down and waited.

Our hero spent three days with Miriam and her aunt, during which time he preached Yeshua to them. Neither Miriam had been very religious in their lives; something they both regretted. Rufus as always alive in the Holy Spirit, brought them a new perspective, and having received the faith from God, they were receptive to the words that the enthusiastic priest taught them.

The two Miriams were Baptised the day before Rufus was due to leave which gave him a wonderful sense of accomplishment. He thanked Yeshua for having given the gift of faith to these two women who were beginning to play an important part in his life. His father Simon's words had come to mind as he performed the Baptismal service.

'It is the Holy Spirit who must give them the faith, we ourselves cannot do it.'

Miriam's aunt said her farewell in the garden. Miriam accompanied Rufus to the door. They stood in the pretty hallway, to say their farewells.

"Come back to me," she said, as the tears in her soft, expressive eyes, told just how much she had grown to love him.

"It is all in the hands of Yeshua," he said pressing her to him. And fondly kissing her forehead, walked out the door.

CHAPTER SIX

THE TEMPLE OF ISIS

A loud knock at the church door echoed through the empty building and reached Senh who though already awake, lay in his room at the back, deciding whether he should get up or lie in a little longer. He made haste however to open the door, and found himself face to face with Rufus, who wore his usual hearty smile and quickly embraced him.

"Its great to see you again," blurted out Senh, allowing Rufus in, and locking the door. They made for the back of the building to Rufus' room.

The priest stopped as they approached the tabernacle, and even though it was empty, knelt down to thank Yeshua for his worthwhile trip and safe return. He then joined Senh, who had taken the travelling bag into his room.

They talked as Rufus unpacked. He was soon brought up to date with the few things that had occurred in Memphis in his absence.

"So nothing of any importance has happened since I left."

"No, nothing really. I had some people ask me when you would be preaching again. Incidentally, there is someone spying on the building constantly."

"Sorry, I forgot to tell you.... So, he is still at it. You know what? Now that I am back and you are also here, we shall recruit Demetrios and Sosegenes, and trap him. We will bring him in for questioning, and if necessary, take him to the authorities."

"Yes, that might put a stop to him and whoever is behind it," said Senh.

"Tonight, I shall go to the park to preach again," announced Rufus.

He then told Senh all about his trip: How they had found Miriam's aunt, how much he had enjoyed his stay, and how they had both wished to be baptised.

"I congratulate you my good friend," said Senh, with a smile."Not just for their conversion, but I see that she is very much in love with you. Yeshua has put her in your way in an extraordinary manner. I hope that eventually you will realise that she can make you happy again."

Rufus nodded in ascent.

* * * * *

The crowd at the park seemed bigger than ever as Rufus began his discourse on one of Yeshua's parables.

"*The kingdom of heaven is like a....*"

"Hey, Priest!" shouted someone, bringing the good news to a halt. Rufus looked around to see who had called out so rudely.

"I have been sent to tell you to come with me quickly. A man is dying, and he needs for you to convert him. He has been here listening to you before, but was too sick to come tonight."

Rufus was not happy, as he had just started his preaching, but how could he refuse someone on his death bed. The man's soul could be lost if he did not go. He apologized to his audience, and asked the man where the sick person was to be found. He was informed that it was on the other side of town and that he could ride on the back of the man's horse. He refused the man's offer, to ride with him. and mounting his donkey, asked the messenger to follow him as he made his way to the church.

Senh was at the church when he arrived. The priest informed him as to where he was going with the stranger, who had been sent for him, and his reason for going.

"Hold the fort until I get back, I shall be away for a while," said Rufus.

The pair rode at the donkey's pace. They travelled for about a half an hour and reached the edge of town. Rufus could see no houses, only desert, and some ruins nearby. At that point he became suspicious of the man, who seemed to be pulling back trying to keep the donkey in front of his horse.

"I cannot see any houses," remarked Rufus, throwing the man a suspicious look.

"We are almost there," answered the man. "The house is just over that mound." He pointed at the dune just ahead of them.

At that moment a number of horsemen galloping up from behind the mound surrounded the priest. The messenger, turning his horse, galloped away.

"What do you all want with me?" asked Rufus needlessly, now realising that he had been tricked.

"Come with us," ordered one of the riders.

"I have no business with you," protested the priest.

"We have business with you though," retorted the other.

Four of the men dismounted, and running at Rufus, overpowered him.

They tied his hands behind his back, blindfolded him, and lifting him back on his donkey took the reins, and led it towards some ruins where a number of people were waiting. The animal was made to turn in a number of different directions so as to disorient the hapless rider before allowing it to come to a stop. Rufus felt himself being pulled off the donkey, and led away. There was a creaking sound, as of a heavy door or gate opening. He was forcibly taken down a ramp, the air feeling cooler as he descended. No one spoke, they just kept pushing him from behind. At last the ramp came to an end and the ground levelled off. He was pulled through a few turns and then, down some steps. Finally, he was thrown into what he imagined to be a cell, and slamming the door, they left him blindfolded and with his hands tied.

He immediately set about trying to loosen the bonds. Finding them difficult to remove, he felt for his little dagger as once again these people whoever they were, had not searched him.

After much squirming he still could not reach it so he tried another approach. He moved around the room uncertainly, feeling around for an exposed edge of stone, sharp enough to cut his bonds. Not finding anything suitable, he retraced his steps to the door, where an arch that surrounded it gave him what he was looking for. He began rubbing what he felt were leather straps, up and down against the rough outside edge of the stone.

Persistence and patience paid off. At last after much work the bonds gave way, freeing his tired hands and allowing him to remove his blindfold.

It was pitch black, and there was a musty smell about the place. He felt his way around the room again, this time searching for a window. There was no window, and the room was also devoid of furniture.

Realising the gravity of the situation, Rufus spent most of the night in prayer. His throat and tongue became very dry. He could hear scampering noises around him, and knowing them to be rats, he dare not lie down. Every now and then one would run over his foot as they pursued each other around the cell.

He had fleeting recollections of falling asleep intermittently, though he felt sure that having hugged the corner of the cell for support, he had succeeded in remaining on his feet all night. He could feel no pain anywhere from scratches or bites, so he was happy to conclude that the rats had not attacked him in his sleep, if indeed he had slept.

He was sure that day had broken, but there was no way of ascertaining his suspicions. Total darkness surrounded him.

Presently, a trickle of light began to creep in under the door. The intensity of the light increased, and suddenly voices could be heard. Moments later, the door of the cell opened to reveal two men. The prisoner, covered his eyes to shield them from the sudden light, as the men entered the cell carrying a lighted torch. A third man stood in the doorway with a naked sword in his hand.

Rufus put his hand on his dagger as he thought of taking the initiative, and attacking the armed man by the door. If he was quick enough, he could strike him and close the door on the other two in the cell. He really had nothing to lose.

Then he realised that if he suffered or died it was for Yeshua's sake, and that was what was expected of him as a Christian, and a man of peace and love.

He removed his hand from the dagger, and accepted instead an earthenware jar that was being offered him, inviting him to drink. Though he was extremely thirsty, he sipped the liquid gingerly, until he ascertained that it was water. Then he quickly drained the vessel.

"That is all you are going to get priest," said the man who had given him the water. "You will be needing food where you are going, but you will not be taking any with you."

"The Afterlife will be a place of suffering for you, as you will not be embalmed and will have no food or possessions with you," scoffed his partner.

"So you are planning to do away with me?" asked the priest, now realising that his captors were not Jews, but Egyptians.

"The next time we come you will be tried and sentenced by our priests," affirmed the same man.

"Where am I?" asked Rufus, not expecting an answer.

"You are in the temple of Isis, under the ruins of a much older temple," explained the jailer. "This dungeon which we reserve for our better guests, will be your comfortable home until you overstay your welcome. We hear that your God works miracles, maybe he will get you out of here," he jeered.

"May I at least have a bench to lie on?" asked the priest.

"I do not know if you will be here long enough to need one," laughed the man.

They walked away, slamming the door, and slipping the bolt. He was in the dark once more.

Senh, became greatly concerned about his friend's prolonged absence, and began to suspect that he may have been harmed. He left the church early in the morning, and went to Demetrios' house hoping that perhaps he had spent the night there for some unaccountable reason. Rufus had not been there. The same negative response was given him at Sosigenes' house

The antiquarian became somewhat alarmed, and decided to rent a horse and go in search of him.

'I remember him saying that the house he was to visit was at the other end of town,' he said to himself, and headed out in that direction without a clue as to where he would find Rufus. Being early morning, there were not too many people about and he made good progress. He knew that the town ended at the ruins of the old Ammon temple which he eventually reached without encountering his missing friend. He was about to turn around and go back, when he spotted a donkey tied up at some distance among the ruins.

Being of a curious nature, (an inherent characteristic of antiquarians and archaeologists,) he rode up to see if it was their donkey. The marking on the animal hidden under the saddle confirmed his suspicions.

He walked around for a short while looking for the pastor. Eventually he gave up, and began to check the ground around the donkey's location carefully. Many foot and hoof prints became apparent in the sand but leading nowhere. He soon came to realise, that Rufus had been abducted and would be somewhere in that vicinity, as evidenced by the plight of the donkey.

After hiding his horse further in among the ruins, he went back to the ass, and taking care to keep himself hidden, waited for developments, if there were to be any.

Rufus continued to pray as the morning advanced. Two hours had elapsed since his jailers had visited him, when again he was aware of light creeping in under the door.

Once more the sudden illumination of the room bothered his eyes; he covered them as his captors entered. This time however, there were more people than the previous time. The sounds of many voices could be heard outside his cell.

"Bring him out and take him to the chamber of penitence!" someone ordered.

Three men came into the cell, tied Rufus' hands, roughly dragged him out, and took him into a chamber illuminated by a number of oil lamps. As his eyes got to tolerate the light, he beheld a room with colourful and skilfully painted walls depicting people undergoing various types of cruel chastisements. In the centre of the room, on an elevated, stepped podium, stood a statue a little larger than life size, of the goddess Isis. Our unfortunate hero remembered seeing that image in some of the scrolls that his friend Senh owned, and whose story had been recounted to him by the knowledgeable antiquarian, along with many other stories of Egyptian mythology.

The wary prisoner, perceived a number of people in the chamber, including three bare breasted women who wore strange head bands with a snake effigy. The women bowed as three men, heads and eyebrows shaved, and wearing leopard skins entered. Each man carried a staff crowned with a lotus head similar to the capitals on the columns. The older of the three priests, by name of Addaya, lifted his staff and looking at the prisoner with a hateful stare, intoned.

"Let the goddess Isis hold this slave of hers for punishment."

The deep voice reverberated around the room and seemed to come from the very depth of the earth.

Two burly attendants stripped to the waist, undressed the prisoner also to the waist and made him kneel in front of the statue. They tied his hands to two rings that were embedded in the stepped podium, and his ankles to two other rings secured to the floor, behind where they stood.

Rufus, now realising that no one could save him other than Yeshua, silently prayed for courage and strength to bear what he was about to undergo and did his best to concentrate on the flagellation that his divine Saviour had endured on his and everyone's behalf.

The old priest's intonation began again. One of the men present, handed a couple of knotted leather whips to the two burly attendants, who took their places on each side of the prisoner.

"Do you repent of spreading the heresies of your God Yeshua in opposition to our sacred beliefs in our great goddess Isis?"

"No!" was Rufus' emphatic reply.

The priest nodded to the chastisers, and the prisoner winced as the first two lashes reached his bare back.

The priest once again intoned, "do you repent?"

Again came the same emphatic "No!" with the same results. The prisoner grit his teeth and prayed for strength as each lash cut into his back, his eyes smarting with involuntary tears.

The scenario was repeated again and again with all three priests now chanting the, "do you repent?"

Rufus bore the lashing bravely, his teeth clenched, his mind on Yeshua and the Holy Spirit, to whom he also appealed in his distress. After a while, he lost consciousness. He awoke, to find himself in another cell lying face down on a long wooden bench. The bench was covered in blood that had rolled off his back, down his sides and had congealed. In his semi-conscious state he realised that the cell was illuminated by a brightly burning torch, and he thanked Yeshua for that. The weakness he felt was not surprising, as he had not eaten for almost two days and the loss of blood from his whipping had been considerable. There was a pitcher with water by the bench and sitting up with great difficulty, he reached for it. His head spun as he lifted the pitcher and drank avidly. Then, lying on his stomach again, he promptly fell asleep.

* * * * *

Senh, sitting at his vantage point among the ruins, was awakened from a light nap by the sound of many voices. Peering gingerly around a large stone, he beheld a large crowd of people entering a cave close to where the donkey was tied. On the ground in front of it was a basin with water, and around its ears, a bag of oats.

It was now evening. The whole day been spent waiting for some development to occur around the donkey. He could not believe his eyes at the influx of people, and particularly, the secret entrance in the rock face. His trained eyes had not noticed anything even remotely resembling a doorway in his earlier inspection of the area.

He quickly left his hiding place, pulled his shawl partially over his face and entered the cavern with the crowd. He was amazed at what he saw as he followed the winding ramp down into the bowels of the place, where a beautifully ornamented temple appeared before his eyes. The very large statue of Isis in the centre of a stepped platform was impressive. It was attended by a few young bare-breasted maidens in white attire with jet black hair and their eyes heavily outlined in black. They performed offerings of flowers to the goddess, and danced around in a slow sensual bare-footed dance to the beat of a muffled drum, and the sound of flutes.

Presently, the scraping noise on the winding ramp ceased. The congregation having now arrived, stood expectantly awaiting the entrance of their priests.

The sound of a horn ushered in the three priests in their leopard skin costumes accompanied by many torch bearers, and followed by a number of bare chested muscular male assistants. The two large containers on each side of the statue of Isis, filled with herbs and incense were set alight, sending great clouds of smoke up into the vortex above the statue and creating a mystical atmosphere.

The priests went through their ceremonial chants. As these came to an end, the horn sounded once more, followed by the deep, ominous percussion of drums, that seemed to come from deep in the earth.

All of a sudden, a man was brought in. He was struggling to gain control of his legs as two powerfully built men naked to the waist carried him in. The man was also stripped to the waist and covered in blood. A collective gasp was heard as the crowd beheld the prisoner. Senh gasped too in sheer horror, as he beheld his friend Rufus in such a sorry plight.

The deep voice of the chief priest captured the attention of all present.

"Here is a man who has been preaching heresy and has perverted some of our people, tearing them from the loving, motherly arms of our beloved Isis. This, as I need not tell you, carries a sentence of death if the individual shows no repentance, and refuses to pay homage to our beloved goddess.

"Yea! Yea!" chorused the congregation in response.

"I shall ask you for the last time Christian," said the chief priest in a deep but loud voice and looking severely at Rufus.

"Do you denounce your God Yeshua and accept our great goddess Isis?"

"No!"

The priest repeated the question. Once again receiving the same negative answer.

"You have all heard his reply," cried the priest with hands raised dramatically and looking at the congregation..

"Yea!" came the confirmation from the people.

"Bring in the cross," ordered the old Addaya with great solemnity in his voice.

Senh was beside himself with concern.

'What are they going to do? Are they going to crucify him?' he wondered, as he realised his utter helplessness in aiding his beloved friend.

The cross was brought in and placed in a hole prepared beforehand for the purpose.

The drums were heard again, and a horn's mournful sound filled the temple as the people held their breath with excitement, and anticipation.

"Tie him to the cross!" ordered the high priest.

"Wait!"

Everyone froze as the word resounded through the cavernous temple.

All eyes were on the prisoner who had shouted the word.

The high priest gave the prisoner a look of scorn, as he waited for him to say what was on his mind.

'Perhaps,' he thought, 'the Christian will still recant.'

But Rufus, fervently and silently praying to the Holy Spirit, addressed the chief priest and all the congregation of Isis.

"A condemned man has the right to speak his mind before he dies has he not?"

A pregnant silence followed and a few reluctant 'yeas' were heard.

"You are punishing me, because I have been preaching a God that you say defies your goddess Isis." Rufus felt his strength come back to him, a feeling of great tranquility such as he had never experienced pervaded his senses and his whole being. He recalled with love, the words of his father, speaking of the feeling that Yeshua had blessed him with on the road to Calvary and later when he was about to work a miracle through him.

"You are all looking for an Afterlife which will bring you happiness forever, are you not?"

"Yea."

"It is vital that you be embalmed so that you will be allowed to enter the happiness of the next life, is it not?"

"Yea."

"How many of you can afford to have yourselves embalmed? And how about your beloved family, can you afford to have them embalmed too?"

There was complete silence from the congregation and the priests as they awaited the Christian priest's next words.

"Yes, I can see that this concerns and saddens you. Only the wealthy will have an Afterlife. Does that seem fair to you? Is that what a goddess whom you worship and depend on does for you?"

Dead silence.

"I am about to die at your hands. But before I do, I shall give you knowledge beyond what you have ever imagined."

The people could be heard stirring as they fidgeted around and whispered to each other in anticipation of the prisoner's intriguing words.

"I preach to you a God who came from his exalted place in heaven, where he is Master of the Afterlife. He became man and gave his life on a cross, to redeem us from our sins, out of love for every person living in this world, the rich and the poor alike, no matter who they are. He loved the poor for their humility, and the difficulties they face in their every day lives. Those who believed in him, he said, would have eternal life and would live happily forever with him in the Afterlife. He came to this world of ours, as a Jew. He spoke of love for one another, performed many miracles; curing the sick, restoring sight to the blind, forgiving people's sins, calming the sea, and even raising some from the dead. But because few of his own people accepted him, he invited all those who were not Jews to believe and follow him. He had come, he said, out of his immense love for all of us to die as a sacrificial lamb, so that all men's sins would be forgiven through him.

The Jews crucified him out of hate. But do you know that he rose again three days later and appeared to his friends; even ate in front of them? What man has ever come back from the dead?" Rufus waited for a few moments, as he knew they had been stunned by those words. Then he continued.

"He said he would come back, and he did. My own father helped him to carry the cross as they led him to his crucifixion." Rufus turned and looked at the cross behind him.

"I know people who knew him, loved him, and followed his teachings. He is a living God, not a god of stone or painted wood. He is the son of Yahweh the God of the Jews, the same God as you have heard, freed his people from slavery at the hands of your pharaoh many years ago.

The story of Isis, Osiris, the virgin birth, and the god Horus, which you are all well acquainted with, though mythological, were perhaps meant as prophesies to you, of Yeshua who was to come. Just as some of the Jew's prophets also prophesied that their Messiah who is Yeshua would come. Your gods were not actual people, they were legends.

Yeshua the Son of God is no legend. Yes, he too was the result of a virgin birth. The Holy Spirit of the God Yahweh is his father. His mother's name is Mary. After her son's death on the cross, she disappeared. Her purity and favour with God, won her the Afterlife, where we believe she ranks next after God; for she was indeed the mother of the son of God.

All this really happened less than fifty years ago. That is no myth. That is the truth, and there are people alive who can prove it. So I say to you rejoice and be glad. If you believe and accept the Lord Yeshua, who is a living God, who loves each and everyone of you more than you can possibly imagine, and gave his life for you and me,...you will not perish. Your Afterlife in paradise with him is assured you without embalming, or riches, which you cannot take with you, or any thing else."

Then turning to the chief priest of Isis, he said.

"I have spoken the truth. Now you may kill me. I am happy to die by the grace of the Holy Spirit, for Yeshua the son of God."

"He must not die, " shouted someone.

"He must not die," shouted Senh at the top of his lungs from the middle of the crowd."

"He must not die,"shouted a few others,...followed still by others, until the cry was taken up by every soul in the temple, repeating it over and over.

Addaya, the chief priest, hearing the acclamations of the crowd, was greatly shaken and convinced by the appeal, as were also his colleagues. He approached Rufus, untied his hands, and falling at his feet, begged his forgiveness for the cruel punishment he had meted out to him.

The Christian priest taking the old man's arm, raised him up and embracing him, forgave him in the name of Yeshua.

The people went wild; rejoicing that they were all to have a happy Afterlife. They mobbed Rufus asking for further instruction.

Fighting his way through the jubilant mob, Senh found his way to his friend and assisted him out of the temple with the help of Djidi the youngest of the three priests. They sat him painfully on his donkey, and Senh finding his horse, accompanied his very injured but happy friend back across town to their church.

.

CHAPTER SEVEN

UNEXPECTED HONOURS

Rufus woke up in his own bed once more. His back felt as if it was on fire, but his joy could not be measured by any earthly standard, for he exulted in having suffered for the Lord.

He gave himself to contemplation on his recent experience, and took delight in the way that Yeshua had been there strengthening him mentally in his time of trial.

How much stronger he now felt.

'That exhilarating inner strength and fearlessness,' he mused, 'must have been what the apostles felt on that Pentecost morning that my father told me about, when he helped James baptise so many people. Oh, how I would have loved to have been there.'

There was a sudden knock at the church door, and he heard Senh call out.

"I'll get it."

A few moments later he returned, and with him was the old Isis priest and a matronly woman carrying a jar.

"Greetings my friend," said Addaya, "I have come to try and undo some of the damage I did you. Please be kind enough to let this lady treat you with an ointment made with spices and oils which she concocts and which will assist greatly in the healing of your back."

"That is most kind of you," answered Rufus, who continuing to lie on his stomach motioned to the woman to apply the ointment.

"When you recover sufficiently," continued the old priest, "I would be extremely grateful, if you would perform Baptism on me and all my people, as they are all most anxious to proclaim

Yeshua as their new God. In fact we have already removed the statues of Isis from our temple, and are awaiting further instructions from you as to what we are to do."

Both Senh and Rufus were overjoyed to hear the enthusiastic request, and the latter promised to attend to it as soon as he felt more comfortable.

* * * * *

The news of Rufus' conversion of around three hundred people in one day, was received with much jubilation by John Mark following the Memphis priest's report. The bishop however was most disturbed by the horrifying ordeal that his Cyrenean friend, had experienced.

'I must arrange for him to have a little time with his daughter and family, as soon as he organizes these new converts,' he said to himself. 'I can then send Annianus to look after his church until he returns.'

* * * * *

A week after his recovery, Rufus proposed to the old converted priest and his colleagues, that a meeting be held at the church so that arrangements could be made for the pending Baptisms.

The meeting took place two days later. Senh, Demetrios, Sosigenes, and Melech, were also there, as the accommodation of so many people in one place at one time appeared quite problematical, and the priest needed as many ideas as he could get.

Rufus, though reluctantly, had been considering using the temple of Isis as the place for the Baptisms; it being at least four times as large as their church.

'Would it be right, to celebrate a Sacrament in what had been a heathen temple?' he asked himself.

'I cannot afford to wait for the bishop's approval. I must do this quickly before some enemy begins to poison their minds again and I lose them. They need the strength of the Holy Spirit at this moment, and Baptism will help them in that regard. I will go to the temple and pray that Yeshua may remove all evil spirits and turn the temple into his Holy church. A rededication service will be performed, and the new church named *Church of the Divine Saviour.'*

He proposed his plan to use the temple for the Baptisms, which was well received by the unbaptised trio, and arrangements were made for the following Christian Sabbath, the 'Dies Solis' of the Romans. The 'Body and Blood' would not be distributed, though it would be received by Rufus alone. Senh, and the others, did not protest. They knew that their beloved priest had a reason for leaving them out of receiving on that particular day.

The unbaptised participants at the meeting gave their approval enthusiastically, and assured Rufus that the statues of Isis had been dismantled and taken outside. It had now become part of the ruins. The wall paintings would be whitewashed right away if it was so mandated. Especially, those of the chamber where Rufus had been so cruelly and severely lashed. Rufus expressed his wish that it be so.

It was a very happy and thankful Christian priest who celebrated the monumental Baptismal service that Sabbath day. The three ex-priests of Isis were quite enthralled, as were the new congregation. They lined up and approached the altar which sat on a newly constructed wooden platform where the old stepped platform had previously stood. The Baptismal font was actually one of the large cauldrons which had been used to burn the incense and herbs, supported on a new ornamental iron framework, and sitting on the platform a few steps away to the side of the altar.

The happy Rufus preached a long sermon prior to the actual Baptisms. He instructed all present on the rudiments of their new faith, the Blessed Trinity, and the importance of what they were about to partake in.

Senh, Demetrios, Sosogenes, and Melech, assisted the priest by holding the water jugs, handing out towels and being generally useful during the service.

After the service, which was a huge success, the ex-priests approached the tired but elated celebrant, and embraced him each in turn, the older one saying:

"Apart from our late congregation, we three priests wish to come to you for instruction in the ways of Yeshua, so that we can continue to serve our people, but in the new way."

"I shall be delighted to teach you all that I know in that regard," promised Rufus. "By the grace of God you have received your faith, and now we must all pray that he continues to guide you and strengthen it every day. I shall begin a program of instruction as will be suitable for you and your two priests. The Lord surely has plans for your lives, and when I find you ready for the ministry, I shall ask the bishop who is my superior, to come up from Alexandria, and ordain you all."

* * * * *

The life of the church in Memphis, became more vibrant, more jubilant, and displayed great enthusiasm. The new Christians were instructed with great love and care by the very dedicated Rufus who worked tirelessly to 'fish men' for Christ. The old and the new converts evangelized their new faith at every opportunity, and the small church, (The Holy Trinity) that Rufus had set up was now used only as a place of teaching during weekdays. The ex-temple church now being the official church for the whole city of Memphis.

The pastor, for so Rufus should now be called, was hard pressed for time and began to contemplate having Senh ordained. The intelligent Egyptian had been well schooled, had been gifted with a very strong faith, and his assistance would soon be crucial to the running of the fast growing church. This would greatly lighten Rufus' work load. With this in mind, he had written to John Mark asking permission. Having obtained it, he sent a very happy and enthusiastic Senh off to Alexandria.

Three weeks later Senh returned as an ordained priest, bringing back a scroll from the bishop confirming his ordination, and praising his beloved friend Rufus for his success and dedication to the ministry. No doubt the dedication and holiness of the Memphis priest had been lauded highly by Senh, who loved his friend and held him in his highest esteem.

The preaching in the park continued, either by the pastor now the senior priest, or Senh who shared the same gift of speech.

Over the next year and a half, the pastor zealously taught the three expectant priests the rudiments of their faith, including any new developments that might be received from the hands of thc apostles. The aspirant priests had been maintained by the monetary contributions of their old congregation. Those who had worshipped Isis before, were used to contributing a portion of what each family made for the support of their priests, as was the case with the Christians. This excellent and responsible practice continued after their conversion.

Rufus realising that soon there might be as many as five priests in Memphis, wondered as to how he would accommodate them in that small church. The bishop of Alexandria had ordained another priest as well. Those were very positive signs that the church in Egypt was growing.

"Perhaps five priests are going to be too many for the present," Rufus pointed out to Senh, as they sat in the church garden one beautiful summer evening.

"You could be right," agreed the other. "Those are a lot of mouths to feed for our congregation at the moment. Their present contributions, might be inadequate, unless we can increase the size of our congregation to suit."

"I have been thinking," continued the pastor, "that when the ex-Isis priests are ordained, the two younger ones, can be sent to another town up river to do some preaching there. They could then with our help, establish another congregation and eventually another church, starting with a building even smaller than this one. Their new congregation would support them.

These men are already experienced in dealing with, and teaching people, and they will not need to have their hand held all the time."

"Yes, we could make real progress there I suppose," agreed Senh.

"However,' continued Senh. "The old priest, even though he is the most experienced of the three, should stay here with us. He will not be up to the rigours imposed on him by such missions."

"You read my mind, my friend," agree Rufus, stroking his short beard. "You and I may be doing a lot of travelling yet, and you know what? The old man could hold the fort very ably whilst we are away. He is a very clever and wise man, and seems to have accepted the faith with great enthusiasm."

A rattling at the garden gate was heard. Both priests looked up to find Addaya, whom they had just been mentioning.

Senh made haste to open the gate and embracing him, said.

"We were just talking about you. Come join us in a cup of juice."

Senh went to the kitchen for another cup. The old man, embraced Rufus who had risen to receive him, and both sat down as the assistant priest returned cup in hand.

"If you don't mind, I would prefer a cup of cool water from that well," said Addaya, pointing to the bucket sitting on the well. Senh hastened to comply as the old man, tired from his long walk, took a seat beside Rufus on the bench under the porch.

The pastor, gazed at the old man's sweaty face, and smiled.

"Soon, God willing, you will be ordained." His eyes searching Addaya's face, as the latter swallowed his water in one uninterrupted motion. An 'aaah' of satisfaction following. Senh hastened to bring the old priest another cupfull.

"Your two colleagues will also be ordained," continued Rufus. "I hope you will not be too disappointed if I ask you stay here with me to advise and help me. I intend to send Ahmes and Djidi on missions, to evangelise a little further upriver."

The old man, taking another mouthful of water, listened without comment.

The pastor rubbed his neck, and continued.

"I feel that owing to your age, you will have a much more comfortable life here with us. You are more experienced in dealing with people than any of us. You are a learned person and being zealous in your new faith, you will serve Yeshua well I know. So, will you accede to my request and remain here as our anchor whilst we are all away?"

"I shall envy my two younger friends as they go on their missions. I am an old man now, and you are well intentioned. How can I refuse?"

"Wonderful! thank you," blurted out Rufus, as his deputy smiled in agreement.

"We are in any event talking about the near future. Ahmes and Djidi and even yourself, still require some further instruction before you are all ready.

Two months later, in the autumn, the pastor travelled by riverboat to Alexandria to meet with the bishop.

* * * * *

The arrival of Rufus in Alexandria was the occasion of much joy to the congregation there, who having heard of the Memphis priest's great work, were most keen to meet him.

Rufus walked once more, unannounced into the little office beside the altar, where every wall was covered with shelves holding scrolls and parchments.

John Mark who was at his customary labour of love, was most jubilant at the sight of his friend the pastor and embraced him heartily.

"I thank our blessed Lord for the joy of seeing you once again," said John Mark.

"I have greatly missed you," declared Rufus. "It is the sad part of our lives, that Yeshua keeps us apart for such great lengths of time. How are you my dear friend?"

"The Lord has given me a strong constitution. I feel well, and my work progresses steadily," explained the bishop, waving his hand at the shelves around him.

"Recently," continued John Mark, reaching for a scroll that lay on his table."Your brother sent me this scroll with details of the Passion of our Lord, which your father had dictated as he promised to do for me some years ago. It agrees beautifully with the testimony of Joseph of Arimathea and that of Nicodemus; though your father was the only one to cover most of the actual journey to Golgotha."

"How I envy my father that journey with the Lord," sighed Rufus, with a very sad countenance, and great regret in his voice. "At that time being the young and worldly boy that I was," he continued, "I had no interest in that unique and sacred event. Instead, I spent the day enjoying myself with my brother and sisters, in Jerusalem." He shook his head, as if to shake off his self disgust, and asked.

"How is Annianus?"

"He is a happily married man, and does his work with great enthusiasm. He has a very good disposition; everyone likes him," replied the bishop.

"I am so glad to hear that. I too am very fond of him."

The two friends spent that day and a good part of that first evening together, deep in discussion, and happy in each other's company.

"By the way," said John Mark. "This time by sheer coincidence, the *Stella Maris* is due to touch at Alexandria only briefly within the next day or so, and so you will have an opportunity of seeing your beloved friend Marius, who does not look a day older each time I see him. As you expected, he got married, and has taken his wife to Cyrene, because of her very close friendship with your sister-in-law, Hannah. He was contemplating selling his ship, but he still seems too attached to the sea and fortunately, strong enough to deal with it."

Rufus was overjoyed to hear that, and thanked God for allowing him such a timely visit to Alexandria. He then brought up a question which he was a little reticent to discuss with his superior, but he simply had to, as there would be no better time.

"I now have a matter to bring before you that is giving me much concern and for which I need your approval my wise friend," began the pastor, and taking a sip of watered wine from his cup, he waited to capture the bishop's complete attention.

"I am about to find myself with four priests."

The bishop frowned. "How come?"

Rufus reminded him, that as per his earlier communications he had been instructing the three ex-Isis priests with particular diligence for the last two years.

"Having undergone their punishment," began Rufus with a slight shiver; recalling the lashing he had received. "I was skeptical of their sincerity as it was their congregation and not them, that demanded the conversions. However, as the months passed, I grew to know them. I became convinced of their sincerity, and now I feel strongly that they would make good priests, as they happen also to be experienced managers. The two young ones, I would like to send out on missions further up river, whilst their old chief who is a very learned man, would stay as anchor in our smaller church."

"You mean as opposed to the cavern church that you converted to the *Church of the Divine Saviour*."

"Exactly."

"Five priests in one city for a congregation of around five hundred sounds like a lot to me. I tell you what, send one down to me," proposed the bishop. "I was considering ordaining one more, and that would suit me. Our congregation here is growing well. I believe that on the last count we have over one thousand souls to look after. Another priest would give poor Annianus some much needed help, as I shall be setting up another church soon, and he will be its pastor."

"So you have no objections to my plan?" queried the Memphis priest with relief.

"None whatever. I love the thought of increasing our reach into the interior. Though God knows what opposition you are going to find there."

"With the help of the Holy Spirit, to whom we must consecrate the mission, we shall be able to do a good 'fishing of men,'" assured Rufus.

Once more, the *Stella Maris* pulled into harbour a day before Rufus was due to leave for Memphis. Marius appeared at the church, greeted Annianus and asked for the bishop. Annianus who knew that Marius was unaware of Rufus being in Alexandria, led the captain to the back of the church without a word, and stepped aside to allow him to enter the little room beside the altar. Marius could not believe his eyes as he beheld his beloved old friend Rufus. I leave you once again my dear reader to imagine the meeting of these two friends.

Marius could not ask Rufus enough questions, and the latter, could not but do the same of the former. John Mark, embracing the captain, left the room and took his assistant with him.

The happy pair sat and talked until the bishop returned and relayed a message from Annianus, inviting them all to supper at his house.

Two days later, Rufus was on his way to Memphis, having spent the following day after Marius' arrival writing letters to his family, and buying a little gift for his daughter, all of which the captain took with him. Sarah, Marius' wife, was now in Cyrene living near Hannah to whom she had been like a mother. The captain, as the bishop had said, was in no hurry to sell his beloved ship, which pleased the pastor no end as it was his only link with home.

Silas was in good health, and sailing the Caesarea, Cyrene, Rome, route which he knew so well.

'Now I am a contented man,' mused Rufus to himself as the riverboat floated up river to his familiar Memphis.

The last evening of his journey, as he looked at the little villages passing him by in the moonlight, he fondly remembered the pleasant hours he had passed with Miriam on that memorable trip almost two years ago.

"I must see her again soon," he promised himself, and leaning his head back against the bulkhead, fell asleep.

Morning broke, waking him up just as the boat pulled into the jetty in Memphis.

An impetuous rattling at the garden gate, brought Senh to his senses. He snapped out of a ridiculous dream, and getting out of bed, staggered uncertainly into the garden; his eyes trying to focuss on the gate. Wake up lazy bones, called out the pastor as he could see that his friend was still half asleep.

Senh opened the gate and embraced Rufus who was most pleased to see him.

Breakfast lasted a good while. The two priests excitedly brought each other up to date with everything that concerned them. They then went into the church, where as usual they spent some time in prayer in front of the tabernacle before starting their day's work.

That month went by without any notable incident; except for the joyful fact that twenty more converts were asking for Baptism. As usual the preaching in the park had paid off. That particular month a number of Greeks and a few Romans, had joined their congregation.

* * * * *

Finally, after two years, the time arrived for the ordinations. Addaya, Ahmes, and Djidi, were very excited as Rufus called them to a meeting with Senh, and himself. During the meeting he informed the expectant trio that they were now ready to become priests in the service of Yeshua, who now filled their lives.

To everyone's surprise, including Rufus', who had sent a message to the bishop informing him that the three priests were ready. John Mark replied with another message saying that he would be visiting Memphis to perform the ordinations.

The three candidates were ecstatic at the news. All prepared to welcome their chief, and made sure that everything would be to his satisfaction.

Four days later, the bishop was at thc church door in Memphis, knocking loudly with his staff, as Rufus had instructed him to do, so that the knocking would be heard from their rooms at the back. The pastor had promised himself that he would install a bell at the church door, but he still had not got around to it.

Both Rufus and Senh ran to open the door suspecting that it would be the bishop. Who else would be knocking so loudly at that time of the morning. They were not wrong. There stood John Mark with a big smile on his face and arms outstretched ready to embrace them both.

Once again a long breakfast followed, as the three men talked, and enjoyed each other's company, until they adjourned for their hour of prayer in front of the tabernacle.

"I wish I could tell you what a beautiful church you have here," remarked the bishop with a critical look in his eyes, observing with some trepidation, the stark whitewashed walls. "But I am afraid I shall have to disappoint you. It is quite bare and unattractive."

"I apologise for that, but unfortunately my dear brother is not here, and I do not have a single artist in my parish. I am afraid my wonderful brother spoilt us both with what he accomplished in Apollonia. That was in the old church; the barn conversion as you will remember. You should see what he did with the one he built up in the town of Cyrene."

"Yes, it is difficult to decorate well without a good artist to carry it out," agreed John Mark, remembering Alexander and his great talent.

"I was very fortunate to find a good artist in my congregation, for which I thank the Lord with all my heart," said the bishop with relief in his voice and a hand on his heart, as the two men walked out of the church, and out to the porch in the garden.

They sat on a long wooden bench in the shade, just outside the kitchen. From there, they could admire the neat and colourful little garden, whilst helping themselves to some fresh figs that were on a table in front of them. A product of their own fig tree in the garden.

"At least," remarked the bishop with a chuckle. "You have a lovely little garden here, which provides all the colour that your church lacks."

"Yes. Thanks to two of my older parishioners, who keep themselves busy tending to it with great love, and not a little knowledge," smiled Rufus, busily peeling his fig.

"I am most keen to see the cavern church, which of course is now your main church," said the bishop."this one is certainly small." He took a bite of his fig. "Perhaps in the future, when you can find the money you will have a much larger one," he continued. "Somehow, a cavern does not seem to me to be the best place for a church, unless it is used as a hiding place."

"That too was our thinking," agreed Rufus, looking at Senh who had as yet not said a word. "We never know when a persecution can start, and the secret entrance to that place is carefully guarded by the faithful."

"There are so many hidden passages and entrances there. It is a veritable labyrinth," added Senh with a knowing look.

"Sounds very mysterious," said the bishop, arising, and walking into the garden to admire at close range, the work of the volunteer gardeners, who having just arrived, were waiting at the back gate, for someone to let them in.

That evening, the three new candidate priests, were invited to meet the bishop, who was quite taken with them. Some parishioners, among them, Demetrios, Sosigenes, and Melech. All accompanied by their wives, and Jeth who was a bachelor, presented themselves with food baskets. Soon, an impromptu celebration was in full sway, to the great surprise and joy of John Mark; who being the congenial person that he was, revelled in meeting all those people who loved the Lord, and made Him a constant part of their lives.

The day of the ordinations arrived. It was a brisk autumn day and there was a wind blowing which made it somewhat unpleasant. Because the 'cavern' church was at the other end of town, the three priest started off early in the morning on foot.

The bishop having now met the priesthood candidates, had arranged for Djidi to go with him to Alexandria. He being the youngest one of the three, John Mark wanted to keep him under his wing for a while.

Nothing could have prepared the visiting bishop for the surprise he received as he beheld the large rock door open on its central pivot following the secret knock. The journey down the winding ziggurat type ramp enthralled him, and he beheld the cavernous main hall of the church with its impressively high roof, in complete wonder and amazement.

The church was as usual illuminated by many torches. Plants of all descriptions and fresh flowers in garlands decorated the wall behind the altar. The altar itself was covered with a white linen cloth and the golden tabernacle glistened majestically in the light of the torches and oil lamps.

The chatter of the expectant congregation ceased, as the bishop stepped up onto the platform and stood to one side of the altar. He cut an imposing figure in his white robe, his thick white hair crowning with dignity his still relatively young face. He held a long wooden staff, formed into what resembled a shepherd's hook at the top, as he surveyed the congregation in front of him. Suddenly he spread out his arms and addressing them as brothers and sisters in Yeshua the Christ, he thanked them all for attending.

The ominous sound of the horn was heard, and the service began.

Old habits are hard to break, and this particular congregation in their pagan days had begun their service to Isis with that sound. Because of their reluctance in abandoning the custom, Rufus did not press them to change their habit as it was irrelevant to the services being performed. He permitted this custom, as also the decoration of the back of the altar, with plants and flowers, which he liked.

John Mark was surprised by that sound which was new to him, but receiving a nod of approval from the pastor, began the service with the usual prayers. By now the service in Alexandria, and Memphis followed a format established by the bishop, following closely the liturgy he witnessed at Cyrene, which as my faithful reader knows, was designed by Simon and Alexander.

Immediately following the reception of the 'Body and Blood" of Christ, which was limited to the celebrants themselves and the three candidates, the latter trio descended the platform and knelt before the altar.

The bishop went around and faced the people, standing in front of the now empty tabernacle. He then performed the 'Laying of Hands' on each candidate pronouncing the words:

"Receive the Holy Spirit. Go forth and teach in the name of the Father, and of the Son, and of the Holy Spirit, and receive the power to forgive sins."

He then bade them stand, and embraced each one with a big smile.

The three new priests were ecstatic, as the congregation cheered enthusiastically for these men who having led them before would now be leading them once again; this time, on the right path.

When the cheering died down, the bishop stepped forward, and motioned to Rufus, to come to him. The pastor walked over to hear what John Mark would ask of him. To his surprise as he stood there, the bishop addressed the congregation with a loud voice.

"I am now going to perform another service which I am sure none of you have ever witnessed."

Rufus became a little alarmed as he wondered what his friend and superior was going to do.

"Rufus! Please kneel," he ordered.

A truly baffled Rufus fell on his knees and held his breath as he saw the bishop take a very small silver crucible with a lid from his white tunic and place it on the altar behind him.

"Rufus, son of Simon of Cyrene," he said, as he spread his hands over the pastor's head, and looking up to heaven, continued.

"By the power vested in me by the apostles in the Blessed Name of Yeshua, I now consecrate you Bishop of Memphis. In the name of the Father, and of the Son, and of the Holy Spirit."

Turning, and taking the crucible from the altar which contained blest olive oil and dipping his thumb into it, he anointed Rufus' forehead forming a cross whilst simultaneously saying.

"I anoint you in the name of the Father, and of the Son, and of the Holy Spirit."

Rufus remembered his father, as he suddenly felt once again, that deep tranquility that his father had spoken of when Yeshua worked through him, and it was with tearful eyes, that he arose to receive a hearty embrace from his beloved friend John Mark, the Bishop of Alexandria; who would later be known to posterity, as the Evangelist,...Saint Mark.

The priests and congregation were stunned. But when they realised the great event that had occurred, they cheered once again. The new bishop, calling for silence, asked for the singing of a hymn by members of the old congregation, many of whom were present. Thus, concluded the unique service to the joy of all.

A sumptuous celebration which had been prepared by the new congregation followed, and it was almost morning when Rufus, Senh, and the bishop arrived back at the old church, and to their beds.

John Mark decided to stay in Memphis a day longer than scheduled. He still felt somewhat fatigued the following morning, after the long celebration of the previous night. He was not used to being up so late, being the very organized man that he was. His normal bedtime was much earlier; his eyes tiring easily from the habitual scribing that took up so much of his time.

Rufus, Senh and a number of parishioners, were at the jetty the following day 'Dies Martis,' to see the bishop off, and wish him a safe journey.

CHAPTER EIGHT

THE COMMITMENT

A month had passed since John Mark's visit. The new bishop of Memphis, was still trying to come to terms with his promotion. Addaya had embraced his new responsibilities with great zeal, even at his age, (for he was in his late sixties) he displayed an energy worthy of a younger man. He was quite satisfied in his new role at which he excelled; visiting the sick members of the congregation and giving them solace and hope. He never complained when he was called out in the middle of the night to pray with, and give consolation to the family of the dying or dead.

This ministry, so ably carried out by the old man, allowed Rufus and Senh more time to deal with other matters of equal importance in the running of the church.

The new bishop had decided that it was time for Ahmes, the middle aged ex-Isis priest to embark on his mission further up the Nile. Senh, was immediately consulted, for he had travelled the Upper Nile extensively as part of his antiquarian work and was very experienced with the different areas and their varying allegiances to Egypt's pantheon of gods.

The bishop sat down with his assistant to discuss the possible location of the mission. What town would offer the best chance of success in their evangelization efforts? He pointed out to Senh that he wished to progress slowly, and not too far from base, as this would ensure quick support for Ahmes in case of difficulties or emergencies.

"Well," said the assistant bishop. "I suppose we cannot go too far wrong if we were to start in Akhetaton. It is about three days and nights away, just a bit further than we are from

Alexandria. It is located a little upriver from Hermopolis where you took Miriam. You could visit her on the way back. Lucky you," laughed Senh, as he saw Rufus' eyes light up.

"I know I'm going to get a 'yes' for Akhetaton, am I wrong?"

"You know me far too well," protested the bishop smiling at his friend.

The following morning Ahmes was called into the bishop's room, and was told of his mission. Ahmes, was a married man, with a family. Rufus told him that as soon he had a congregation of fifty, he would help finance the establishing of a church, and he could then take his family with him. In the meantime, they would be supported by the Memphis church.

The new priest, excited at having the opportunity of starting out on his own, lost no time in relating the news to his old chief Addaya, who had been like a Father to him and Djidi.

"I am glad for you my son," said the old man. "I know that with the help of the Holy Spirit you will win many souls for Yeshua. If the bishop gives me permission, I may come and visit you sometime. Or,...perhaps you will come back and visit me, when you have someone to take care of the congregation which you are sure to have in time. That would be much more probable I think, as my wife is constantly ailing, and I cannot very well leave her to herself for long. In the meantime, I shall keep an eye, on Kema and the children for you, and assist them any way I can."

Rufus accompanied Ahmes on his trip upriver. They travelled by riverboat which he had grown to trust, rather than by land. As Senh had foretold, it took them three days and three nights to get to Akhetaton which was a smaller town than Memphis but quite charming in its own way. There were some very important ruins there just as in Memphis. It had also for a brief period, been the capital of the country many years earlier in antiquity. The priestly pair found adequate lodgings, and after having eaten, started off on their quest for a place where Ahmes could preach every night.

The priest, was a capable physician in his own right, which was the way that he would make a living whilst he 'fished for men,' in the evenings.

Rufus attended the first three days of preaching to assess the new priest's performance, and was reasonably pleased. However, there were points that needed to be discussed and some that needed minor corrections. He decided to delay his departure for a couple more days to ensure that his priest's delivery was according to the format that he had prescribed.

Ahmes was told not to attempt answering any questions of which he might be ignorant or uncertain of the answer. The bishop told him that if he was in doubt, he should admit that he did not know, and promise to seek the right information given a few days.

Arrangements were made with a riverboat captain, who would act as courier and carry messages from Akhetaton to Memphis and vice versa. This would enable Ahmes to write out the question, and Rufus, or in the bishop's absence, Senh, to answer.

Rufus was not happy having to leave Ahmes to preach by himself. It was something that needed experience, and though the man's instruction had been very thorough over the past year, he found that he was rather green in that type of preaching. It was quite different from the service that the priest had performed in the service of Isis, where preaching had been minimal. He would wait and see how things would develop. He made a mental note for the future, to have his priests preach near their church for a period of time. There, he could instruct them in their oratorial skills before sending them out on their missions.

'The Lord would surely help. In his own way, and in his own time.'

With these thoughts, he boarded the riverboat on his way back to Memphis, with a projected stop over at Hermopolis.

Ahmes accompanied him to the boat, and thanked him for taking the time to further instruct him.

"You should have enough money," said Rufus," to keep you for at least a month. By then, I feel sure that you will have visited a few patients, and made some money. Let me know if you need any more, and remember to keep some for your fare back to Memphis, you never know how things are going to go. Be a man of peace. Do not get angry with anyone. We Christians must be known as people of peace, and love. Farewell my friend, and may Yeshua protect you and the Holy Spirit guide you."

The two men embraced, and the bishop shouldering his baggage, jumped into the boat as it left the jetty.

It was late afternoon when Rufus disembarked, and made his way to the house of the two Miriams. A buxom young maid opened the door and asked his business there.

"I have come to visit both your mistresses young woman," said Rufus with enthusiasm. " Be kind enough to say that a friend wishes to see them."

The maid bowed, and leaving him at the door went to give her message.

"My goodness," what a lovely surprise chanted the elder Miriam, as she, coming to the door, recognised the visitor, and moved quickly to embrace him.

"Please come in. Miriam will be overjoyed to see you; she is in her room."

The excited aunt stepped down into the garden, and called out to her niece.

"I have a lovely surprise for you. Come out," she sang, throwing a wink, and a happy smile at the visitor.

A few moments later, Miriam appeared, more beautiful than ever, and with a joyful scream she hastened to Rufus, lovingly embracing him. Tears of joy flooded her eyes.

"You are more beautiful than I remember," he said, as he embraced her again, and turning to her aunt, he remarked:

"You both look so well, it makes me very happy to see you in such good health."

They sat in the little nook in the garden where the stone benches were. Thc tantalising scent of the bougainvilleas soon transported our hero into a different world. A world that he had almost forgotten. One that spoke of warmth, comfort, sympathy and love. The rigours and deep concerns of his priestly life seemed to evaporate, as he sat there with the two Miriams, and listened to them telling him how he had been missed; the young one's eyes glowing with love.

'How wonderful it must be to come home to a woman like her every day,' thought Rufus. 'It would make life so much easier to deal with. She would understand my commitment to the Lord, and help me if only by listening and supporting me in my work; smoothening those bumps that I meet along the way, which are hard for me to bear by myself. This woman's sympathy is worth more to me than that of anyone else.'

After a brief spell, aunt Miriam left the two together, with the excuse that she had supper to prepare.

"You have been constantly on my mind," said Miriam with sadness in her eyes."It's been a very long time. You cannot imagine how I have missed you and worried about you. Also, the possibility that you might perhaps not wish to come back to me."

"I have been so busy and involved with God's work that I have had no time of my own," said Rufus, with a compassionate look.

"I have thought of you often," he continued with a loving smile. "Mostly, in the quiet of night, when it relaxed me to picture your lovely face, and think of the dear moments we have had together. From now on I am hopeful that the Lord will allow me to see you more often. I have left a colleague of mine up in Akhetaton which is only a short day's boat ride from here. I shall need to keep an eye on him. He is one of my priests."

"That's wonderful, I shall see you more often. Thank the Lord."

"Hopefully, I shall be coming to evangelise here also, once I know that I have a strong team behind in Memphis."

"My aunt and I pray to Yeshua every day, but we greatly regret that there is no one here to perform the 'Breaking of the Bread' for us, and tell us stories of Yeshua's life, as you did when you were last here."

"Yes, unfortunately there are not enough priests to go around once the people are converted to Yeshua. I am by the grace of God, a bishop now."

"What is a bishop?" she asked.

He smiled at her as if saying, 'how would you know?'

"A bishop is a man of the church who has a few priests under his charge, and is responsible for many people in his care. He has the privilege of ordaining priests.

My father is the bishop of Cyrene, and when he dies, my brother will be the next bishop there, if my father consecrates him before he dies.

"That is wonderful! I congratulate you. You must be very good at your work when you have been so favoured," she smiled, reaching for his hand.

"The Lord has been good to me, especially allowing me to be here. I feel so rested and happy with you," he said taking her hand and looking into her eyes.

"I do love you very much, and I shall never be completely happy until we are together."

"I have dreamt of this moment, but I never thought I would ever hear you say that," she said, and leaning forward she passionately kissed him over the little stone table that stood between them.

"You will marry me then?"

"Of course! would I kiss a man who I was not going to marry?"

"Supper is ready!" was the aunt's call from the kitchen.

Their betrothal was announced to her aunt who was overcome with emotion, tears rolling down her cheeks.

"I hope you don't take her away from me," she cried, embracing him. He could not reply, it was all in Yeshua's hands.

During the meal, the 'Breaking of the Bread' was performed, much to the women's delight. Rufus took care to have them say the prayer that he had taught them on his first visit after their Baptism, and which he now said with them before receiving the sacrament.

"Lord Yeshua, I humbly and repent-fully ask your forgiveness for my sins, purely through love of You."

After supper, Rufus brought his future wife and her aunt up to date with his life in Memphis; his visit to Alexandria; his meetings with Marius; and his new cavern church. But made no mention of his ordeal to win the congregation of Isis for the Lord.

They spent a truly restful evening. The aunt played her harp, and Miriam who was learning to play the flute, accompanied her, handling her new instrument quite convincingly. They coaxed Rufus into singing a couple of songs, and were very pleasantly surprised when he exhibited a very capable baritone voice.

Later, he helped the maid move Miriam's bed into her aunt's larger room, and once again, he slept on a pile of comfortable cushions in the vacated room.

They were all up early next morning ready to enjoy another day together.

Rufus who had been doing some heavy thinking during the night, decided that he would remain in Hermopolis for a whole week. He would do some preaching in that city, in the hope of winning a few more souls for Yeshua. The new converts would also provide some religious company for the Miriams, who now played such an important part in his life, and would need spiritual support during his forthcoming absence.

He could easily have Ahmes come over occasionally from Akhetaton and perform a service for the new group, which would grow by the grace of the Holy Spirit, and by their own testimony to their friends and acquaintances.

'Yes, that should work quite well with the help of God,' he said to himself as he performed his ablutions and made ready to go across the little garden for breakfast.

After having eaten, the three of them, leaving the maid to care for the house, and have a lunch ready for their return, went in search of a good place from which to preach. After eliminating many options, they unanimously decided on a location which would set the preacher in a prominent setting; albeit a trifle theatrical, appealing strongly to the romantic inclinations of all three.

The place chosen was in the very heart of the town. It was an old ruin comprised of a number of steps leading up to a small stone platform. On the platform, stood one solitary column devoid of superstructure, and crowned by a lotus capital. Despite the age of the column and capital, there was still evidence of its original colouration. In its hey day, accompanied by many others like it, and carrying their remarkable superstructures it must have presented a veritable feast for the eyes.

That evening, promptly after an early supper, the excited trio headed for their chosen site. Rufus mounted the steps carrying a simple and light cross a little taller than himself. After some forethought, he had had, a local carpenter make it to his specifications earlier that day. The two women standing at the bottom of the steps, waited with bated breath for the beginning of the preaching and results to follow.

Rufus held up the cross well over his head, and after a short silent prayer to the Holy Spirit, called out to passersby with a loud voice.

"People of Hermopolis! Come, and hear news that will change your lives!"

He repeated this a number of times, until a few of those passing by, stopped, and approached the steps below him. He waited a little longer, smiling in the meantime at those who were there. Again he called out once more.

A group who were evidently conversing with one another nearby, now took notice of his call and they too came nearer to listen. The bishop was now ready to begin; seeing that he now had a small assembly of around twenty people.

"You are doubtlessly wondering why I am standing here before you with this cross in my hand?"

He then began to preach to them the Lord Yeshua, with great knowledge and enthusiasm. The reason for the Lord's coming was expounded with great emphasis on the Afterlife, which he knew would arouse immediate interest in the Egyptian mind.

Every now and then he would stop, look at the crowd, and ask for confirmation to some suggestion he had made; thus getting them involved. He related a few of the Gospels with such conviction, that those listening were enthralled with the stories. He then explained to them their meaning, the application of the messages that they conveyed, and how their lives would be affected by them.

The two Miriams listened with ever increasing admiration at the words that flowed from Rufus' mouth. It was apparent to them, that his words were endowed with a supernatural fluidity, and sounded something akin to music. Every note synchronised with the next as they grew and swelled to culminate in a glorious final crescendo.

An unprecedented crowd of more than fifty people had now gathered. Their attention and interest was so marked, that when a couple of young jeerers began to create a disturbance, the crowd quickly and forcefully ushered them on their way.

When Rufus finished an hour later, there were numerous calls for Baptism, but the bishop being unprepared, and knowing that they would return to hear him, informed them that he would be there for another four days.

"If you return tomorrow at this same time, I shall be most happy to baptise you," he told them with a big smile on his face, and blessing them with the sign of the Cross.

Descending the steps amidst cries of acclamation, Rufus, joined the happy women and the trio made their way home rejoicing and thanking God.

Thus ended another very profitable day in the life of the Bishop of Memphis.

Five days later, after having baptised no less than twenty people, Rufus took leave of his beloved espoused and her aunt. He promised to return soon with his friend and assistant Senh, who would perform the marriage ceremony for them.

As he sailed down the Nile back to Memphis, his mind was at rest with regard to the new infant community that he had now established in Hermopolis. He had no doubt in his mind, that both Miriams would take charge of the new converts, and organize their prayer meetings.

"I did not expect you back any sooner," greeted Senh, as Rufus walked into the church. Both approached the tabernacle, knelt down, and prayed.

A little later, having finished their prayers, they both went out into the garden.

"I would have stayed longer, but I thought I would surprise you by returning earlier than you expected," joked Rufus in reply to Senh's earlier remark.

"How is Miriam?'

"Very well," thank you. "She and her aunt Miriam get along like sisters."

"Of course, she was not one bit happy to see you," quipped the assistant with a big smile.

"Very well. Since you will tease me until you completely exhaust me. Yes. We are betrothed....there! Now you know."

Senh gave his friend a big hug, grasped his hand, and congratulated him with all sincerity

"When is the big day?" he asked.

"God alone knows. We shall have to wait and see. By the way, I made twenty converts there, all baptised in public, and assisted by both Miriams."

"So that is what held you up. I might have known you would not waste a moment. How did you get along with Ahmes in Akhetaton?"

"That is another matter. He is eager enough and clever enough, but I am not sure about his delivery. It is rather stiff and his presentation is somewhat awkward.

He has an odd way of explaining things which troubles me. I arranged with a riverboat captain who does the run between here and there to carry messages, so that if Ahmes is stuck for answers he can write us and we can help him out."

For the next two months, the business of the church in Memphis continued as usual, with a total of forty new parishioners being added to the congregation; of which twenty five were Jews. There had been however no further trouble from the Jewish community. They seemed to be reconciled to the fact that some of their members would be lost to the Christians.

Rufus had had only one communication with Ahmes during that time. The latter asked for money, but gave no report, other than he was having some difficulties. The bishop had asked his missionary, to send a report back every month. He now began to be concerned, and wondered whether to send Senh out to investigate the reason for the negligence. However, on second thought, he remembered how ably Senh had looked after the home front during his last voyage, and decided to go himself. It would also give him the opportunity of seeing the man personally, and visiting Miriam on the way back.

"Why don't you get Ahmes to marry you whilst you are up there?" asked the assistant priest.

"Because I want *you* to do that at the first opportunity."

"I am honoured, sir," answered Senh with a mocking bow, though he was elated by his friend's preference for him.

"The Lord knows when. We can't both get away at the same time," lamented the bishop.

A few days later, Rufus was on his way to Akhetaton to investigate Ahmes' lack of communication. On arrival, he made his way to the lodgings that he had stayed at on his last visit.

"He left a month ago, and I do not know where he is staying now." said the landlord with a note of disgust in his voice.

Rufus had no idea where to find his priest, so he took a room there again. He stayed for lunch before going out on the town to kill time until evening, when he would go to the park where Ahmes would as expected, be preaching.

Whilst he was having his lunch in the dining room, which he shared with another couple, he overheard a conversation that was taking place in the kitchen, between his landlord and landlady, and which gave him great concern.

"Someone has to tell him. He should know, since he is his superior, or so he told us," said the wife in a low tone of voice.

"No. I am not telling him. It is no business of ours. He will find out in time."

"It's not right, he is supposed to be a holy man," said the wife.

"You tell him then. I'm not doing it."

"You men are such cowards at times."

Rufus looked up as the landlady entered the room and sat down on a cushion across from him. She talked in a hushed voice so that her other two guests would not hear.

"Are you in charge of the preacher Ahmes?"

"Yes," whispered back the bishop.

"I understand that you are trying to find him?"

"Yes, that is correct. I do not know where he has gone."

"That man is not behaving as he preaches people should behave."

"Have you heard him preaching?"

"Yes, my husband and I attended some of his meetings in the park. He spoke of your God's son Yeshua, and how he loves us all and how he is hurt every time someone sins," she said with sincerity.

"Yes, that is true," asserted the bishop, pleased that the woman had learnt about Yeshua and his love for all.

"He spoke out against fornication, killing, robbing, and telling lies about one's neighbour, and called these things great sins. He said that people who committed these things and did not repent, would be tormented in the Afterlife, and would not be allowed into heaven where only the pure hearted were permitted to enter."

"All that is true," confirmed the bishop wondering with some apprehension as to where all the conversation was leading.

"Your priest, does not do what he preaches. He has angered many people that trusted in him and believed in what he was telling them."

The bishop felt a cold chill run down his spine, as he began to understand the woman's complaint.

"What, may I ask, is the man's transgression?" he enquired with fallen countenance, and shifting uneasily on his cushion.

"He keeps a small boy with him constantly, and abuses him in many ways. We told him to go. We could not stand the boy crying at night and at times, even during the day."

"Did you see anything?" Rufus lent forward, eyes in wide open expectancy.

"No. We only heard the crying, and the boy's complaints," she concluded with a look of disgust on her face.

"I shall see to this," promised Rufus," and if you are right in your suspicions, he shall be stopped and disciplined. In the meantime, I will stay here with you for the rest of my stay. Thank you for making me aware of the situation."

"I am sorry to have distressed you," pouted the woman, with a sympathetic look at the bishop." He has disappointed us, and many good people who were overjoyed by his message," she concluded, gathering her robe around her and arising.

"Have no fear in that regard. I shall be preaching in the park and reassuring the people that we are not hypocrites, but follow what we teach. There is a bad apple in every basket." With these words, the bishop got up, left his hostess, and went for a long walk to gather his wits about him.

'What shall I do if he is guilty?' he said to himself, with a sinking heart.

Evening could not come soon enough for Rufus who liked to meet a problem head on, and as quickly as possible. In his younger days he had been impulsive, but now his status as bishop demanded he take his time, and deliberate carefully on anything that may have repercussions. The problem he faced now would certainly have ramifications and make decision taking very precarious.

Finally evening arrived, and having had a very light and hasty supper for a lack of appetite, he made his way to the park.

Ahmes had not as yet arrived. Rufus sat on a rock and waited for him.

A small boy with a sad pensive look walked passed him, and as Rufus looked up to scrutinise the boy, he caught sight of the priest.

Ahmes approached, his eyes scanning the mound from where he would be preaching. He was startled to see Rufus, who getting up went up to him and embraced him with a certain coldness that the other answered in a similar vein.

"What are you doing here bishop?" asked Ahmes, with what seemed to Rufus a guilty intonation in his serious voice.

"I came because I suspected that your work as a physician was not going well, since you needed monetary support from us."

"Unfortunately, I have had difficulties finding patients, and as many again, 'fishing for men.'

"That is most distressing to hear," remarked Rufus.

"I am inclined to suspect an intended alienation of you personally by the people of this town. You have done something to offend them, and you know what it is."

"Who have you been talking to?" asked the priest with a touch of anger.

"To be perfectly honest with you, it was your former landlady who told me that you had behaved atrociously, taking advantage of a young boy sexually and in other manners." The bishop looked at the boy, who was sitting up on the mound watching them.

"They are disparaging me, and spreading their venomous suspicions around the town so that no one will have anything to do with me," said the angry priest with his arms in the air.

Rufus looked him in the eye with a long enquiring look which the other could not sustain; turning his eyes away.

"For a Christian priest to lie in a grave matter like this is a great and mortal sin, as you learnt during your period of instruction," admonished the bishop with a grave countenance. "We live by the truth, because Yeshua was himself the very truth. We must all accept the consequences of our sinful actions as truth is paramount. The devil, the father of lies, goes around as the apostle Peter said, *seeking whom he may devour.* It appears to me that he has reached you and made you do abominable things.

You have done great harm to the church, as well as to yourself, and what is even worse, you have perverted an innocent child. The Lord Yeshua said *it would be better if one tied a mill stone around one's own neck and cast oneself into the sea, than pervert an innocent child.* To these people who came to hear you preach, you are their Judas."

The priest did not flinch, he just stood there as if petrified. Rufus held up as it were a mirror in which he, Ahmes, could see his inner self, and repentance began to sprout in his soul.

"Yes! A Judas," continued Rufus. "You have betrayed them in not practicing what you preached. You convinced them of a new and better moral life, and dashed their beliefs by violating the rules yourself. These poor souls are disenchanted. A budding faith which by the grace of the Holy Spirit you sowed in them,...you shattered. I shall have a very difficult time winning them back. But I shall not leave this place until I have reversed the harm that you have done, and win all those souls back for our beloved Yeshua."

Ahmes, fell on his knees in front of the angry bishop, and begged forgiveness; tears falling down his brown cheeks as he clasped his arms around the bishop. A crowd had gathered by then. Rufus, putting his hands on his priest's head, and looking up to heaven said. "Your sins are forgiven in the name of the

Holy Trinity." He then raised up Ahmes as the crowd watched, and said in a loud voice, so that those gathered could hear him. "Your sins have been forgiven, go and sin no more. You must now make restitution for what you have done.

Go up the mound, and embrace the boy, and tell him you are sorry for what you did to him. Then apologise to these good people, after which I shall also speak to them."

The shamed priest began to ascend the mound, but the boy seeing him coming, ran away with a frightened look on his little face. Ahmes continued until he had reached the top, and turning around faced the people, who after witnessing the scene between him and Rufus, stood there in silent expectation of what he might have to say.

The priest duly apologized to all, admitting his wrong doing, and making sure to stress that the sin was strictly his, and that his preaching was the truth.

"I have been weak," he lamented, with tears in his eyes. " I have not lived up to what my faith taught."

Rufus, then standing beside him addressed the gathering. He held their attention for the next hour as he with his great oratorial ability satisfied the crowd who had grown larger as his discourse continued. Many questions were asked, all of which he answered with truthfulness and enthusiasm. In the end, he converted many, who as usual, asked for Baptism.

"We are not prepared today to baptise you, but if you come again tomorrow evening, we will be most happy to perform the sacrament," he announced with regret.

All dispersed, and Rufus told Ahmes to go to his lodgings and stay there until the next evening when they were to meet again at the mound, for the Baptisms.

Having got rid of his unhappy priest, the bishop went back to his own lodgings and informed the landlord and his wife, that he had spoken to the people, and that they now understood the situation.

"I was there nearby," said his host, "I heard everything, we will both be there for you to baptise us tomorrow."

"No need for that," said the bishop with a smile, "I can do that for you right now."

The Baptisms followed, to the joy of Manetho, and Phile, for those were their names. They gave their esteemed lodger a good supper, witnessing for the first time, the 'Breaking of the Bread' of which they partook; the bishop having explained the significance of the Sacrament, and forgiven their sins.

As the three sat at table, Rufus mentioned with concern, the boy who had ran away from the mound, and asked how he might be found.

Phile told him with some emotion in her voice, that the child was only six years old, an orphan, and that as soon as he grew hungry again, he would probably run back to the priest, regardless of the treatment he might receive. Tears appeared in her large black eyes as she spoke, her full-lipped shapely mouth pouted, as she looked across the table at her husband eliciting his sympathy. Manetho who was in his early forties as was his wife, shook his head slowly at Phile's words, and said.

"We can go look for the boy after supper if you like," casting a glance first at the lodger, and then at the hostess.

"Thank you," said the bishop. "I really need to talk to that little boy. Much harm has been done him and he will need a lot of love to enable him to become a normal boy again. Though I doubt he will ever completely recover from so horrible an experience at such an early age. We can but pray."

The hopeful trio took off after supper in search of the boy. They looked around the park and the immediate vicinity, but to no avail. After about an hour of fruitless searching they decided to go to Ahmes' new lodgings, which they found by asking people of their neighbourhood whom the couple knew, and happened to meet during their walk.

As they came upon the house, they heard crying coming from behind a low wall appertaining to the house. Looking over it, they found the boy sitting there on the ground crying.

"He won't let me into his room, and I am hungry," cried the boy."

"Come with us," said Phile reaching for his hand. "We will give you something nice to eat."

The boy looked up, and recognising Phile, jumped up on the wall with her help, and all started back to their house.

The bishop spoke to the boy with great love, as they all sat in the dining room after he had eaten. Phile embraced the child, and kept him by her side all evening, which calmed him. Soon, they had him smiling.

Manetho, seeing that the boy made his wife happy as she sat there contentedly hugging him, and knowing that she could never have a child of her own, surprised her and Rufus with the suggestion that they keep the child who had no one to love or care for him. The little boys eyes widened with joy, as Phile, her motherly instinct aroused, gave the child a kiss and another to her contented husband.

The Baptisms in the park went well, with eighteen people being baptised.

The bishop informed them that he would be leaving the following day, and would be taking the priest with him. There were no objections to that, as they were glad to get rid of him.

"You will now remain at the church in Memphis, with Addaya," said the bishop as the riverboat in which they were travelling, left the jetty in Akhetaton.

"Your family being near, you will best be able to overcome any future temptation. I myself will look after the new congregations in Akhetaton and Heliopolis."

Ahmed made no answer. In fact, he did not utter a single word. He would not eat what the bishop gave him, and just stared at the shore lost in his thoughts.

Rufus who felt weary and upset, cat-napped as the heat of the day made him drowsy. He was suddenly roused out of his sleep, by shouts that appeared to come from the captain of the vessel.

"Come back! Come back here you fool. There are crocodiles in these waters."

Rufus turned to look for Ahmes, and could not see him. All of a sudden, it dawned on him that it must be his priest that was in the water, and swimming away from the boat.

"Please turn the boat around and pick him up," begged the concerned bishop.

"It's no good," said thc captain, "the currents here will not permit that, I'm sorry."

Rufus took off his tunic and got to the rail, but was apprehended from behind by the arms of two strong oarsmen who pulled him back into the boat, just as a dreadful scream was heard from the direction in which Ahmes had been swimming.

"That man must have wanted to die... Fool!" said the captain, with disdain.

The bishop was distraught.

'Lord why did you let him do that?' he prayed. 'He would not have sinned that way any more, I was going to keep him away from children other than his own, for the rest of his life. He was repentant Lord, and I forgave him in Your name. He also made retribution. Have mercy on him Lord and receive him into thy kingdom.'

Weary of heart and soul, Rufus interrupted his passage, and left the boat at, Heliopolis, where he made his way to Miriam's house with a very heavy heart.

Miriam, who was alone in the house was besides herself with joy at seeing him again sooner than expected, and looked past him as she let him in, expecting another priest who might be coming to marry them.

"How wonderful to see you," she sang as she ardently embraced and kissed him.

"Come, sit down," said Miriam, with a look of concern in her lovely eyes. "My aunt will be back shortly; she and Ita, went to the bazaars. You do not look happy my love, what ails you?"

Rufus told her the whole story of Ahmes' misdemeanour and subsequent fate.

She sat beside him, hugged him, and consoled him, which gave him some relief. They both remained in their embrace, for a long time until she, realising that he had probably not eaten, got up and brought him some fruit which they shared as they looked at each other in silent admiration.

This, thought Rufus, is what a wife is really for; feeling the aura of love that surrounded him in his misery.

'Why did he do it? I do not think he wanted to die. He did not know that there were crocodiles in the water there. He was probably so ashamed that he wanted to get away and be by himself. Why did God let him do that?' His mind could find no rest, it was sheer torment.

The door suddenly opened and in walked the two shoppers, laden with things that the aunt had bought. Again, the elder Miriam was delighted to see him.

After a pleasant lunch, and having recovered somewhat from his depressed state, the bishop asked if it would be possible to assemble the tiny Christian congregation so that he could perform a 'Breaking of the Bread' service for them all.

Aunt Miriam, sent Ita the maid, to spread the news and ask all of the faithful to meet at their house the following evening.

"It will be tight,"said Miriam, "but I feel sure that we can get them all in, even if they are a little crushed. They will not want to miss the service.

The bishop stayed another week in Hermopolis, where the congregation had augmented to forty eight souls by the time he boarded the riverboat for Memphis. A meeting place had been found for them in an old building that one of their affluent members had donated, as was often the case, and which they would be patching up and renovating as best they could.

Once again, Rufus was on his way back to Memphis on his own; his mind in turmoil. He knew that he had missed an opportunity to take Miriam with him and have Senh marry them, but he was too upset at having lost Ahmes.

How was he going to tell the man's family the truth without tarnishing his memory?

These thoughts tore at the fabric of his very being, and relegated the consideration of his marriage to second place in his mental list of priorities.

"Are you still a bachelor?" were Senh's welcoming words as the bishop walked into the church. The former was busy filling the oil lamps, and getting things ready for the instruction classes. Those were given to the congregation twice every week, as had been arranged by Rufus and himself.

"I'm afraid so," answered the bishop, embracing his assistant.

"I thought surely this time you would be bringing her with you. I am dying to make an honest man of you," laughed Senh in his good natured, joking way.

"I have the most horrible news to tell you," said Rufus with a grave countenance.

"She is well, no?" asked the Egyptian with much concern.

"Yes, thank God."

"What then?"

"We have lost Ahmes."

"Could you not find him in Akhetaton?"

"I shall explain after prayers," said the bishop as he knelt in front of the tabernacle followed by his assistant.

"Come my friend let us sit down in my room and I shall explain all," said Rufus as he got to his feet and bowed to the tabernacle.

Needless to say, the rest of the afternoon was taken up with the bishop explaining the tragic affair to his friend. The latter became as depressed as Rufus himself, with the many considerations and ramifications that the disastrous affair had spawned.

"I must talk with Addaya as soon possible," said Rufus, I need his advice and help.

"He may be in later. If not, I shall send word to his house," said Senh.

"No. Better still, let us go to his house right now, maybe he's there," suggested the bishop.

"There is a good chance that he is, as his wife is very ill and he spends a lot of time with her these days," assured Senh with a sad look.

The two clerics found their way to the old priest's house, and knocking loudly on the door (the old priest was somewhat deaf), waited for him to appear.

"Bishop! I am most happy to see you. When did you get back?" greeted Addaya, with a big smile.

"Earlier today, and I need to see you most urgently my friend," answered Rufus embracing the old man.

"Please come in," invited the old priest as he led the way to the family room where they all sat down.

"How is your good wife faring?" asked the bishop with some concern in his voice.

"She is in a very bad way," Addaya whispered, so that his wife would not hear.

"May I see her?" asked Rufus.

The three men entered the bedroom and found her lying in bed surrounded by a few women friends who had come to visit her fearing the worst. Though she was much younger than the old priest, she looked old; her face deathly pale and thin, her eyes surrounded by purple rings and her lips bloodless. She smiled feebly when she saw the men.

The bishop approached her and took her hand. As he did, he felt that great tranquility once again, followed by an impulse he could not resist, and with his eyes raised to heaven said.

"Berenice! In the name of Yeshua, and by the power of the Holy Spirit, be cured."

The woman shook slightly, the colour began to come back into her face, the purple rings disappeared and she sat up in bed. Tears of joy ran down her face as she embraced Rufus who was as surprised as she was at what had happened. Addaya came forward and embraced the bishop also, thanking him with many tears. Berenice, was now up on her feet embracing her friends, who were flabbergasted by the miracle they had just witnessed.

"I want you all to know," explained Rufus, "that I did not perform any miracle. It was Yeshua working through me who cured Berenice. It was His divine will."

There was much celebration in that house that evening. However as night came, the women left, and Berenice, giving Rufus one last affectionate hug, went off to bed leaving the men to talk.

The bishop and Senh, tactfully broke the news of Ahmes to Addaya. The old priest's jubilant mood dissipated, he looked at the bishop with incredulity as he digested the tragic story that the pair had related. His head drooped sadly. He said; his voice breaking:

"He was as a son to me. How could he have done such a thing?"

"The devil took possession of him, I have no doubt on that score," replied Rufus, "for he was most repentant afterwards. I do not think he wanted to die, merely to be on his own to reconcile himself, and face life again."

"It is going to be so difficult to tell his wife and children," sighed Addaya.

"And yet, I must be the one to tell them."

Rufus and Senh left shortly afterwards, leaving the old priest in a bittersweet situation.

Senh wanted to know how the bishop had performed the miraculous cure.

"I assure you," said Rufus, "that I was as surprised as you were." He remembered the miraculous cures of Marcus and the woman in the village in Cyrene by his father.

He then explained to his friend what he felt and how out of his control the miracle had been.

"We are so fortunate," said Senh, "to have been given the grace to believe in our powerful God. We must continue to try and get as many souls as we can to believe in him also. And we must pray that Ahmes be with him."

* * * * *

Three months went by, and Rufus felt stagnated in his work as pastor. He was itching to go out and continue to spread the good news further up river, even further than Hermopolis and Akhetaton. Senh was a good orator, and made converts every week, so the bishop was quite content to leave him in Memphis. The church in Memphis had now over six hundred members, and even the 'cavern church' was proving small as two services for the 'Breaking of the Bread' were required every Sabbath day.

John Mark had been very distressed by the Ahmes incident and subsequent tragedy and included a prayer in the Sabbath service for constant spiritual protection of priests by the Holy Spirit. The church in Alexandria had also been growing, and the head bishop had ordained another priest after Djidi; giving his bishopric three priests. They were restricting their evangelization to the Delta area, which had a large and mixed population.

Rufus now felt the need to begin a school for the training of future priests, who would soon be required for missions up river into Upper Egypt. The closer areas such as Akhetaton and Hermopolis, however would have to grow to at least two hundred souls in each before he would consider sending priests to take care of both those towns. The school would produce a priest every two years which seemed more than adequate for their projected plans. It would be run by Senh mostly, with Rufus as an advisor. They would immediately recruit six young candidates, from which two would be chosen to continue their studies for the next two years. After that, one priest every two years would be more than adequate, it was felt.

CHAPTER NINE

THE STATUE

Four years had now elapsed since Rufus had come to Egypt. Little Letitia was now ten years of age, and though she thought of her father often and prayed for him all the time, she felt abandoned; despite having all her family around her.

Simon gave her more of his time than any of his other grandchildren though he loved them all equally. At age fifty nine, the Bishop of Cyrene was still full of vigour, and 'fishing' many souls for Yeshua. He had spread the faith all around Cyrene, and had established a sizeable community in Ptolemais, where he had built a church which was run by his assistant Saul. His grandson, young Simon, now assisted him and Alexander as the need arose, whilst they awaited the ordination of another young man that was in training for the priesthood.

Simon learnt from Marius that Rufus, was now a bishop, which made him very proud, as he recalled with regret, the difficult start that his son had had in embracing the faith. He thanked the Lord for having claimed him for his service, even if it had been through the truly hurtful experience occasioned by the loss of his beloved Letitia, and daughter. He now yearned to see him again if only briefly, but his work and responsibilities in Cyrene made it as difficult for him to travel, as it did for Rufus in Memphis. He felt it would be wonderful if he could visit him and take little Letitia along.

'I shall pray for that, and leave it as usual in the good Lord's hands,' he consoled himself.

* * * * *

Rufus knelt in front of the tabernacle in his little church in town, which he had named 'Church of the Holy Trinity.' A name which had irked the Judeans considerably when the church was built and as my good reader will recall, had been part of the cause of the church fire.

'Lord I am still greatly distressed by the loss of Ahmes,' prayed the worried bishop. 'If he did willfully kill himself I feel very responsible. I called him a Judas. I may have put it into his head to follow his example. I do not think he knew of the crocodiles in that part of the river, though it is possible that it may have been rumoured in Akhetaton. Please Lord, grant that he have died accidentally out of ignorance of that danger, and not willfully by his own hand.'

The wayward priest's death weighed heavily on the bishop's shoulders as he knelt and prayed. It had filled his mind with an obsession, that precluded even the thought of his soon-to-be marriage. Two months had now elapsed since Ahmes' death which had changed his life considerably.

'In future,' he told himself. 'I shall have to be more careful as to who I send out. Surely this has to be an exceptional case.' His mind turned to his pending mission.

'It's time I visit the two little congregations in Akhetaton and Hermopolis,' thought Rufus, half talking to Yeshua, and half to himself.

'I shall leave tomorrow. I have to brief Senh and make sure that someone remains here at all times. Perhaps one of the young men that we are training can spend the day here, whilst Senh is out doing his preaching with the other one, or, fulfilling other duties which may be required of him. The cook will be here too, so they won't have to go out to eat.'

His rambling thoughts dispersed, as he made the sign of the Cross; an innovation that had come via John Mark from Judea and which all Christians were practicing ardently in their prayers. Also in liturgical services and as a means of blessing.

The following morning found the bishop boarding a riverboat once more on his way to Akhetaton. He prayed as he passed the stretch of river where his unfortunate priest had died, and once again asked the Lord's forgiveness if he was to blame. He spotted as many as eight crocodiles sunning themselves on the far shore. It was common knowledge that crocodiles swam the river, but there were not many incidents of people being attacked by them. Animals that came to drink at night were the game they mostly fed on, and which kept them satisfied. During the day, they lay on sandy banks or merely floated among the papyrus reeds. So he reasoned, in an effort to shake off 'the monkey' that he now constantly carried on his back.

'Yes. This seems to be the place where they concentrate; the captain was right,' thought Rufus. He spent the rest of the voyage counting in comparison, the rather sparse number of the creatures that lay elsewhere on the riverbank, sunning themselves in the warm early morning sun.

Once again, he stayed with Manetho and Phile, to whom he appealed for help in rounding up the faithful, so that arrangements could be made to assemble them for the 'Breaking of the Bread' which he was so eager to perform for them.

As he sat together with his landlord and wife at lunch the day of his arrival, the bishop had occasion to observe the boy who was now a vital part of that household. He seemed content, and having gained a little weight, looked much healthier. The boy was silently playing with a toy; a little donkey which Manetho who was a wood carver had made for him. The boy, named Pah, never answered when the lodger asked him anything. He merely drew closer to Phile, and looked at him with sadness and fear in his eyes, even though he talked quite freely with his new parents. Of a sudden looking at the bishop, he asked. "Are you a priest?"

Rufus was taken by surprise having resigned himself to receiving no communication from the boy.

"Yes, my son," he answered.

Again the boy said nothing, but took refuge in the arms of Phile who could feel the fear and apathy that had gripped the child.

Rufus felt a need to instruct Pah that all priests were not the same, and that Ahmes had been punished for his comportment. But on second thought, he would ask Phile to do that for him later.

The little congregation gathered in the garden behind the house, where the service was performed to everyone's joy. The bishop having as usual explained the sacrament and forgiven their sins.

They all drank from the bishop's cup, that travelled with him. The little cups had not as yet been given them at Baptism as was done in Cyrene, Alexandria, Memphis and possibly other places. A sum of money was left with Manetho to have a local silversmith make them, following a sketch that the carver drew. A jug with a thin spout was also to be made. The congregation would contribute at each weekly Sabbath day prayer meeting, whatever money each could afford to give, and Manetho was to collect it and reimburse the Memphis church for their cost. Any money in excess of that, would be held by Manetho on behalf of the congregation, but would be accountable to the Memphis church, who would direct the way the money would be spent. It was also agreed, that the contributions collected after each meeting would be counted there and then in front of the whole congregation. Someone was to record the amount, prior to the wood carver or anyone else, taking charge of the money.

Rufus preached at Akhetaton for the next four days, winning another ten people whom he baptised on the mound where he preached. That way, others would learn from the Sacrament that was meant to open a new life for them.

The landlord, his wife, and the boy, were there to see him off at the jetty. He blessed them with the sign of the Cross from the boat, as it floated away downriver.

The younger Miriam was just leaving, accompanied by Ita her servant as Rufus approached the house.

"Oh Rufus! What a wonderful surprise," she sang, at the sight of him. She quickly embraced him with great joy in her heart, and a beautiful smile on her lovely face.

"How are you my love, and how is your aunt?" he asked with a smile, pressing her to him, and kissing her brow.

"We are both well, thank you. Why don't you accompany me to the bazaars, just for a little while....It won't take long?"

"Ita, you can stay....Take this bag," she said, taking the bishop's bag from him, and handing it to her sturdy maid with some difficulty. "Please tell my aunt that we will be back in a little while."

"It will give me great pleasure to accompany you my dear," replied her betrothed. They both walked away, and Ita made her way back to the house. Contentment filled their hearts, as they walked down the street together, smiling at each other, and enjoying the warm sunny morning, which gave life to everything around them.

"How are you feeling Rufus? Is that man's death still bothering you?"

"Yes. I cannot seem to be able to shake it off, my love. It weighs heavily on my conscience. I feel I was too hard on him, and he could not deal with the remorse he felt. He had a wife and children you know, and they had to be told everything."

"You are much too hard on yourself," she said taking his arm. "You are very soft hearted with everyone, but with yourself, you are a hard judge. What you did, was what your position as bishop demanded of you. You are a man of authority and difficult decisions are expected of you. God will not hold it against you if you have done your best to see that his commandments are followed by those under you."

"You are a wise woman Miriam, and you have a gift for consoling me. Surely Yeshua has put you in my life for that very purpose, I am so fortunate," he said as he pressed her hand and entered one of the bazaar that she was leading him to.

The remainder of the day was very pleasantly spent. Rufus and Miriam having greatly enjoyed browsing the bazaars and shops, returned to the house where the lovers had much time to themselves sitting in the garden together whilst the elder Miriam serenaded them with her harp from the living room.

These visits to the Miriams' house, though infrequent, answered to Rufus' inherent need for a woman's love, which was perhaps constituted a weakness in his nature. It was the elixir that invigorated him and restored a completeness that marked his zeal for life, helping him to embrace reality in its palpable sense. The natural and supernatural qualities which composed his life, blended together in such a way that they gave an added and profound meaning to his humanitarianism. He was as a result able to interact with greater charity and understanding with the members of his flock. He felt a great responsibility for them, as also for those who were as yet floundering in their beliefs, or mislead into the worship of false gods. His 'persona' as a result, was greatly enhanced, and he inspired confidence, even respect, in all who came into contact with him.

"I am having much trouble arranging for Senh to come and marry us," said Rufus in answer to Miriam's question." I have no one to leave behind to look after the church duties. I'm afraid that the only way is for you to come with me and be married there in the church at Memphis. Once we are married, then you can come back and stay with your aunt which I am sure will make her very happy. I shall, God willing come and be with you every two months or so, as I must keep an eye on my priests who will be spreading out on their missions. Even if you were to stay in Memphis you would be alone much of the time. My work will keep me travelling, and I do not like the idea of your living in the church, as we have enemies and you would not necessarily be safe."

"I shall be ready next time you come," she said with a gleam in her eye.

"Why don't you come with me now? Senh hinted that he would like to go to Karnak to visit his family. He has not seen them in over two years. He also needs to see an old client there, who has been asking him to authenticate a statue which could generate a good bit of money for our church. So this would be a good time for us to get married. We would hold the fort in Memphis until he returns, and then I shall bring you back to your aunt. What do you say to that?"

"Oh, my, that sounds wonderful...Yes! Let's do that."

Aunt Miriam was disappointed at having to miss the wedding, but as the plan was to bring her niece back soon, she gave them her blessing

As the riverboat bearing the happy couple, floated down the river towards Memphis, Miriam noticed, with some concern, that Rufus was distracted. She suspected that at the root of it was the Ahmes tragedy. She attempted to clear his mind of the matter.

"Have you the bishop of Alexandria's approval for our wedding? Miriam asked.

"What did you say? he asked absentmindedly as his eyes scanned the river bank.

She repeated it for him.

"Yes!... Oh no. He will not disapprove; we have talked about it a number of times," he replied, making an effort to smile, as his mind had indeed wandered back to Ahmes.

Senh, who was busy closing the shutters for the night, was delighted to see Miriam with the bishop walking into the church. He embraced them both at the same time, with a big smile on his face.

"At last I am going to make an honest man of you," he said, putting his arm around his friend's shoulders and winking mischievously at Miriam.

They walked through the church to the house, where the two young student priests were sitting in the colonnaded porch chatting away and awaiting the return of Senh to complete a lesson that he had been giving them.

"You two fellows will have to go back home tonight," said Senh as all three walked into the porch.

The student priests arose on seeing the bishop and cast an enquiring look in the direction of Miriam, who gave them a lovely smile as Rufus introduced her to them as his betrothed. They both bowed their heads in recognition and produced charming smiles; their eyes betraying their admiration at her beauty.

"These two young men, will soon be carrying the good news up river once they are ordained. This is Alceres, and this is Bek," said the bishop with a paternal smile, putting his arm around each one as he introduced them.

Shortly after, the student's bedroom was cleaned and vacated by them. They departed each to their own homes leaving it ready for Miriam's use.

"We should have built another bedroom perhaps?" said Senh without stopping to think

"Ha! Ha!" laughed the bishop, "you forget that by the end of the week, this room will be empty again."

Senh suddenly realised that the bishop and his wife would only require one bedroom.

"I did not stop to think. That is so different to what we are used to," he said casting them a sheepish look.

Again they all laughed as they made their way to the kitchen to prepare something to eat; the cook having already left.

They sat and discussed the arrangements for the wedding, which even though a very understated one, still needed planning as indeed every wedding does, regardless of size.

"You should ask bishop John Mark to come and marry you, he would be delighted, and he certainly outranks me," suggested Senh honestly and with a smile, though with a pang of sadness in his heart.

Miriam looked at her betrothed as if asking, 'why not?'

"No, no, I cannot disturb him, even though he would willingly come. His work is of immense value to the church and he has a large diocese to look after. To tell you the truth, I always thought of you to be the one to marry us," he said addressing Senh, "it never entered my mind to ask anyone else," concluded the soon-to-be bridegroom.

The three of them moved out to the porch. By the light of a few oil lamps and a full moon, they conversed as was their custom, until late into the night.

The day of the wedding arrived. It came exactly one week after the couple's arrival. The little church was filled to overflowing as a result of the young priests having spread the news around the parish. The bishop was flabbergasted to see the turnout. He had only invited a few close friends, meaning it to be a quiet wedding.

The parishioners had gone out of their way to decorate the old church under the direction of young Bek, who with the help of his eager colleague had painted arches on all the hitherto insipid whitewashed walls, and placing a palm branch in each, created an avenue of palm branches which greatly improved the ambience of the stark church.

The altar was radiant with palm leaves, fresh flowers, and the light of many oil lamps. These imparted a warmth which pervaded the whole church and lent solemnity to the service in which the 'Body and Blood ' would be administered solely to the bride and groom.

Miriam who was a stranger to the congregation was much admired for her beauty and elegance. Sophia her only friend in Memphis, was there to assist her at the altar. Demetrios, assisted Rufus and held the rings.

Senh began with the customary 'Breaking of the Bread' service with Addaya assisting. The bride and groom knelt on handsomely woven cushions where they remained for most of the service, shortened by the absence of the sermon. Instead, Sehn made a short congratulatory speech, which was enthusiastically received by the congregation, all of whom held their beloved bishop in such high esteem.

Hymns were sung and accompanied by harp, lute and lyre, adding much to the festive feeling of the service.

Later, the parishioners milled around the house and garden, eating and drinking the provisions which they themselves had prepared, and brought with them. The newlyweds circulated among the impromptu guests, chatting amiably, and receiving endless congratulations and best wishes.

Rufus thanked the congregation and associates for their love and dedication in making the day a memorable one for himself and Miriam, who had now won the admiration of the whole parish. Slowly during the course of the afternoon, the guests drifted away.

Senh was the last to leave. He was to stay at Melech and Esther's house for the next couple of days prior to his leaving for Karnak, as had been previously arranged with those two absentee parishioners. Melech was in bed recovering from injuries, after having been attacked a few days earlier on the street.The church door was finally closed by the bridegroom behind his assistant, and turning, lamp in hand, made his way back to his waiting bride.

Both Rufus and Miriam were at the jetty to see Senh off two days after their wedding.

"It will be difficult to send you word since I shall be so far up river," said Senh as he stepped into the riverboat and in answer to Miriam's question.

"Yeshua will protect you my brother. Don't stay too long, you will be missed," called out the bishop as the boat drifted away.

During their walk back to the church, Rufus informed Miriam, that if all went well, Senh would return with a good sum of money. His clients were in a position to buy and subsequently sell a very rare piece of antiquity if it proved to be authentic.

"If that venture of his works out, we will be able to sell the church and pool our resources to buy a larger building to convert into a much more suitable one."

"Will he make that much money?" she asked incredulously.

"Oh yes, those antique statues and artifacts are worth fortunes," assured Rufus with a nod of the head. " Senh's expertise is what the people in that business rely on to accomplish their goals. In any event," he continued. "I believe he is from a very good and wealthy family, and will surely help us in a monetary way whenever he can. He has never mentioned anything, but from his demeanour, education and comments that have slipped out every now and then, I strongly suspect that he is heir to quite a fortune, even though he is so genuinely humble."

* * * * *

Senh had just arrived in his home town after six nights on the river and two on land, where at least he found comfortable beds. Trying to sleep all those nights sitting up on a cushion was just too tiring. Every second night he had left the boat and gone ashore, catching another boat the morning after. Riverboats constantly plied the river and not much time was lost by that mode of travelling. Humble but clean lodgings, providing reasonably good meals, could be found very close to the jetties or sand banks where the boats docked, so it was easy for the long distance traveller who could afford it, to rest his weary bones intermittently.

Senh made his way to his father's house with the great anticipation of seeing his family again; his mother in particular, whom he dearly loved, and who had always spoilt him. He rang a bell which hung outside the wall that surrounded the house and garden.

"Debi! Debi!" called out Senh as he stood at the gate and waited for the old servant to open it for him. The gatekeeper hastened to his call.

From where he stood, he could see the family chapel atop a multi stepped platform, and he bit his lip in frustration at the thought of the family still paying homage to that useless piece of inanimate stone; the god Ammon.

"Master Senh, what a delight to see you," said the old man with a reverential bow, as he opened the gate of that huge house.

"I rejoice to see you again, my worthy old friend. You are looking well for your age," said Senh embracing the old man who had been very good to him when he was little. He often hid him in the garden at his own risk, when his father looked to disciplining him for having been mischievous. Later when the master of the house had calmed down, he would surrender him to his mother.

"Everyone is at home, master. Shall I go and announce you?"

"No, thank you Debi, I shall surprise them." With those words the priest made his way to the main hall of that opulent house. There was no one in the very richly decorated and formal outer chamber, but as he approached the tall double doorway to the sumptuous main hall, the chatter of voices became readily apparent.

"I'm home!" He announced loudly as he stepped into the room.

All chatter stopped. The family looked in his direction, and then the avalanche came. His mother was the first to reach and embrace him with tears of joy in her eyes, as one by one all followed her example. His father, who was the last to embrace him, asked somewhat severely where had he been for such a long time.

"I have had business down in Memphis, and I have come to see Anen with regard to some very pressing and lucrative venture of his with regard to a statue."

"Yes, he was telling me about it, and has been anxiously awaiting your arrival for over three weeks. I do not know if he bought the statue or not. They were rushing him for a decision as they said that someone else was keen to have it."

"I must go see him right away," said the son as his younger brother Merenre pulled him away to introduce him to his new girl friend, who had been attracting much attention among the family.

The girl was talking with his mother and sister Naporaye as thc brothers approached.

"This is my brother Senh," said Merenre addressing his girlfriend.

The girl looked at Senh with a mocking look in her lovely black eyes.

"I am pleased to meet you," she said with a mocking bow and a smug look.

"And I am surprised to see you again Nebitia," replied Senh with cynicism in his voice. He walked away taking his mother by the arm.

"You better keep an eye on that one mother; she is as wily as she is beautiful. She tried to seduce me, and now she will try again with Merenre. She is after our money you may be sure of that," warned the concerned brother.

Lunch was served in the garden, where the family with the exception of Merenre and Nebitia sat under the shade of a large, impressively designed pergola, enjoying their midday meal.

Senh was very vague about his business in Memphis. His father being a very prominent member of the temple of Amon, would be quite angry if he knew that his son was a priest in the service of another god. Later on, he would confide in his mother and explain to her his joy in being a Christian, and ask her to keep it from her father and brother.

That same night after the family had retired to their beds, Senh's mother whose name was Laret, stole into her son's room, and asked him to tell her just what he had been up to all that time in Memphis.

"Was it a woman that kept you there?" she asked with motherly concern.

"If I tell you Mother, you must promise that you will keep it a secret. Father will likely disown me if he ever finds out."

"Oh, dear boy, what are you going to tell me?" she asked with a frightened look on her handsome face.

"It is nothing frightening or horrible. In fact it is something very beautiful and fulfilling.... I am a Christian priest."

Laret's eyes squinted at her son, incomprehensibly.

"What is that religion about? I think I have heard something of it. You are one of its priests?"

"Yes Mother, it is a beautiful religion. I shall tell you all about it during the time that I am here; which will not be long I fear. Just long enough to complete some business that I have with Anen, and then I shall go back to Memphis, as I am needed there."

The mother sat and listened to all that her son told her of Yeshua, and marvelled at the things she heard.

"Tomorrow morning," she said, "after your father leaves with Merenre, you and I and Naporaye will sit in the garden and you can tell us more about this Yeshua who is now your God." Kissing her son, she left him to himself.

All next morning Senh sat in their beautiful garden by the pool. His mother and sister sitting on the stone ledge that surrounded it. He sat on the ground looking at them, the warm morning sun at his back. The priest expounded the life of Yeshua to them in considerable detail, holding both of his two loved ones in a state of total absorption. An occasional "Ah!" was heard, particularly at the mention of Yeshua's resurrection, which completely captivated the intrigued pair.

"If your religion ever comes here, my son," said his mother with a touch of panic in her voice, "your father will lose most of his people."

"Certainly all of the poorer ones," added his sister with concern marked all over her pretty face.

"Eventually it will find its way up here, as it is my good friend Rufus' intention to continue to carry the good news of Yeshua all the way up river to the very desert itself. We have established communities all the way from Alexandria, to Memphis, Akhetaton and Hermopolis," explained Senh with a touch of pride.

"Rufus, a close friend of mine, and my superior, is the bishop of Memphis." His eyes sparkled with enthusiasm as he continued. "He has already converted, almost at the cost of his life, a whole temple of Isis in one day. A total of three hundred people including its three priests, who are now priests of our religion. Actually two only, since one behaved abominably and when he was shown what a disgraceful thing he had done, he jumped off the riverboat and was killed by crocodiles which were prevalent in that part of the river."

A sumptuous lunch under the flower scented pergola followed, as the threesome thought of the repercussions this might have in Senh's life if either his father or brother were to find out.

"I'm off to find Anen," said Senh having finished his lunch. He picked up his shawl that lay beside him, gave both his mother and sister a kiss, and walked away.

"Try not to be late for supper," admonished his mother by way of farewell.

Senh made his way past the chapel, around the house and into the stables, where he chose one of his father's many excellent and pampered horses. His, he was told, had had to be killed, having broken its leg during a hunting accident. This caused him some immediate grief, as he had been quite attached to the beautiful animal. He rode out through the back gate just beside the stables, which was opened for him by the stable master.

A nimble white horse creating a cloud of dust behind it, galloped with power and grace of movement over the desert sands; much to the exhilaration and enjoyment of the rider, no other than our noble Sehn.

The path he followed, led, after a considerable ride, to the archeological site or 'dig' as it was commonly known, of a very ancient temple of Re, the sun god. It was in the process of excavation and lay midway between Karnak and Thebes.

Arriving at the site, Sehn rode over to the largest tent, (for there were several) dismounted, and handed the reigns to one of the workers who stood there admiring his horse.

"You have ridden him hard, Master," said the man with a bow. "May I rub him down?"

"Yes. Certainly, if you know your way around horses," said the priest.

The man smiled, made another shallow bow, and walked the horse away behind some rocks. Sehn went into the tent to find Anen. He was not there. Instead, a man with a bald head and long pointed nose who had been examining an open scroll, turned to him with large, black, enquiring eyes.

"I have come to see Anen, can you tell me where he is?" asked Senh.

"He is at work in the temple. The man outside can take you to him if you like. I have been waiting for him for quite a while. If he knows that there are two of us here, he will return sooner I hope," he raised his arms in desperation.

"The man outside is rubbing down my horse. I shall go and find him myself, I have been here before." So saying, Senh left the man who had not introduced himself, and walked off to the 'dig' to find his client and friend.

As he passed, he saw the labourer lovingly rubbing down the beautiful animal that seemed to be enjoying the pampering.

After having maneuvered around a few corridors and down some ramps, by the light of occasional oil lamps placed in niches in the rock walls, Rufus found himself in the better lit, austere belly of the dig.

"You are happier here than you are in the daylight upstairs," he said loudly, putting his arm around his friend who was so engrossed with his work that he had not noticed him coming into the burial chamber.

"By the very gods, if it isn't you," he laughed as he straightened up and embraced his friend the antiquarian.

"I have been waiting for you for over a month," he continued. "I am being bullied by a group of people to buy a piece of statuary. The god Amon. It was found by a goatherd two months ago in the desert in a most unusual location near here. I have been resisting them until I could have your opinion and hopefully,...your blessing." He stopped, scratched his sparsely haired head, and continued again.

"I met the goatherd. He was a young boy, perhaps twelve years old. Later, I visited the family to ascertain the truth of the finding. But that means very little; they could all have been bribed. Why a statue of moderate size, just slightly larger than life size, should have been abandoned in a desert cave, I cannot think. If it is authentic it is definitely 'old Kingdom.' My backers, a group; your father among them, will offer much. They already have a client lined up who will pay hugely for it."

"Where is it now?"

"Just where they found it. In that same cave. They have been guarding it day and night."

"Who are these people?"

"They are a group from Luxor who exist solely to aid widows, orphans and the crippled etc., some sort of charitable society. Whom I am too busy to investigate."

The archaeologist threw his hands up in exasperation as he said this, scrutinizing for the umpteenth time the decrepit mummy that lay in the sarcophagus in front of him.

Senh promised his friend that he would immediately attend to his request. He proposed they meet on the following morning and ride out to the cave in question, where he could examine the mysterious statue.

"Oh, by the way," said Senh. "There is a man waiting for you in your tent. He did not introduce himself, but he was looking over some parchments and said he had been waiting for you for quite some time."

"He is one of them. The one designated to prod and prod me endlessly. That, is why I make him wait."

"Ha!Ha!Ha," chuckled Senh. "You have not changed one bit. Come on, I want to see what he has to say."

He threw his arm amicably over his old friend's shoulder, and they walked out of the burial chamber and into the welcomed light of day.

The bright morning sun accompanied three riders the following day. They rode through the hot, barren, Egyptian desert to where the cave that housed the enigmatic statue was to be found.

On arrival, the guard questioned them, and receiving assurance in the form of a secret password; whispered in his ear by the representative of the charitable group, allowed them to pass into the cave.

The group representative whose name was Ensaf, quickly made himself busy lighting a series of torches affixed to the walls, providing ample light for the inspection of the statue.

Senh immediately got to work. He examined the object with consummate care.

It had been stood up, so that the underside of the base was not discernible. But this did not bother him at that time. Later if necessary, it could be toppled.

After a considerable time, the antiquarian gave notice that his examination of the piece was over.

"Well ?" asked the archeologist. Ensaf listened attentively.

"I am not sure," said Senh. "The chiselling baffles me. It may very well be authentic, but I must study some notes which I have at the house, to be sure."

They then left the cave and rode back to Karnak where Ensaf parted company with them.

"Come home with me," invited the antiquarian with a wave of the hand." We shall have supper and then we can talk. "I am very suspicious about that statue, but I did not want to say anything in front of him."

The two friends sat out in the garden of Senh's sumptuous house under a crescent moon and delightful starry sky, drinking some excellent beer. They had supped with the family, and Anen had conversed with Senh's father for a good while. Now it was the son's turn to discuss with his friend the topic that they were both so involved in.

"Are you ready to start?" asked Anen.

"I am quite confident my good friend," began Senh, stroking his short beard, "that the statue that you have all set your hearts on is a clever fake."

Anen took a mouthful of his beer and looked enquiringly at his young friend.

"How come?" he asked.

"Old Kingdom tools were mostly copper or later bronze as you well know," said Senh taking a sip of his own beer, and continuing with a faint smile.

"Because the statue was not in a finished state, or polished, all the chisel marks were apparent if observed closely enough. There should have been an inconsistency in the chiselling marks but I could not detect any."

"Why were you looking for inconsistency in the chiselling?" enquired the archaeologist, scratching his chin.

"If copper, or even bronze tools had been used on the limestone, which as you know is what the statue is made of, the chisels, especially toothed chisels, which apparently they were, would have lost a tooth every now and then, due to the softness of the metal. On continuing the work with a new chisel, the carver would not have gone over the same mark to correct it, but would have just continued working, leaving the mark made by four teeth instead of the usual five.

"Quite so," nodded the archaeologist.

"But in this sculpture every chisel stroke was perfect, showing no evidence of broken teeth, so iron or steel chisels must have been used. As you are well aware, these came into use later, in the late Middle Kingdom," concluded Senh, taking a good gulp of his beer.

"Mmmm...The rascals. Now we shall investigate them," assured Anen, raising a finger, and his bushy eyebrow simultaneously. He leaned over, and laid a hand on Senh's shoulder.

"As usual my dear fellow, you have served me well, even though I am disappointed. I shall see that you are adequately compensated. But what do we do with those thieves?"

"Simply tell them what I said," replied Senh with his habitual honesty. "And turn down the offer."

The friends parted for the night after agreeing to meet at the 'dig' next morning, when they would inform Ensaf that they had decided against purchasing the statue which had been declared a fake.

Whilst Senh and Anen were having their supper and later their discussions in the garden, Ensaf, unaware that the archaeologist and the antiquarian were spending the evening together, was having his supper with other members of his group, or, should they be called 'gang'.

"The antiquarian, is reserving his verdict until he meets with Anen and myself tomorrow morning. I am almost certain as I read between the lines, that he is going to uncover the fake," said Ensaf with a knowing look, walking around the room and turning as he reached the window.

"He must not make it to that meeting then," said one of the gang with authority.

"How are we going to stop him?" asked another, his hands in the air, "Are we to kill him?"

"If he was not Hemon's son we probably could," said one of them half jokingly, as he took a mouthful of beer and snickered at his companions around the table.

"All we can do though," he continued, "is way-lay him and hold him captive until we can wear out Anen and have him buy the statue. We were pretty close until this fellow showed up."

"He must not see or suspect any of us," interposed a heavy set, snub nosed, bearded man, who kept blinking his eyes nervously as he spoke.

"This game is getting a bit out of hand," he muttered repentantly.

"Leave it to me," said Ensaf. "I shall take care of it."

Riding the same beautiful horse, Senh galloped off the following morning to meet with Anen and Ensaf. He was busy thinking how much money he had lost in having to advise his friend to walk away from the deal. That money would have helped buy the new larger church in Memphis, and how disappointed Rufus was going to be.

'I shall be on my way very soon now. After I spend another week with the family and have some more fun riding this great beast,' he mused.

Suddenly three horses emerging from behind some rocks cut across his path. The riders, their faces covered and swords in their hands, rushed their steeds at him. He tried to steer his mount into a sharp turn, but one of the men grabbed his reins whilst another jumped on him from his own horse pulling Sehn down with him and tumbling to the sand.

The other two were on him very quickly, and soon he found himself tied up and blind folded. They then lifted him back onto his horse and led him away.

"I wonder why he is taking so long getting here," commented Anen, as he and the prospective seller awaited the arrival of the antiquarian at the 'dig' location.

"He has obviously been delayed," answered the other feigning interest. "Is he normally punctual?"

"Oh yes! He is a man of his word....from an excellent family you know."

The morning wore off and in the early afternoon, Anen becoming very concerned, called the meeting off and went in search of Senh. He promised to meet the man there again the following morning.

Anen's enquiries at Senh's home produced no results as to his whereabouts. The family had seen him leave for the meeting on his white horse and knew nothing further. His mother was very worried about him as was natural, and sent word to her husband immediately. It was agreed that if he did not return home that evening, a general alert would be given to all Hemon's friends and acquaintances to begin a search for his son.

The cellar in which Senh found himself after having his blindfold removed and hands untied by his hooded kidnappers was damp and cold. It had no windows, and the floor was of stone. An old bench long enough to serve as a bed, took up one corner of the narrow cell, and the ceiling was only two hands over a man 's head, as Senh discovered when he tried to stretch. A table with a jug of water, a cup, and a wooden stool, completed the furnishings of the room, with the exception of the inevitable pot with a handle that sat under the bench. The room's light came from one solitary oil lamp which sat in a small niche in the wall. A small jar filled with oil, some spare wicks and two pieces of flint sat beside it. The wooden door as he observed with annoyance, opened to the outside, putting the hinges beyond his reach.

Except for the water, there was nothing else to satisfy his alimentary needs, as he patiently awaited someone to appear with something in the way of food.

In the meantime, seeing there was no means of escape, he spent his time in prayer asking Yeshua to find a way for him to extricate himself from his predicament. If not, he would bear his captivity with patience and resignation in atonement for his sins, and the greater Glory of God

He guessed it must have been four or five hours since he had been incarcerated, when he heard footsteps coming down the wooden stairs. The door opened, and there stood the same three hooded men, with weapons in their hands. They told him to go sit on the bench, one of them keeping a short Roman type sword pointed menacingly at him.

Another of the trio, after having tied Senh to the bench, began to pull out some tools from a leather bag he had with him, and opening the cell door wide, began to drill a number of holes through the upper part of the door, whilst the third member of the group put some food on the table which he had brought for the prisoner.

The alterations to the door took over an hour to accomplish. Senh was then untied, and left to eat the food that had been brought him, and which he attacked with 'gusto.'

'I am going to be here for quite a while,' thought the unhappy prisoner, as he eyed the small door that had been installed for the passage of food, and waste.

'They have not robbed me, beaten me, or ill treated me. So, what do they want with me?' thought Senh. 'I wonder if these people are involved with the statue? Why would anybody want to detain me? I have only been back for three days and have offended no one....No! it cannot be my father; he was most happy to see me. There is no way that he or anyone would know that I am a Christian priest. My mother or sister would never betray me." He sat up on the couch and stared blankly at the door. 'I could have been kidnapped for ransom money, or it could be because of the statue. It simply has to be the statue, there's a lot of money riding on it if they can persuade Anen to buy it. Which of course he never will now.'

It dawned on him, that they did not know his verdict, but they probably suspected that he was going to uncover the fake. He realised, looking at it from their point of view, that if they could keep him away long enough, they might put pressure on the archaeologist into buying it. Using the same reason they had used already; that there was another buyer waiting eagerly and could not be put off any longer.

'It all depends on Anen. if it is the statue, the moment he refuses to buy I shall be set free. These three bandits are just the workers. I suspect that Ensaf and possibly other more powerful people are behind this. It is all one big game and I am the plaything.'

Anen was at his wits end. Senh had disappeared on his way to the meeting, as his mother had attested.

'Could Ensaf have anything to do with it?' he wondered.

'No. The man was a well known merchant in good standing in Luxor, he would not get involved in an abduction. I had better let him know that I am not buying the statue, though I shall not give him the real reason.'

Next morning, as usual, Ensaf visited Anen at the 'digs.'

"Good morning my friend," greeted Ensaf, with apparent enthusiasm.

"And to you," answered the concerned archaeologist.

"Our mutual friend has abandoned us it seems. After hinting that he felt the statue could be authentic, he disappears, and leaves us in the lurch."

"I don't care anymore, one way or the other, my people have changed their minds and the deal is off. You are free to sell it to your other interested party."

"They seemed so keen, what do you think made them change their minds?"

"How can I know that? " answered Anen. "I was hired to buy it, and now they have rescinded. I cannot change things. I am busy enough with my dig. Who knows what we are going to uncover. In the meantime it is costing the group a lot of money to keep things going here. Maybe they are concerned about that too. In any event the deal is off."

Ensaf, attentively listening, grew very worried, thinking of the extreme measures that they had adopted by sequestering Senh.

'His father is a powerful man,' he said to himself, 'and once we release his son, he may begin to investigate. The man has no proof that we abducted him of course, so we should remain unsuspected. However, I must continue to treat him well, and release him with the utmost caution so as to leave no trace behind him.'

"Very well then," said Ensaf, " I shall relay it on to my people," and so saying, they shook hands and parted.

"Perhaps if we release him without presenting another reason for his abduction, it will be too obvious that we did it to obtain the statue. We will be strongly suspect, and an investigation is sure to follow. We must think up another plausible reason for his abduction." These words from one of the group, following an explanation from Ensaf as to how the game had come to a swift end.

"A fine pickle' we have got ourselves into now," lamented the snub nosed man, in whose house they had assembled. He sat, with his head bowed, his hands covering his ears, his elbows on the table and surrounded by the his cronies.

"We shall just increase the stakes," stated the joker of the group in a nonchalant sort of way.

Ensaf got up and walked over to the window, as if the view of his associate's garden was going to give him the solution that he was seeking in his troubled mind.

Turning around with a look of concern, he looked at his three friends.

"It seems to me that if we are to continue with this, the only other thought that comes to mind, is that we demand a ransom, and hold him until we get it."

"We are really going to become a bunch of criminals now," said a lanky, thin faced, member of the party, who had sat there quietly bewailing the mess that they had all got themselves into.

"That's life," declared the joker. We have all made our money by our wits. I for one have few scruples when it comes to making money. If we are successful, we shall have a bundle more of it as Hemon is very well heeled, and he will pay, as long as we do not ask for too much.

"That is the answer," broke in Ensaf, clapping his hands in relief.

"If we keep the amount of the ransom well down, they will think that the abductors are just a bunch of cheap crooks and will be less likely to suspect us, as people of our caliber would have asked for a much higher sum."

"We shall have to keep the horse hidden and sell it as soon as possible," remarked the lanky one.

The joker smiled and making a twisting motion with his hands as he looked at his friend, said.

"Why not just kill it and bury it. After all it has been branded, and it will give us away."

"Oh, my goodness," said the snub-nosed one, such a beautiful creature. It would be a crime to kill it."

"You can ride it all the way to prison. Ha.Ha.Ha." Laughed the joker, his big mouth displaying a very bad set of teeth.

There was silence for a while, as the four heads searched for a more honourable solution to their problem.

"Perhaps," exploded Ensaf of a sudden, turning away from the window, once again.

"Perhaps," he repeated, with a hopeful but cunning look in his eyes. "He can be allowed to escape, whilst he is being moved from one location to another. After all, the son is not aware of any reason for his confinement, though he might suspect that that the statue is the reason. On the other hand, his father's wealth could have given some cheap criminals the idea of abducting him."

"That sound like the best idea, to me," said the master of the house, with a number of rapid blinks, and wringing his hands nervously.

At this point in the conversation, a maid appeared carrying a tray with refreshments for the group with the complements of the lady of the house. A temporary hush fell over the room.

They continued their discussion as they ate and drank, all feeling very guilty. The whole aspect of the meeting was an unfamiliar one. They all regretted the matter which had started as a business game, and had gotten out of hand. After all they were all well known merchants with good reputations, and they and their families could get badly hurt if things turned out badly.

The meeting came to an end a couple of hours later. It was decided that the plan they had decided on, be carried out under Ensaf's direction, since he was in the worst predicament. The prisoner should continue to be treated well. A ransom note for a small amount of money should be sent, with instructions as to where the payment should be left. After that, and before the money was actually collected, which would put the collector at risk, the antiquarian was to be moved out of Ensaf's house and somehow, he should be given without his suspecting it, an opportunity to escape taking the horse with him.

Three days had passed, and Ensaf still hesitated. The money was now at the collection point and the prisoner had as yet not been released. He had no reliable place to move him to without giving himself away. The ransom money, was presently sitting in a cave outside of the city, through which a small stream ran.

Ensaf had played there as a boy with his young friends, and was well acquainted with its layout which afforded a number of ways of entering or exiting. The subterranean stream ran into a river, which was a tributary of a tributary of the Nile. He had given directions, that the money should be in a bag and placed in a certain spot which he could access without exposing himself.

Ensaf decided that he would collect the ransom money himself and enlisted his brother-in-crime, the 'joker' to assist him in his unlawful and risky endeavour.

The plan was to approach the cave by way of the river. The joker, was to sit in the boat tied up on the river bank, and await Ensaf. The latter would enter the cave following the stream and take the money bag from its collection point, without exposing himself; merely by reaching for it.

It was early evening, slightly before dusk. The boat reached its destination. Ensaf jumped out, tied the boat to a large stone on the bank, and asking the joker to have the oars at the ready, proceeded to wade into the stream and work his way up the cave to the chamber where the money was expected to be.

It had been many years since the misguided merchant had played around that cave as a boy, and his size had increased considerably. He found the opening through which the stream ran very restricting, and slipped a number of times getting much wetter than anticipated. As he continued, he had to submerge almost completely in order to pass through the very low ceiling that the cave afforded. The sides of the walls were mossy and slippery, and caused him to fall and be swept back down stream losing all the advantage that he had gained.

After two more tries, and feeling rather sore from a number of bumps and scratches he had received, he finally reached the part of the cave where the money would be. At last, there it was. All he had to do was reach for it. He waited and listened, his eyes carefully scrutinising the cave, in the scanty evening light. Feeling he had to be sure that there was no one there, he sat and waited for a long while. Finally, convinced that there was no one in the immediate vicinity, he gingerly reached for the bag. To his great surprise and frustration, he could not reach it. He strained and strained forcing himself into the opening in the cave wall that he used to squirm through as a boy. Much as he tried, his arm could not reach the bag. Fearing that he would get jammed in and not be able to extricate himself, he sat back down and felt around for a stick or something that would allow him to snag the bag and bring it to him. There was nothing around that would assist him.

It had grown dark now, and it would be more hazardous for him to find his way back down stream to the boat. But what option did he have?

It would have frustrated him even more, if he had known that Hemon disdaining the small sum of money that had been demanded of him, had not bothered to keep vigilance on the money. All he wanted was for his son to be set free as soon as possible.

It was a very wet and half drowned Ensaf, that finally made it to the boat where Joker was waiting, and rowed his exhausted friend home after a futile and frustrating day.

The following day, Ensaf who had the gift of perseverance, visited the cave once again with his dedicated friend the joker, and completed his mission, claiming the moneybag with the aid of two well chosen sticks that he took with him. He ended up just as soaked as he had been on his first attempt, but at least he had succeeded.

Having now the ransom money in his possession, he was in a good position to release his prisoner directly from his house, rather than attempting to move him to a different location and risk more problems. He was now content that Hemon and his son would be quite convinced that a group of cheap criminals were to blame, and he and his repentant group, would not be suspected.

The astute Ensaf, amidst much coughing, and nose blowing, as a result of a bad cold brought on by his recent wet encounters, resolved to change the characteristics of the cellar as soon as the prisoner had been released. The tell-tale doctored door would be removed and burned, and a curtain take its place. The couch would be removed, and the niche that had accommodated the oil lamp, would be filled in and repainted. That way, if he should be suspected, and his house searched, there would be no evidence to incriminate him.

The captive sat peacefully in his cell awaiting another meal, for he was quite hungry and very bored. He had been in confinement for four days. The only relief from his boredom was the time he spent eating. The food had been good. He was almost sure now that he was just being held until the statue was sold, and his mind was at ease. In which case Ensaf was certainly incriminated, he being the agent for the mysterious group. But where was the proof?

Footsteps on the stairs, brought the prisoner out of his reverie, and presently the door opened and the same three armed hooded bandits entered. They proceeded to tie his hands behind his back and blindfold him once more, not a word being spoken. They pulled him up the stairs, and led him through what he supposed to be a corridor followed by rooms inside a house, and finally exiting into the fresh air.

Feeling no heat from the sun Senh realised that it was night. He soon found himself in the stables judging by the familiar odour. He was then helped up onto a horse, which he hoped would be his father's white beauty, and immediately led away; the reins in the bandit's hands.

They must have travelled for about half an hour in what he felt was desert, as the sound of the horses hooves could hardly be heard. Of a sudden, all came to a halt. It was a little while before he felt he was alone. He spoke out, but got no answer. His horse was gently and noiselessly moving around.

Jumping down he began to work on his bonds, which had not been too securely tied. After much wiggling and wriggling, they began to loosen, and soon he was free of the bonds and blindfold. Rejoicing at seeing his horse once again, he began to ride around by the light of a full moon, looking for his way back to Karnak. Morning would be breaking soon, and as he was making no progress, he dismounted. Opting to simply remain where he was, he kept the horse's reins in his hands and concentrated on staying awake.

With the tranquil, vapoury, turquoise sky of morning, came distant sounds as of people singing and talking. He rode up one of the dunes following the direction of the sounds and was rewarded with an animated scenario in the form of a caravan. He hastened to hail it, hands raised in greeting.

"Good morning," he shouted as he surveyed the people who were in high spirits. "Which way to Karnak?"

"Stay with us,....that is our destination," someone replied with gusto, as they continued with their singing to the rhythm of a tambourine and reed flute.

Senh rode up to the caravan master introduced himself, and struck up a conversation, as they all headed for the town.

CHAPTER TEN

THE NEW CHURCH

The riverboat plied its way steadily down river bound for Memphis. Senh sat near the rear of the boat, surrounded mainly by farmers, with their menageries. They were travelling to nearby markets, where they would sell the few animals that they had with them and catch a later boat back home in the evening. These boats, which carried a mixture of human and animal cargo with regularity, offered the people a reliable and safe means of travel. The only obstacle was that of overcrowding, which though never allowed by the vessels' crews to become a real danger, was the source of much discomfort to passengers.

'That was quite a different visit to the one I had envisaged,' thought Senh to himself, as he contemplated the murky brown-green of the water gliding past him.

I wonder if my father is ever going to catch those rascals. They played their cards very cleverly, and since they treated me as well as the circumstances would allow, the whole episode might well be forgotten before long. Which is just as well, the last thing I want is to be called back to provide evidence in a trial which would surely be held, and would drag on as most trials have a habit of doing.

The captain announced the first stop of the journey, and a number of farmers prepared to disembark with their cumbersome animals in tow.

Sehn continued his reverie as the boat once again pulled away from the jetty.

He pondered over the talks he had enjoyed with his mother and sister. Yeshua, was now present in their minds, and though he had not baptised either one, much to his regret, he felt that his sister would be willing indeed the next time he went home. He felt with sadness that his mother would not convert in deference to his father whilst he lived; he being such a high member of that pagan church. His brother, for the moment was beyond reach, and given that he was following in his father's footsteps, might never be open for conversion. He would non-the-less continue to pray for them all.

'It was a disappointing trip in many ways,' he said to himself as the boat finally pulled into the jetty in Memphis.

'But at least, Anen paid me well for helping him out, and my father gave me a good sum too. That should help us with the purchase of the new church. And,...mmm, did I ever enjoy riding that wonderful white horse.'

"You have certainly had an exciting time," remarked Rufus, as Senh finished the story of his stay in Karnak. "I envy you the rides on that horse. I used to have a pretty spirited horse too, many years ago. I called him Pepper, but he did not match up to the one that you have described. Surely, he must be a thoroughbred?

"Yes, all my father's horses are such."

"Come on and don't be so secretive," interposed Miriam with a smile and curiosity in her lovely eyes. "Describe your father's house to us, so that we too can enjoy its grandeur, for I feel sure it must be so."

"Very well! how can I refuse when you ask so prettily?" replied a smiling Senh.

They continued to sit on the porch as he described his father's house, and many other things in Karnak. A town which neither Rufus or his new wife had ever visited.

The evening proved to be a most enjoyable one for the three; chatting until late into the night. It was decided, that the search for the church should begin the following morning. The bishop and Miriam had found a couple of possible locations, but were unconvinced as to their suitability.

Senh, retired to his old room which Miriam had kept ready for him for some time, there having been no certainty as to the date of his return.

It was after midday the following day, that the trio stopped to rest and enjoy a meal at one of the food shops in the centre of town. They had looked at three locations but only from the outside. All three members of the search party favoured one in particular. It was situated in such a manner as would make it more convenient for most of the present congregation to attend and at the same time permit new members from other parts of town, equal access.

After lunch, they revisited their preferred site, and finding the owner, were given a tour of the building.

The area that would be allocated to the actual church was large enough to meet their demands. The remainder of the building was also of a good size and had a back garden and porch, but there were no rooms as such. It did have a well in the garden, and the garden itself was enclosed with a high wall. There was no gate however and that would have to be incorporated.

All in all, it spelt one thing....*money.*

"Unless we can buy the building really cheap we cannot afford it since the additions are extensive, not to mention the renovations, and even the structure itself needs some attention," declared Rufus when they were out of earshot of the owner.

The owner was asked what he wanted for the property, and they were pleasantly surprised at the price that he asked.

"We need time to think this over and decide whether we can afford it, since we will require to do extensive work to convert this place into a church," said the bishop.

"A church! What is a church?" asked the owner.

"It is like a temple," replied Senh, "and it needs to have rooms for the priest and family, so we have to build a few to accommodate our needs."

"Oh, a temple," said the owner scratching his chin. "Well, I tell you what. If it will make things easier for you to give me a good deposit, and pay me so much every month with a little interest until you have paid off the full amount; I can let you have it for the price that I require."

"Sounds good, but we have not yet agreed to your price even so. We shall take a day or two to think about it and get back to you. There are two other places that we are also considering. We have to make up our minds," stated the bishop, who then took his leave followed by his two partners.

The following day the trio visited the next location in order of priority and which they had also surveyed from the outside. It was further from their present church location but still at an acceptable distance. This building was somewhat larger than the one previously inspected. It was in better condition, had a number of rooms at the rear, along with a sizeable gated enclosed garden with a well, and colonnaded porch to boot.

The price asked was a little higher than the previous one, but there would be no further building required.

"Why don't we propose to put down a goodly sum of money. As much as we can afford, and have him take the rest back on a monthly basis as the other man suggested," proposed Senh.

"Yes, we learnt something from that man, didn't we?" remarked Miriam.

"We did indeed," responded the bishop with an approving nod.

The following day the site was purchased on the condition that the old church would be sold. The owner agreed to the terms proposed by the trio. It was estimated that the new church would be paid off in six years.

A month later, the old church was sold for a better price than the bishop and his partners had expected. After settling on a date for possession of the new, and the release of the old church, the 'Church of the Holy Trinity' was about to grow in size and at a new location.

It was the fifty third year of our Lord. Rufus was in his thirty ninth year, when the new 'church of the Holy Trinity,' was finally completed. It had taken a full year of construction and had involved many of the congregation who contributed their work enthusiastically, helping the various trades who kept their prices, well below their norm. All the decoration and artwork was executed by young Bek, who proved to be a talented artist, and who along with Alceres, was now only a few months from ordination. Miriam, also quite a talented painter, assisted Bek in his endeavours, which greatly pleased the bishop.

The congregation now stood at six hundred and sixty three souls, and grew daily.

The new church could hold around twelve hundred at a time. There were usually two services every Sabbath day, so there was for the present, plenty of room to accommodate the faithful. Most of the congregation stood up during the service, only the older and handicapped members sat on the benches at the front of the altar.

Miriam, who had been at work on the new church all year, helping her husband in many ways, was now long overdue for a visit to her aunt. It was arranged, that Rufus would take her back to Hermopolis. That would give the bishop an opportunity to pay a visit to Akhetaton which like Hermopolis, had only received two brief visits from Senh over the past year. The work on the new church having kept the bishop too busy to go himself.

The bishop and his wife left for Hermopolis, leaving Senh in charge as pastor of the new church with Addaya assisting. The two student priests were also there to help in many ways, thus ensuring that the affairs of the church would continue smoothly.

Senh, taking one of the students with him, preached to the general public almost every evening, constantly winning souls for God. Apart from having the students learn from his rhetoric, he had them preach part of the sermon. This allowed them to develop their preaching skills, and the Ahmes' lack of skill would never be repeated. Addaya continued with his ministry to the sick and dying whenever called for, and was generally useful around the parish in many other ways.

Whilst things were proceeding well with God's guidance in Memphis and Alexandria, some unpleasant occurrences had taken place in Akhetaton.

It had come to the attention of Rufus, that the Christians in that city, were being watched very closely by a group of people connected with the embalming trade. Also, by makers and sellers of artifacts such as silver and gold vessels, and statues used in Egyptian burial chambers. A petition had been presented by those trades to the Roman authorities, but since the matter had religious undertones, they refused to interfere. However these people had begun to take the law into their own hands, and a few Christians had been attacked at night and beaten rather badly. There was talk of things getting much worse as the Christian ranks grew.

There was little evidence of any trouble as yet in Hermopolis. Rufus encountered none during the week he spent there with the Miriams, after returning his wife to her aunt. The preaching from his accustomed spot in the evenings, had gone well, and no hostility of any kind had marred his work.

It was however a different matter when he arrived at Manetho's house in Akhetaton directly after Hermopolis, and ran into an unruly mob shouting obscenities and insults at the members of the household. A Roman soldier had been posted outside the house, keeping them in check as far as vandalism was concerned, but their mouths were as powerful as weapons. He found his friends very unhappy when with the permission of the Roman sentry, he gained access to the house, and embraced them.

"What is to be done?" asked Manetho. "We have tried to reason with them, but they are led by a couple of power happy maniacs who keep kindling the fire of apathy towards us."

"Who placed the guard at your door?" asked Rufus.

"The centurion in charge of patrolling this area; he is a fair man and understands that it is not our intent to cause these people trouble. We have also had a tough time keeping our own people from coming to blows with them, as they have to protect their families."

"Yes, that is always a problematic matter to deal with. Our religion is a religion of peace, since Yeshua said, *when they strike you in the face, turn the other cheek*. This is such a difficult thing to do, especially when one's family is attacked," pointed out the bishop, with uncertainty. I am going out to talk to them, perhaps they will listen to me," said Rufus, and stepped outside.

'It is providential that I came at this time,' mused the worried bishop, as he looked at the crowd, and prepared to confront them.

"People of Akhetaton, please hear what I have to say."

The Roman soldier looked a little nervous as Rufus waited for silence.

"People of Akhetaton!" he repeated once more in a louder tone of voice.

The noise began to subside as the crowd showed interest in hearing what the bishop was about to tell them.

"Friends! For so I consider you all. You are displeased with the Christians, because you say they are taking work away from you. Is that not so? Or have I been misinformed?

"Yea, that's right."

"You work at different trades. There are some among you for example, who are artists and make your living from painting pictures on walls. How many of you are here? Show me please." A number of hands were raised. "How many sculptors and carvers are here?" More hands shot up. "How many silversmiths that work in silver and gold?" Yet a few more were visible.

"Who tells you that the Christians are losing you income from your work?

I am here to assure you that your work will continue to grow as the Christian religion grows.

Which of you made fifty or more little silver cups and a jug for the Christians a number of months ago?" Rufus looked enquiring around and waited for a response.

"I did," came the answer from the back of the crowd.

"Were you paid fairly?"

"Yes."

"Why are you here then?" The man did not answer.

"Just as this good man was employed, so also will all you who are artists, and sculptors, and carvers. The Christians need your work the same as anybody else.

Churches have to be decorated and the holy vessels are made of silver and gold. So please keep the peace, and go home all will be well. Christians are peaceful people they will never knowingly hurt you, their faith dictates that. Don't be guided by those who advise you otherwise when they do not know."

"You are robbing us of our work," shouted another man, shaking his fist at Rufus.

"What work do you do?"

"I am an embalmer," he shouted back, as others sang. "That's right! That's right!"

"To you I can only say, that we do not need your work because we believe that we will achieve the Afterlife without having to embalm our people."

As he said this, the bishop noticed that the crowd had dwindled to less than half, and was encouraged. But he knew that those left would probably not be convinced, and prayed for the Holy Spirit's assistance.

"We do not intend to hurt you or rob you of your living, every man is entitled to make a living. But we cannot change what we believe, and the fact that people come to believe like us Christians is something we encourage. It allows everyone to be happy in the Afterlife simply by living a good life, being a good neighbour to all, and loving one another as we have been taught to do.

You see, we worship a God who was killed twenty years ago, and came back to life. Yes, incredible is it not? After all no one ever comes back from the Afterlife. Well, he did. He appeared to men whom I know. They knew him, lived with him, and saw him eat in front of them when he came back from the Afterlife. He also brought other people back to life. Yes!"affirmed Rufus, his gaze on a man in the crowd who had motioned with his hand in disbelief.

"He cured the sick, calmed storms at sea, and walked on water. This is the God that we worship. So you see, we do not need to have ourselves embalmed. He promised us that if we loved him, and one another as he loved us, and kept his precepts, we would live happily forever in the Afterlife. He came down to earth, and was born of a woman, and died for us all, you and me, on a cross, so that all our sins might be forgiven and we would be allowed to enter into a joyous Afterlife.

The silence was ominous.

"If any one of you wishes to gain the Afterlife, I am here for the next few days, come and I shall baptise you and you will save your souls without having to be embalmed. There are so many people who cannot afford to have you embalm them, many are friends of yours,....are they all to perish because they are poor? The Afterlife is for everyone; rich and poor."

Rufus then turned, and went into house, leaving a silent and concerned crowd outside. Slowly after some muttering among themselves, they dispersed to the soldier's relief, and went off to their home

"They are quiet for now," pointed out the bishop to Manetho, 'but when the troublemakers among them begin to goad them again, some will be back; but secretly, which poses more danger for all the congregation. You will have to be vigilant and try to stay on the right side of the law, that way you can solicit the aid of the Romans. See that everyone keeps a level head, and be peaceful. Yeshua will be with you as you pray for his help."

Once again Rufus, baptised a number of people, including some of those who had heard his talk to the tradesmen. Manetho had previously converted some, and these the bishop also baptised. The boy Pah continued to keep his distance from

Rufus, much to the latter's disappointment, as the boy was of the same age as little Letitia. He really wished for him to get over his innate fear of the clergy. Phile's continuous efforts to enlighten him, and have him baptised, had not as yet borne fruit.

The bishop left his little flock once more, after performing the 'Breaking of the Bread' service, and promised to send a permanent priest to look after their spiritual needs within a few months.

On his way back, Rufus did not make a stop at Hermopolis, but sailed directly to Memphis, where he was as usual, happily received by his congregation who were very fond of their enterprising missionary bishop.

* * * * *

The next two years, furthered the growth of the Church in Egypt, which had augmented to a considerable size. The church in Alexandria, had a few Christian parishes, each with its own priest. John Mark was still the head of the Church in Egypt, with two assistant priests in his own large parish, as he continued his work of recording the life, works, and teachings of Yeshua, which were being called Gospels, and would provide strict guidance for all future generations.

Whilst the Church in Alexandria constituted the anchor of the Christian faith in Egypt, Memphis was its missionary arm. Rufus as its bishop had extended his bishopric well up river, and was, with the indirect help of Sehn attempting to evangelise Karnak.

Akhetaton was shepherded by Alceres, and Hermopolis by a recently ordained young priest named Iteti. The new mission at Abydos, was placed in the hands of Bek, who had shown much courage and ability as a missionary and become somewhat of a favourite with the bishop, who saw much of himself in the young priest.

Despite many resolutions, Rufus in the fifty fifth year of our Lord, had still not been able to find the time to visit his daughter Letitia, who was then sixteen years old. He visited Miriam his wife, on as many occasions as he could. She lived with her aunt all the time, which allowed him to travel up and down the river keeping an eye on his various congregations, and encouraging his priests.

He had visited John Mark only three times over the past five years. On each occasion timing his visit to coincide with the *Stella Maris* being in port there; thus kindling his old friendship with Marius and exchanging news of Cyrene and Memphis.

On this latest occasion, Marius and Rufus sat on the deck of the *Stella*, talking of home. The captain informed his friend that the Simon family continued with no apparent change. Marcus, and Julia were also well, and little Letitia was not so little any more much to her father's regret at not having been there as she grew up. Marius had narrated to the bishop how his sister Rachel had made a name for herself by forming a group of women dedicated to the service of God, among them Julia, who assisted her most ably, and together they performed many works of mercy among the people of Apollonia, Cyrene, and all around the countryside. Letitia would often visit the sick or needy with her grandmother or her aunt, and this greatly impressed her father.

"She is growing up to be a beautiful woman," stressed Marius with great joy, as he saw Rufus' face light up with pleasure. "One could hardly expect anything else remembering her mother."

The bishop gave a sad smile, as his mind went back to that 'other life' as it seemed to him. A life full of the exuberance of youth and the joy of living for living's sake. Not that he was in any way unhappy in his present 'new life', but it was a life of great gravity and commitment, accompanied by much responsibility. This 'new life' had perhaps been made endurable and satisfying, not only by the grace of God, but also as a result of that energy and lust for life that had driven him in his youth.

"I feel so guilty about not having been with my little one when she needed a father," he admitted to the captain as they chatted of home.

"You did what the Lord asked of you, and she can understand that now. She bears you no grudge on that account I assure you; though she is dying to see you and get to know you."

Since that last meeting with Marius, Rufus thought more and more of his daughter, and felt very strongly the need to see her again. It was perhaps providential but non the less a great and happy surprise, when a few months later, he received wonderful news from John Mark.

Marius had arrived in Alexandria with his sister Rachel and his daughter Letitia, and the captain would personally accompany them on their way to Memphis by riverboat. Their arrival would follow eight days, after the courier message.

Rufus was beside himself with joy and anticipation.

'Thank you Yeshua, what a wonderful gift. Not only my daughter, but my dear sister also. How can I possibly thank you Lord,' prayed the bishop; his heart overflowing.

The days following the news, dragged by at a torturous pace, anticipating the arrival of his loved ones.

Finally the day so anxiously expected, arrived. The bishop stood at the jetty by himself, scrutinising every boat that came in. At last, in mid afternoon, he spotted Marius' unique head standing above many other heads in the crowded boat.

Soon after, Rufus was embracing his beloved daughter, his sister, and Marius, amidst many tears of joy, emanating from all four as the years of separation dissolved into one ecstatic moment, excluding all other concerns.

"My, you really are the picture of your beautiful mother my love," he said to Letitia, as he dried his eyes with his shawl.

"How I have longed to see you Father,... we shall never be separated again, cried Letitia, taking her father's arm.

His daughter on one arm and his sister on the other, Rufus nodded to Marius to follow with the donkey which had been burdened with the baggage as they made their way to the church.

"I might have known you would not let them come up river alone," said the grateful bishop, addressing his friend the captain as they approached the church, which was a fair walk from the jetty.

On arriving at the church, the door was opened by one of the student priests who after being introduced to the newcomers, took charge of the donkey and baggage. The four of them made straight for the tabernacle to thank Yeshua for their safe arrival, after which they followed Rufus into the residential section of the church.

Senh, who was in the garden, and had not heard them come in, greeted them with great joy in his humble heart. He looked at Rachel with particular admiration.

The cook was still there, and she was soon busy preparing supper for all. They sat in the colonnaded porch and talked about many of the things that had waited so long to be said.

Supper was served and eaten right there in the open air, beside the carefully tended garden, with its pretty well, beautiful flowers, and clay pots. The date palms swayed gently in the evening breeze reaching over the high wall of the garden, as if trying to fan that soothing air onto happy gathering.

It was late that night when they finally dispersed, each to their own room. Letitia and Rachel shared the room that Miriam and Rufus normally occupied.

The bishop awoke early next morning, with the realisation that Miriam had not been mentioned at all in the course of the previous evening, and took advantage of his sister's early presence in the kitchen to acquaint her with his married status.

Rachel was most surprised, but happy that her brother had found someone who loved him and could return his love.

"I am very worried," he said, "about Letitia being told. I have no idea as to how she is going to react to the news."

"It is difficult to say," replied Rachel, "she is sometimes quite unpredictable,...not surprising at her age."

"I have in all honesty to tell her right away. I pray that she understands how terribly lonely it has been for me. I needed an understanding soul to comfort me in my many difficult moments. Yeshua sent her I am sure out of his love for me."

"I have no doubt," agreed Rachel, just as Letitia appeared at the kitchen door.

"What have you no doubt about auntie?" asked Letitia simply as a way of greeting.

Rufus nodded to his sister to leave them, and after embracing his daughter he took her hand, sat her on a stool nearby; he, sitting on another, facing her.

"Now my dear, I have something to tell you, and I do not know how you are going to receive the news." He looked at her with anxiety in his eyes. She looked at him with a touch of apprehension.

"I have been married for the last five years to a wonderful person."

Letitia's eyes filmed over and a gush of tears flowed down her lovely reddened cheeks. Her father cast a saddened and alarmed look at her.

"That is why you never came to see me," she cried running out the door, and into her room.

A greatly concerned Rufus followed his daughter, but was stopped by Rachel, who had been talking with Senh and Marius on the porch, awaiting the outcome of the conversation between father and daughter in the kitchen

"Leave this to me," said the aunt, and immediately joined her niece in the bedroom.

It took some time before Rachel re-emerged, and reported that Letitia was still quite upset and would be staying in her room for a while.

Rufus was devastated by his daughters behaviour. It took Senh and Marius some time before they calmed him down. He had not stopped to consider the effect his marriage would have on his abandoned daughter. He went into the church and spent the rest of the morning in front of the tabernacle asking Yeshua to help her see things in a better light.

It was not until later, past noon, when Rachel went to see if Letitia wanted something to eat, that she found the room empty. A search was immediately started by all four members of the household, but the offended girl was nowhere in the building.

Distressed with grief, the bishop and his two male companions took off in search of his daughter leaving Rachel in the house with one of the student priests in case she returned whilst they were out.

The searchers looked all around the vicinity with great anxiety. A girl all alone, would be easy prey for any rogue who happened to be about. The three men split up, and searched aimlessly whilst praying fervently for help.

It suddenly occurred to Rufus, that perhaps she might be headed back to the jetty, as that was the only road she knew. He made haste down that road. He shuddered as he wondered how she could possibly be contemplating going on the riverboat back to Alexandria all by herself.

Finally, reaching the jetty which was beginning to fill with people waiting for the boat, he spotted her among the crowd and hastened to her side.

"My darling," he began, "I had no idea that I would hurt you so badly by my marriage." Letitia's eyes were quite raw with crying. She gazed at her father with a look of betrayal on her face. Rufus taking a hold of her hand, and with a loving look in his eyes, continued:

"After more than four years without your wonderful mother, I, unlike you, had no one to console or comfort me in my sorrow at losing her. I was so far away from you all, and even though I was happy to be doing God's work, I still missed you all terribly,... especially you. I kept telling myself that I simply had to find the time to go and see you and spend some time with you. You have no idea how badly I wanted to be with you my love. But you know from seeing your grandfather how busy a bishop is, and what a great responsibility he has. He cannot abandon his flock for any more than a month or so, and I would have needed at least two or three months to go to Cyrene and back.

"You chose to abandon me when mother and Marcia died," cried the girl, as tears filled her eyes.

"Come now," he coaxed, putting his arm around her.

"I did not abandon you for any earthly reason my love. I answered God's call to serve him; just as my father, brother and sister did."

They walked away from the jetty together without further word for some time.

Then she asked. "Do you love her very much?"

"Yes, she is a wonderful person."

"How is it that she does not live with you?"

"She knows that I am not like other husbands. I have to travel around the Nile, to either preach in a new town, or visit my young priests and their congregations. Rather than leave her here alone, I left her with her aunt up river in Hermopolis. I visit her whenever I am in the area, and stay there for a few days every two months or so."

"Will I meet her?"

"Yes, of course if you want to. I am sure you will like her, and she will be overjoyed to meet you."

Father and daughter arrived at the church to the relief of everyone there; including a number of parishioners who had joined in the search at Senh's request, and were all discussing as to where to look next.

Rachel came running to her and embraced her lovingly with tears of joy, as she realised that father and daughter were apparently reconciled.

The next few days were happy days for all, as the bishop prepared to sail with the two visitors up river to have them meet Miriam. Senh would be left to hold the fort with one of the student priests. Addaya was now living at home where he was most comfortable in his semi retirement.

"Just when I was getting to know you," said Senh with regret, "your brother steals you away." He and Rachel were enjoying a little time together, walking in the garden.

"My brother says we shall be back within a week or so."

"I shall miss you just the same; I so love your company."

"I enjoy talking to you too," said Rachel as she headed for the kitchen with some flowers that she had picked. "I shall put these in a jar, and place them beside the tabernacle."

Letitia, seeing Senh in the garden, went over to ask him how long the riverboat would take to get to Hermopolis, and would she be able to see the crocodiles that had eaten a priest as she had overheard her father telling her aunt.

"What's this about crocodiles?" Marius' deep voice was heard as he joined Senh and Letitia in the garden.

Small talk ensued for a while between the three, until Rufus announced that he would conduct a full service with the 'Breaking of the Bread' in honour of Marius. That the Lord might give him one more safe passage back to Cyrene.

"I cannot get used to thinking that you are done with your sailing," said Rufus putting his arm over his beloved friend. "What is to become of the dear *Stella Maris*?"

"Marcus may buy her. Jason and Lucius will be sailing her with one new deckhand. If that is the case, he will give the two sailors an opportunity to buy the *Stella* from him over a set period of time. It would be a great thing for them," explained Marius, stressing his words with his hands as he spoke.

"That is typical of my father-in-law, always generous to a fault. I am so glad thatthe Lord has continued to give him good health. He is a very important member of the church in Cyrene, and my father loves him as a brother," said the bishop with great conviction. He then summoned all to church taking the captain along with him; his arm over his friend's shoulder.

"In the name of the Father, and of the Son, and of the Holy Spirit." And with those awesome words, the service was under way; the bishop officiating, Senh assisting, and the others kneeling on their cushions on the stone floor in front of the first bench.

The following day found Rufus taking leave of his beloved old friend Marius. That gallant and selfless man who had so nobly served the needs of the Simon family over the years,(as you my esteemed reader may well recall) and had been for quite some time lovingly ensconced as a member of that exemplary Christian family.

"This could be goodbye for ever my beloved friend," said Rufus as he embraced his mariner friend. "Only the good Lord knows if we shall meet again. I thank him for giving me the great happiness of having known you. May he continue to bless and keep you well for many more years."

"Goodbye dear Rufus. Please Yeshua, we will see each other again. I'll pray for that. I shall tell your father what a great man of faith you have become, and I will always love you as a son." With moistened eyes, the captain stepped into the riverboat bound for Alexandria; then home to Cyrene on his beloved *Stella Maris.*

CHAPTER ELEVEN

THE MEETING

It was the third morning out of Memphis. The riverboat docked at the crowded jetty in Hermopolis. Three passengers; Rufus, Rachel, and Letitia, each harbouring dubious and disquieting thoughts, prepared to leave the loaded vessel.

Miriam had as usual no way of knowing of their arrival. The troubled trio, made their way to aunt Miriam's house, each carrying their scanty luggage. They chatted lightly, exchanging mundane remarks at their surroundings as they contemplated the unattractive, poorer area around the jetty. Soon however, on approaching the street where the two Miriam's lived, they became aware of a better neighbourhood, more to their liking.

Rufus knocked loudly at the door, suspecting the women to be in the garden breakfasting. As he waited, he offered up a final prayer to Yeshua, asking for understanding among the women. His innate sense of humour which had abandoned him of late, and perhaps out of place in this particular instance, made him remark to the good Lord, ever his companion. 'Help Lord, I am out-numbered and at the mercy of these women.'

The door opened...."Rufus my love!" Those words of Miriam's filled with joy, fell over the expectant trio like a powerful cataract. Hot, as it tumbled over the happy bishop, warm, as it covered an uncertain Rachel, and chilling, as Letitia received its heaviest impact.

Yeshua must have heard Rufus' plea. Letitia's heart, when her turn came to embrace and be embraced, melted at the warmth and beauty of her step-mother. The bishop's face was a sight to see, as he rejoiced in the way the Lord had manipulated at his bidding, that uncertain little episode in his humble life.

The good man enjoyed the company of these beautiful women who comprised his augmented family, and by God's grace were becoming acquainted with each other in the most endearing fashion.

'How can I ever thank you Lord for your blessings,' prayed Rufus as he sat in that delightful garden, his eyes admiring each of those extraordinarily handsome women, bent on spoiling him every minute of the day.

'I have work to do,' he said to himself with earnestness after the second day in that earthly paradise. 'There are many out there who do not have this peace and love which Yeshua gives us each day.'

That evening after supper, Rufus, in the company of the women and a few of the faithful, stood at his customary post expounding 'the good news' once more to the people of Hermopolis. The preaching, which captured the interest of a good number, was followed by a visit to the church. It had been consecrated the previous year; named the "Church of the Resurrection," and was under the guidance of young Iteti, as its pastor.

Despite the loud protests of the women, Rufus left after four days, with a promise of dropping in again on the way back from Akhetaton, after seeing Alceres.

Manetho and Phile received him with their usual warmth and attentiveness. The boy Pah, now sixteen years of age, was not living with them at the time. He had found employment up river as a carpenter and carver. Phile was not happy with her foster son being away from home at such a young age, but the boy was of a rebellious nature, and they were unable to convince him to stay.

Alceres received his superior most cordially, and insisted that he stay with him at the church house where they could discuss things at leisure.

"I am a good cook, so you will not go hungry," he said to the bishop as they both took their seats under the porch in the garden just outside the kitchen.

The little church; "Yeshua the Redeemer," had been bought three years earlier with money collected from the parishioners which now numbered around three hundred, and included three or four very wealthy members. In any event, they had arranged to pay for the church over a period of time, which was the way preferred by Rufus, since it would put the least strain on the parishioners and church funds.

"Is Manetho still in charge of collecting and disbursing the money?" asked the bishop in the course of a good supper that the young priest had prepared.

"Yes, the parishioners seem to have confidence in him, and I am always invited to their meetings when any expenditures are involved. There are four members in charge of the church funds. Everyone in the congregation contributes regularly both here and in Hermopolis where Miriam your charming wife, along with three members of the parish, is very involved in the church finances there."

"I see that young Pah, Manetho's foster child, is gone."

"That boy is a problem. He dislikes me and makes no bones about it. He is disrespectful and never comes to church."

"I am not surprised, I feared something like this would happen when he grew up.

It is not his fault, and certainly not Manetho's or Phile's either. You heard the story of Ahmes did you not?"

"Yes, the priest that abused him when he was six years old."

"Exactly." Said the bishop with great regret in his voice, as the persistency of that unhappy event continued to torture his soul.

"I had a presentiment that that very disturbing incident would have repercussions," lamented the bishop. "Unless he comes to you for help, do not interfere with him. Phile is the only one who may be able to keep him in line. I am afraid that his earlier fear of priests, has now developed into hatred, and I fear the consequences. We must pray for him with constancy, he is a disturbed soul and could cause us trouble. Please keep me informed."

The two priests continued to talk over matters related to the functioning of the church as the night wore on. There was a spare room in the church house, and so the bishop decided to stay there. Alceres, quickly retrieved the bishops baggage from Manetho's house.

Rufus was pleased with the growth of the church in Akhetaton. The young pastor was running things very ably, which allowed the bishop to concentrate on the mission that was further up river at Abydos, and which was managed by young Bek. Rufus decided on the spur of the moment to visit him. He had not seen him for almost three months. Though he had not received any call for assistance from the young pastor, he had a feeling that he should go to him. As yet there was no 'stone and mortar,' church in Abydos and he had to look into that possibility if the number of converts warranted it.

Three days and three nights on the river stretched to four days and nights, as he took to Senh's method of travelling, and stopped over one night only on shore, where he enjoyed the comfort of a proper bed and a couple of decent meals. Thus he reached his destination, where he was soon knocking at the door of his subordinate's lodgings.

The landlady, Menevi,whom he knew, opened the door and greeted him with a big smile on her pleasant round face.

"Bek!" she called out, "your bishop is here to see you."

Bek quickly appeared, straightening his tunic as he went, and embraced his superior with great joy.

"It's so good to see you," he chanted.

"You look well," said Rufus looking at Bek, and pointing at Menevi.

"She feeds you well."

"He eats like a horse, but I manage to keep him fed," smiled the landlady with satisfaction in her voice. "I shall get your usual room ready, right away," she added, addressing the bishop and leaving the two men to themselves.

"How many have you in your congregation now?" asked the chief.

"At the last count a week ago, there are sixty four," replied the priest.

"Soon it will be a problem as to where you are going to celebrate the 'Breaking of the Bread' service. How do you manage now?" asked Rufus.

"One member of the faithful has a large house and garden, so we meet there every Sabbath day and perform the service along with any new Baptisms."

"Who collects the money, and looks after it?"

"I follow your instructions," assured Bek, his eyebrows raised, and with a nod of the head. "One member receives the collection after the service, and another three work with him. I preside at all meetings requiring expenditures. That way I keep my eye on things. I believe we have somewhere in the neighbourhood of three hundred denarii and we have paid fully the purchase of a long spouted silver jar, and a hundred silver cups; sixty of which we have already given away.

"That is very good, I am well pleased," said the bishop with a smile and an approving nod.

The following evening, Rufus went to listen to Bek's preaching, and was impressed with the well delivered sermon. However as the priest was finishing, a voice was suddenly heard from among the crowd not far from where the bishop stood. Rufus had pulled his shawl over his head and mingled with the people so as to listen to their remarks whilst his young priest preached.

"You are tricking these people with all your stories," shouted a young man in the crowd, and turning to the people he continued. "All the things he is telling you are lies. He does not believe anything he is telling you. He will convert you with his fancy talk and then take advantage of you any way he can."

Bek, was taken aback by the accusations.

"What reason have you to throw these accusations at me? You do not know me. What I am telling these good people is completely true and for their own good.

I do firmly believe in what I am saying, which is all good. Come up here and look at these good citizens in the eye and tell them where you heard me contradict myself." Bek's eyes searched the crowd as he continued, gently waiving his hand.

"Many of you have friends who have embraced the faith that I am expounding to you. Ask them before you go any further if they feel cheated by my teachings."

Some of the crowd looked at the angry boy with disdain, and told him to go away. Rufus went over to the boy with a view to pacifying him.

"Pah, why are you doing this? Your parents would be very unhappy indeed if they knew how badly you are behaving."

The boy was greatly surprised to see the bishop, and turning, quickly ran off.

The crowd began to disperse, Bek joined his chief, and they made their way to their lodging.

"You handled that very well," said the bishop, "that boy will probably continue to give you trouble. He has a hatred for the clergy. I know who he is. His parents, or rather, his foster parents, were wondering where he was. Now they shall know."

The bishop explained Pah's problem and asked the pastor to stay alert, as he did not know to what extremes the delinquent boy would go.

"He is up in Abydos," said Rufus as he sat with Manetho and Phile, in Akhetaton on his way back.

"We were concerned that he would start giving priests a problem. He says he hates all priests," cried Phile drying her eyes with her sleeve.

"I have told my priest there to be very alert, as the boy is quite disturbed."

The bishop soon left Akhetaton once again. He returned to Hermopolis, to visit the Miriams for a couple of days, and then take his sister and Letitia back to Memphis.

The women were anxious at his having taken such a long time to complete his tour. He explained to them the need to see Bek, and the problem with the boy Pah.

"We have been having some problems here too," said Miriam with regret.

"Oh?" asked the concerned bishop.

"The church was stoned three days ago, and a parishioner badly beaten by some people who accuse us of robbing them of their livelihood."

"The embalmers no doubt, and others that they have influenced," said Rufus, "just like in Akhetaton, a while back. I thought they would have been over that by now....I would like to see the injured parishioner."

"How are you going to stop them?" asked Letitia with concern, looking up at her father's face, as she hung on his arm. Though she so closely resembled her mother, her smile was that of her father. Miriam watched the girl with maternal sympathy, as she imagined how this lovely, warm natured, sensitive child, must have missed her handsome father all those years of her growing up.

"I did once before, but this time it might be much tougher," responded Rufus, with a drop of his eyebrow, and doubt in his eyes.

"Cannot we appeal to the Roman authorities? " asked Rachel addressing the bishop's young wife.

"Yes, but they would only give us protection at the preaching spot, or perhaps post a guard at the church, but they cannot prevent Christians being attacked in the alleyways and fields, or even in their homes," replied Miriam with fear in her lovely black eyes.

"Enough of all this alarming talk, the Lord will protect his people as we all pray. Lunch is ready!" called out aunt Miriam as she emerged from the kitchen followed by her buxom maid carrying a tray of steaming vegetables.

Lunch was eaten amidst much talk of the welfare of the church, and their part in furthering its progress.

"There will come a day God willing," said Rufus, "when we will not have to concern ourselves with these problems and fears; as most people will worship the Blessed Trinity, as Christians. We will carry on praying to our beloved Yeshua for that day to come soon. We must continue to work hard. It is our duty in life to serve the Lord, with all our strength, regardless of the consequences. May God come to our assistance as we need him."

So ended the bishop's little discourse. Lunch being over, he asked his wife to take him to the house of the injured man.

"I am most reluctant to leave you and your aunt all alone here," lamented Rufus as he walked arm in arm with his contented wife.

"We will be alright, the parishioners will keep an eye on us, and aunt Miriam is so well known here, that we can solicit help from our own authorities as well as the Romans. Just now, I am enjoying your company, and that is all I want to think about," she said, smiling at him and drawing closer.

The man they visited was slowly recovering from his wounds, which had been caused with an eye to hurt rather than kill. But he had, apart from a couple of nasty wounds to his right arm which were bandaged up, a very badly swollen face, and a purple tinted broken nose, which had in Miriam's eyes the appearance of a fig.

Consolation and spiritual joy was Rufus' gift to the suffering young man, who as the bishop left the house, thanked him and smiled, for pointing out to him that he had suffered purely for Yeshua's sake. "That!" The bishop had told him, "was a great blessing and would go a long way towards his salvation."

The time to leave his beloved wife arrived once more two days later, when with some apprehensions at leaving, Rufus accompanied by his daughter and sister, walked out of the Miriams' house, and found their way to the jetty.

It was very early in the morning, and as the bishop left, a pair of sinister eyes were observing his departure with great interest.

Senh was beside himself with joy at their safe return.

"You had me really worried this time Rufus. I knew that you would not be sitting with all those lovely ladies gossiping, despite the temptation. You did well to visit young Bek. He is a very clever fellow, but he is still somewhat green, and I too worry about him."

They all sat on the porch, enjoying their morning amidst the beauty and aroma of the garden that Miriam, had, with the help of a couple of dedicated elderly parishioners, designed and tended with such loving care during her stay in Memphis.

It was not long before Rachel began to pay visits to the infirm, as was her custom and a part of her mission of mercy. Addaya, who had great experience also in this ministry, but now beginning to feel his years, accompanied her as many times as he could. He knew all the parishioners and introduced as the 'bishop's sister.' On occasion, Letitia who had inherited a soft heart from both her parents, accompanied her aunt on some of those visits, which were carried out mostly during the day and appealed to her Christian and humanitarian disposition.

Rufus delighted in having his daughter and sister with him, but wondered if they would not be more comfortable and happier at home in Cyrene. His father must be missing them terribly too, and he felt he had to ask them what they planned to do.

One afternoon, the day following the feast of Pentecost, as father and daughter strolled arm in arm around the garden, the bishop with a slight hesitation, addressed her.

"Are you feeling homesick?"

"No Father, not really. I miss grandfather the most, and all the others of course, but I am very happy here with you. I have had them around me all my life and now it is your turn to put up with me," she said with a happy smile and getting up on tip toes, she gave him a kiss and a big hug, which greatly moved her admiring father.

The bishop was not as concerned when it came to his sister's wishes to stay or go back home. He knew that like himself, she had given her life to the Lord, and that she would be content anywhere his providential wish sent her regardless of family, whom she deeply loved. Her mission had come directly in a palpable way from Yeshua himself, and that gave her the joy of life and contentment that her persona exuded; she was an example to everyone who met her.

"The garden behind you, creates an appropriate background for your beauty."

Those words, from Senh, as he talked with Rachel in the church garden.

"You make me blush my friend," she protested, but with a certain feeling of satisfaction, the words fanning her semi dormant female vanity, which she endlessly attempted to control, her admirers being many and constant.

"You are easily flustered. Have you not noticed how much I admire you?"

He would have said 'love', but knew by now how self-defacing she was, and did not know how such a definite advance would be received.

"You must not admire me too much, after all, just like yourself, I am doing the work of Yeshua, whom I love with all my heart and soul," she said as she looked at him with those beautiful, bewildering, but innocent green eyes. They seemed to search his very soul, and spark within him a torrent of emotions which he found hard to control.

"Is there not even a little love left for anyone else?" he, asked with a touch of anxiety.

"Oh yes, I have great love for my 'neighbour' as Yeshua asked of us."

"Don't you like me just a little?"

"Oh yes, I am quite fond of you. You are a good and holy man, and I find your company very pleasant indeed," she answered in a truthful way, as she was taken by his pleasant manner and appearance.

"So, I shall not despair," he continued testily.

"Despair is a sin as you well know. I hope I shall never give you cause for that."

There was certainty in her voice as she spoke those words which he took as encouragement.

'Women like to string men along. I shall let her have her little fling for a while. She is not a child, but a very mature, intelligent, and experienced woman and we are well suited to one another. I wonder why she needs to play this silly game. I feel sure she knows that I am in love with her.' So thought Senh as he looked at her with adoring eyes.

The routine of parish life made for habit forming ways with respect to the day to day activities in and around the Church of the Holy Trinity. The preaching in the evenings continued, and was carried out by the bishop or his assistant. They made excellent progress as usual and the church welcomed new members on a monthly basis. Two 'Breaking of the Bread' services, were performed every Sabbath morning and were always well attended, the faith of the parishioners being strong, and active. The ministering to the sick was well managed by Addaya with Rachel's help.

Young Letitia however was beginning to show signs of home sickness as her fourth month in Egypt came to a close. Though she would not admit it or complain, her father began to seriously consider having Rachel take her back home to Cyrene. After all she was now sixteen and he remembered with pleasure and sadness, her amorous mother whom he met when she was sixteen.

He realised that the church garden was no place for his daughter to spend her time, away from her young friends and admirers.

"I have been thinking that it is getting time for you to take Letitia back to the family," he said to his sister one evening as they walked around the garden reminiscing.

"It seems to me that she is happy here," replied Rachel with a surprised look in her eyes, as she tickled her nose with a flower she had plucked from one of the bushes.

"She has very few friends apart from you and Senh. She needs young people in her life. At this time of life a beautiful girl wants to be seen and admired...Yes, and loved. Think back, you had a string of boys constantly after you. She is a very warmhearted person as was her mother, and like her she needs a boy's companionship at the moment. Later on the Lord will determine what her life will be. But right now, I think it is our responsibility to see that she has that opportunity."

Rachel looked at her brother with sadness in her eyes, and a tear appeared on each one and glistened in the moonlight. She said nothing but pressed close to him and squeezed his arm.

'What am I to tell him?' thought Rachel, with sadness in her heart. 'He is not really thinking of my position. How can he? I have not told him of my love for Senh. That impossible love which I know will never lead to anything but frustration. I have given myself to Yeshua, and no one, not even Senh can change that. I can see that my brother has not noticed our unspoken love for each other. Or,...perhaps he has,' she said to herself with sudden awareness. 'Oh! This is his way of helping me out, by sending me back home. He is killing two birds, actual three, with one stone.' These thoughts raced around her head as she walked arm in arm through the garden with her clever but seemingly ruthless brother.

"You are suddenly very quiet my dear," remarked the wily bishop, realising that his intelligent sister was wrestling with the implications of his suggestion.

"You have given me much to think about. Little wonder you were such a successful business man," she responded so as to make him aware that she saw through his cunning scheme.

A few more weeks passed. Rufus, Senh and Letitia, sat in the porch one evening awaiting the return of Rachel and Addaya. They had gone to minister to a sick parishioner who had undergone a difficult child birth, lost her child, and was severely depressed.

There was an urgent ringing of a newly installed bell which hung outside the church door. Senh made haste to answer it. As he opened, Addaya fell into his arms panting for breath and very upset.

"What is the matter? Where is Rachel?"

"She has been abducted by a Roman soldier on horse back. He rode off towards the desert probably where the fourteenth Legion is encamped. They are in the middle of some exercises there as I have heard," he panted.

Senh left the old priest sitting on the church floor, and ran back to his room, shouting as he went that Rachel had been abducted. He grabbed his money belt, dashed through the church like a madman, and hurrying past the sitting priest rushed out the door. He ran all the way to the stables where they hired horses and very shortly after, rode off into the desert in the direction of the Roman encampment.

"Has a soldier carrying a woman on his horse gone in through here in the last hour?" asked the priest as he pulled up his horse in front of the guard at the camp entrance.

"No! Soldiers are not allowed to bring women into the camp," responded the guard. "He has probably taken her up into the caves over there," he continued, pointing to a cliff face at some distance, punctured by a number of natural openings or caves.

"May I talk to the officer on duty please?"

"Just a moment," said the guard, and turning to his mate who stood quietly beside him, asked him to go fetch the centurion.

Senh dismounted, and waited impatiently. A centurion conversing with the guard, walked out of his tent, and approached him..

"You say a Roman soldier rode off with a woman?"

"Yes. He abducted her in town, after knocking her escort down, and headed in this direction, he was recognised as a member of the fourteenth Legion."

"What is this woman to you?"

Senh was surprised by the question, which naturally had to be answered quickly.

"My sister," he said, as he silently apologized to Yeshua.

The officer gave a command, and a soldier broke away from a group, ran to where there were a number of horses, and untying one of them, brought it with him to the camp entrance.

"This man has had his sister abducted by one of our men," said the centurion with firmness. "I want you to accompany him up to those caves over there and help him look for her before he gets her into trouble. And make sure you get the man's name and number."

"Thank you very much," shouted back Senh as the two horses galloped off in the direction of the caves.

Rachel swooned on feeling herself held roughly around the waist, whilst struggling to keep her balance as the horse she had been forced onto, galloped down the city streets and out into the desert.

The smiling face of the young Roman soldier who had abducted her, mocked her as he squeezed her closer to him. He was a man in his very early twenties, fairly good looking but with hard, cruel, steel-grey eyes.

As they travelled through the desert the light began to fade.

'Soon it will be dark,' she thought, 'they will never find me in time to save me from this lustful, cruel man.' She prayed as they rode, hoping for a miracle from Yeshua.

"I have had my eye on you for a while my pretty little Christian," he snickered with resentment in his gruff voice.

"I've even got a bet on with one of the fellows in my turma, that I would get you first. I can't wait to see his stupid face when I show him that I have won."

Rachel shuddered to think how he would do that.

The galloping horse slowed down as they started to climb a hilly path that led to some caves high up in the mountain. The poor woman was beside herself with fear, there was not a soul in sight. 'Only God can help me now,' she thought.

'I have never known a man,...and what is he going to do with me when he is finished? He cannot take me with him anywhere, and he would be stupid to let me go. He could not trust me to keep the matter a secret,' she mused.

"If you let me go," she said naively, "I shall tell no one. I can swear that to you. It's a terrible thing that you are about to do."

"Ha! Ha! Ha!" laughed the man, and forcing her face towards him, gave her a rough kiss on the lips, his hand reaching for her breast. She pushed his hand away with all her strength.

"Aha! there is some spirit in this meek Christian maid. I thought your religion teaches to turn the other cheek?" he remarked with sarcasm. "You see, I know a few things about your religion. How old are you?" She did not answer.

"You must be thirty if you are a day. But I like older women, there is something about them, especially beauties like you. You must have had a pile of men in bed with you by now I reckon. I saw no husband accompany you, just that old fool. Who is he, your father?"

"He is an old priest," she said with tears in her eyes, "and I have never had a man in bed with me, neither will I ever," she blurted out in desperation amidst a torrent of tears, as she pleaded with Yeshua to preserve her virginity.

"Oh! this is my lucky day," he said giving her another of his lusty, hateful kisses.

After much climbing and passing a number of caves, they came to a stop at the mouth of one of them and rode in. He jumped off the horse and lifting her down, grabbed her by the hand and pulled her along a dark winding tunnel. At its end, a large cavern opened up before them, lit by rays of light from the setting sun, which came through a large opening in the wall.

All of a sudden she found herself free, as another soldier appearing from nowhere it seemed, and with a hideous war cry and drawn sword, accosted her abductor who quickly drew his sword also and pushed her out of the way. They sprang apart, swords clashing as they battled at the entrance to the cavern, cursing and shouting obscenities at each other as they fought.

Rachel slowly approached the two fighters amidst the clanging of steel, with the thought of running past them and back to the horses whilst the two were fiercely engaged and not looking at her. She kept tight to the cave wall, carefully gaining ground as they moved away,... only to come back again. After several attempts to escape, she could at last see her way clear. Surely she could get to the horse before they could free themselves and go after her? She took a deep breath and broke into a run close to the wall.

As she drew abreast of the fighters, one of them backed into the wall immediately in front of her, and as she stopped and turned to go back, she felt a great blow across her buttocks and found herself on the cavern floor with the way to the tunnel blocked once again. The battle continued.

She rose, and retreated across the cavern to the opening. A ledge, wide enough to stand on just outside the cavern, caught her attention and she went over to inspect it. It was an unnerving experience. In the failing light of dusk, she could see, the desert sands interspersed with rocks far below. Stepping back into the cave with a shudder, she remained near the opening.

The battle raged on and on, thrust and parry, forwards and backwards, until at length, an agonising, " Aaaah!" followed by a string of curses, brought the battle to an end. The victor threw his bloodied sword on the cave floor breathing heavily in a semi-exhausted state. Blood ran down one of his arms, and he had a bleeding gash on his face. Struggling to catch his breath, and with evil in his eyes, he leered at his defenceless quarry, and said:

"Now, he knows I have won. And now! For my prize.... Come over here little Christian, you better start praying harder than you have up to now, maybe your God will save you yet. Ha! Ha!...Ha! Ha!"

He slowly approached Rachel as he laughed. She, paralyzed with fear, and seeing no way out of the situation, commended herself to Yeshua, and went through the opening. She stood on the ledge, praying and keeping her eyes on the soldier who kept coming.

"I have you now," he said reaching for her, his foot on the ledge.

As his hand touched hers, the ledge suddenly gave way, sending both of them hurtling down the cliff.

Senh and the soldier riding with him arrived at the mouth of the caves.

"We will need a torch or else in half an hour we will see nothing," said Senh with some trepidation. They dismounted and searched around for some firewood. There was nothing that caught their eye in those arid desert surroundings.

"Let's look in the cave," suggested the soldier. "Our fellows often come here with their women, and they may have left some torches behind."

They looked into the first cave and found nothing, but in the second cave they found two,...one half burnt and the other unused. Nearby there were some pieces of flint which had been used to light them, and they did likewise.

Now armed with the torches, they began to check each cave they passed, pulling their horses in with them as they quickly searched. They looked through four or five without much success other than finding more unused torches. As they approached the next one on their route, they heard the neighing of a horse, and hastened to look inside.

"Hello! anybody here?" shouted the soldier.

There was no answer, but a horse's hooves could be heard stomping on the rocky floor of the cave. Except for the horse, however, the cave was empty, which greatly puzzled the pair.

They again heard the neighing of a horse, but coming from somewhere else. A quick investigation uncovered many things. The neighing came from the cave next to them and entering they found the horse. Venturing yet further into a tunnel which led to the heart of the cave, they heard deep groans, and following the sound they happened upon a badly wounded soldier, bleeding profusely and seemingly on the point of expiring.

"The dirty swine, he cheated me and took the girl. She was mine! he cheated me.

He chea..." those were his last words, as his head slumped down on the cave floor.

Senh's heart sank when he heard what the dying soldier had said.

"Look here!" said his military companion as he bent down. "Here is another bloody sword. These fellows must have had a battle going for your sister. The horse is out here, but where is the victor if there is one?"

As the distraught priest listened to the soldier's remarks, he could see the moon shining ominously in the middle of the opening in the cave wall. He approached it with great apprehension, as if not wanting to find what was inescapable that he should discover. A great presentiment gripped his heart and seemed to be ripping it from his chest. He reached the place where the ledge had been, but by the faint light of the crescent moon, he could discern nothing of the ground below the caves, it was just too dark.

"I don't understand it," said the soldier, "there has been a fight to the death by the look of it, and there is blood here on the cave floor, but no other body."

By the light of the torch they discovered that the trail of blood reached as far as the opening in the cave wall and out onto the edge.

Suddenly it was very clear to Senh who slumped against the cave wall and almost fainted at the thought.

"Are you all right?" asked the soldier. The priest could feel the soldier's slap on his face as he came to his senses again.

"Yes, thank you," he replied as he shook off his stupor.

"They both fell through this opening. I know we will find them below," cried Senh his head reeling.

A half hour later, after much searching along the foot of the cliff by thc light of the moon and the torches, Senh and his sympathetic companion in uniform found the two bodies. The victor of the cave fight lay over a jagged rock, his face smashed, his body covered with blood and seemingly broken in various places. Near him and lying peacefully on her back on the desert sand as if reposing, her beautiful green eyes looking up at the starry night sky, lay Rachel's elegant but now lifeless body.

Senh contemplated the lifeless woman before him with dry eyes, his teeth tightly clenched, his eyes breathing fury, hatred filling his soul as he looked over at the perpetrator lying lifeless on the rock.

" I hope you are in hell!" he shouted at the dead murderer. His hands reaching for the sky in despair. Black fury seething and storming in his soul.

The soldier accompanying him gave Senh his condolences, and told him that the matter would be reported. He handed the body of Rachel with care to his companion of that terrible evening, who, sitting on his horse, received it with great reverence. He sat her in front of him, her beautiful head resting on his shoulder, and supporting her lifeless body in his arms. The distraught Sehn made his way through the dark desert night, back into town and to the church, his heart filled with an indescribable sadness which had slowly taken over the place of the hatred that had overcome him at the scene.

At the sound of the church door bell, all those waiting inside ran through the church and opened the door.

There sat Senh on a horse, his face wet with tears, with their beloved Rachel in his arms waiting for help it seemed, to get her down. Despite her fall, there seemed to be nothing broken and no bruises showing. They thought she was asleep. So, she appeared to them. Then it became clear she was dead, and all were devastated by the terrible tragedy which unfolded before their eyes.

Rufus fell on his knees his hands over his face, trying to stop the flow of tears that drowned his eyes. Letitia wailed pitifully, Addaya was in tears, and Senh was standing there completely stupefied, his world with all his hopes and dreams, having been dashed into a thousand pieces.

When the terrible shock had passed, Rachel's body was placed on cushions at the foot of the altar, and they sat in vigil all night praying for consolation for themselves mostly; for they knew without a shade of doubt that she was with her beloved Yeshua, and did not need their prayers.

The burial, took place the next day following a 'Breaking of the Bread' service.

The body was taken for burial to a field that the bishop had acquired a few years before, and where all the Christians of Memphis were now being buried.

The burial service from the Liturgy was read by Rufus with great difficulty, his voice continuously faltering. When the service was over, an upright wooden cross was hammered into the ground to mark the plot that held her coffin. A stone with her name, date of birth, and death carved on it, would be placed later, on the ground in front of the cross. Prayers were then recited once more, and all withdrew. Except Senh. He stood there, his eyes fixed on the grave, his heart telling her of his love, and wondering whether she could hear him.

'If she is asleep until judgement day," he thought, 'she will not hear me. If her soul has gone straight to the Lord, which I feel is the case, she will probably not hear me either. We do not know if the souls of the departed are allowed to see or hear those left on earth.'

'Lord what a mystery death is. We can only trust in you,' he muttered to himself as he finally left the grave sadly shaking his head and made his weary way back to the church.

It took Senh a whole week to come out of his depression. He took to his bed and would not leave it. He spent his days sulking and staring into space.

"I loved her dearly," he told Rufus, as he recovered from the terrible blow, "all my future happiness rested with her."

"Did she say she loved you?" asked her brother.

"No. Not in as many words, but I know she did, but for some reason she could not say it, and I was unhappy about that. I felt, in time she would have told me."

"Senh, you know I love you like a brother, and I would not hurt you for the world," said Rufus, with anguish in his voice, his eyes showing great sympathy for his ailing friend. "But I must tell you something that she obviously did not tell you. Yes! I believe she was in love with you,...but it was an impossible love."

"Why would that have been?" asked Senh with a surprised look.

"When she was quite young, in her very early twenties, she had a fabulous experience. Such as few people ever have the privilege of having."

Senh looked at his friend with great interest, as the latter continued.

"She was kneeling in front of the tabernacle one day, and a voice coming from within it, asked her to dedicate her life to Him. Yeshua actually spoke to her. She accepted his request, and consecrated her life to Him. So you can see now why she could not tell you she loved you, though in fact she did. You can imagine the stress that she lived under these last few months. There is no doubt in my my mind that she was a great woman, and an exemplary Christian. I absolutely know, that she is with her beloved Yeshua in heaven, and we should all be happy and proud to have been a part of her saintly life."

The bishop, head bowed, remembering his dear sister, was about to walk away, when Senh, falling on his knees, asked with sudden urgency for Rufus to hear his confession. The bishop stopped, and turning to face his friend made the sign of the cross, and waited for him to start.

Senh asked him to forgive him on Yeshua's behalf, the sin of hatred of which he had been guilty that dreadful night at the scene of the crime, in wishing with all his heart, that Rachel's assailant had gone to hell.

"We are such weak creatures," said the bishop, who, absolving his priest from his serious sin with the sign of the cross, added:

"Here we are, denouncing hate and promoting love, and circumstances no doubt of the devil's making, surprise, and overcome us with their malevolence. We sin inadvertently on the spur of the moment; our well intended spirituality overshadowed by our weak human nature. It is a good thing that we are given the gift of repentance, for it is a great gift indeed. We correct ourselves by the grace of God, and try in our small insignificant way to offer God an inadequate token of atonement in sympathy with that great sacrifice of Christ, by which those same sins were actually and previously atoned for. How else are we to aspire to purity of spirit?"

"Add one extra quarter of an hour of prayer to your day for the next two weeks as atonement, " directed Rufus, and helping his friend back on his feet, he warmly embraced him.

CHAPTER TWELVE

INVASION

Two weeks after Rachel's untimely death, Rufus, seeing that Senh had now fully recovered from his depression, prepared to go up river with Letitia, to give the sad news to the Miriams.

"You are in charge once more my dear friend," said the bishop slinging his travelling bag over his shoulder. Carrying Letitia's bag in his hand, he walked out the church door with her, leaving a trustworthy Senh to hold the fort with all its implications.

"The Lord go with you, and give my love to the ladies," shouted the acting bishop, waving farewell to his mentor and daughter.

The scene on arrival at the Miriams, was an extremely sad one. Those women's lives had been so touched with the beauty both of body and soul of the bishop's sister, that the one consoling factor they all held to, was her saintliness. That, along with her apparent martyrdom, had won her they firmly believed, Divine acceptance into the kingdom of heaven.

"My goodness, what a terrible fate," lamented the bishop's wife.

"She must have been so terribly frightened, poor gentle soul," sighed aunt Miriam with tears returning to her eyes.

Rufus said nothing of Senh's subsequent depression. In fact he glazed over the part that his assistant had played in the tragic drama. But Letitia with the carelessness of youth expounded the story in great detail, and before long there was an interested and animated discussion on the whole tragic saga.

"He must have been very much in love with her," proposed Letitia with romantic tears gleaming in her eyes, bringing sad but beautiful memories to her father, as his mind took him back to a scene at the gate of her mother's house in Apollonia, so many years ago.

Young Iteti, the pastor in charge of the Hermopolis church, had been given leave to visit his family down river, for a month, as he had not seen them for over two years. In his absence, Alceres would look after Hermopolis following the bishop's return to Memphis after his visit. Rufus prepared to do the preaching at his usual place in the priest's absence, for the duration of his stay.

He stood on the platform by the column and waited to be noticed by people who would perhaps have heard him before. He waited, lost in prayer; his hands clasped in front of him; his head held high; a far away look in his eyes, focusing on his beloved Yeshua, and his saintly sister. The bishop cut a grand statuesque figure; almost monumental, on that elevated podium. He would never consider himself thus. But Rufus, Bishop of Memphis, had grown to become a personality of note.His figure, now a little fuller than that which had constituted the more youthful Rufus, gave him by virtue of his erectness of posture and persisting athletic demeanor, an imposing and distinguished presence, which gained him much respect and attention from all who crossed his path.

Presently people began to gather around him.

"Greetings preacher!" called out one well meaning citizen, who had, it seemed to the bishop, a familiar face.

"God's blessings on you my good man," retorted the preacher with a smile. "I feel sure you have listened to me a number of times."

"Yes. That is so," responded the man, half mumbling, and with a nod of the head.

"Have my words not yet convinced you to accept the Lord Yeshua as the Son of God?"

Before the man could answer, other people approached and a crowd began to gather. The man, being of a rather reserved disposition, shied away from the question. The bishop made no further comment in that regard, but prayed that the man might find the courage to come to him or Iteti at some future time.

"My friends from Hermopolis, I rejoice to be here among you once more, and to relate to you the good news of the wonderful Afterlife which awaits everyone. Whether rich or poor, master or slave...."

The introduction was like a magnet to those Egyptians whose beliefs in the Afterlife, as my reader well knows, involved a disturbing selectivity and by corollary,... exclusivity, in its attainment.

As the sermon continued, the preacher noticed a small group of people standing aloof from his captivated crowd, and who were observing him with what appeared to the alert bishop, to be hatred in their eyes.. They talked among themselves, and threw the occasional critical glance in his direction. No attempt was made by them however, to interfere with the proceedings.

The sermon came to an end, and a number of people met the bishop at the bottom of the steps, expressing their desire to be baptised. Since there was now a small church in that city, and not too distant from where they were, the prospective Christians were directed to follow him there.

An old man opened the church door for Rufus and his eager party. Soon, all the catechumens (for so they would later be called,) were standing around the water font as the satisfied bishop performed the Sacrament single handed on each one.

"Now, by the grace of God you are members of the Church of Christ. You will now be known as Christians, and this church will be your place of worship from now on." With those encouraging words the man of God blest his new converts and after embracing each one,... left. He walked contentedly back to the house where the women were eagerly awaiting his return.

It was late in the evening when Rufus walked in the door of aunt Miriam's house. The Baptisms, had taken a while to perform, and he felt tired. After conversing for a while, they retired to their beds. Aunt Miriam shared her bedroom. which now had another bed, with Letitia. The married couple occupied their usual room. The maid, the last to retire, found her way sleepily to her little room at the back of the garden by the well.

It was a dark, cloudy night. The stars and moon were obliterated from view. The house was in repose; its occupants slumbering peacefully,... with one exception. Rufus who had recurring thoughts of the seemingly malicious group at his sermon, was out of synchronization with the rest of the family. He kept vigil in a somewhat semiconscious state. A wooden cudgel at hand under his bed.

A human howl followed by a colossal splash of water, broke the pristine silence of the Egyptian night. The household was rudely awakened. Rufus, club in one hand, his tunic in the other, emerged from his room and crossed the garden towards the well from which the sounds emanated. Looking up at the wall, he perceived, silhouetted against the greyness of the clouds, two figures sitting on it ready to jump into the garden. They remained static, as from the well immediately below them, came sounds of splashing and screams for help.

Hearing the distress of their companion in mischief, they crawled along the wall intending to jump down into the garden from a safer location. Our hero followed their movements as a cat watches a mouse on whom it intends to pounce. All of a sudden there was light, if only from one solitary oil lamp, as the buxom maid, having heard the screams of the man in the well, and quick to suspect some trouble amiss, quickly lit a lamp and ventured out into the garden, a big stick in her hand.

"One is in the well," she screamed. "Leave him there."

The other two were now in the garden wielding large knives. Rufus who had met them as they jumped down, parried their thrusts with his cudgel and a wooden lid he had snatched from a nearby water barrel, and which he used as a shield as he attempted to hold them in the corner of the garden by the toilet. The maid put down her lamp on the well's sill and came running to the bishop's aid. The other women of the house looked for things which they could use as weapons in case they had to defend themselves.

The two invaders fought fiercely with Rufus who using his feet as well as the cudgel, was, with difficulty, keeping the men at bay. His arm with which he had to block a number of blows was wrapped in his tunic, as he valiantly battled in his scanty undergarment. Suddenly, the maid threw her stick at one of the assailants. It struck him in the face, allowing Rufus one quick opening of which he quickly took advantage. He gave the one, who ducked as the maid's weapon flew past him, a great clout in the head with his club, sending him reeling against the back wall, unconscious. The bishop then delivered his crowning blow on the head of the one the maid's stick had struck, with similar results.

Rufus, quite exhausted after his ordeal, called to the women to find some ropes or tear up a bed sheet to provide bonds for tying up the unconscious men. He then approached the well and by the light of the oil lamp, saw a man struggling to stay alive a number of arm lengths below. The garden was now aglow with lights that the women had lit. The tired bishop with the help of Ita the buxom maid, busied themselves rescuing the bandit from the well. Letitia became aware to her horror of the marks across her father's naked back. Miriam explained the story which she had eventually cajoled Rufus into telling her, as they continued to bind the unconscious invaders' hands and feet with the strips of linen, urgently torn from their bed sheets.

By letting the well bucket down and allowing the half drowned man to clutch onto it and the rope, they managed with some difficulty to pull him out, and laying the exhausted swimmer on his belly, they tied him up.

A knocking at the front door, announced the presence of the law. The Roman law in that case. A passing night patrol having heard the commotion, were investigating the noisy confrontation. The maid showed them in, and soon the whole matter was properly aired. The soldiers took the prisoners out, including an unconscious one who had to be carried between two of them.

The local authorities then arrived, having been alerted by a neighbour. It was soon established, that the trio were embalmers and that they had planned to murder the bishop and the whole household with him.

When all was over and the prisoners gone, Rufus called his wife, and asked her to join him in the bedroom. She went to him with an enquiring look on her face.

Once inside, Rufus removed the tunic which had been wrapped around his left arm, went over to the water basin stand, and exposed his arm. She, seeing the nasty, bleeding gashes, quickly stuck her head out the bedroom door and screamed for Ita to get the physician immediately. The tunic was soaked in blood. The bishop felt a little wobbly and sat on his bed. Miriam, in very flustered condition used what was left of the bed sheet to bandage his arm as tightly as she could.

On hearing Miriam call out to Ita, Letitia and the aunt, hastened into the room. The daughter became quite distraught at seeing her father's bandaged arm and his blood soaked tunic, and sitting on the bed beside him wept hysterically on his shoulder.

"I shall, if I can stay awake, tell you an amusing little story, as we wait for the physician," said Rufus in an effort to distract his daughter and wife.

The story of the young Rufus battling the bandit, on the pale horse, (as you my faithful reader will recall,) was being colourfully narrated by the bishop when the physician, who lived just a few houses away, made his appearance. The latter, dismissing the other women, allowed the wife to stay in the room with the patient whilst he performed the required painful salting and suturing of the wounds. He remarked to the couple's relief, that the wounds, though many, were not deep, and had as a result not caused the tendons any appreciable damage.

Later in the day, when all the horrors of the night took on a more tolerant perspective, the bishop's unfinished story was brought to a stirring conclusion. It recounted, how the young hero, having surrendered his captive to the Roman authorities, yearned sympathy for his wounded arm from his women folks who were too far away to oblige.

The pending trials of the three embalmers kept Rufus waiting longer than expected in Hermopolis. He was also growing increasingly concerned with the man who had not regained consciousness. He and the family began daily prayers for the man's life. A daily visit to the prison became a ritual for the bishop, where he met the man's wife and tried to comfort her as best he could.

"What am I to do now? lamented the poor woman, "I have two little ones to feed, and this crazy man has got himself into all this trouble because of hatred. I told him not to follow those two friends of his. They are a couple of hot heads and have no little ones depending on them. The Romans will either crucify him, or send him to the mines until he dies of exhaustion." Her sympathetic listener tried to pacify her sorrow.

'I should not have hit him so hard,' bewailed the troubled bishop to himself. I should never have used force, what was I thinking? No! I wasn't thinking, that's the thing. There is no doubt in my mind that one of the most difficult things that our Lord wants of us is this *turning of the other cheek.'* The kind hearted bishop was most distressed at the possibility that the injured man should die as a result of a blow from his hand.

'I profess to be a man of God, and yet. Oh my, Oh my, I shall be guilty of a terrible sin, such as could lose me my soul. It was no accident, I hit him as hard as I could. Sure it was self defence on behalf of my family. Does a man not have a right to do that? Or an obligation to defenceless souls, such as children, invalids, the sick or abused? We fight devils that we cannot see, why not also those that we can see, and who do so much evil. Would I not have fought to save my sister from that devil?'

This mental torture continued to accost Rufus' head day and night, whenever his mind was supposedly at rest. Miriam listened to him in the night as he slept uneasily wrestling with his demons.

'The only respite is the knowledge that God will forgive me, as long as I am sorry. Sorry? Sorrow is driving me out of my mind. He has already forgiven me. But how do I forgive myself for letting Him down so badly? How can I say that I will never do it again? If the man dies, I must immediately seek Alceres and have him forgive me on Yeshua's behalf, as I am not worthy to 'Break Bread' or receive, until I have been absolved from my terrible sin.'

Despite all of the bishop's prayers,...the prisoner died.

Rufus was overwhelmed with grief. He was stricken with a fever shortly after word of the man's death was received, and now in his delirium he longed with a great longing to see Alceres. Miriam volunteered to go and find the needed priest in Akhetaton, but her aunt talked to some men of the parish, and two of them willingly consented to go and bring him back.

Two days later, Alceres arrived, greatly distressed to learn of the bishop's condition and of all that had occurred in Hermopolis.

"I am here my dear bishop," said Alceres with great love and reverence. Rufus, hearing his voice, rallied enough to understand that salvation was near in the form of his beloved young priest.

"I am aware of your sin, and am here to absolve you of it. I know that you are more than repentant, but I must hear it from your lips," said Alceres with regret.

"Oh! How sorry I am. So, so, sorry," bewailed the bishop, as his subordinate uttered,...I absolve you of your sins, in the name of the Father, the Son, and the Holy Spirit.

"The Lord be praised," rejoiced Rufus as the grey cloud that had been suffocating him dispersed shortly after.

The bishop's recovery was remarkable; within two days he was back to himself; having been fed royally and spoilt by the women of the household who had such great love for him.

A week later, the trial of the house invaders was held. It came as no surprise to anyone, that the two embalmers were sentenced to twenty years in the copper mines; which gave the bishop no satisfaction whatsoever. He would rather they had been converted, and their souls saved. He did however meet with the widow of the one who died, and promised sustenance for herself and her children at the hands of the diocese. He hoped that in time, she might, by the example of the congregation, convert to Christianity, and thus be saved along with her children.

Having had some time with Alceres after his recovery, Rufus would not have to visit Akhetaton on that trip. All that was left for him to do, was for him and Letitia to take their leave of the Miriams and return to Memphis. Once in Memphis, they would wait there until they got word from Annianus of the *Stella Maris'* arrival in Alexandria.

"I do not know whether we shall see each other again," said a tearful Miriam to Letitia, hugging her for the last time before they parted. "I have grown to love you as a daughter, and my prayers and best wishes will accompany you always. Goodbye my beautiful little one, may the Lord give you an adoring and loving husband. Speak kindly of me to your lovely family, whom though I have never met, I feel I know."

"Goodbye my love, do not be afraid, there will be no further trouble now from anyone," assured Rufus. "They have all learnt the price they must pay for attacking Christians. I have already asked the congregation to protect you, and not to provoke any one outside our faith. Iteti who will be returning very soon now, will look after you as usual. I shall miss you terribly." Having said these words to his wife, the bishop embraced her, kissed her, and made his way to the door.

Miriam came to him again, and kissing him warmly, wished him and Letitia a safe and pleasant trip home.

With his arm recovering nicely, the grey clouds of his recent mental anguish temporarily dispersed. Rufus now concentrated on his upcoming journey to Cyrene after so many years. He would carry with him the terrible news of the loss of Rachel, whom he had constantly in mind, and which was going to cause such devastation at home.

The bishop climbed out of the riverboat as it drew up to the jetty in Memphis. He extended his hand to Letitia who took it and followed him out.

'Senh will be surprised at our having taken so long, but he should be used to it by now, I always seem to take longer than planned on these uncertain trips,' he said to himself.

The church door bell was rung with enthusiasm, with the hope that Senh would interpret the ring as being theirs.

"Aha!" he said, as he opened the door. "I knew it was you ringing. Come in, come in." He embraced Letitia first, and then the bishop.

"It has been very quiet around here, I hope you have something interesting to tell me," smiled the assistant bishop.

"We are going to surprise him aren't we my dear?" said Rufus winking at his daughter.

"But we are not going to say one word until we have been given a nice breakfast," interjected Letitia taking hold of Senh's arm, and dragging him towards the kitchen.

"How can you put up with this little bully?" asked the assistant, enjoying every moment of Letitia's play.

"She is unbearable. That is why I am taking her back to her grandfather. Let him deal with her," replied the doting father, stopping to kneel in front of the tabernacle.

Twelve days later, having been alerted by Annianus of the pending arrival of the *Stella Maris*,... and briefing Senh yet again. Rufus and Letitia parted company with the assistant bishop. He, with a big hug and moist eyes, wished the young beauty, love, happiness, and the Lord's protection throughout her life.

CHAPTER THIRTEEN

HOME AGAIN

Loud animated sounds, in the form of exuberant male voices emanated from a small, rickety old building which sat at the town end of the wharf in Apollonia Harbour. On entering, a visitor would have been surprised to see a small representation of Rome's mercantile mariners chatting and laughing, as they ate their meal and enjoyed themselves in the company of their mates. If the visitor felt a further tinge of curiosity, he, or she, would proceed past this loud boisterous company, travel down a narrow corridor, and opening a solid oak door, encounter another group of mariners of a more sober bent. These were happily enjoying their meal with their brother captains, whilst relating to one another the latest news of the sea.

In this august group of mercantile marine elite, at the head of the large well attended table, sat one of our heroes,...Captain Marius. He looked every inch a sailor, and possessed a certain bearing which won him the respect of his fellow members. As founder and head of the Apollonia Seamen's Club, and with his habitual congenial disposition, he had endeared himself to all those tough weather-beaten men with whom he had shared a lifetime of struggle with the sea.

This new mode of existence provided him not only with an income, but kept him in touch with what would always be, 'his breath of life,'..the sea. His good wife Sarah led a contented new life, as she now spent all her time around her beloved Hannah and her quite grown up children.

The heavy oak door to the room where Marius sat, suddenly opened and a sailor peering in, announced to the room, the berthing of the captain's former ship the *Stella Maris.*

"Just pulled in from Alexandria," added the man.

Marius quickly got up, and made for the door, hoping that Rufus had finally managed to find the time to visit the family. As he drew near the ship, he saw the passengers disembarking, and among them, to his utter delight, he recognised Rufus, with young Letitia beside him. She looked the very figure of her mother, her long golden hair blowing in the wind, her palla resting on her shoulders.

He hurried to the bottom of the gang plank, disappointed at not seeing Rachel, whom he expected would be in their company.

A few moments later, a surprised Rufus was embracing his old friend Marius, as Letitia awaited her turn to do likewise.

"At last, welcome home!" Greeted Marius as he parted from Letitia's embrace.

"Where is Rachel?" he asked, looking back up the gang plank.

"We bring horrible news with us," lamented Rufus, as his old friend's face dropped.

"She is dead," he sighed, taking hold of both of Marius' arms and squeezing them as if to drive his point home. Big tears welled up in the old sailor's eyes and rolled down his weather beaten cheeks; dozens of beautiful memories of Rachel whirling around his head, all gnawing at his heart. He embraced Rufus once again and remained frozen for a little while, trying to recover his composure. At length, he recovered, and nodding his readiness, all three made for Marcus' house. Marius carried Letitia's bag, his head still reeling from the shock.

Needless to say, (and as you my dear reader can well imagine) the scene just witnessed with our three heroes at the wharf, repeated itself pitifully at each meeting with all members of the Simon and Marcus families. This was also the case with all the faithful of the Christian community in Cyrene and Apollonia, whose members Rachel had ministered to, and comforted for so many years. A trail of sorrow was left as the news travelled. It would be a trail covered with the jagged stones of tragedy, and would take a long time to smoothen by the normal usage of life.

A day of celebration as opposed to the usual mourning, was proclaimed in Rachel's honour, by the Cyrenean Christian community, for the triumph of the soul of their 'saint' and 'martyr', as they all declared her.

Services were held in both churches; upper and lower Cyrene. Each brother officiated in their own parish. Alexander at the "Church of the Holy Spirit" in upper Cyrene, and Rufus at the "Christian Church of Yeshua of Nazareth," in lower Cyrene.

Simon, who had fallen ill at the news of his daughter's death, sat behind the altar; his lips moving almost imperceptibly, trying to come to grips with his terrible loss. He conversed silently and intimately with his beloved Yeshua, asking,...'why Lord?'

Rufus recovered slowly from his resentment at being the bearer of such bad news, and began to feel more like himself as the days passed. He often thought of his beloved Miriam's sequestered existence with only her aunt to fill her life, when she could be enjoying the company of those two wonderful families. Especially, as Julia did not fault him for his marriage to her. His mother-in-law had told him that she could remember with great satisfaction, the ardent love that he had had for her daughter, and she was genuinely happy that he had found someone who could return the love that he had always been so capable of giving.

Alexander shared with his brother his concern for Simon's health. It had not been good since their mother died. He was given to periods of loss of energy, followed by an annoying tingling all over his body, at which time he was almost unable to move. The physician who tended to him was very suspicious that his heart might be not be functioning as it should, but he was not entirely sure. Since Simon was forbidden from doing anything strenuous, the missionary journeys were now left to Alexander and Saul his assistant.

"If God forbid, Father should suddenly die, I shall have to find you, and have you consecrate me as his successor," said Alexander with much concern.

"No, no," we shall get him to do it you right now, and consecrate you as assistant bishop. But you will nevertheless be a bishop. If and when Father dies, you will be the next bishop of Cyrene, as you well deserve. We cannot risk anyone coming from outside with no knowledge of this bishopric's requirements. Besides, where is such a man going to come from, and who better than you?" queried the Bishop of Memphis.

"If Father agrees, we shall do that whilst you are here, it will give us all great joy to have you partake in the service," asserted Alexander.

The brothers spent much time together catching up with the many years that they had missed together. They often sat in the garden in Alexander's house overlooking the sea, and enjoying the cool, calm, summer evenings. The mistress of the house fussed around the pair with a joyful heart at seeing the brothers together.

Hannah could not hear enough of her brother-in-law's adventures.

"It seems that the Lord, planned a truly adventurous life for you, to which you are well suited," she said one night, throwing a loving arm over Rufus' shoulder.

"Alexander!" she said, looking at her husband, as they all sat in her terrace enjoying the evening breeze. "You were given a more sedate life, with your gifts of painting, sculpting, and decorating. But in the end, you are both serving Yeshua with all your heart, making use of all the gifts that the Lord has given you both; truly a blessed, and a wonderful thing. Your father is so proud of his boys, as indeed we all are," assured the still beautiful Hannah with a lovely smile.

The consecration of Alexander as the assistant bishop of Cyrene was duly performed two weeks later. Rufus intended to leave shortly after, and would inform John Mark of the auspicious event, on his arrival in Alexandria.

Rufus had now been in Cyrene for over a month, and was beginning to feel a little uneasy at staying any longer much as he would like to. He had met all his nephews, and nieces, and had spent most of his time with Letitia who followed him everywhere. Marcus and Julia had been wonderful to him. Zaphira, Tecuno and Silia, now virtually part of the family, (all having been released from their bondage) were enthralled with his adventures and were most unhappy at the prospect of not being able to continue to serve him.

Damian brought him up to date on his own continued dealings with the firm of Erasmus, and informed him that Vibia was the proud mother of a seven year old boy. She and Tertius, had been enquiring after him. Lavinia and Linus were well, and were thinking of visiting Cyrene the coming year.

His life now revitalized, Rufus was ready to return to his duties in Memphis.

He spent the last two days exclusively with Letitia who was despondent about losing her father again.

Rufus boarded the *Stella Maris* once more; Lucius at the helm, Marius and every member of his family waving from the wharf. He, the Bishop of Memphis, suspecting that this would be his last visit to Cyrene, blessed them with the 'sign of the cross,' as the ship pulled away from the wharf.

Simon, feeling he would never see his son again on this earth, prayed silently, 'Lord, why does life have to be so tough.'

* * * * *

On arrival in Alexandria, and as the gang plank was being raised onto the *Stella Maris,* Rufus took leave of his friend Lucius. He thought of Letitia's promise of visiting him again soon, and hoped it would be so.

'Perhaps, she will come on her honeymoon with her husband,' he said to himself.

John Mark was elated at seeing him again, and it took all evening for Rufus to bring his chief up to date with all the happenings in his native city which the holy Evangelist was eager to hear.

"Your father is not well," repeated the bishop of Alexandria shaking his head with regret.

"Yes, I approve of your brother being consecrated as assistant bishop. Who else could better fill your father's shoes?"

"How is Simon the tanner? Is he still at work there?"

"Yes," replied Rufus with a smile, "but I believe he is about to leave his business to his grandson Bartholomew, the youngest of Hannah's boys."

"He and your father will surely entertain each other in their retirement, talking about their exciting old days."

"Any young ones for the priesthood?" asked John Mark ending his many questions.

"Yes, as a matter of fact, young Simon, my brother's oldest boy has been very active in the church for the past four years. Alexander was thinking of ordaining him this year, since he is more than ready, and seems like a very intelligent and dedicated lad. He is twenty one years old, you know." said the proud uncle.

"Maybe the bishopric of Cyrene is well established for the next fifty years." joked the head bishop, who in future times would be known as archbishop.

Annianus, accompanied Rufus to the riverboat, and announced that he was, by God's grace, soon to become a father. If the baby was a boy, he intended to call him Rufus.

"You do me great honour my friend, I assure you of my prayers for a safe delivery, and a healthy baby, whether boy or girl. Please send me word, and give my warm regards to your lovely wife. Please God I shall have the pleasure of seeing her again sometime soon."

And so, the two friends parted. The boat pulled silently away from the jetty, its bow pointed up river towards Memphis.

Kyros, one of the student priests, appeared at the front door of the church, in answer to the bishop's ring.

"Bishop, it is so good to have you back, let me take your baggage." So saying, the happy young student took the bag and quickly carried it to the church house, where he immediately made Senh aware of his superior's presence.

Senh dashed into the church, to find Rufus in prayer in front of the tabernacle.

He knelt down beside his friend, and thanked the Lord for returning him safely to the parish. Later, as was their custom, they sat in the porch exchanging news with one another.

"Have you heard anything of Miriam?" asked Rufus anxiously.

"Just once, about three weeks ago. Young Alceres had visited Hermopolis to meet with Iteti, and she invited them both over for the cena, a couple of evenings."

"I shall leave the day after tomorrow, and make a call at Akhetaton also.

In fact you know what? I think I shall go further up and see young Bek."

"So I shall loose you again for another three weeks at least."

"Worse things than that could happen. By the way, how is Addaya doing?"

"He plods on, slower every day, but the man has persistence on his side, and is very reliable. He is still hurting as I am from Rachel's loss, blaming himself for not having prevented the abduction," explained Senh with sadness.

True to his word, the bishop was on his way the third day after his arrival in Memphis. His first stop was at Hermopolis, where he was received with great joy by his wife and her aunt.

"My love," said Miriam, "I was beginning to get concerned about you; though I really had not expected you any sooner." They kissed with great love and joy.

"How did you find everyone there? Come, sit with us in the garden and tell us all the exciting news which we are dying to hear," smiled his wife with anticipation.

"I told everyone about you and they are all praying that I take you to meet them some day. Letitia's grandmother sends you her love, and asks you to be good to me. I told her what a terrible woman you were," joked Rufus. His wife threw a menacing glance at him.

The bishop and his wife made the most of their time together. He stayed for four days, and left the 'Dies Lunar,' after having performed the Sabbath service in the little church the day before, to the great joy of Iteti and everyone in the congregation.

In Akhetaton, Alceres received his beloved superior with great rejoicing, and arranged for a few members who assisted him in his ministry, to meet two days from hence at the house of a wealthy merchant; also a member of the congregation, where they would celebrate the bishop's return with a sumptuous cena, in his honour.

Rufus was pleasantly surprised with the number of people that attended the impromptu gathering. Besides Alceres, Manetho and Phile, there were six other members of the parish which included the master and mistress of the house. In addition, another five persons had also been invited by the host, among them, a Roman Centurion and his wife who were close friends of the family.

The guests were enjoying the garden, where a table with delicacies and beverages had been placed at their disposal prior to the cena in the house. It was late afternoon, the heat of the day was beginning to slowly dissipate. The cool of the evening arrived as a soothing balm enhanced by the delicious aroma of the surrounding flowers. An eye catching shallow pool, surrounded by potted flowers and plants was the centre of attraction. It was well stocked with small fish which swam lazily around the lilly pads and rocks that had been placed there, giving it a natural ambience and providing shelter for the fish.

Rufus was reminded of the parties that he and Letitia had occasionally given in their beautiful house in Rome, with Lavinia and Linus always in attendance.

The bishop was deep in conversation with the hostess and the centurion, when a shrill, hate filled voice, interrupted their conversation. There was a sudden silence as the party gave ear to the menacing outburst. Manetho and Phile froze, as they realised that the voice shouting obscenities aimed at the bishop came from the person of their mentally unstable foster child Pah.

The disturbed creature slowly walked up to the bishop with fiery hatred in his eyes, cursing and swearing. Rufus was about to speak to the boy, when the latter sprang at him, a knife suddenly appearing in his hand, and striking at the bishop's heart. Rufus, whose reflexes had always been quick, managed to divert the dagger's thrust with his left hand, whilst holding a cup of wine in his right. The knife, missed its mark but pierced the bishop's chest near the arm pit, inflicting a deep wound, and causing the holy man to stagger into the arms of the centurion. The latter quickly drew his sword in readiness of any further attack from the boy; who foaming at the mouth, his eyes glowing with satisfaction, was taken hold of by two of the guests.

"Take him away and bind him!"ordered the centurion, putting his sword back in the scabbard and assisting the bishop onto a nearby garden bench.

"Wait!" shouted a bleeding Rufus, as the two men, one of them Manetho, were taking Pah away,

"Bring the boy here!" he said, as he painfully but swiftly removed the knife from his wound.

They brought him back and held him firmly. The bishop got to his feet with great difficulty. Suddenly, he felt that mysterious calmness possessing him as Yeshua took over, and he said in a loud and authoritative voice.

"I command you evil spirit, in the name of Yeshua, and by the power of the Holy Spirit, to leave the boy. Get out! Go into the fish over there, where you will remain." He pointed at the pool as he spoke.

There was a sudden upheaval in the pool, which attracted everyone's attention. The fish jumped out of the water, did turns in the air, and fell back into the pond swimming around recklessly; possessed by the vanquished demon.

When all turned around, they found the bishop lying in pain on the bench, the knife on the ground, and the boy crying inconsolably, looking at his afflicted victim with repentant eyes.

"Let the boy go back to his parents," said the holy man raising his head. "The devil that possessed him is now a prisoner in the fish and will never enter the boy, or anyone else again," he then passed out.

Rufus had lain in bed at the house of the merchant for a week; he was accosted with a fever, and in a constant state of delirium. A physician attended to him daily, but his condition did not improve. His wound had been properly sutured and well tended to. The bleeding had stopped completely, but the fever continued.

Alceres, somewhat alarmed, went off to Hermopolis to fetch the bishop's wife.

Miriam arriving in the middle of the second week, took over the nursing of her husband, and did her best to pull him out of his delirium. On examining the wound two days after her arrival, she noticed some pus exuding from it, and called the physician's attention to it. The latter realizing that the the wound was festering, removed the sutures and applied a mixture of salt, seaweed extract and herbs, that he had found efficacious in other cases. He gave instructions, that the treatment continue three times daily. All they could do was wait and pray.

The host of the house, a man by name of Fabianus along with his wife Gratiana, did everything they could to aid Miriam in her effort to save her husbands life. They even took turns watching over him during the night, so that she might get some badly needed sleep. Thankfully by the beginning of the third week, the issue of pus had stopped, the fever lightened up, and little by little the invalid began to talk more coherently. By the end of that week, Rufus was at last fever free though rather weak.

The cook of the household proved to be a God-send. She concocted dishes of meat, chicken, fresh vegetables, and potent soups, which began to work wonders on the invalid. By the time the following week had elapsed, Rufus was his old self again, and most anxious to resume his preaching and make up for lost time.

Fabianus and his good wife, bade goodbye to the bishop and his wife. They thankfully rejoiced at the private 'Breaking of the Bread' he had performed at their house the previous evening. An indebted Rufus blessed them, and the house, on leaving with Miriam for Hermopolis.

"Well, I expect you to behave yourself from now on young man," said Rufus as he addressed Pah, who was now a different person. He and his foster parents were there at the jetty in Akhetaton, to wish him and Miriam farewell. With them also was Alceres who thanked Yeshua for having cured his much revered bishop, and promising to baptise Pah, who now it seemed, had received the faith.

* * * * *

The Church in Upper Egypt as the sixty third year of our Lord came to a close, continued to flourish under Rufus' direction. Bek, became one of the unsung heroes of the early Church, as he continued to organize and maintain new missions once they were spearheaded and established by the indefatigable Bishop of Memphis. A few years earlier, the bishop had had to cut down on the number of priests ordained. One every two years had proved to be too many. Most missionary churches were now run by one senior priest or pastor and one auxiliary priest. That way, Rufus could get a representative of every parish to attend to his summons every now and then. Without leaving their parish unattended, they could bring him up to date with their progress and problems. It cut down on his travels, and left the communication channels open.

Miriam proved an exemplary cleric's wife. She accepted with grace and resignation, the interrupted marital life that she had been called to lead for the 'Greater Glory of God,' and the good of the Church. When not enjoying her husband's company, she busied herself with the work of the church and the maintenance of her parish, where she was highly respected and revered. She often thought with great love and admiration of her sister-in-law Rachel whose saintly life had been completely dedicated to the Church, and whose example she tried to follow.

She thanked God with all her heart that she had been given a wonderful God-serving husband like Rufus, to encourage and guide her.

As for our hero the tireless and holy Bishop of Memphis, he knew he was very blest with a wife like Miriam. He looked forward to going back to her after every battle, and be comforted from his weariness by her never failing love and sympathy. To live in the service of God was to him a very great privilege, and when he met with success in the 'fishing of men' he felt pleased with himself and life was exhilarating and rewarding. But what of those nights of doubt as to his performance in the eyes of God; the judge of all. His errors, his difficulty in turning the other cheek in the light of injustice or aggression, the occasional lack of proper consideration for the individual soul in his preoccupation for the greater number. Was that justified? How would Yeshua have handled that and many other situations that a man of his responsibility had to deal with.

At times like those it was good to know, that another kindred soul shared his concern and was there after each campaign to revitalize him with her love and encouragement. He was content that the Lord had not given them children. Miriam was not as happy with that, as she would have loved to have had a son or a daughter by Rufus, whom she dearly loved and respected. But she resigned herself to the will of God. She knew it was meant to be that way, so that her husband would not be distracted from his important work by further responsibilities for small children. Those, as he already knew and regretted, needed a father's constant attention which he was not in a position to give.

The good bishop advised his priests of the importance of choosing an appropriate wife:

"We who are in the service of God," he would say. "Have to be most careful in our choice of a wife. She should if possible be a Christian. If she is not, but is receptive to conversion, that is also good as you will have gained a soul for Christ. However you must be very sure that she will accept the difficulties that our lives entail, and understand that in everything we do, God comes first. She must be ready for that sacrifice at her own cost, and even at the cost of her children, which will always makes things more difficult for her to accept. Most of you, will have the advantage of permanency, in that you will not be sent out on missions. The missionaries however are best to stay celibate if they can, or, as in my case, be fortunate enough to find a wife that resigns herself to God's will. In other words, her faith has to match yours. Pray that Yeshua and the Holy Spirit put some wonderful woman in your way who will meet the necessary requirements. That is my advice to you. The rest is in your hands. Please bear in mind, that a bad choice can cause damage to yourselves and by extension, to the Church. For those of you who can tolerate a life of celibacy, dedicated solely and exclusively to God,... that is the best possible mode of life."

* * * * *

The church had now reached all the way to Luxor, with Bek holding the fort there in his very able, pioneering way. Karnak had presented problems, in as much as Senh who would have been the best choice for the evangelization of that particular city, would have had to do battle with his father. Rufus opted to leave him in Memphis, where he had consecrated him as assistant bishop of that city with John Mark's blessing, just as Annianus, was now the assistant bishop of Alexandria, and had two sons. Alceres had married and had a daughter.

Old Addaya had passed away two years back. His wife Berenice however was still alive and in good health. She was looked after by the parish. Senh had two young priests assisting him in place of the old man,

A fair number of young priests had been ordained, and had been sent out to the various new churches after Bek had organized them and moved on following Rufus, who would venture into the unknown and establish a foothold. As a result there were many fast growing Christian communities a good way up river, and John Mark was extremely pleased with the Church's progress in Egypt.

Back in Cyrene the years had taken their toll. Simon the tanner, had succumbed to a stomach ailment from which he had suffered for four years. Julia had also died, and Simon, was in very poor health. Alexander was virtually running the Church in Cyrene, with the help of his son Simon, who was an ordained priest. Marius was still in reasonably good health.

Letitia who had visited her father in Memphis on her honeymoon, now gave notice that she wanted to see her father again, and would be bringing her little seven year old son Marcus with her. She had married a merchant from Cyrene, the son of a close friend of Marcus'. They had a son and daughter, and lived in her grandfather's house which would be part of her inheritance when he died.

In Rome the Christian Church had been meeting with much opposition, and even persecution, from the Roman authorities and the people. Even though many souls were being won to Yeshua, they could not organize themselves into having proper 'stone and mortar' churches as was the case in some Roman Provinces, such as Egypt and Cyrene. Their's was a militant Church in constant motion. The faithful would meet in private houses and could not go around professing their faith openly.

It was rumoured of late, it being the year of our Lord sixty four, that things were going to get worse for the Christians of Rome. The apostle Paul had gone to Rome, and was under house arrest there. There was fear, that he might even be executed. The Emperor Nero was sporadically persecuting Jews and Christians, in response to complaints from Roman citizens who had suspicions regarding those two religions that refused to join in the sacrificial rites and religious holidays of the Romans. Strange rumours circulated about Christian worship and practices, which they did not understand, but were ready to condemn.

It became known to the bishop of Alexandria, that Peter was in Rome, as the latter had heard that the Christian community in Rome was a large one, and felt a need to visit them to strengthen their faith. The fact that he could talk of Yeshua directly, he hoped would inspire them in their tribulations. Peter also wanted to get to know the men in charge of the various congregations, and ascertain that the Gospels were being accurately preached. He was also aware and disturbed by the news that a certain Simon Magus was influencing many in Rome with his magical powers and false teachings, and feared for the weaker members of his flock in the Imperial City.

A short while after Peter's arrival in Rome, the city had been set ablaze, and the fire had destroyed a major part of that city. The Christians were falsely accused of having started the horrendous conflagration which took thousands of lives. A great persecution of the Christians of Rome followed.

John Mark sent a message to Rufus, asking him to visit Rome and see if he could get Peter out of there, his life being very much in danger. The Bishop of Alexandria was aware that the Bishop of Memphis knew Rome well, and had connections there. Though he was loath to endanger his very dear friend, he felt that Rufus had the best chance of bringing Peter back alive. The apostle was the key figure in the life of thousands of Christians all over the world, and his life being endangered, was of the utmost concern.

Rufus consented to his superior's request, and hastened to put his bishopric in order prior to his leaving. Senh was to act as bishop during Rufus' absence. The latter, would continue to have two priests living with him at the church house. All missionary work would stop until his return. Bek's present outpost position in Luxor was to be maintained, and augmented as best he could.

Having organized his forces to his satisfaction, Rufus left for a final run prior to his departure for Rome. Ignoring Karnak, and Luxor, he visited Abydos, then Akhetaton to confer with Alceres, whom he asked to visit Luxor and acquaint Bek with his voyage to Rome.

He then sailed down to Hermopolis to spend a few days with Miriam. She felt most uneasy about Rufus' forthcoming voyage, but did not discourage him.

"I shall not rest easy my love until I see you back," she told him.

"I know Rome well my dear, and with God's help, I shall bring Peter back," he said, with a determined look in his eyes.

The four days passed quickly, and soon he was kissing his wife goodbye, at the jetty, where she was accompanied by her aunt and a few members of the local congregation.

"May Yeshua accompany you, protect you, and bring you back to me soon," she said, as she wished him 'God Speed' with tears in her eyes.

As the boat drew away from the jetty, Rufus wondered if he would ever see his beloved Miriam again.

CHAPTER FOURTEEN

A DIFFERENT ROME

The Mediterranean Sea sparkled in the morning sun. John Mark and Annianus, who had come to see Rufus off, embraced him each in turn, and assured him of their constant prayers. Silas waited patiently for the farewells to finish as he looked on with joy and anticipation at having his friend of so many years on board once again.

Rufus waived back at his friends on the wharf. The captain guided the ship out of the Alexandria harbour and onto the open white crested sea under full sail; the Sirocco wind at their backs.

"I hear that there is not much of Rome left," said Silas with a concerned look.

"When were you last there?" asked the bishop.

"About a month and a half ago."

"How did you know to pick me up?

"John Mark had sent word with a captain bound for Caesarea, and the Registry Office there, passed on the message to me when I arrived," explained Silas, his nose twitching as he spoke. "I had to pass Alexandria anyway since it's on my route to Rome. So picking you up lost me only one day."

The two old friends talked animatedly, as the other fifteen passengers leaned over the railing watching the dolphins, who always seemed to be around to provide entertainment.

Rufus had the cabin to himself for the voyage, and as he sat there having his lunch, his thoughts flew off to Miriam in Hermopolis.

'What would she do if he did not return? he asked himself as he sat in his cabin having lunch. 'She would receive contributions from the Church for her sustenance, and would eventually inherit all that her aunt possessed. That would give her ample means to continue life as she was accustomed to. Iteti would no doubt look after her spiritual needs, and Senh would surely look in on her every now and then,' he confided to himself.

'Why am I being so morose in the middle of the day? Yeshua has always looked after me, and will probably see me home safe after this adventure too.'

He wiped his mouth, having just finished his lunch, and went out on deck.

Being almost winter the choppiness of the sea, had a number of people leaning over the side, feeling its effects. He thanked God that he had been blessed with a sturdy stomach.

"There, you are!" came the voice of Silas as he joined Rufus by the rail.

"One of the passengers was just telling me that the Christians in Rome are being hunted down like wild animals. They are escaping from there by the thousands. It seems the Emperor Nero is blaming them for having set Rome on fire."

"Christians would never do that," said the bishop with conviction.

"You and I, know that, but the average Roman believes what the Emperor tells him. You must keep your faith secret,... tell no one that you are a Christian. As you know, I shall be in Ostia for the next seven days after our arrival. If you get into trouble and are pursued, get over to me in a hurry. Should you need to hide after I am gone, either Neta or Bashir will hide you I am sure."

"Thank you my friend. I know I can count on you and them also, but I shall be in God's good hands, and whatever he wills for me is what will happen."

The long trip came to an end with Ostia coming into sight. Soon, Rufus and Silas were parting with their habitual warm embrace.

"Remember what I told you, and may your God look after you," were Silas' last words. Rufus descended the gang plank and made his way to Neta's house, as had been his custom on arrival in that town for so many years.

"No! it can't be," screamed Neta as she opened the door and encountered her favourite lodger. She threw herself at him in a joyful embrace, which was just as happily reciprocated.

"I thought I would never see you again," said the tearful, aging landlady.

"How are you Neta, and how is your daughter?"

She looked at him with sadness in her eyes. "I am well for an old woman, but my poor Lydia died seven years ago. She got very sick and was gone within twenty days. Her husband married again, as they have three children; two boys and one girl, and they needed a mother. I am too old now to care for them."

The bishop comforted her as best he could and spent the rest of the day bringing her up to date with everything. She insisted on hearing every detail of his life since he had last visited her.

"I am glad you found such a considerate and lovely wife. Or should I say....glad that she found you. My goodness, you have come up in the world. You are now such an important man. Your life as you well know, is going to be in danger the moment you set foot in Rome. You are not safe even here, though things are much quieter."

"Are you a Christian?" asked Rufus.

"No. One of my lodgers explained it all to me once. Your God seems to be a very loving God, and one who actually lived until a few years ago. It must be a good religion if you are one of its chief priests."

"It is a wonderful religion, one that tells all men to love their brothers. That is why I know that the Christians did not set Rome ablaze as they are saying."

"There is a rumour going around, that Nero himself set the blaze so that he could build his new palace where all the houses and buildings had stood," whispered Neta, as if afraid of being overheard.

"Would you like to become a Christian?" asked the bishop hopefully.

"Perhaps some time later; right now I am too afraid. You be very careful, and keep your beliefs to yourself," warned the old woman, and raising her hands suddenly added, as the thought came to mind.

"I had some Christian friends of yours stay with me a while back. Jeth and Agafya and their children. They were escaping Rome after the fire, and were taken back to Egypt by Silas. I had them with me for almost three weeks. They spoke to me of you, and explained what a bishop was, as I did not know at the time."

"Yes, they are parishioners of mine," owned the bishop. "Very good people. I greatly esteem them. They were very unfortunate to lose everything they had here in Rome."

The following morning, Rufus took leave of his anxious landlady, and began his long walk to Rome. He came to the farm that had sheltered him once on that route, when he had been beaten up and felt so badly. He needed to see those friendly people once again.

As he approached, he was stopped by a black dog which was tied to the gate post barking fiercely at him.

He waited for a few moments until the dog stopped to catch its breath, and shouted, "Tita! Manius! Tita!" A few moments later a figure appeared at the door. A very old man leaning heavily on a stick came towards him and stood at the gate.

"You called me?" he asked.

"Yes, Manius, you don't remember me, do you?"

"No, I cannot say I do," he avowed with a gentle shake of his head, and scratching his neck.

"It's been many years since we last saw each other. My name is Rufus, and when I was a young man, and had suffered a beating in Ostia, you and Tita your good wife, gave me shelter, and treated me most kindly. You had a big Hispanian dog then."

"His name was Lupus," said the old man. "Now I remember you. Yes! Now I remember. Tita became very fond of you. She has been dead for over ten years now, I am here all by myself. A neighbour comes and cooks for me and looks after the house. Come in, come in," he insisted.

The dog followed the pair as they entered the house, and lay on the floor at its old master's feet.

"What brings you here?" asked Manius.

"I have business in Rome," answered Rufus, not wanting to give the old man too much information. He did not know how stable his friend's mind was at his advanced age, and he might betray him unwittingly.

"I don't know how much business you will be able to do in Rome, unless you happen to be a builder," said Manius with some humour and a smile.

"They tell me that most of the city has burnt down," volunteered the bishop.

"Yes, that is so, and they are blaming the Christians for starting it."

"Do you think they did it?"

"I don't know what to think. One says one thing and the other says another.

I just mind my own business, that is enough for me."

Shortly after, the bishop took leave of his old friend, but kept in mind the farm as another hiding place if it should ever be needed.

Two hours later, Rufus was standing on one of the seven hills of Rome once again. The same spot he had stood on so many years ago when he first visited that Imperial city. From there, he could see the devastation that the whole world was talking about. In happier times, he would have seen Drucila's house with the green shutters, and a little further down Erasmus' shop; where he worked for those two wonderful, adventurous years; full of ambition, persistently searching for

Letitia, with a burning love that he had never felt again; even for Miriam. Youth could conquer everything he then believed, and it was good to remember that in his case,...it had. Even if at the time he hardly acknowledged his debt to the Lord, who saw him through thick and thin.

'Now Lord! What have you waiting for me here?' he prayed, as he started down his old street which was nothing but rubble. 'Please stay by my side. Help me do my work, and allow me to rescue your beloved Apostle.'

He passed the charred remains of his old lodgings and wondered what had happened to Drucila. 'Was she alive or had she perished in the fire?'

His old shop was just a heap of rubble with some of the walls still standing, but badly charred by the smoke. Everything that could burn had burnt. He continued on for a while until he arrived at Erasmus' house. That too was gone, and he wondered if Vibia had been able to save the silver in the underground cellar. There were many people among the ruins, clearing up as much as possible and living in tents set up where their houses or shops had been. There was activity everywhere. Carts filled with debris, were being driven towards the outskirts, where gangs of workers were engaged in heaping up the remains of the city, creating huge ugly mounds. He walked in, stepping gingerly over the black charred beams of the house and made his way to where the cellar door had been. Clearing away some debris with his feet, he found the cellar. It was still covered by that same stone trap door that they had designed so as to make it as unobtrusive as they could.

'Perhaps the silver stock is still in there?' he mused.

As he was pondering these thoughts, someone walked up behind him.

"What are you looking for?" rang in his ear.

Rufus turned to find himself face to face with his old partner Tertius.

For a moment the latter looked at Rufus as in a daze. Then it hit him.

"Rufus!" he exclaimed immediately embracing him. "By Jupiter, what a surprise."

"It is good to see you my dear friend. How is Vibia and your son?"

"Alas, she and the boy died in the fire as well as her mother Gaia," he said, tears filling his eyes. "It was horrible, flames everywhere, the whole street was engulfed in flames, and as they tried to flee, a building collapsed on top of them as I later heard. I was at work in the shop and came running as fast as I could. The streets were blocked with people running in my direction as the wind spread the fire, and it was impossible to get through. I too had to retreat, as the flames came at me along with mounds of people, many of them on fire. It was an absolute nightmare," he stopped to catch his breath and swallow his tears.

Rufus held him for a few moments until he recovered himself.

"Life is hard is it not? said the bishop in a conciliatory tone, giving his friend a sympathetic smile. We all suffer sooner or later. We mortals are exactly that....Mortals".

"You were looking to see if the cellar had been opened?"asked Tertius.

"Yes, I see that it is still untouched, or so it seems."

"That is exactly right, and I am leaving it alone for now until I see which way the wind blows," said Tertius, as he kicked back some of the debris that Rufus had cleared. "It is possible that it has all melted into one great big blob, and will be very difficult to remove. However, only time will tell. Right now, I do not even want to think of it. I am sure no one will find it, as the joints fit so closely. Besides, they cannot release the hidden mechanism. In any event, my happiness is gone forever, and that down there is not going to bring it back."

The two men left. They walked away surrounded by devastation. The occasional remnants of a house totally destitute and crumbling, were the only indicators of this having once been a thriving, pulsating city. Tents were everywhere, as people struggled to eek out a day to day existence. Pedlars with their wheel barrows pushed their way along the busy streets.

Tent shops of all kinds had sprouted up in the same locations that they had previously occupied in the buildings, and life continued in its new and precarious fashion. There was talk of immediate rebuilding by the authorities, and the people, the city's merchants in particular, were hopeful that government compensation would help them rebuild again.

"Where are you living now?" asked Rufus.

"Come and see," said Tertius as the other followed.

After much walking, and having passed the ruins of the temple of Venus, bringing back so many memories to Rufus, they finally came to where some houses were still standing, and though damaged in varying ways, seemed habitable. Into one of these houses entered Tertius, motioning his ex-partner to follow. The abode consisted of one room with a fireplace, a table, a number of cushions and two low tables on a rug. There was a bed in one corner, and on the other stood a chest. An ablutions table, with basin, jug and towels, comprised the remaining features of the room.

"This is all I could find, and it is not cheap. The owner was fortunate in not having the house catch fire and since there is such a demand for housing, he is charging all he can," explained the merchant with a wave of the hand. "Our warehouse did not burn; being in the Great Aventine area, south west of the Circus Maximus as you know. The fire started on the south eastern side of it. Besides, being so close to the river, those buildings were well doused with water, which kept the sparks from causing any vital damage. I carry on the business from there, since the shop is gone." Tertius crossed the room, repositioned a few cushions, sat and motioned Rufus to sit.

"Come visit me there any time you like. In fact, I was considering taking a small portion of the warehouse, and turning it into a few rooms. I could live there all the time. Work is the only thing that is keeping me from going crazy. You are welcome to stay there with me. I shall make an extra room, which you can have. I can really use your company my friend."

The bishop thanked his distraught friend, and throwing a fond arm over him, promised to keep in touch, and perhaps even take him up on his generous offer.

"What a disaster," sighed the bishop; having lived and known Rome so intimately, and feeling great sadness at the extent of the devastation.

Rufus got up and made for the door. "Now that I know where to find you my friend, I shall go search for my wife's family up in the Sallustiani area beyond the Thermae of Diocletian."

"They may have been fortunate, as that part of the city escaped much of the fire; the wind dropping around the eighth day and changing direction at the same time," explained Tertius, with a sad wag of his head.

"We will see each other again soon," promised Rufus, who walking back to his friend put a hand on his shoulder.

"Keep your mind on your work for now. Later on, when the great black cloud that weighs upon your heart lightens," (by the grace of God' was almost on his lips, but he prayed the words in his mind) you will be able little by little, to think of your beloved family with more resignation in your heart." He embraced his beleaguered friend once again, took his leave, and set out to find the house of the Tricius family.

The streets continued to bustle with people.

'People are so resilient,' thought Rufus to himself, 'even a disaster like this one does not kill their spirit. Here they are, trying to normalise their lives even in such adverse conditions. Survival is such a strong instinct. And then of course, there is always hope, even if it is often Godless.'

His next shock came as he approached his old house; now without the cherished gate that matched that of Marcus' house in Cyrene. The house had been reduced to a blackened shell, some of its walls still standing, the roof and gate gone.

The saddened bishop stood there gazing at the scene in a trance, as he dreamily entered the gateway to get away from the crowd on the street. He could almost hear the laughing and running of his two little daughters, followed by the ever watchful Zaphira. His beautiful Letitia looking on with pleasure glowing in her lovely blue eyes. Oh, what happy times those had been. No matter what happened to him now, he resolved to hold that picture in his mind, to dispel all future sad moments.

Rufus turned away, and prayed as he continued his walk, that he might find the Tricius residence still intact. He was encouraged on passing houses that were showing lighter damage. As the walk progressed, he rejoiced that there was no further evidence of the fire.

Shortly after, he arrived at the house and rang the bell outside the closed gate. A new face appeared shortly after, and enquired as to the visitor's business.

"I am a member of the family my dear fellow. You may announce me as Rufus."

The man nodded in assent, and walked away through the beautiful garden towards the house.

To the bishop's great joy, Lavinia arrived at the gate and waited to embrace him as the gardener opened it.

"Oh, Rufus, what a wonderful surprise," she declared, tears of joy streaming down her still lovely but now more matronly face.

The bishop fought back tears of his own as he embraced her.

"I am so relieved to see you well and safe after this terrible disaster," he said. "Are you all well? Linus, the children, your mother and father?"

"Yes! thank the Lord we are all well, except my father whom we lost six years ago."

When the bishop heard her exclamation, he was surprised, and rejoiced that she had now accepted Yeshua, but saddened to hear of her father's death. It seemed to him that death was everywhere these days, now that many people he knew and loved were reaching the end of their lives. 'The Lord giveth, and the Lord taketh away,' he said to himself with a conciliatory sigh.

"I am so sorry to hear you lost your father; he had a great sense of humour, and you were the apple of his eye."

"I fell off the tree when the grandchildren arrived," she laughed in her habitual, musical, vivacious way, which had always coaxed her cousin Letitia out of her grey moods during those days of sequestration in that very house; frustrated and unhappy at being kept away from her darling Rufus.

She took his arm and led him toward the house where her mother was waiting for them at the door. Lucia, now in her sixty eighth year, embraced the visitor lovingly. In answer to Rufus' condolences, she explained with sadness in her eyes the manner in which her husband had died. She then embarked on her favourite topic. That of her dear grandchildren; who she greatly missed, and how eagerly she awaited their infrequent visits.

"We were quite distraught to learn of Rachel's horrible death," lamented Lavinia. "It must have torn the heart off the whole family. She was such a beautiful woman and so dedicated to Yeshua. Her name was known even to some of my friends in Rome. They say she actually worked miracles."

"I have never heard of that," he assured her. "But she was so humble and self effacing that she probably forbad the sick person from saying anything once they had recovered."

"You will stay with us here," said Lavinia with her habitual directness, as she gave the contented bishop a loving smile. Linus will be here soon. He has been extremely busy in the Senate since this disaster occurred, and much will be happening soon in Rome. These are very difficult and disturbing times.

"When did you accept Yeshua?" asked the bishop in a hushed tone.

"How did you know that?" she asked in turn, with an enquiring look in her lovely eyes.

He looked at her and smiled, "you said: "Thank the Lord." When I asked you how your family was keeping."

"Oh! That was careless of me. It is force of habit now. My mother and I are Christians, though we keep it very secret these days. They are killing us by the hundreds everyday. We are living in terror."

"By the hundreds?" reiterated the shocked bishop.

"Yes. They take us to the Coliseum and feed us to the beasts."

"Is that possible, how can that be?...Is Linus one of us?

"No. He wants nothing to interfere with his work, which is his life.

"I'm sorry to hear that, we need voices in high places. Does he know that you are a Christian?"

"I think he does, but we never talk about it, and I have said nothing to him."

"My mother and I are so proud of you. Silas who keeps us up to date with all that happens in Cyrene and Egypt, tells me that you are the Bishop of Memphis, and that you have spread the good news way up the Nile beyond Karnak."

She called out to one of her servants, and ordered some juice and wine to be brought to them.

"Incidentally, I had a visitor some time ago. A parishioner of yours. I believe his name was Jeth. He was a sculptor, and brought me a scroll you had given him for me. It was a good number of years ago. He was searching for his son and espoused, who had been abducted by the boy's grandfather I think."

Rufus nodded and smiled. "That man has quite a story, I shall tell it to you, sometime."

Oh! How is your new wife?" asked Lavinia with a big smile, and much curiosity.

"She is well. We have no children, which in a way is good for me, but bad for her as she spends much time alone with her widowed aunt Miriam, whose name she shares. They live in Hermopolis, up river, three days away by boat from Memphis. I only see her when I stop over on my missionary trips, every two months or so," explained Rufus, picking up a silver cup with some juice that Lavinia had poured for him.

"Poor soul, she must be a very good woman to put up with that," said his hostess with a pretty pout on her shapely mouth.

"She is also a very beautiful woman, and still in her thirties. Yeshua put her in my way in an extraordinary manner."

Rufus proceeded to relate his first meeting with Miriam, as they continued to sit in the peristyle of that lovely house, bringing each other up to date with all the news of their very different lives; Lucia interposing every now and then.

Lunch was eaten. The afternoon wore off very quickly and enjoyably. The cena being next in line was fast approaching, as the gate bell announced Linus' arrival. His wife made haste to greet him at the door, and on passing whispered something in Rufus' ear. Her mother who was present, gave him a knowing look.

Linus looking well, a trifle heavier than the last time the bishop had seen him, walked in and immediately embraced his friend.

"I am very glad to see you Rufus. You are looking well old man," he laughed.

"I can say the same for you, its great to see you again. Lavinia tells me that you are the busiest man in Rome."

"I don't know whether I qualify for that title, but these are truly crazy times, and none of us know where this tragic situation is going to take us. As you see we have been extremely fortunate in having our house in one piece. Did you see yours on the way up?"

"Yes, it was a very sad moment for me."

"To be sure.... What brings you to Rome?"

"I am afraid that if I tell you, it may compromise you, and I have no wish to do that. A man must be left free to do his best in what he believes without encumbrances."

"That is very considerate of you Rufus; but then, you were always considerate. It is a very plausible quality in you. One which we have always appreciated. Come let's sit down to our cena, which is I am sure, more than ready."

After the excellent cena, which was a real treat for Rufus who had had to contend with so many bad and mediocre meals during his travels, they sat back in peristyle, and talked of all the things that they found entertaining. They completely avoided the subject of religion.

From what Linus gave the bishop to understand, the Senate was deeply suspicious that the Emperor himself was responsible for the fire, and that the Christians were being used by him as a scape goat. The reason being that he wanted to build a very large complex, which would also include his new palace, in the part of the city that now lay destroyed. Thousands of workers were being put to work clearing up that particular area, leaving the rest of the city to be attended to by the citizens and merchants. However, no one dare make any allegations until the evidence was found to weigh overwhelmingly in favour of the Senate.

He lamented the terrible loss of life that occurred every day, and which he knew was done to pacify and entertain the frustrated and angry mobs, who were blood thirsty for revenge, and for no other reason. The senators were walking a tightrope, and had to be most careful with the agendas that they proposed, until something more concrete presented itself. There had also been a rumour that the very popular General Galba, had taken exception to some fiscal matters that Nero had unilaterally implemented, and which the man declared, were self-serving and detrimental to the populace and the army. Being a powerful man, people were wondering whether he might yet arrive in Rome and take over the Government.

As the talk continued, Linus who did not know if Lavinia or her mother had brought Rufus up to date with their children's lives, began to relate to the bishop, each of the girls' situations as a result of their marriages.

"As you probably know, our youngest daughter Priscilla though only eighteen, recently married a young centurion, and lives in Antium near her aunt Lydia, whose husband is now a legate, and at the moment serving in Hispania.

Which incidentally is where our Victoria lives. She married a Hispanic wine merchant whose father, my father-in-law, traded with and befriended, by name of Decimus."

"My goodness! exploded the bishop. "What a small world it is. I know the young man's father.

"How can you possibly?" asked Linus his eyes wide with amazement as he looked at Rufus in expectation.

"Yes, I met him as a young man, whilst my Letitia was here in this very house. You were courting Lavinia at the time." Rufus continued, with a knowing smile.

"I travelled from Rome to Tingis in Africa, by way of Gaul and Hispania, as you may remember, finding suppliers for our markets. Decimus who lived in Carthago Nova was recommended to me by a friend of his, Cassius, in Tarraco, whom you have met. He visited me here in Rome on two occasions. I stayed in Decimus' house for two days. He took me to his vineyards, and I ordered a cargo of wine from him. He was a very nice fellow, and as I remember, he had a squint in one eye."

Linus' face was a picture to see. His large blue eyes looked as if they were about to jump clean out of their sockets; his mouth wide open in strong disbelief. He exploded into a long, loud, and merry laugh. Rufus joined in heartily; much amused at the surprising situation.

Lavinia, having left the men in the atrium whilst checking on her mother, who had gone to her room earlier, came running back at the sound of the laughter; fearing she would miss something highly amusing. She could not believe Rufus' story, until Linus told her of the squint in Decimus' eye. Then she, bursting with laughter, her hands spread over her heart, accompanied the two as they broke into laughter once again, sending its merry sound reverberating around the house.

After breakfast the following morning, Rufus sat with Lavinia and her mother, following Linus' departure to the Senate.

"Do you think Linus knows that I am a Christian bishop?"

"Yes, I think so, though he has said nothing to me. I believe he appreciates your tactful reservation. I feel sure he will help you anyway he can, but secretly of course. He is such an honourable person, and like yourself very dedicated to his work.

He is an excellent husband and father, and I love him very much."

"You are very fortunate indeed, and I know you thank the Lord for it."

Rufus got up from his cushion.

"Now, I shall leave you. I have work to do," said Rufus, looking around for his bag.

"I will look up Octavius as you advise, and see if he can take me to Peter. Though you are dying to spoil me here, I will have to stay wherever I can find refuge from now on. I will not put you and the family in danger by seeking shelter with you. Should I find myself in trouble; which being more than likely, I shall do my best to avoid. I shall be well away from you.

Pitching his bag onto his shoulder, he gave the two women a one armed hug and walked away.

Lavinia accompanied him out, and with a heavy heart wished him Yeshua's protection. He, passing the garden gate, stopped, turned, and waived; his habitual warm smile on his face.

The address that Lavinia had given him was not easily found. The soot left by the smoke covered the street signs, which were carved on the crumbled walls of the corner houses. An hour and a half after he left Lavinia, he was still floundering around somewhat lost.

"I am looking for Via Castra," he asked pretty young woman who stood on the side of the street in front of a baker's shop, waiting for someone it seemed.

"You are standing in it," she replied, with a mocking smile in her long, somewhat narrow, but pleasant face.

"You must pardon me, I am a stranger to this area, and without the signs,..." and he pointed at the illegible blackened blobs, "it is difficult to be sure."

"Who are you looking for?" she asked.

"I am looking for a man by name of Octavius."

"Come with me. It will be difficult for you to find him; all these tent shops look alike." She led the way.

"But you will miss the person you were obviously waiting for," protested Rufus.

"Oh, that doesn't bother me, he's always late. He'll just wait there until I get back," she replied with certainty in her voice, and a mischievous smile.

"There! is your man," she pointed him out as they reached the tent. Octavius the leather carver, looking up, greeted the girl with a big toothy smile.

"Good morning Athena, who do you bring here?" he asked getting up and observing Rufus.

"This good man was asking for you," replied the Roman maiden with a smile for both men to share. Turning, she retraced her steps to the baker's shop.

"Charming young woman," commented the bishop, sitting on a leather cushion pushed over to him by his new friend.

"This cushion brings back many exciting memories," began Rufus unwittingly. He explained without really meaning to, his adventure in Tingis so many years ago, and how Vibia had fussed around with the choosing of cushions.

"We have something in common then," said the artisan with a friendly smile.

"We have much more than that in common I assure you," said the bishop with a somber countenance. Then, looking straight into Octavius' eyes, he said.

"We have our beloved Yeshua in common."

The man was stunned. He was not sure what to answer, fearing the stranger to be a spy trying to extract an admission from him as to his being a Christian. He made no answer, but waited to allow the suspected spy to continue.

The bishop, realising the man's position, stretched out his hand, and pressing the man's arm, said, "don't be afraid. Your name was given me by Lavinia, who is a cousin of my deceased wife."

"Forgive me, but Rome is a dangerous place to live in these unhappy times, and one cannot be too careful."

"I quite understand. Can we talk here?" asked Rufus.

"With all that din going on out there I dare say we can, as long as we keep our voices down and give the impression that we are doing business."

"Can you take me to Peter? I have come looking for him. The church in Egypt where I come from, has sent me to take him back with me to a safer place," said Rufus with hope in his heart, and a pout on his lips.

"Normally, I could have, but at the moment the authorities have him under arrest and allow no one to see him. Two of the faithful who bravely went to visit him, were themselves incarcerated."

"Oh my! I have arrived too late," sighed the bishop.

"Who is in charge here in Rome?"

"There are three bishops here, all consecrated by Peter. They are Linus, Cletus and Clement. There are a number of priests such as I am. The Christians of Rome are many, and there are never enough hands to cope. We organize clandestine prayer meetings in safe houses, and outside the city in the various secret places. The faithful are only told at the last moment so as to avoid having traps set for us," explained the Roman priest with a sad countenance.

"Oh my goodness," lamented Rufus. "Truly, this is a Church in crisis."

"Where do you perform the 'Breaking of the Bread' service?"

"I have performed only a few. Mostly in rich men's houses. But now we cannot compromise them. They help us when and how they can."

Rufus took the next hour to inform the man of the churches and services that flourished in Cyrene and Egypt. Poor Octavius, though he had heard of those churches, listened with open mouthed amazement at the wonders that he was hearing. The bishop described many details of the liturgy and other important ceremonies, now in use in those churches.

"You are obviously a priest," remarked Octavius, his eyes searching Rufus'.

"Yes, and I am the Bishop of Memphis in Egypt; even though I am a Cyrenean. I spent a number of years in Rome, where I was a successful merchant and lived here with my family."

"By Jove, I am honoured to meet you," said the priest extending his hand to the visitor, who took it with an amiable smile, and warmly pressed it.

"Lavinia has spoken to me of you. Also, many years ago a visitor from Egypt whose name I do not recall, also mentioned you. But I never thought I would actually meet you." Octavius got up, took a jar that was at hand, and offered some dates to his visitor, who took a few as the conversation continued.

"I must set up a meeting," said the priest, "to introduce you to Linus who is the bishop in this part of the city. Later, with his help, you will meet Cletus and Clement," said the priest taking a few dates from the jar, and putting one in his mouth. He pinched his long straight nose and looking at Rufus with admiration in his light brown eyes, said:

"I may be able to arrange a meeting which you can address tonight, or tomorrow, God permitting. I shall take you to meet Linus another day, if Athena's brother to whom I am teaching the trade can look after the shop whilst we are away."

The bishop thanked him. Observing aimlessly the tent under which they sat, brought Saul the tent maker to mind. He turned to his new friend, and asked.

"Tell me, Saul is here in Rome, but under house arrest. Is that not so?"

"Yes, and he is allowed to see and talk to people. We have a man who keeps us informed, and brings us messages from him. But most of us keep clear of visiting him as it exposes us as possible Christians, and the authorities have many spies who watch out for us. It appears he will be judged by Nero soon. There is little hope for him, especially after Peter having been arrested also."

"Where are you staying?"asked Octavius.

"I have no place to stay."

"You can stay right here, if you don't mind living in a tent."

"I have had tougher lodgings in my life, I assure you," answered the bishop.

CHAPTER FIFTEEN

PERSECUTION

The meeting of the faithful, had been arranged two hours before it was due to begin. It was to take place on the other side of the river where many of the Christians lived. There, the devastation of the fire had not reached, and the houses though poor, were still standing. That neighbourhood was shared by Christians and Jews. Both being susceptible to persecution by the Roman authorities from time to time, they maintained a 'live and let live' unspoken arrangement between them; a strictly Roman phenomenon that precluded betrayal of one another.

The Christians gathered in a little valley surrounded by trees, which shielded them from the observation of passers by on the main road and the prying eyes of ill wishers. Sentries had been posted along the perimeter of the valley and an escape route marked out and ready for use.

Octavius, stood up on a large rock which set him above his brethren, and was thus in full view of all present. Dusk had now settled in, and a few torches lit.

The meeting began with a prayer to Yeshua for protection of the faithful and the expansion of the Church. Then the leather carver motioned Rufus on to the rough podium and after welcoming him on behalf of all present, left him to introduce himself, and to tell them whatever he thought relevant to his mission.

"Brothers and sisters in Christ! People of the Church of Rome! It is an honour to be here with you tonight," began Rufus. "I bow to your bravery and strong faith in the Blessed Trinity in the midst of this horrendous persecution that menaces you every day of your lives, and is taking such a terrible toll.

The world of Christendom applauds you and prays for you. Your commitment to the Lord is exemplary, and I personally wish to express my admiration for your strength and courage.

Our brother Octavius tells me that Saul constantly instructs you through his messages, on your expected comportment as Christians. How to live pure lives and love your neighbour.

He also tells me that Peter had something beautiful to add to, and illustrate Saul's messages by way of little stories. Those stories about the Lord Yeshua, that Peter his beloved and saintly apostle related to you before his arrest, are now called Gospels. They tell of the things he said and did, so the you might follow his teachings, imitate his ways, and so save your immortal souls.

Peter, who was at Yeshua's side constantly, is the best and truest witness to our divine Lord's life. The words that he has spoken to you explaining those parables which our divine Master uttered, are at this very moment being written down by a few holy people under the guidance of the Holy Spirit. They will enable you, your children, and all future generations to understand and keep the words of our blessed Lord in a way that cannot be changed, or misunderstood. Tonight, I will relate to you a few of those wonderful stories. Try to remember them exactly as I tell them to you, so that when you retell them they will not vary in the least."

The bishop related a few of the gospels. For the next two hours, he held the people in total suspense as they listened most attentively to his every word.

Twice during the meeting however, the torches were quickly extinguished, and a guarded silence reigned. The lookout members, had heard or observed something suspicious and gave the alarm by extinguishing the torches in their water buckets. On this occasion they were false alarms, for which the whole congregation was thankful. The meeting continued thereafter, by moon light.

The meeting over, Rufus, prayed with them, blessed them, and all dispersed. He and Octavius made for the river, and crossing a bridge found their way back to the latter's tent.

Rufus arose early next morning. He went out, bought some food and returned to the tent shop. He woke up his host, made herbal tea, prepared bread with olive oil, cut up some goat cheese, and shared his breakfast with his new friend.

"I am going to find out where Peter is," said the bishop with determination, and rising from his cushion with urgency prepared to leave.

"I have no idea where they are holding him," admitted the other.

"See you later," said the bishop. "When I get back tonight, if you like, we can try to organize another meeting with a different group."

"Good day!" sang Rufus, and off he went in the direction of Lavinia's house. He felt sure that as yet he had not attracted any undue attention.

Arriving at his cousin's gate, he stopped, and looked around to see if he could spot any suspicious character that might have been following him. Convinced that he had not been followed, he rang the bell and waited.

The gardener opened the gate for him, bowed his head in recognition, bade him good morning, and hastened to announce him. As he reached the door of the house, he saw Lavinia crossing the atrium, busily arranging her hair as she approached to meet him.

"Rufus, how nice to see you again.... You look a little concerned, are you in trouble?"

"No, nobody knows me in Rome, apart from some Christians whom I preached to last evening. Octavius set the meeting up, and there was a fair attendance, considering."

"Oh, good. I am happy to hear that," she said as she took his shawl and carried it into the peristyle, where they sat on their cushions once again, to chat.

"Lavinia, do you have any friends in the military here?"

"One of Linus' closest friends is a legate. How would you need his help?"

"Would he find out where they are holding Peter?

"I don't know. Connecting you with Peter may get you into trouble."

"Do you think Linus could find out without arousing suspicion?"

"I could ask him, but then he would know what you are here for. I shall ask him tonight, but you must not be here."

"No. I shall be with Octavius. Have you means of sending me word? Or, perhaps I could meet you somewhere near here tomorrow morning, where you could come accompanied by your maid as if you were out shopping."

"I shall send you word through Octavius."

Rufus walked away slowly from Lavinia's house checking every now and then to see if he was being followed. He ducked into a doorway thinking someone was tailing him. His thoughts were with Peter. He stayed there for some time. The phantom pursuer did not materialise. He then proceeded towards the north end of town, where he had heard that a large encampment of troops was situated.

'Perhaps, that is where they are holding Peter,' he thought as he walked. 'It is a wild guess, but if I am meant to find him, the Lord will surely guide me.'

After a considerable walk, he came upon it. There were many rows of tents accommodating the soldiers; there being no building standing in that part of the city which was in the vicinity of the destroyed Circus of Nero.

He was suddenly confronted with a terrible sight. There, in front of him, was a long line of people. Each person was chained to the other, and all being driven like cattle by Roman soldiers using horse whips.

"You will all get to see your leader as you pass," shouted the sergeant with a big laugh. The prisoners followed him dragging their chains. Men, women and children, struggled on; their ankles bleeding; their clothes torn; their faces with the fear of death stamped upon them.

The bishop watched them with a sickish feeling in his stomach. He followed; curious to see what leader the guard was referring to. As they passed a large stone obelisk such as he had sometimes seen in Egypt, and the only thing standing, he noticed that all heads turned in its direction. Some bowed, and some simply stared sadly as they passed.

He crossed over to the other side of the line of prisoners. He froze at what he saw. There in front of him, hanging upside down on a cross was a white haired man, stripped to the waist, and more dead than alive.

His dream of many years past, rushed into his head as he could hear his father's words, 'Perhaps your dream is prophetic in some way or other, only God knows.'

Without thinking, he approached the figure who he now suspected to be Peter. The guard, being distracted for the moment, did not notice him as he bent down, his face close to the old man's, whose lips were moving as in the dream. He listened..." Guide my sheep!"

"Get away from there!" came the gruff voice of the soldier, who suddenly noticing Rufus, gave him a hard push, bowling him over. He got up, and quietly walked away to one side and stood there looking at Peter; the rock, as Yeshua had called him,... and silently prayed. Others came, and soon a group of people looked on and waited; some mocking, and some quietly, with tears in their eyes. Late in the evening just as dusk began to settle, the saintly man gave a loud gasp and died. A very sad Rufus made his way quickly to Octavius' tent as night began to fall.

Those whispered words kept resounding like bells in the bishop's ears, as he walked and wondered what Peter meant. He knew he had asked for help for his sheep.

'What sheep? His Roman sheep? They have other shepherds to look after them, I am only a stranger here. There must be something that he expected me to do right here to benefit them. What is it that I can do for Peter's flock that the other bishops cannot do? Was it my people in Egypt that he meant?' These thoughts greatly troubled Rufus as he directed his steps to the leather carver's shop.

Octavius received him with a sorrowful heart as he heard the bad news, and surprised Rufus by quickly getting up, and asking him to follow. They took off at a brisk pace cross-town again towards what seemed to the bishop, the place of Peter's execution which he had just left. They arrived just in time to see two soldiers riding on a cart with Peter's body in it. The cross was lying on top of the apostle's body and they were headed for the country.

"We must know where they bury him," said Octavius, as they prepared to follow.

"Later tonight," continued the priest, "we shall dig him up and take him to our own burial place, where the faithful can visit and pray to him for help now that he is with the Lord. We all knew him and loved him."

The two men followed the cart at a distance so as not to arouse suspicion.

Eventually, the soldiers stopped in a field where there were a number of mounds, and jumping off the cart, lit two torches, stuck them in the ground and began to dig. The Christian duo drew noiselessly closer, and hiding behind a large boulder nearby, made sure of the actual location of the grave.

"I am off," whispered the priest. "Please stay until I return with help. We too shall need a cart."

Rufus nodded ascent, and away went Octavius, stealthily disappearing into the night.

An hour later, the soldiers having finished the burial, left; taking their torches with them and leaving the bishop to his thoughts in the dark.

As he sat there, his back against the boulder, Rufus had ample time to mentally revisit his life and family. For some unknown reason his mind insistently dwelled on his father Simon. 'How privileged he has been,' he mused. 'He actually touched the Son of God, and was thanked by His holy mother. How proud I am to be his son. If I get out of this mess in one piece, I shall stop at Cyrene on my way back to Egypt, and see my wonderful old father again, perhaps for the last time,' he promised himself.

His thoughts strayed once again to the words of Peter.

'How can I help?' he continued to muse. Then, of a sudden, it struck him. He was to teach the liturgy to his brother bishops in Rome, who had not had the opportunity of formulating one in their constant strive for sheer existence.

'That is why he had said 'guide' and not 'feed,' as Yeshua had told him. Yes! It had to be the liturgy,' he assured himself with conviction.

'When all these horrible persecutions are over, and they build stone and mortar churches, they must have a liturgy that is already orthodox in nature with ours in Egypt, Cyrene and Antioch. I must stay and write it all out and leave it with the bishops here. They in turn will have further copies made, and give them to their priests. The 'Breaking of the Bread' service will then be the same all over the Christian world.'

After more than two hours of waiting, he heard the sound of wheels on the stone road, and snapped out of his reveries to welcome his friends; all four of them.

Within a half hour, the body of Peter was exhumed. They put back the soil over some boulders mimicking the shape of the mound, and went on their way with the beloved apostle's body in the cart, covered with hay.

They did not go back to the city, but took to a country road instead. Eventually they entered an orchard, and after weaving their way among lemon trees, they came to a clearing. On approaching, they beheld by the light of two torches, an underground vault with its stone cover lying by the side of the opening. Three young men sat on it awaiting their arrival.

The body of the saintly Peter was most reverently uncovered as Rufus drew near the cart. Peter's face, caught in the light of the torches, had the appearance of wax. His prominent features registering with authority the strength and enthusiasm with which be had fought his battles against the evils of the world, on behalf of his beloved Yeshua.

Rufus spreading his hands, and with his eyes lifted to heaven, prayed to Yeshua on behalf of all Christians for consolation at the great loss of one of their chiefs on earth.

And, that the Lord might continue to guide the Church in this hour of need with Peter at his side.

"We thank you for Peter Lord," prayed the bishop. "He was an inspiration to us all, and we felt closer to You because we were close to him. We will honour his memory always because he was a saintly man, who lived only for you Lord. Help us to follow his example and so, like him, to gain a place with You in heaven, not by our poor efforts, but by Thy grace and love."

The Lord's Prayer was then recited. The body was wrapped in a linen shroud and carried with great love and care into the small vault, which could hold only two bodies each on separate slabs. It was decided that a thin stone pillow with Peter's name carved on its side, would be brought another day and placed under his head. Markings on the outside of the grave were out of the question as attention would be drawn to it.

The stone was then slid into place, soil and leaves were strewn over it, and all withdrew. One man alone drove the empty cart, whilst the others split up so as not to attract attention on their way home.

CHAPTER SIXTEEN

THE SCROLLS

Rufus made his way to his former warehouse by the river. It had been a week since Peter's death, and he had met with bishops Linus and Cletus, though not as yet with Clement. The Roman bishop had had to cancel the meeting on the spur of the moment because of a potentially dangerous situation.

He had discussed the liturgy question with the two bishops. They had shown great enthusiasm for the project, and agreed with him that that, had been Peter's request, seeing that little else made any sense. He, as Bishop of Memphis, had been most warmly received by them and he in turn, had assured them of his help in whatever they needed. His identity was to be kept secret for the safety of the Church in the Roman Provinces.

Tertius, was as expected in the warehouse office, and rose to greet Rufus as he entered.

"Welcome Rufus. I am very glad to see you again."

"I came in answer to your kind offer of allowing me to stay with you here, once the changes you spoke about have been made. I being a carpenter, even if a little out of practice, can help considerably in doing the work."

"You, a carpenter? I don't believe it," laughed the merchant.

"I was a carpenter for close to five years before I became a merchant. I will tell you all about that some other time, since it seems I had never mentioned it to you," replied the bishop, throwing an arm over his friend's shoulder.

"Show me the area that you are intending to change."

They walked to the back of the warehouse where there were some high windows, and Tertius waived his hand in the general direction as to where he thought they should cut the area off from the main warehouse.

"Very well, let me measure it," said Rufus, "and I shall draw up a rough plan showing the partition walls. Then, once we are sure that they are where we need them to be, I shall mark the stone floor and go from there. I think we should also put in a wooden platform overhead, to serve as a ceiling and to seal the living area against, rats and mice, since there will be food around. We can use the platform for light storage, the roof here is high enough to allow that."

Tertius listened attentively, as he began to realise that his friend knew much more than he had given him credit for, even jokingly. Thinking back, he remembered that Rufus had once told him that he came from a family of carpenters.

The rough plans were soon drawn up and the bishop presented them to his friend.

"Are you sure you want to spend all this money?" asked Rufus.

"Of course, it is much cheaper than building a house, and what would I want with a house now in any event?"

"We must contract a mason first of all to put up the partition walls," advised Rufus. "Materials, are going to be very costly these days, as we will be competing with the Emperor who will be hoarding all the materials for that palace complex that he is going to build."

"Indeed you are right," answered the merchant.

"Why don't you import building materials right away. You will make a lot of money and yours will come cheap," suggested Rufus suddenly feeling his mercantile juices flowing.

"I should get you back in the business," joked Tertius; but really in earnest.

"I have other important things to do my friend. But I will help you any way I can. I need to have a quiet place to write, and this would give me that. I must be honest with you."

"I shall be delighted to have you here no matter the reason," said Tertius.

"That is very good of you. I don't have much money these days but I shall help you and that way earn my keep," assured Rufus, with a tilt of the head.

"Why don't you have any money? Have you given it all to your daughter?"

"Yes, that is part of it. But there is another part which I would rather not tell you as it could make trouble for you. As it is, I suppose I shall be putting you in jeopardy by living here with you in any event."

"You would never do anything wrong Rufus. My father-in-law told me that you were the only person he had ever put his trust in."

"To be sure, and I would do anything for you also, but you may find me a burden and a risk. You see, I am a Christian; and not just a Christian, but a bishop of that faith. I am the Bishop of Memphis in Egypt."

Tertius' mouth opened involuntarily at this news. His gaze was intense.

"I did not believe you when you said you were a carpenter, and you have proved me wrong, I dare not say the same with regard to your position, but I am stunned...Absolutely stunned."

"So you see, priests do not have money of their own, they are supported by their congregations. They are meant to be humble people and be content with the ordinary things in life. Extravagance or any unnecessary luxuries are not permitted. Though, if the priest has a family, it will be looked after also, by the parish."

"Are you not permitted to work at anything else?"

"It depends on its not interfering with one's priestly duties which always come first. In our case, I can help you with some work in exchange for staying here and eating your food whilst I perform my priestly duties."

"We will get along just fine, and of course it goes without saying, your faith will never be mentioned by me to anyone. It can get you killed as you well know."

Three days later, the work in the warehouse began. The brick layers started the new partitions, and Rufus eagerly awaited his turn to get to work on the carpentry.

The sooner the place was finished the sooner he could start his work on the liturgy.

Tertius employed two clerks and two warehouse men, who were there all day. Rufus would have to be careful that they knew nothing about him other than that he was a close friend, also a clerk, and was to assist Tertius with the accounting. That, would be done in the new section at the back of the warehouse. In actual fact Tertius would be doing the accounting most of the time whilst he would be writing the Liturgy.

Another thing that was being done at the same time as the walls, was the cleaning and renovating of the old vault, readying it for the silver which was still at the ruin of the old house. Rufus waited two weeks before he could begin his work, during which time he lived in Octavius' tent.

One morning, whilst Rufus was still a guest of Octavius, young Athena brought a message for him from Lavinia, asking him to come to her house as soon as possible.

It was mid morning when he reached Lavinia's gate. He did not have to ring, as the gardener was working nearby and came immediately to let him in.

"Good morning!" chanted the bishop with a wave of the hand that almost became the sign of the Cross.

"And to you master," answered the slave with a smile.

Rufus walked up the garden path, stood at the ornamented wrought iron outer door of the atrium's hallway, and waited. He looked to see if he could catch the eye of a servant who would announce him. Seeing no one around, he called out.

"Anybody home?"

A servant came running, apologized for no good reason, and said she would inform her mistress of his arrival. A few moments later Lavinia came to him.

Her habitual smile was gone, and there was a grave look on her face. Rufus reflected that her aspect did not typify her habitual pleasant manner, and wondered at its meaning.

She embraced him warmly, and said.

"I have bad news for you Rufus," and looking sadly into his eyes, said, "your father died,... I am so terribly sorry."

The bishop was taken aback by the sudden tragic news. Tears appeared in his eyes as Lavinia took his hand, and they sat down in the peristyle to mourn and brood.

"I had a presentiment the other night; the night that Peter was buried," said the grieving son. "I was hoping I could see him once more when my work here was finished. But now all hope is gone. He is with Yeshua, Peter, my mother and sister. That gives me the consolation I need. He had an extraordinary life may he now rest in the peace of the Lord."

"Silas sent me the news," she said, "along with his sincere condolences."

"Your brother Alexander is now Bishop of Cyrene, and I am sure he will be a great bishop too."

"I have no doubt of that. He will also be as grieved as I am. To quote a favourite saying of my father," his voice faltered. "Why does life have to be so tough."

"So you found Peter?" she asked, hoping to change the subject.

"Yes, but I was too late. He was almost dead on that upside down cross when I found him. He whispered three words to me, and died a few hours later."

"Can you tell me what he said?"

Rufus went on to explain his dream on the *Pretoria,* and the story connected to it.

"That is extraordinary. My goodness Rufus, you do come up with some incredible coincidences. Though this one sounds more like a prophesy."

"Your mission here is over. Now you can go back to Egypt and your wife. Silas is in port for the next four days," she continued.

"No, I am not ready to go just yet, I have some scribing to do if I have interpreted Peter's words correctly. It should not take me more than a month, so I shall be ready to sail with him God willing, the next time he comes."

"Why don't you stay and do your writing here. No one knows you, and you can remain here sequestered in the house, and work until you are ready to sail. Perhaps Peter meant you to look after your own sheep in Memphis."

"That struck me too, but the bishops here all agreed with me. Because they need the liturgy we have in Cyrene and Alexandria tied down for the sake of orthodoxy, they felt it was what Peter meant. Besides, I promised to help them out in the preaching of the good news. After all, we are all 'fishers of men," as our divine Lord asked us to be. I shall try to see Silas before he sails, as he must take with him the news of Peter's death. Incidentally, no one in Rome must ever know that I am the Bishop of Memphis, it could endanger my flock."

Rufus did not wait for lunch, his appetite had abandoned him. His thoughts were in Cyrene and the family grieving over his father's tomb, even though the news was over a month old. He thoughtfully made his way to Octavius' tent shop.

The leather carver priest, who was busy stitching together one of his beautiful leather cushions, looked up and greeted the bishop with an enquiring look as he beheld his friend's grave countenance.

"My father has died," said Rufus, pushing back his shawl and sitting on a cushion opposite his Roman friend.

"I am very sorry to hear it," responded Octavius, with a meaningful tilt of the head, and momentarily closing his eyes. "How did he die, may I ask?"

"His heart had been troubling him for a good while now, and he finally succumbed to it."

They talked for a little while, and then Rufus, remembering that Silas had to be told of Peter's death, prepared to leave. He informed his friend that he would not be back for a couple of days, and the reason for his going. He then began the long walk to Ostia, where the *Felicia* was berthed.

Silas and Rufus, sat on the deck on board the *Felicia,* sharing their latest news, which naturally concerned events in Cyrene with regard to Simon's death. As might have been expected, the funeral there had been a large and memorable one. Simon had been an exemplary human being, and his memory would be revered not just by his congregation, but by Christians all around the country. Even a fair number of those outside the faith had attended the funeral. Alexander, who would now fill his father's shoes and inherit his flock, had organized the beautiful funeral service which was held at "The Christian church of Yeshua of Nazareth" the first church of Cyrene, and seat of the diocese.

The bishop, listened attentively to the news that Silas unfolded for his edification, and greatly regretted not having been there with the family to share their grief at losing such an extraordinary and God-favoured human being.

He now got up, and invited his friend to go with him to Neta's for the 'cena'. There he would give him the details of his adventures and work in Rome. Especially, his being with Peter at his death; the writing of the liturgy at the latter's request, and the distributing of the various copies to the bishops of Rome. All this information was to be relayed on to John Mark on his next visit to Alexandria, who in turn, would make sure that Senh and the Miriams, would be brought up to date with his exploits.

"What news in my absence?" asked the bishop, as he greeted Octavius on his return to Rome.

"We have a meeting arranged for tomorrow evening, at the same place as the last time, but the congregation will be a different one Bishop," pointed out Octavius. "Shu....sh, please, never call me that again, remember, no one must know that. Only you, Linus, Cletus, Lavinia, and my ex-partner Tertius know. He is not yet a Christian, but I have hopes. I shall be staying with him soon, as we are creating a living space in his warehouse where I can do my work on the scrolls. He would never betray me," assured Rufus.

The following evening, gave way to a starry, clear night. The people were arriving in small groups by the light of a full Roman moon which lit the stony paths that led into the little hidden valley. By day the valley was a delight for the eye, with its mixture of rocks, grass, trees, wild flowers, and even a fair sized stream, which tumbled over green, moss covered stones, and disappeared into a cavern that lay hidden in a pine forest thick with colourful underbrush and flowering bushes.

By the time Octavius and Rufus, reached the valley, the flow of expectant souls had halted, and all were ardently awaiting their arrival. There were no torches burning. There was a full moon and visibility sufficed for their needs.

"I greet you in the name of our Lord and Master, Yeshua," began Rufus, eyeing the crowd that must have numbered over a hundred.

The bishop was in the midst of explaining the last of three parables he had planned for that night, when swishing noises caught his ear, followed by groans and then screams as the group began to break up running in all directions. Particularly into the forest. One of the arrows (for indeed they were arrows,) tore the bishop's tunic as it grazed past his arm. Octavius, who had planned their escape routes, quickly took Rufus's arm, pulled him down off the rock which had acted as a podium, and told him to run by his side.

The bishop, seeing the flock scatter and being pursued, stopped for a moment to see if he could help anyone. The carver however, took his arm again and they both ran into the woods where many had already gone. Rufus, along with his guide and perhaps thirty others, soon found themselves inside a cavern through which the stream ran, and which they had entered on their hands and knees, crawling over the slippery mossy stones. The cavern was of a fair size with smaller tunnels branching off in various directions.

"This place has saved our skins a few times already. Let us silently pray that tonight be no exception," said Octavius.

"Give a hand here," he asked. With the help of Rufus, and another, he began to roll a large stone into the opening through which they had entered, closing it off. They then secured it with another stone tightly wedged in behind it.

The cries of the wounded and the captured could be heard in the distance, as everyone in the cavern remained silent. All prayed for their hapless brothers and sisters. Suddenly the tramping of feet was heard approaching the cavern. All quietly backed up and dividing themselves into groups, took refuge in the tunnels, leaving the main chamber empty.

The light from a torch filtered in through the mouth of the cavern. Then a splash was heard, followed by a number of obscenities and the light disappeared.

"Light me another torch!" ordered a loud gruff voice.

"We don't have any more with us, and this one's soppin wet."

"We don't need it, the opening is too small for anyone to get through. I am all soaked. We have enough of them to make the tribune happy," said the gruff voice once again.

"Ah! wait, here comes another torch, at least I can get a look in, and then we can be sure," asserted the same voice.

Everyone in the cave waited with bated breath. A lighted torch followed by an arm, penetrated through the opening; the torch changing positions as it allowed the soldier holding it to peer into and all around the main chamber of the cavern. The light was dim though, as one solitary torch was insufficient to provide adequate lighting.

"See anything?" asked another soldier.

"No, the place is empty."

The torch was pulled out, and a few moments later, the tramping of feet began again. The soldiers making their way, cursing and swearing, back to the road from where they had initiated their attack.

In the cave no one moved, they were not sure yet if they were being tricked by the soldiers into thinking they had gone.

They sat down and prepared to wait it out even if it took all night.

A few of them had been separated from loved ones and were in some distress.

The bishop and the priest, quietly made their way to each of them, prayed with them, and gave them some consolation and hope. As Rufus approached one of them, a woman, who was quietly sobbing, he realised to his great horror that it was Lavinia.

"Oh, my goodness, what a shock to find you here my dear. Don't be frightened, you will be safe soon. Why would you risk coming here? asked Rufus with a startled look in his eyes.

"My maid, Angeliki, separated from me just before we reached the cavern, she kept running into the woods. God knows if they've got her. She told me it would be dangerous, but I wanted to hear you preach. You are truly inspired," she whispered, giving his cheek a light caress. "May the Lord protect you. Letitia would be so proud of you if she could see you."

"Maybe she can, who knows what God allows his saints to do. We know so very little in that respect."

An hour later, a coded tap was heard at the mouth of the cave, indicating that all was clear. Octavius moved gingerly and noiselessly towards the small opening and looked out. There, by the light of the moon which lit her pretty face was Athena, beckoning to the priest to bring his people out.

The blocking stone was then pulled back, and one by one, the faithful crawled out. Two thin young men entered the cave, lit a torch which they had brought with them, and replacing the stone found their way out through one of the tunnels, that allowed a very restricted and secret exit deep in the woods at some distance from the cavern.

Rufus walked Lavinia home, both keeping their faces well covered. She was very flustered on account of the missing servant, and he promised to enquire after her in the morning.

They both secretly prayed however, that she would turn up during the night.

"Linus is going to be furious with me when I tell him the truth as to where I have been tonight," lamented Lavinia.

"I told him that I would be spending the night with a friend who was not feeling well, and whose husband was away on business. I have never lied to him before and he does not deserve that, but he would never have given his consent to my going."

"In the future," admonished Rufus, "you should stay home until this madness subsides. You know how to pray. You have heard a number of Yeshua's parables which you can think about. Soon, I hope there will be a scroll that you will be able to get with all of Yeshua's life and stories in them. I have a very good friend; in fact he is my superior, who is truly inspired by the Holy Spirit. He has been working on that for years now, and like him there are a few others who have learnt all those things from the apostles themselves, and are guided by the unerring hand of the Holy Spirit. Those stories, are known as Gospels."

"What about the 'Breaking of the Bread'?" she asked.

"Octavius can sneak up here every now and then in some disguise, and perform the service for you, your mother, and a handful of your Christian friends and servants."

By this time they had reached the rear gate of the house which was adjacent to the servants' quarters. The mistress of the house pulled on a short piece of rope, setting off a little bell inside the house. The gatekeeper soon appeared and opened the door for her.

"Good night Rufus, and thank you for bringing me home. God Bless you and keep you safe," she said and smiling at him, disappeared into the house.

As the bishop found his way back to Octavius' tent, wondering if by some miracle, Angeliki, Lavinia's maid, had been found alive and free, her mistress walked into her bedroom to find her husband fast asleep.

Knowing him to be as most men, a heavy sleeper, she undressed and slipped into bed beside him. She lay awake for the rest of the night revisiting the frightening events of the night and deeply concerned about Angeliki, who was more of a sister to her than a slave. She fervently prayed to Yeshua that she might have escaped unharmed.

Morning had not quite arrived, when breaking with all normality in his nocturnal behaviour, Linus woke up, and feeling her next to him, jumped up with a start.

"How come you are here? When did you get in?"

"When you are wide awake my love, I shall tell you."

Linus had never awoke quicker in his life.

"Go ahead my dear," he said as he rustled his hair, rubbed his eyes and sat bolt upright on the bed. She followed his example, their shoulders pressing together.

"I have a confession to make," began Lavinia with tears starting in her eyes.

"I have deceived you," she said, " and you do not deserve that."

He turned to look at her with a pained expression as he waited for her to continue.

"I did not visit Marcellina today. I lied to you. I attended a Christian gathering instead, where Rufus was preaching."

Linus looked with incredulity at his wife. "Did he ask you?"

"Oh no, on the contrary, he scolded me for it when he eventually found me in the cave where we were hiding."

"So there was trouble even?"

"Yes, big trouble. I was so scared. I got separated from Angeliki and I don't know where she is?" continued the distressed wife bursting into tears.

"By Jupiter you really risked your life tonight. What were you thinking?" He put his arms around her with tenderness and concern.

"It is impossible for me to explain it to you, but when one becomes a Christian, something happens," she said amidst her tears. "It changes one's life. There is an Afterlife you know Linus. A much longer one than this one; in fact it lasts forever, which is difficult for us to understand. Can you imagine, 'endless?"'

"All I can imagine, is that I could have lost you just like Rufus lost Letitia," he said pulling away from her; touch of anger in his voice. "I shudder to think what he went through, and I would not want to go through that."

"Rufus told me to stay here in future," she said cuddling up to her husband.

"And, if I needed to have a service which is of the utmost importance to us..."

"The 'Breaking of the Bread ' service," cut in Linus, with a look of certainty in his eyes.

"Yes! how did you know that?" she asked incredulously.

"Because I knew you were a Christian, and I made it my business to know what your faith is all about. Yes, of course I understand, but I cannot get involved in that. My duty is to this life. To keep you happy and safe, and to get us to a ripe old age, enjoying our children when we can, our friends, and all the things that we are used to. I want you to promise me right now, that you will do as Rufus has advised you to do, and never, and I mean, *never*, run off to another of those gatherings again."

"I promise," she said, and with tears in her eyes hugged and kissed him.

"One last thing," admonished her husband with some pretended seriousness.

"What is that?" she asked, fearing that she had got away too lightly.

"You have sinned against me very badly," he said with a mischievous smile.

"You will have to confess that to your priest."

She sat there in mouth open wonder. He got up and began to dress.

Rufus arrived at the carver's tent as morning began to break. He quietly went to his side of the tent, lay on the cushions, and promptly fell asleep.

Street sounds woke the bishop up to find his friend working away on the other side of their partitioning curtain.

"Good morning," he greeted, sticking his head out.

The carver looked up from his work and smiled,"hello," and continued with his work. Rufus began his ablutions, and dumping the water at the rear outside the tent, got dressed. He then joined his roommate in the shop, where there was some bread and oil ready for him to eat along with a piece of cheese and some beer.

"How many were lost last night?" asked the bishop anxiously.

"Too many,...at least thirty,"

"Poor souls, it was their turn," said Rufus,"what a horrible way to have to live. I just cannot get used to that. We try to do only good, but the devil runs loose, lying and spreading false stories about us to those in authority, causing havoc."

"Have you heard anything of Angeliki, Lavinia's maid?"

"I am waiting for Athena's report," answered Octavius with a shake of the head.

"You are so well organized," commented Rufus. "You were a brave leader last night my friend, and in time you will be doing great things. May the Lord protect you and allow you to grow in his service."

"Thank you, I value your opinion my august friend," said the priest.

It was mid afternoon when Athena appeared at the leather carver's tent to report all the dead, wounded, and arrested. She had a list of names written down and Rufus scanned the columns in search of Angeliki's name.

There it was; in the group of those arrested. Which meant that she would die in the Coliseum within a day or two at the most.

At the request of the bishop, Athena sent news to Lavinia of Angeliki's plight.

Lavinia received the message from Athena with great anxiety, and immediately calling one of her servants to accompany her, headed with haste to the new temporary Senate building. Fortunately, it was nearby, in her own neighbourhood. A large building which had escaped the ravages of the great fire, had been quickly renovated and redesigned to suit its vital function.

One of the attendants, a very young, fair haired man, received her and ushered her into one of the makeshift waiting rooms whilst he went to announce her presence to Linus.

The latter, having already finished his speech a little earlier, left the Senate chamber and followed the young man to where Lavinia was waiting.

"My love, what are you doing here?"

"Angeliki is being held it seems in the Coliseum, and you know what that means."

"Yes, I have to act quickly. Leave it with me I shall get right onto it. Fortunately my work here is done for the day."

"Flavius!" called out Linus as the young assistant was walking away.

"Yes, Senator?"

"Please run and find Legatus Aemilius and ask him to wait for me. I am on my way down to see him right now."

With another "yes, Senator," the young messenger took off.

"You go home now dear and try not to worry. I shall do my best to get her out."

With those words and a hasty kiss, husband and wife parted each to their own destination.

Linus arrived at his military friend's camp. He was received with great respect, and shown into a ruined courtyard surrounded by broken walls tinged with soot but with a small but well tended garden at its centre. A series of army tents, surrounding the courtyard could be seen through the broken walls. It was replete with a fish pond which had somehow survived the great fire. Flowers were once again blooming in their many clay pots, and a few very attractively carved stone benches, and sculptures had been placed at intervals along a stone path, that meandered artfully around the courtyard.

The senator adjusted his immaculate white toga, and sat on one of the benches awaiting his childhood friend.

A short while later, the tall, elegant, uniformed figure of Aemilius walked into the courtyard and embraced his friend. " I am honoured to have such an illustrious personage visit my humble place of business," he joked, as he put his arm around his equally tall friend.

"The honour is mine, most august defender of the empire," reiterated Linus with a mocking grin as they sat down.

"What can I do for you my friend?"

"Save me from my wife's wrath."

"How have you misbehaved this time?" joked Aemilius, knowing full well that there was more to it than that. 'But then, what were friends for?' he thought to himself. 'Man's joy in life is his family and his friends, everything else is humdrum and mostly troublesome.'

"I swear that on this occasion I am innocent." laughed Linus.

"Explain!"

"My wife has a highly cultured and useful Greek maid by name of Angeliki, who has got herself into quite a pickle because of her religious beliefs, and is now detained along with other Christians in the Coliseum."

"Surely you can do something," she complains. "I need her, and am very fond of her. I don't want to have to train another."

"I shall have to move quickly, otherwise, she will be some lion's supper," asserted Aemilius, with a pout and a tilt of the head. "It amazes me that some of our most productive citizens are being destroyed for no good reason. Just so that a blood thirsty rabble can be entertained, and distracted from others' ambitions. We live in a difficult age. Hopefully it won't last much longer."

"I thank you honourable Legatus."

"There is a condition."

"And that is?"

"Come with Lavinia this coming Dies Saturni for the cena," said Aemelius with a smile. "I want to show you an excellent horse. I shall even let you ride her. She is North African and has real spirit,...I got her just a week ago. Bring 'Argos' with you, we can put her through her paces, and see how she does against him.

Linus, rose from his bench and smoothened his toga.

"I shall look forward to that. And thank you, my friend."

The two friends embraced, and parted.

The senator stopped on his way home, to buy Lavinia a little trinket in one of the tent shops.

There was rejoicing in the Senator's house that evening, as Angeliki was rescued and sent home to her mistress with the admonition that a second offence would carry a death sentence with it.

Octavius was busy as usual with his leather work when news came that Angeliki had been released and sent home. The news was later passed on to Rufus who received it with joy, and knew that Linus had put his considerable weight behind the effort.

'Linus is a good man," thought Rufus. 'Perhaps in time, when things become more peaceful, he might be won over to Yeshua. I will pray for him. At the moment though, I shall concentrate on Tertius, who is another good man, and is more within my reach.' He headed with some urgency in the direction of the latter's warehouse.

CHAPTER SEVENTEEN

FAREWELL

One month had passed since the partitioning off of the warehouse had begun.

Rufus and Tertius, had both moved in, and were very satisfied with the results.

They each had their own bedroom with a high window fitted with shutters closing from the inside. A lock on the door to their new area ensured privacy from the employees. There was a kitchen, a common room, and a very small toilet with a little door to the outside for the removal of their waste; making it easy for its disposal into the river which was only a few steps away. Each room had a desk and stool, as well as a comfortable bed, an ablution stand with basin, jug, towel hook and polished brass mirror.

"This was a great idea of yours," said Rufus as they sat in the common room which also served as dining room.

"These accommodations are much better than that room I had that was so expensive. Now all I need to do is remove the silver. But I have no idea how to do that. It could take a few days to accomplish and cannot be done in the open."

Rufus stopped to think for a few moments.

"Why don't we put a tent over it. That way, we will be able to inspect it without being seen, and assess the damage if any to the silver."

"I might have known you would come up with a sensible solution," chuckled Tertius.

"First," said Rufus, "we have to get a new door with the secret latch installed here, on the old vault. You don't want the employees to know you have silver down here. Do you?"

"How can I keep it from them?"

"Erasmus moved the silver to his house, so that the employees would never know that he kept any. If we do things properly," said Rufus, "they will never know."

The bishop sketched up a stone slab and secret locking device made of iron, and they quickly employed a stone cutter, and a blacksmith to provide and install the new door to the old vault. The work being done at night.

A day after the vault was completed, the two friends, after having measured Erasmus' ruins, ordered a tent of appropriate size to be made for them. Four days later they installed it in the afternoon, providing them with the necessary privacy. They opened the vault and Rufus descended to inspect the silver. Much to his relief, and that of Tertius, the bars had not melted and could be removed one at a time.

Tertius hired a donkey and cart, and as soon as the light failed they began to load the cart by moonlight. Lamps were out of the question.Their shadows on the tent walls, would give them away. It would require two trips to remove all the silver, so they had to risk leaving the vault unguarded until they got back. All four hands were needed to do the job. The cover of the vault was replaced, the remote security latch set, and off they went; the donkey labouring hard to pull the heavy load. They worked at unloading throughout the night in the privacy of the warehouse. The employees did not suspect that the old vault had been opened, as the customary large wooden box was replaced over the trap door, and everything looked the same as it had for years.

The same procedure was repeated the following night, after a day of vigilance at the old site by the owner. The silver was finally secured once and for all. Tertius decided that in future, all silver transactions would be conducted during the night when the clerks and storekeepers were absent. This way all silver sales would be known only to Tertius, who would keep secret the books pertaining to it. His customers would collect their orders and provide their own transportation.

"Now let's try and get some sleep, and let the staff do their work and keep an eye on the place," said Tertius yawning mightily as the first member of his staff appeared. The tired pair took off to their beds, having left instructions that they were not to be disturbed unless there was an emergency.

The end of the first week saw the conclusion of the first of the scrolls on the liturgy for the 'Breaking of the Bread' service. The marriage liturgy followed three days later, and the birth and burial liturgies three days after that. The bishop was quite happy with his progress, and all that remained for him to do, was to make another two copies. One for Bishop Cletus, and another and Bishop Linus, who would arrange to have more copies made by other scribes. With God's help, there would be a fair number within a few months to start distributing where needed, in Rome and elsewhere. The original, he kept for himself.

Rufus, now knowing that he would be ready to sail with Silas whenever he pulled into port, set out for Ostia to check out the expected date of arrival of the *Felicia*.

After having been informed by the Registry Office that Silas was expected within two weeks, he dropped in to see Neta, as usual. He spent the night there, and began his walk back to Rome the following morning, this time bypassing old Manius' farmhouse.

Tertius was at his desk when the bishop made his appearance.

"Now I have an excuse for finishing with work for the day," he said on seeing Rufus, and getting off his stool closed the door to the warehouse; the staff having left. Both men retired to the back to prepare something to eat, and rest for the night.

"Soon, I shall be gone and I shall have to leave you a pagan," said Rufus.

"I am content with what I am," said the merchant.

"Will you permit me to talk to you about my God? You have nothing to lose and who knows, it may impress and interest you."

"Since I have no interest except my work, you may as well entertain me with your wonderful stories, it will help pass the time."

That was all the bishop needed to begin working to save his friend's soul.

The rays of the morning sun entered through the high window in Tertius' room bathing in its light, the new Christian, who was blissfully enjoying his third hour of sleep after a long night of attentive listening to Rufus' convincing sermons. The latter was also fast asleep; resting after his ardent effort in winning and baptising his friend for Yeshua.

Later that morning, the bishop set off to find Octavius, with the object of setting up a meeting with bishops Linus and Cletus to hand them their copies of the liturgy, and to take leave of them.

"I shall find out right away," promised the leather carver, in answer to Rufus request. "Chances are you can meet with one of them today, and the other hopefully tomorrow." With these words, Octavius departed.

Rufus, having nothing better to do whilst the priest was away, walked up to the baker shop and bought himself a pastry, which he took back to the tent to eat.

He was halfway through his pastry, when two soldiers rushed into the tent and took a hold of him.

"Come with us leather carver, we want to talk to you," said one of them.

They led him up the street, and as they passed the butcher shop, Athena was standing there waiting for her lover as usual. She saw Rufus being taken by the soldiers, and heard him say as he passed with an accompanying wink in her direction,

"I am not the leather carver I tell you."

"What were you doing sitting and eating in his tent? "

"I was waiting for him to return."

"The soldiers looked around, and seeing Athena, asked her.

"Do you know the leather carver who has a shop down the street?"

"Yes, I know him."

"Is this he?"

"No." she said with a positive tone in her voice.

"You can go," said one of the soldiers. Reluctantly, releasing Rufus, they walked back to Octavius' tent to await their quarry.

"Would you please stay here Athena and warn Octavius before they see him. He has gone to see the bishop,"requested Rufus. "I shall make myself scarce for now....In what direction is Bishop Linus' lodgings?"

"Keep going straight up," she said. "If that is where the priest went, he will likely come back the same way. If you see him, please tell him to send me word with Claudius, I shall stay around here until I hear from him."

Rufus walked away, thanking God that the soldiers had not asked him any more questions, or searched him, as the scrolls were in his possession. Once out of sight of his would-be captors, he slowed down, stopped, and waited for Octavius to appear.

At long last the carver approached. The bishop, taking a quick look around, took his friend by the arm, pulled him aside, and explained all that had happened.

"I cannot go back anymore," lamented Octavius. "From now on, I shall have to keep a low profile. I shall probably lose all my materials and tools, unless someone, maybe Athena's brother, can steal them another day when they get tired of waiting for me. Incidentally, your meeting with the bishop is set for tonight. I shall take you myself since I have nothing else to do now; other than to find Claudius and send him back to Athena.

Bishop Linus was very pleased to see Rufus again, and was greatly impressed when he opened the scroll, looked at the beautifully scribed liturgy, and examined the contents with great interest and enthusiasm.

"You have done us a great service my good friend," he said as he finished reading it. "I shall have someone make us some copies, and soon we shall have enough to give one to each of our priests. God willing, easier times will come soon, and we can begin to have our own churches as you have in Egypt."

"I shall be leaving next week," said Rufus. " When I get back to Egypt, we will have our congregations pray harder for your welfare here. That you may soon be free of this horrible persecution," assured Rufus as he took leave of Linus with a warm embrace.

He left, accompanied by Octavius, who now had to look for new lodgings among his parishioners.

The following day, Rufus gave his other scroll to Bishop Cletus, who was very pleased with it and promised to have it duplicated, a copy given to Bishop Clement, and the others distributed among his priests.

The Bishop of Memphis retreated to Tertius' warehouse, where he would now remain sequestered until it was time for him to board ship in Ostia, hopefully within ten days or so.

Linus and Lavinia came to take leave of him at the warehouse, as it was less compromising than at their house. It was a sad farewell, as chances were they would never see each other again. They promised to keep in touch through Silas, and talked of perhaps visiting Memphis at some future time. They had heard much about the pyramids, and expressed a wish to visit them. Also to have an opportunity of meeting Miriam who they had heard so much about.

Seven days later, Rufus having said his farewells to Tertius, Octavius, and Athena, was on his way to Ostia, where he would stay with Neta for the last couple of days until he sailed off with Silas again.

The *Felicia*, pulled into port two days later than scheduled, and after having some minor repairs done, cargoes exchanged, and Rufus in the cabin, sailed away; leaving Neta, waving a tearful goodbye to the bishop and the captain.

No sooner had the ship found open sea, than the choppy waters, began once more to play havoc among many of the passengers who lined up along the rail with their intermittent vomiting.

"It's going to be a tough crossing for them, poor souls," said Rufus as he and Silas stood on deck leaning against the captain's cabin.

"This is typical of winter sailing," commented Silas' his nose twitching.

"That is why many ships lay in for the winter in a sheltered port. I cannot afford that luxury. So, here we are," he continued with another twitch of his nose.

"If my guess is right, these people are being forced by circumstance to travel. I suspect they are all escaping Rome, as there are over forty seven on board this trip as you can see, compared with my usual sixteen or so."

"I wonder how many are Christians?" sighed the bishop, throwing a pitying look at the passengers.

"Those children worry me the most," said the captain with regret, and ignoring the bishop's question."If the weather gets worse, they are going to suffer badly. I have no shelter to offer them."

"You do not have any little tents, as Marius had on the *Stella Maris*?"

"No, I talked to the owners about them once, but they kept putting it off, and then it never got done. At least the little ones could have had some shelter.

"How many children are there?" asked Rufus.

"Six I think, under seven years of age."

"Any babies?"

"Thank goodness, no."

They walked around the deck talking to the passengers. The bishop being most anxious to find out how many were Christians. They were not going to tell him that easily, he felt, so he refrained from asking them individually. Instead, he climbed up the ladder onto the roof of captain's cabin, and standing in front of the helmsman, where all could see him, called out to get their attention.

"We are out of sight of land now. All of you who are Christians are quite safe. The persecution exists only in Rome; in the Provinces there is relative peace. For for the time being, I shall say no more."

The sea became less choppy as the *Felicia* travelled south along the coast to Rhegium. However, once that city had been left behind and the open sea once more encountered, it became turbulent again, and another round of sea sickness became the order of the day.

Soon the winds that had been favouring them changed, and they began to be blown away from their intended course, and towards Syracuse.

Silas became concerned as he could detect a storm brewing. As yet it was not apparent to the passengers. The captain's many years at sea, had sharpened his senses to the nuances in the weather, and he kept a close vigil on the clouds.

Eight hours later, his fears were justified, as the wind piped up considerably, and the ship was forced to follow the tack of the wind which carried it on a south westerly route. All night long the *Felicia* was driven in the same direction. Silas had cut to half sail to slow the ship down, as the coast could not be discerned through the heavy rain.

The light of morning was most welcome. The coast of Sicily could be made out, and navigating became somewhat easier.

Everyone was soaked through with the exception of the children, who Rufus had accommodated in his cabin where they were protected from the elements. The ship tossed around considerably, and everyone was hanging on to the railing for dear life.

Eventually, Syracuse came into sight, and though Silas thought of pulling in for temporary refuge, he could not manage it for fear of some rocks that appeared in that direction and he did not want to take a chance maneuvering around them.

Despite the discomfort of all on board, the captain kept to his forced route awaiting a change in the wind that he could take advantage of and get back on track.

Night fell once again, and with it came the fear of drifting in to land.

Once again the sail was cut to half, and the ship sailed on; everyone keenly awaiting the dawn, when better visibility would give them greater peace of mind.

Meals were eaten with great difficulty by those who were not sea sick, and the rain was constant. The cabins, both the captain's and the bishop's gave the mothers an opportunity to feed the children more comfortably and get out of the rain for a short while.

The storm would not abate, and continued for the next two days, when another coastline met their eyes. Silas guessed it must be the island of Malta. They were much closer to land than the captain wished, and despite dedicated tacking, they could not get clear of the coast which kept getting closer and closer.

"I cannot pull out," shouted the helmsman.

"Go in then," shouted Silas, "head for that beach. We cannot afford to miss it....Full sail!" he shouted. He and the mate let down the half furled sail and the ship was steered at full speed turning slowly towards the beach.

It was now a race between getting the *Felicia* on to the beach, or smashing her into the rocks menacing them at its end. For the next half hour the crew battled the current and waves, as the helmsman tried to keep the bow lined up with the beach. Then at last, Silas shouting for everyone to hang firmly on to the railings, let the ship glide forcibly into the sand. The force of the impact as the ship dug into the sand, sent many sliding forward into one another causing some minor injuries. The breakers hammered the ship's stern, as the sail was furled up quickly by the crew, hoping to keep the ship upright. All of a sudden it toppled on its side, everyone sliding across the deck causing further injuries, as incoming breakers continued to lash the ship. The passengers began to jump off and wade ashore between waves. Silas, Rufus and the crew, helped as many as they could, including getting the children out of the cabins, where they had been safe so far and getting them ashore.

Silas remembered with great consternation his attempted rescue of Rufus' family from the cabin of the ill fated *Pretoria,* and tears clouded his eyes as he looked at his friend and helper, who was being haunted by similar thoughts. Some of the passengers who had made it to shore returned to help, and after a while all were lying safely on the beach resting from the ordeal.

The ship, though on its side, stayed entrenched in the sand, which gave Silas much hope. Three hours later, the rain stopped at last, and though the sun did not appear everyone breathed a sigh of relief.

"All Christians, please follow me in a thanksgiving prayer," called out Rufus, starting the Lord's prayer.

As the words were pronounced by the bishop, others began to join in, and by the time it finished, it seemed to our hero, that everyone was praying. Once again he began. "Our Father Who art..."

Most were with him. He then prayed aloud his own prayer of thanks, to which they answered, "Amen."

"I am overjoyed that so many of you have escaped from Rome. In Egypt you will be able to practice your faith without much interference. Certainly none from the Romans, though the Judeans interfere with us every now and then," said the bishop in a loud voice for all to hear.

At this juncture, the passengers were surprised by the appearance of a number of people native to the island, who approached carrying baskets of food and water skins.

Soon all were enjoying the hospitality of those friendly people who addressed them in Latin. Silas and Rufus went over to greet them and thank them for their hospitality.

A group of men appeared, carrying heavy ropes which they began to tie on to the ship, and wrap them around large rocks that were a little further up the beach.

Silas went to help them.

"We will leave things as they are for tonight, as the storm has almost abated," said one of them to Silas in Latin.

"Tomorrow," he continued, "we can start unloading the cargo and see if we can get the ship upright and relaunched.... We shall have a lot more help then."

All the passengers were led away to the village, which could not be seen from the beach as it was back on higher ground. There, they were accommodated in various ways. The women and children were given shelter in some of the villagers own homes. The men were given the run of a barn, that the villagers used as a place of assembly, and was large enough to accommodate them all.

Next morning, having dried out, enjoyed a good night's sleep, and with all the injured having been tended to, the grateful visitors began to fraternise with the inhabitants, and acquaint themselves with their customs.

After a communal breakfast provided by the locals, and the storm having spent itself, the men went off to the beach. They began the unloading of the cargo. It would take a few days to accomplish. The sun breaking through the passing clouds, made the start of their work more pleasant. Most of the male passengers helped with the unloading, as donkeys and mules, were brought to the ship to carry away crates containing miscellaneous merchandise; mostly glass and metal artifacts, to another barn in the village.

A week later, after much work, the now lighter ship was righted again. Wooden trusses were installed to keep it in that manner, ready for relaunching at the next high tide.

The bishop who did not lose an opportunity when it came to the 'fishing of men,' sat on a rock overlooking the serene and impressive bay before him, talking of Yeshua with the village chief whose name was Cato. He was a fisherman, as were the majority of the villagers.

"Yes, I have heard of your religion," said Cato. "In fact, our Island Chief, Publius, who lives in the next bay down the coast from here, is a Christian, and has been to our village preaching to us his God Yeshua."

He turned, and called out:

"Crispinus!" Waiving to a young man who was sitting further away amidst a group repairing their nets.

A well built young man possibly nineteen years old, walked over and joined the pair.

"Yes Cato, what is it you wish of me?" he asked, throwing an enquiring look at the older man, and smiling at Rufus.

"Do you know where Publius is at the moment?"

"Yes, I think I can find him. He is in his village, though he travels a lot around the island preaching that new living God of his.They almost killed him a month ago further down the coast." He said turning to Rufus,"Those Dagonians were angry at his having converted some of their people."

"Could you take me to this man?" asked the bishop with enthusiasm.

"Certainly, anytime you wish, provided Cato here, approves," he answered, looking plaintively at the older man. "It is a good day's march from here."

"You can go early tomorrow morning," said Cato his dark eyes focused on Crispinus' pleasant swarthy face. "That way, we shall have you back the day after tomorrow in the evening. We must make the most of this calm sea, it will not last long."

"I can wait, until the weather is less favourable for your fishing," offered the bishop with a resigned smile.

"No, no, he can take you, we won't miss him anyway; the lazy lout," snickered the chief with a wink at Rufus, and receiving a look of complete indignation from the young fisherman who knew he was being teased.

Next morning, after having assembled his transient flock together, as all of the passengers, save five, were Christians, the bishop said morning prayers with them. Shortly after, he went with the young villager in search of Publius.

Whilst Rufus was away, Silas, was very busy with the repairs on the ship, and the unloading of the cargo. He settled a good sum of money which he had on board, with Cato. To pay for their work, and sustenance of his passengers. All that money he hoped, would be recovered later from the insurers of the ship. He could hardly wait for high tide so that the *Felicia* could be afloat again. Everything was ready for that event.

"We have all the logs ready to be set in place and rocks to weigh them down," said one of the Islanders.

"We can put forty men to the task with ropes and poles to maintain the ship upright as it slips back, and guide it for those last few cubits until the surf takes over.

Who knows, tomorrow might well be the awaited day." So spoke the confident Cato, as if the launching of a ship, was an everyday occurrence.

"I chose this more arduous route, as it is shorter by far, than following the coastal path," said Crispinus, as he and Rufus laboured up the mountainous path that led to the adjoining bay. That bay, unbeknownst to the bishop, was where Saul of Tarsus had previously landed after having been shipwrecked there.

"It does not bother me, I come from a hilly country also, and I am quite enjoying the walk, especially in full view of that beautiful sea," attested the Cyrenean inhaling heartily the fresh briny sea air.

As predicted by the young native, they reached the village by early evening having kept up a very steady pace. They had stopped only once, for their midday repast, which they enjoyed in the company of many seagulls that kept pestering them for scraps.

Some villagers approached the pair as they walked into the village, and enquired as to their business there.

"Yes, Publius is in the village, you will find him down at the beach," they replied, in their own language, in answer to Crispinus' enquiry.

The visiting duo, made their way to the beach below the village, where a solitary man sat on a rock in a statuesque pose, the shallow surf swirling gently around him.

"The Lord be with you," cried Rufus loudly, in Latin.

Publius gave a start, as the bishop's strong voice pulled him out of his reverie.

He turned, jumped off the rock, and went quickly over to the bishop. Having heard the manner of greeting offered him, he embraced the visitor without the least hesitation, simultaneously casting a friendly smile at his young compatriot.

"My dear brother in Christ, for so you are. What a wonderful surprise. Where do you hail from?" asked the chief in wonderment, and in Latin, as he had been addressed.

"The ship in which I was travelling from Rome and bound for Alexandria, was run aground on the beach at this young man's village just over yonder hill," explained Rufus pointing to the heights from which they had just descended.

"You are both most welcome. Come, let us go up to my house and my good wife will give us a nice supper, and we can talk," he said as he lead the way up a rocky path to the village.

"And how is everything at your village?" asked Publius, addressing his young compatriot, in Latin.

"Very well, thank you. We are doing our best to put the beached ship back into circulation," replied Crispinus with a smile.

"His is a good village, they will take good care of you all. Unfortunately, they are not yet Christians, but I am not giving up hope by any means," assured the chief of the island.

"By the grace of God, and undeservedly on my part, I am Bishop and also Chief of this island we call Malta. Saul of Tarsus consecrated me during his stay a number of months ago after having been shipwrecked here. He lived with us for three months and he converted many of my people during his sojourn. We have had no news of him since, and I am concerned, as he was to be tried in Rome by the Emperor."

"I am the Bishop of Memphis in Egypt and a Cyrenean by birth," stated Rufus, with his characteristic smile.

"As for Saul, I know that he is awaiting trial, and though allowed to have visitors, has a soldier guarding him all the time. Not that he would escape, but that is his present situation. I don't suppose you know that the apostle Peter, was crucified upside down in Rome a little over a month ago?"

"Oh no. That is terrible news," declared the chief with a troubled countenance.

"Yes! I was sent by John Mark, Bishop of Alexandria and actually my superior, to get him out of that troubled city, where he was in great danger. Unfortunately, I was too late."

By that time they had arrived at Publius' house. Both men were introduced to the latter's wife; a buxom, fair haired, handsome woman, with a friendly smile. She asked them to make themselves comfortable on the many floor cushions that surrounded a number of very attractive low tables, and then, she disappeared into the kitchen.

"I suppose you will be leaving as soon as your ship is seaworthy again," said the Bishop of Malta.

"Yes, I have been away from my congregations for almost three months, and I am anxious to get back. I have five churches in my diocese, stretching up the Nile river, and the pastors there are sometimes aggressively challenged by members of other religions."

"What do you mean by churches?" asked Crispinus who had not said a word since they arrived at the house.

Rufus explained, as the other two listened intently, to his description of actual stone and mortar churches.

"Similar to temples and synagogues," he concluded.

Publius who had already heard of them, was most enthralled, as he pictured his beautiful island covered with churches, all worshipping the Blessed Trinity.

"How do you perform the services in those churches? Especially the 'Breaking of the Bread,'" enquired the chief, as the young pagan listened.

Rufus hastened to acquaint his host with some of the liturgy and promised to give him the scrolls that he had brought with him, and had left at the village. He related to his brother bishop, the last words of Peter, and his mandate concerning the liturgy, and advised him to duplicate them and give them out to his priests.

The mistress of the house suddenly appeared with two servant girls laden with bowls of food; fried fish, and fish stew, the smell of which tantalized Rufus as they were placed before him on the little tables.

The women were followed by a very attractive girl in her mid teens with an angelic face and lithe figure.

"This is my daughter Vibiana," said the woman whose name was Drusa. She sat with her guests and her youthful daughter, who smiled sweetly at the visitorswith special attention to young Crispinus. He, returning her smile with obvious admiration in his large, dark Maltese eyes.

Vibiana's father did not miss the ocular exchange between the two youngsters, as he winked knowingly at his cleric friend whose attention was completely taken up with his favourite food;...'fresh fish.'

The evening was spent in a most rewarding and convivial way in the porch of that large comfortable stone house. The two churchmen made plans for venturing out together to 'fish for men'. The young people conversed enthusiastically under the watchful eye of the protective mother, who sat there a little distanced from them, contemplating the stars, and listening to the lapping of the now gentle surf.

A bright sunny morning greeted the well rested duo as they started out for Crispinus' village. Their hosts had put the two up for the night, as the chief's house being the largest and best appointed in the village, had provided all the necessary comforts.

The two bishops had agreed to go in a combined missionary journey further down the coast, with the express purpose of converting a particular sect who worshipped Isis. Another sect on that same side of the island, who worshipped the god Dagon, had given Publius a very hard time on his last encounter with them, and it was mutually decided that they would not preach to them, as they were not receptive to the word of God. These Dagonites however, lived in close proximity to the Isis worshipers and to access the latter, who inhabited a small isthmus, they would have to traverse Dagonian territory. It was a risky business, but there were some two hundred souls to be won, and Rufus, remembering his success in winning the Isis people in Memphis, was keen to try.

On arriving back at the village, the bishop was pleasantly surprised to see the *Felicia,* happily floating in the bay as she lay at anchor with row boats busily going back and forth. The reloading of the cargo was proceeding with great efficiency. Fearing that Silas would want to sail as soon as the cargo had been loaded, and seeing that the villagers had so far been resisting Publius' efforts to win them over to Yeshua, Rufus decided to address them that same evening as soon as supper was over.

He asked Crispinus about the god whom they worshipped. He was informed that it was 'Yamm,' the god of the sea. This presented a problem for the bishop as he knew nothing of that particular god who seemed to make sense to these fishermen.

"Do you believe in an Afterlife?" asked Rufus tentatively.

"Oh, yes," answered the young man with a positive bow of the head.

"Do you need to embalm your dead so that they may enter the Afterlife and be happy?"

"No. We believe that when we die, if it is in the sea, we will gain the Afterlife. So naturally, if we die in the sea we cannot be embalmed. Similarly, those who do not die in the sea would not need embalming either. Our god who looks after us at sea, will hopefully, look after us on land also and see that we gain the Afterlife."

"But you are not sure he will, as you say, 'hopefully.'"

"I had not given that too much thought," replied the fisherman.

"Thank you," said the bishop, and walked off to find Cato.

That evening the whole village assembled to hear Rufus; including the Christian passengers, who had won the hearts of the villagers, and done much by their example and brotherly conversation to promote the faith.

Rufus began by profusely thanking them all. Then, he spoke to them of Yeshua; emphasising as usual his love for all and his guarantee of eternal life. He stressed guarantee, and told them that Yeshua was the son of the God who had created the whole universe, and the sea was as much part of his creation as was the land, as indeed they themselves also were.

"You, being such peace loving people would hold a high place in his great love. Yeshua's closest disciples, the apostles, were all fishermen," he told them.

By the end of his discourse, he had won over just about every soul in the village. The few who still doubted, he left to the further persuasion of Publius, who would take over their spiritual welfare once he was gone.

After having heard his first sermon, and influenced by the enthusiasm of the villagers, Silas became very keen to be baptised. As Rufus finished, he approached him and asked if he could receive the sacrament..

"I rejoice my beloved friend," said the bishop with love in his eyes. "I have prayed for this moment. Yeshua has heard and answered my prayer. Marius also, will greatly rejoice when you tell him the next time you see him."

He embraced his sailor friend with much gladness in his big heart, then, beginning to walk away, stopped, turned, and said.

"Maybe you can win over Neta for the Lord."

The following morning which was actually a Dies Solis or Sabbath, the captain and all the villagers who had been converted, were baptised, including Crispinus, who held the towels whilst Cato held the basin. After a short period of preparatory instruction, and absolution of their sins, the 'Breaking of the Bread,' service was subsequently performed, as each villager received the body and blood of Christ for the very first time.

Later in the day, Publius arrived at the village with two other young men, and was received with great acclamation by the villagers who told him of their conversion by Rufus.

The two bishops embraced, much to the delight of the people. They broke into their native songs and soon the merriment of the occasion gave rise to an evening of festivity. Food and drink were produced, instruments played, and the people danced in the street.

As the following day dawned, the bishop woke the captain up, and asked if he would mind holding off his departure until his return from the impending mission further down the coast.

Silas was reluctant to lose any more time, but consented to his friend's request as it was to serve such an important cause.

"I shall be ready for you," said Silas. "But we should be taking advantage of the weather which is now favourable for our sailing. In fact, as your destination is further down the coast, we will gain time if I take my leave of these kind people here, sail down, and await your return to the ship there. You say it is an isthmus?" enquired Silas.

"Yes, and not a large one at that," assured Rufus. "Perhaps that is a good idea of yours, since the other passengers are probably keen to resume their journey. Though I understand that quite a number have opted to remain here in Malta, as they find the people so congenial, and there is no persecution here as yet," pointed out the bishop with an approving smile.

At this stage of the conversation, Publius appeared, and wishing them a good morning, proposed that they prepare to leave as soon as breakfast was over.

"Ah!" chirped Rufus, "just the man we wanted to see. A good morning to you," he retorted with a big smile.

"What can you tell us about the isthmus, that you will be visiting?" broke in Silas.

"It is small, very rocky, and quite pretty actually, and has approximately nine hundred inhabitants. There is a temple of Isis, a synagogue; as Judeans make up a good portion of the population, and also a barracks for the Roman soldiers who patrol the surrounding area, " explained Publius, with apparent satisfaction.

"No beaches, or harbour?" asked the concerned captain.

"There is a natural inlet with a quay as I remember, but no beaches." Stated the Chief." It is quite a rocky area, cliffs all around. A steep, winding path leads down to the quay."

Rufus listened attentively to his friends' conversation without comment.

"I shall let you off there. You can act as my guide since you obviously know your coast well," said Silas, and looking at Rufus continued.

"I will pull into the quay there, and await your return.

You and the others," he said, addressing the chief. "Can find your way back on foot, as you would otherwise have done, and I will just sail on."

He gave an enquiring look at Publius, giving him an opportunity to make further comment, or simply agree with his plan.

Silas' plan, being to both bishops' liking, was then implemented. Word was immediately given for all passengers wishing to continue on their voyage, to be rowed out to the *Felicia.*

The party of six people which comprised the missionary expedition, including the two bishops, were the last to board as anchors were weighed. The ship, with eight remaining adult passengers waiving to all on shore, glided serenely out on the calm blue morning sea.

As the light was fading, Silas dropped anchor opposite, but well away from a beach they had encountered on their passage down the coast, and which would hopefully allow them to reach their goal the following day around midday. The beach in question, was discovered just after having passed a large town, where many ships were harboured, some actually wintering there. Silas had found it prudent, not to get into the hustle and bustle of that considerably crowded harbour, (which would many years later, be known as Valetta. The capital of Malta). The weather presented no threat at the time.

Midday, as predicted by the captain, saw their arrival and berthing of the ship, as a few hands appeared seemingly from nowhere to man the ropes, pulling the ship safely alongside the short quay, which was otherwise deserted.

Publius, Rufus, Crispinus and the three other young men with them, descended the gang plank, and began their journey up the steep path towards the town. They expected to spend at least two days, having planned to preach to the Isis congregation just outside their temple, where they hoped to attract their attention and enjoy addressing a sizeable crowd.

The town was small but had considerable charm. The buildings, with that bright ocherish hue that characterized the native stone, were crisp in design, and well kept. The arch was a prominent feature of the architecture as was readily apparent in many of the buildings. The temple to which the determined missionaries were headed was quite small. It followed the classic Roman model, with its colonnaded portico and composite capitals, gloriously crowning the attractively fluted columns. To the keen observer however, a definite Egyptian influence could be detected in the frontal facade in the shape of its imposing entrance way. That hinted unashamedly at the mythological origin of the resident but inanimate Egyptian goddess.

Rufus approached the temple of Isis accompanied by Publius and his party of young men. He looked around for an elevated spot from which he could preach within view and earshot of the Isis people. It seemed providential to him that there was an old decrepit stone wall right opposite the main entrance of their temple which afforded them a good platform for their preaching.

The Isis followers, would have to be enticed to assemble at his and Publius' invitation. He wondered how many sermons he would have to preach to reach a significant number of them. The old wall was fairly thick and would certainly accommodate two persons standing on it.

He asked Publius to join him. From there they would both be clearly seen. Presently, a crowd began to gather following Rufus' bold call for the attention of all passers by. They responded as usual, out of sheer curiosity.

The chief of the island, who was known to many of them introduced his visiting colleague as the Bishop of Memphis.

"He is our honoured guest who hails from Egypt and is keen to address you all on a most important matter," he announced in a loud well toned voice.

Rufus, invoked the Holy Spirit, spread his arms in friendly exuberance, and addressed the crowd in Latin. Two Roman soldiers kept watch, as was the custom whenever a crowd assembled, for whatever reason.

The address which followed once a fair crowd had gathered, resembled greatly in content, the spirit and thrust of the bishop's sermon in the cavern church. The Afterlife and the embalming, being the object of his inspired rhetoric, as he was consistently receptive to the promptings of the Holy Spirit. Intermingling with the crowd were some Jews, and the two Isis priests with some of their people, who standing on the steps of the temple listened to Rufus' preaching. As the sermon progressed, they were slowly being turned from their original indignation and hushed anger, to a condition of tolerance, and finally, as the preaching finished, to enthusiastic acceptance of his inspired salvific message.

The two Isis priests approached Rufus, and after introducing themselves, asked if he could instruct them further concerning the faith.

The bishop lost no time in informing them of the conversion of the Memphis temple and the fact that three of his priests had been Isis priests.

"Will you and your companions stay as our guests tonight so that we can discuss things at leisure?" asked one of the priests with marked enthusiasm and sincerity.

"We would be honoured," replied Rufus, throwing a glance of approval at Publius who was beside himself with joy.

A general clambering for baptism from the crowd was heard, which summoned Crispinus and his young friends to action as they produced, a jug and some towels, from their bags. With water being nearby in the form of a water fountain, the Sacrament was administered by both the bishops with the same zeal as the apostles had performed it on that first Pentecost Sunday. Rufus remembered his father relating the event with relish to his beloved family, back in those happy, nostalgic days.

Promising to return the following day so as to allow the good news to circulate, the missionaries accepted the hospitality of the two priests of Isis, who like those of Memphis, were eager to lead their flock in the new and true way to salvation.

It was a confident Rufus, who began his preaching the following day. The two ex-Isis priests stood there beside the bishops and their helpers; most of the Isis congregation around them. They, having received word to attend the meeting.

By the time the preaching was over, the Isis congregation was clamouring for Baptism, and the missionaries rejoiced that the temple of Isis would soon be stripped of all its statuary, and consecrated as the first Christian Church of Malta.

Publius who was beside himself with joy, promised to keep a close eye on the new converts, and send a resident priest, who would remain there to train the ex-Isis priests until they could be ordained.

The mission had been a huge success. The Isis cult on the island though small, had been mortally wounded. Their new priests, once ordained, would carry much weight in their goal of converting any remaining vestiges of that religion to Christianity.

A small number of Judeans had also been won over to Yeshua. But that was a tougher battle which would continue for generations to come.

It was the evening of the second day. The mission having been completed, Rufus, Publius and the group, jubilantly made their way back to the waiting ship as dusk fell.

Arriving at the top of the path leading down to the ship, their progress was suddenly impeded. A number of men emerging from behind some rocks, attacked the party with knives and swords shouting.

"Dagon! Dagon! Kill the Christians!" A battle ensued. The Christians defending themselves as best they could. Publius dodged the first lunge from one of the attackers. Crispinus took hold of another, and was rolling on the ground vying for control of the weapon. Rufus parried a thrust and took a strangle hold of another. The other three young men were dodging and parrying thrusts as the assailants accosted them. Publius had one opponent held down, having disarmed him. There was blood on the sleeve of his tunic. Just then, some of the converted Isis people who had followed the missionaries in the hope of talking to them again, hearing the sound of the struggle, rushed in. Some were armed, and the others picked up stones. They set upon the attackers changing the tide of the battle and turning it in favour of the Christians. Soon it was all over. Two men lay on the ground. One of them, a young man from Crispinus' village who lay motionless, and Rufus, who lay there with a knife in his back, bleeding profusely.

The young man was pronounced dead. Rufus was rushed on board the ship, where he was immediately taken to the passenger cabin and laid on his stomach on one of the beds. Two of the Dagonians were taken prisoner, five others, two of them wounded, escaped. A young man from the Isis camp ran off in search of a physician.

Publius stayed by Rufus side, nursing the wound in his own arm, which was crudely bandaged up by Silas as they awaited the physician's arrival.

The latter arrived, shortly after, removed the knife from Rufus's back with great care, and began to mop up the blood with some clean cloths that he had brought with him.

"He has been very fortunate," declared the physician, after a careful inspection of the wound. "Unless I am very mistaken no vital organs have been damaged." He put some salt into the wound causing the bishop extraordinary pain, and then proceeded to cauterise the wound; heating the metal instrument with the flame of an oil lamp that Silas brought him.

Rufus having passed out, was left undisturbed. The man of medicine now cleaned, salted and sutured Publius' wounded arm. It was borne with much clenching of teeth and groaning, by the recipient of those well meant but tortuous attentions.

Publius, Crispinus, and the other two young men left the ship, bidding farewell to Silas and his passengers. They all returned to the town, carrying their dead comrade with them on a makeshift stretcher that the captain had made for them.

From there, they would get a Roman escort through the Dagonian territory and then find their way home.

The two Dagonian prisoners had already been taken to the Roman authorities by the ex-Isis people.

Silas sailed away with a sad heart, as Rufus regaining consciousness, asked for some water, and bewailed the fact that he had not been able to bid farewell to Publius with whom he had left the last remaining scrolls of the liturgy..

'I am so glad that I decided to give him the scrolls,' said Rufus as Silas sat beside him on the other bed.

He could picture all the future services for the 'Breaking of the Bread', that would be performed in Malta over the years; consistent with the way it was celebrated in Cyrene, Alexandria, Memphis, Antioch, and even Rome.

Silas kept a close eye on Rufus as the days passed. The latter, informed him of the conversion of the Isis people, and how pleased, John Mark would be to learn that. The captain was optimistic. The wound seemed to be clean, the inflammation slowly decreasing. He, and the Christians on board, held a prayer service every evening for the bishop's recovery.

The weather was beginning to deteriorate. The choppy seas began to pitch and toss the ship causing discomfort to the passengers who lined up at the rail emptying their nauseated stomachs into the sea.

The winds began to change, and act against their intended course. Excessive tacking was also slowing up their progress considerably.

The fourth day out, on examining Rufus' wound, Silas found that it had began to fester, and became very concerned. The physician had alerted him to the possibility that it could occur, and added that it could be fatal if it persisted. The man had recommended bathing the wound with the residual fluid from sea weed boiled in sea water.

Silas followed the prescribed treatment faithfully. However, two days later, he realised to his distress, that it did not seem to help, as Rufus began to develop a fever and suffer spells of delirium. At such times, the sick man talked of Miriam and his love for her and at other times he would talk of Letitia, and his love for 'her.'

The evening of the fifth day out of Malta, having finished the prayer meeting, he visited his friend again. On seeing no improvement but a possible worsening of his condition, he decided to stop at Cyrene as it was directly on course. Though the sea continued to be choppy there was fortunately no rain, and with a sudden change of wind, their speed increased allowing for much better progress.

Finally, after eight days at sea, Cyrene came into sight. Silas was beside himself with worry as Rufus had become more and more delirious. His fever continued, and the captain was very concerned that he would die before he could get him ashore to a physician and his family.

The moment the ship berthed in Apollonia, Silas ran ashore and directly into the Seamen's Club in search of his friend Marius. The latter, sitting in his habitual place at the the far end of the large table in the captains' room, sprang up in alarm at seeing Silas' face; which displayed with frightening accuracy the panic and anxiety under which his heart was labouring.

"I have him with me in the ship, and I am sure he is dying," announced Silas.

"Who! have you got in the ship?" asked a bewildered Marius, his hands up in the air.

"Rufus! Rufus!" cried the distraught Silas.

"I need help!" called out Marius in an authoritative but appealing voice, looking around at his fellow captains. I need a cart and two horses right away. Can anyone oblige me?"

Mariners scrambled out of the door and onto the quay in search of the much needed horses and cart. The two concerned captains ran up the *Felicia's* gang plank and into the passenger cabin where the deteriorating bishop lay in his delirium as they awaited the arrival of the cart.

"When is that confounded cart going to get here?" complained Marius as the panic that had seized his mariner friend found its way into his heart also.

A half an hour later, two club captains riding on a cart drawn by a pair of horses, arrived at the bottom of the gang plank. One of them jumped off and ran up onto the deck carrying a folded stretcher under his arm.

Slowly and with loving care, Rufus was lifted up, slid onto the stretcher, out the cabin, and down the gang plank onto the cart.

Marius and Silas rode the cart to Marcus' house which was close by; praying that Letitia would be there. The passengers of the *Felicia* were left in the hands of the crew, who made it known that the ship would be sailing again shortly. They were advised to go ashore for a few hours and return to the ship before nightfall, when the captain would hopefully be back. At that time decisions would be made, as to those wishing to stay in Cyrene, and those continuing to Alexandria.

Tecuno who happened to be near the gate as the cart arrived at Marcus' house, recognised the two captains, and quickly opened it for them.

"We have a very sick bishop with us," announced Marius as they passed the shocked servant, who seeing Rufus lying on his stomach at the back of the cart, turned, and ran on ahead to alert his master.

The latter came out to receive them. On seeing his son-in-law in such a serious condition, he instructed Tecuno to go for their physician. He, assisted the captains, who with the greatest of care, were extricating Rufus from the cart. Marcus yelled for Damian, who quickly appeared and gave a hand. The bishop was laid on the bed in the guest room just as Letitia joined them with an enquiring look on her face. Recognising her father, and seeing him in such a sorry state, she burst into tears and fell on her knees beside the bed taking one of his hands and kissing it ardently. Marius left Silas with Marcus, and drove the cart uphill to Lucila's house. Having relayed to her the bad news, he continued up to Cyrene in search of Alexander and Hannah.

Lucila, in her usual excitable way, her eyes clouded by tears, quickly sent her daughter Ruthie to find her brother Rufie, and get down to Marcus' house as fast as they could. She, covering her head with her 'palla', made haste to go to her beloved brother; leaving hasty news for David as she passed his parent's house.

Hannah was home when Marius arrived. Alexander was at the church with their son Simon. Her daughter Judith and her son Bart were home, and soon all four were riding the cart on their way to the church.

Alexander was beside himself with concern as he heard the bad news from Marius regarding his brother's condition. He told his son Simon to ride in the cart with the captain, his mother and siblings. He quickly mounted his horse that was tied up nearby, and took off ahead of them.

The physician having arrived at Marcus' house, was busy with Rufus' wound.

Realising that the wound had been festering for days, he was attempting to reopen it and apply a solution of heavily salted water with a herbal mixture containing seaweed. Rufus remained in his semiconscious state as the fever continued to ravage his body.

"He is very weak, and the fever has taken a very a heavy toll," said the Physician as Marcus and Zaphira listened for his instructions.

"The prognosis is not good, but he may have a chance if you bathe the wound four times a day with this solution that I will leave here with you. Nothing further can be done, other than wait," said the physician closing his medicine bag and preparing to leave.

"Keep me informed as to his condition, but don't build up your hopes," he said as he walked out of the room.

"Let us all pray that the Lord save our beloved Bishop, so that he can continue his wonderful work for Him," suggested Marcus, just as Alexander rushed into the peristyle and made straight for his brother's bed. He took out a small vial of Holy oil from his tunic; and after some prayers, he anointed Rufus' head making the sign of the Cross. With eyes lifted to heaven, he implored Yeshua to save that life that meant so much to him, his family, and the Church.

They all began their prayers. Rufus lay oblivious to what was happening; his delirium kept him in a world of his own. Letitia sat by her father, intermittently applying a damp cold cloth to his forehead in the hope of cooling down the fever which continued to burn him up.

Suddenly Lucila burst into the room with her children. Tears ran down her lovely face, showing the distress that tortured her soul, as as she beheld her helpless, dying brother. Memories of their youth flooded her boggled mind, and came back to haunt her as she gave him a tender final kiss. She remembered those happy innocent days when she so greatly admired him; and their constant teasing of one another which they both enjoyed so much. Now, she fervently prayed for Yeshua to work a miracle and save his life.

Shortly after, Marius appeared. With him were Hannah, Simon, Bart and Judy, who quickly gathered around the sick bed, their faces racked with concern.

Alexander, totally distraught and having heard of the physician's dismal prognosis, immediately got everyone present to begin praying once again.

If the sincerity and intensity of prayer could guarantee the miracle prayed for, the prayers of this family would certainly have been efficacious. But it is God who determines the outcome, and this particular group of believers were well aware of that. Still however, they prayed hopefully with great love and reverence to Yeshua all that afternoon, evening, and through the night.

The prescribed treatments were being administered by Zaphira, with great care and love. As she worked, she thought of her mistress, and wondered if she would soon be welcoming her beloved husband into that wonderful and incomprehensible world that Yeshua's Father ruled with his divine Son and the Holy Spirit; which would last for all eternity, and where by God's grace, she too, aspired to be one day.

Dawn was breaking. The soft tranquil light of morning gently illuminated the beautiful peristyle; dispersing the solemn grayness of the night, and giving those present, hope of a brighter day. The young ones of the family were fast asleep on the many cushions that covered the floor. The others, feeling the discomfort of a vigilant and tortuous night, sat in prayerful contemplation trying hard to stay awake; their fingers intertwined, and gazing interminably and expectantly at Rufus. He, lay on his stomach in what appeared to be in an unconscious state, as the tireless Zaphira continued her loving tending of the ugly open wound in his back.

Suddenly to everyone's surprise, Rufus, turning over, sat up; his eyes wide awake, giving all present, one of his wonderful happy smiles. Letitia, eyes brightening, got up, and took her father's hand. Hope stirring in her breast as her tired eyes met his. After a moment, he looked away, his gaze slowly and deliberately sweeping the room, his smile persisting, but with tears in his eyes, as they came to rest on Silas, and said.

"Dear friend, make sure my beloved wife hears of my passing. Give her my love: As also to her aunt, John Mark,

Annianus, Senh and all my beloved priests. He smiled again, this time at his two grandchildren who now stood with their mother beside the bed, and taking Letitia's hand, kissed it, held it to his cheek, and falling back on the bed, his eyes closing, whispered.

"Into Thy hands Lord, I commend my spi..r........."

Joseph L. Cavilla is a writer and visual artist.
He lives and works in Hanover, Ontario.

CPSIA information can be obtained
at www.ICGtesting.com
Printed in the USA
LVOW07s0126150917
548754LV00001B/65/P

9 781537 443966